PRAISE FOR SEANA
WAYWARD CHILDREN SERIES

EVERY HEART A DOORWAY

"A jewel of a book that deserves to be shelved with Lewis Carroll's and C. S. Lewis' classics, even as it carves its own precocious space between them."
—NPR

"This is a gorgeous story: sometimes mean, sometimes angry, and always exciting."
—Cory Doctorow for *Boing Boing*

"So mind-blowingly good, it hurts."
—*io9*

DOWN AMONG THE STICKS AND BONES

"McGuire has a miraculous talent for examining adolescent discontent, wedding the strange with the poignant, the fearsome with the fascinating."
—*RT Book Reviews* Top Pick, 4½ stars

"Exquisitely crafted, this is the rare companion novel that can stand alone."
—*Booklist* (starred review)

"McGuire's exquisitely written fairy tale is about the choices that can alter the course of a life forever, lost innocence, and what it is to love and be loved."
—*Publishers Weekly* (starred review)

BENEATH THE SUGAR SKY

"Readers will be thrilled to see old friends and meet new ones in this scrumptious tale that emphasizes acceptance, kindness, and the enduring value of friendship."
—*Publishers Weekly*

"Fully dimensional characterization and a compelling story arc keep this series moving."
—*Kirkus Reviews*

BY THE SAME AUTHOR

Dusk or Dark or Dawn or Day
Sparrow Hill Road
Deadlands: Boneyard
Dying with Her Cheer Pants On

THE WAYWARD CHILDREN SERIES

Every Heart a Doorway
Down Among the Sticks and Bones
Beneath the Sugar Sky
In an Absent Dream
Come Tumbling Down
Across the Green Grass Fields
Where the Drowned Girls Go
Lost in the Moment and Found
Seanan McGuire's Wayward Children, Volumes 1–3 (boxed set)

THE ALCHEMICAL JOURNEYS SERIES

Middlegame
Seasonal Fears

THE OCTOBER DAYE SERIES

Rosemary and Rue
A Local Habitation
An Artificial Night
Late Eclipses
One Salt Sea
Ashes of Honor
Chimes at Midnight
The Winter Long
A Red-Rose Chain
Once Broken Faith
The Brightest Fell
Night and Silence
The Unkindest Tide
A Killing Frost
When Sorrows Come
Be the Serpent

THE INCRYPTID SERIES

Discount Armageddon
Midnight Blue-Light Special
Half-Off Ragnarok
Pocket Apocalypse
Chaos Choreography
Magic for Nothing
Tricks for Free
That Ain't Witchcraft
Imaginary Numbers
Calculated Risks
Spelunking Through Hell
Backpacking Through Bedlam

THE INDEXING SERIES

Indexing

Indexing: Reflections

AS A. DEBORAH BAKER

THE UP-AND-UNDER SERIES

Over the Woodward Wall

Along the Saltwise Sea

Into the Windwracked Wilds

AS MIRA GRANT

THE NEWSFLESH SERIES

Feed

Deadline

Blackout

Feedback

Rise: The Complete Newsflesh Collection (short stories)

THE PARASITOLOGY SERIES

Parasite

Symbiont

Chimera

Rolling in the Deep

Into the Drowning Deep

Laughter at the Academy

Final Girls

In the Shadow of Spindrift House

Kingdom of Needle and Bone

Square^3

BE SURE

SEANAN
McGUIRE

Collecting

EVERY HEART A DOORWAY

DOWN AMONG THE STICKS AND BONES

BENEATH THE SUGAR SKY

TOR PUBLISHING GROUP

NEW YORK

This is a work of fiction. All of the characters, organizations, and events portrayed in these novellas are either products of the author's imagination or are used fictitiously.

BE SURE

Interior illustrations by Rovina Cai

A Tordotcom Book
Published by Tom Doherty Associates / Tor Publishing Group
120 Broadway
New York, NY 10271

www.tor.com

The Library of Congress Cataloging-in-Publication Data
is available upon request.

ISBN 978-1-250-19892-1 (trade paperback)
ISBN 978-1-250-86287-7 (hardcover)

First Edition: 2023

Printed in the United States of America

0 9 8 7 6 5 4 3 2 1

EVERY HEART A DOORWAY

FOR THE WICKED

PART I

THE GOLDEN AFTERNOONS

THERE WAS A LITTLE GIRL

THE GIRLS WERE NEVER present for the entrance interviews. Only their parents, their guardians, their confused siblings, who wanted so much to help them but didn't know how. It would have been too hard on the prospective students to sit there and listen as the people they loved most in all the world—all this world, at least—dismissed their memories as delusions, their experiences as fantasy, their lives as some intractable illness.

What's more, it would have damaged their ability to trust the school if their first experience of Eleanor had been seeing her dressed in respectable grays and lilacs, with her hair styled just so, like the kind of stolid elderly aunt who only really existed in children's stories. The real Eleanor was nothing like that. Hearing the things she said would have only made it worse, as she sat there and explained, so earnestly, so sincerely, that her school would help to cure the things that had gone wrong in the minds of all those little lost lambs. She could take the broken children and make them whole again.

She was lying, of course, but there was no way for her potential students to know that. So she demanded that she meet with their legal guardians in private, and she sold her bill of goods with the focus and skill of a born con artist. If those guardians had ever come together to compare notes, they would have found that her script was well-practiced and honed like the weapon that it was.

"This is a rare but not unique disorder that manifests in young girls just stepping across the border into womanhood," she would say, making careful eye contact with the desperate, overwhelmed guardians of her latest wandering girl. On the rare occasion when she had to speak to the parents of a boy, she would vary her speech, but only as much as the situation demanded. She had been working on this routine for a long time, and she knew how to play upon the fears and desires of adults. They wanted what was best for their charges, as did she. It was simply that they had very different ideas of what "best" meant.

To the parents, she said, "This is a delusion, and some time away may help to cure it."

To the aunts and uncles, she said, "This is not your fault, and I can be the solution."

To the grandparents, she said, "Let me help. Please, let me help you."

Not every family agreed on boarding school as the best

solution. About one out of every three potential students slipped through her fingers, and she mourned for them, those whose lives would be so much harder than they needed to be, when they could have been saved. But she rejoiced for those who were given to her care. At least while they were with her, they would be with someone who understood. Even if they would never have the opportunity to go back home, they would have someone who understood, and the company of their peers, which was a treasure beyond reckoning.

Eleanor West spent her days giving them what she had never had, and hoped that someday, it would be enough to pay her passage back to the place where she belonged.

1 COMING HOME, LEAVING HOME

THE HABIT OF NARRATION, of crafting something miraculous out of the commonplace, was hard to break. Narration came naturally after a time spent in the company of talking scarecrows or disappearing cats; it was, in its own way, a method of keeping oneself grounded, connected to the thin thread of continuity that ran through all lives, no matter how strange they might become. Narrate the impossible things, turn them into a story, and they could be controlled. So:

The manor sat in the center of what would have been considered a field, had it not been used to frame a private home. The grass was perfectly green, the trees clustered around the structure perfectly pruned, and the garden grew in a profusion of colors that normally existed together only in a rainbow, or in a child's toy box. The thin black ribbon of the driveway curved from the distant gate to form a loop in front of the manor itself, feeding elegantly into a slightly wider waiting area at the base of the porch. A single car pulled up, tawdry yellow and seeming somehow shabby against the carefully curated scene. The rear passenger door slammed, and the car pulled away again, leaving a teenage girl behind.

She was tall and willowy and couldn't have been more than seventeen; there was still something of the unformed around her eyes and mouth, leaving her a work in progress, meant to be finished by time. She wore black—black jeans, black ankle boots with tiny black buttons marching like soldiers from toe to calf—and she wore white—a loose tank top, the faux pearl bands around her wrists—and she had a ribbon the color of pomegranate seeds tied around the base of her ponytail. Her hair was bone-white streaked with runnels of black, like oil spilled on a marble floor, and her eyes were pale as ice. She squinted in the daylight. From the look of her, it had been quite some time since she had seen the sun. Her small wheeled suitcase was bright pink, covered with cartoon daisies. She had not, in all likelihood, purchased it herself.

Raising her hand to shield her eyes, the girl looked toward the manor, pausing when she saw the sign that hung from the porch eaves. ELEANOR WEST'S HOME FOR WAYWARD CHILDREN it read, in large letters. Below, in smaller letters, it continued NO SOLICITATION, NO VISITORS, NO QUESTS.

The girl blinked. The girl lowered her hand. And slowly, the girl made her way toward the steps.

On the third floor of the manor, Eleanor West let go of the curtain and turned toward the door while the fabric was still fluttering back into its original position. She appeared to be a well-preserved woman in her late sixties, although her true age was closer to a hundred: travel through the lands she had once frequented had a tendency to scramble the internal clock, making it difficult for time to get a proper grip upon the body. Some days she was grateful for her longevity, which had allowed her to help so many more children than she would ever have lived to see if she hadn't opened the doors she had, if she had never chosen to stray from her proper path. Other days, she wondered whether this world would ever discover that she existed—that she was little Ely West the Wayward Girl, somehow alive after all these years—and what would happen to her when that happened.

Still, for the time being, her back was strong and her eyes were as clear as they had been on the day when, as a girl of seven, she had seen the opening between the roots of a tree on her father's estate. If her hair was white now, and her skin was soft with wrinkles and memories, well, that was no matter at all. There was still something unfinished around her eyes; she wasn't done yet. She was a story, not an epilogue. And if she chose to narrate her own life one word at a time as she descended the stairs to meet her newest arrival, that wasn't hurting anyone. Narration was a hard habit to break, after all.

Sometimes it was all a body had.

NANCY STOOD FROZEN in the center of the foyer, her hand locked on the handle of her suitcase as she looked around, trying to find her bearings. She wasn't sure what she'd been expecting from the "special school" her parents were sending her to, but it certainly hadn't been this . . . this elegant country home. The walls were papered in an old-fashioned floral print of roses and twining clematis vines, and the furnishings—such as they were in this intentionally underfurnished entryway—were all antiques, good, well-polished wood with brass fittings that matched the curving sweep of the banister. The floor was cherrywood, and when she glanced upward, trying to move her eyes without lifting her chin, she found herself looking at an elaborate chandelier shaped like a blooming flower.

"That was made by one of our alumni, actually," said a voice. Nancy wrenched her gaze from the chandelier and turned it toward the stairs.

The woman who was descending was thin, as elderly women sometimes were, but her back was straight, and the hand resting on the banister seemed to be using it only as a guide, not as any form of support. Her hair was as white as Nancy's own, without the streaks of defiant black, and styled in a puffbull of a perm, like a dandelion that had gone to seed. She would have looked perfectly respectable, if not for her electric orange trousers, paired with a hand-knit sweater knit of rainbow wool and a necklace of semiprecious stones in a dozen colors, all of them clashing. Nancy felt her eyes widen despite her best efforts, and hated herself for it. She was losing hold of her stillness one day at a time.

Soon, she would be as jittery and unstable as any of the living, and then she would never find her way back home.

"It's virtually all glass, of course, except for the bits that aren't," continued the woman, seemingly untroubled by Nancy's blatant staring. "I'm not at all sure how you make that sort of thing. Probably by melting sand, I assume. I contributed those large teardrop-shaped prisms at the center, however. All twelve of them were of my making. I'm rather proud of that." The woman paused, apparently expecting Nancy to say something.

Nancy swallowed. Her throat was so *dry* these days, and nothing seemed to chase the dust away. "If you don't know how to make glass, how did you make the prisms?" she asked.

The woman smiled. "Out of my tears, of course. Always assume the simplest answer is the true one, here, because most of the time, it will be. I'm Eleanor West. Welcome to my home. You must be Nancy."

"Yes," Nancy said slowly. "How did you . . . ?"

"Well, you're the only student we were expecting to receive today. There aren't as many of you as there once were. Either the doors are getting rarer, or you're all getting better about not coming back. Now, be quiet a moment, and let me look at you." Eleanor descended the last three steps and stopped in front of Nancy, studying her intently for a moment before she walked a slow circle around her. "Hmm. Tall, thin, and very pale. You must have been someplace with no sun—but no vampires either, I think, given the skin on your neck. Jack and Jill will be awfully pleased to meet you. They get tired of all the sunlight and sweetness people bring through here."

"Vampires?" said Nancy blankly. "Those aren't real."

"None of this is *real,* my dear. Not this house, not this conversation, not those shoes you're wearing—which are several years out of style if you're trying to reacclimatize yourself to the ways of your peers, and are not proper mourning shoes if you're trying to hold fast to your recent past—and not either one of us. 'Real' is a four-letter word, and I'll thank you to use it as little as possible while you live under my roof." Eleanor stopped in front of Nancy again. "It's the hair that betrays you. Were you in an Underworld or a Netherworld? You can't have been in an Afterlife. No one comes back from those."

Nancy gaped at her, mouth moving silently as she tried to find her voice. The old woman said those things—those cruelly impossible things—so casually, like she was asking after nothing more important than Nancy's vaccination records.

Eleanor's expression transformed, turning soft and apologetic. "Oh, I see I've upset you. I'm afraid I have a tendency to do that. I went to a Nonsense world, you see, six times before I turned sixteen, and while I eventually had to stop crossing over, I never quite learned to rein my tongue back in. You must be tired from your journey, and curious about what's to happen here. Is that so? I can show you to your room as soon as I know where you fall on the compass. I'm afraid that really does matter for things like housing; you can't put a Nonsense traveler in with someone who went walking through Logic, not unless you feel like explaining a remarkable amount of violence to the local police. They *do* check up on us here, even if we can usually get them to look the other way. It's all part of our remaining accredited as a school, although I suppose we're more of a sanitarium, of sorts. I do like that word, don't you? 'Sanitarium.' It sounds so official, while meaning absolutely nothing at all."

"I don't understand anything you're saying right now," said Nancy. She was ashamed to hear her voice come out in a tinny squeak, even as she was proud of herself for finding it at all.

Eleanor's face softened further. "You don't have to pretend anymore, Nancy. I know what you've been going through—where you've been. I went through something a long time ago, when I came back from my own voyages. This isn't a place for lies or pretending everything is all right. We know everything is not all right. If it were, you wouldn't be here. Now. Where did you go?"

"I don't . . ."

"Forget about words like 'Nonsense' and 'Logic.' We can work out those details later. Just answer. Where did you *go*?"

"I went to the Halls of the Dead." Saying the words aloud was an almost painful relief. Nancy froze again, staring into space as if she could see her voice hanging there, shining garnet-dark and perfect in the air. Then she swallowed, still not chasing away the dryness, and said, "It was . . . I was looking for a bucket in the cellar of our house, and I found this door I'd never seen before. When I went through, I was in a grove of pomegranate trees. I thought I'd fallen and hit my head. I kept going because . . . because . . ."

Because the air had smelled so sweet, and the sky had been black velvet, spangled with points of diamond light that didn't flicker at all, only burned constant and cold. Because the grass had been wet with dew, and the trees had been heavy with fruit. Because she had wanted to know what was at the end of the long path between the trees, and because she hadn't wanted to turn back before she understood everything. Because for the first time in forever, she'd felt like she was going home, and that feeling had been enough to move her feet, slowly at first, and then faster, and faster, until she had been running through the clean night air, and nothing else had mattered, or would ever matter again—

"How long were you gone?"

The question was meaningless. Nancy shook her head. "Forever. Years . . . I was there for years. I didn't want to come back. Ever."

"I know, dear." Eleanor's hand was gentle on Nancy's elbow, guiding her toward the door behind the stairs. The old woman's perfume smelled of dandelions and gingersnaps, a combination as nonsensical as everything else about her. "Come with me. I have the perfect room for you."

ELEANOR'S "PERFECT ROOM" was on the first floor, in the shadow of a great old elm that blocked almost all the light that would otherwise have come in through the single window. It was eternal twilight in that room, and Nancy felt the weight drop from her shoulders as she stepped inside and looked around. One half of the room—the half with the window—was a jumble of clothing, books, and knickknacks. A fiddle was tossed carelessly on the bed, and the associated bow was balanced on the edge of the bookshelf, ready to fall at the slightest provocation. The air smelled of mint and mud.

The other half of the room was as neutral as a hotel. There was a bed, a small dresser, a bookshelf, and a desk, all in pale, unvarnished wood. The walls were blank. Nancy looked to Eleanor long enough to receive the nod of approval before walking over and placing her suitcase primly in the middle of what would be her bed.

"Thank you," she said. "I'm sure this will be fine."

"I admit, I'm not as confident," said Eleanor, frowning at Nancy's suitcase. It had been placed so *precisely*. . . . "Anyplace called 'the Halls of the Dead' is going to have been an Underworld, and most of those fall more under the banner of Nonsense than Logic. It seems like yours may have been more regimented. Well, no matter. We can always move you if you and Sumi prove ill-suited. Who knows? You might provide her with some of the grounding she currently lacks. And if you can't do that, well, hopefully you won't actually kill one another."

"Sumi?"

"Your roommate." Eleanor picked her way through the mess on the floor until she reached the window. Pushing it open, she leaned out and scanned the branches of the elm tree until she found what she was looking for. "One and two and three, I see you, Sumi. Come inside and meet your roommate."

"Roommate?" The voice was female, young, and annoyed.

"I warned you," said Eleanor as she pulled her head back inside and returned to the center of the room. She moved with remarkable assurance, especially given how cluttered the floor was; Nancy kept expecting her to fall, and somehow, she didn't. "I told you a new student was arriving this week, and that if it was a girl from a compatible background, she would be taking the spare bed. Do you remember any of this?"

"I thought you were just talking to hear yourself talk. You *do* that. Everyone *does* that." A head appeared in the window, upside down, its owner apparently hanging from the elm tree. She looked to be about Nancy's age, of Japanese descent, with long black hair tied into two childish pigtails, one above each ear. She looked at Nancy with unconcealed suspicion before asking, "Are you a servant of the Queen of Cakes, here to punish me for my transgressions against the Countess of Candy Floss? Because I don't feel like going to war right now."

"No," said Nancy blankly. "I'm Nancy."

"That's a boring name. How can you be here with such a boring name?" Sumi flipped around and dropped out of

the tree, vanishing for a moment before she popped back up, leaned on the windowsill, and asked, "Eleanor-Ely, are you *sure*? I mean, sure-sure? She doesn't look like she's supposed to be here at *all*. Maybe when you looked at her records, you saw what wasn't there again and really she's supposed to be in a school for juvenile victims of bad dye jobs."

"I don't dye my hair!" Nancy's protest was heated. Sumi stopped talking and blinked at her. Eleanor turned to look at her. Nancy's cheeks grew hot as the blood rose in her face, but she stood her ground, somehow keeping herself from reaching up to stroke her hair as she said, "It used to be all black, like my mother's. When I danced with the Lord of the Dead for the first time, he said it was beautiful, and he ran his fingers through it. All the hair turned white around them, out of jealousy. That's why I only have five black streaks left. Those are the parts he touched."

Looking at her with a critical eye, Eleanor could see how those five streaks formed the phantom outline of a hand, a place where the pale young woman in front of her had been touched once and never more. "I see," she said.

"I don't *dye* it," said Nancy, still heated. "I would never *dye* it. That would be disrespectful."

Sumi was still blinking, eyes wide and round. Then she grinned. "Oh, I *like* you," she said. "You're the craziest card in the deck, aren't you?"

"We don't use that word here," snapped Eleanor.

"But it's true," said Sumi. "She thinks she's going back. Don't you, *Nan*cy? You think you're going to open the right-wrong door and see your stairway to Heaven on the other side, and then it's one step, two step, how d'you do step, and you're right back in your story. Crazy girl. *Stupid* girl. You can't go back. Once they throw you out, you can't go back."

Nancy felt as if her heart were trying to scramble up her throat and choke her. She swallowed it back down, and said, in a whisper, "You're wrong."

Sumi's eyes were bright. "Am I?"

Eleanor clapped her hands, pulling their attention back to her. "Nancy, why don't you unpack and get settled? Dinner is at six thirty, and group therapy will follow at eight. Sumi, please don't inspire her to murder you before she's been here for a full day."

"We all have our own ways of trying to go home," said Sumi, and disappeared from the window's frame, heading off to whatever she'd been doing before Eleanor disturbed her. Eleanor shot Nancy a quick, apologetic look, and then she too was gone, shutting the door behind herself. Nancy was, quite abruptly, alone.

She stayed where she was for a count of ten, enjoying the stillness. When she had been in the Halls of the Dead, she had sometimes been expected to hold her position for days at a time, blending in with the rest of the living statuary. Serving girls who were less skilled at stillness had come through with sponges soaked in pomegranate juice and sugar, pressing them to the lips of the unmoving. Nancy had learned to let the juice trickle down her throat without swallowing, taking it in passively, like a stone takes in the moonlight. It had taken her months, years even, to become perfectly motionless, but she had done it: oh, yes, she had done it, and the Lady of Shadows had proclaimed her beautiful beyond measure, little mortal girl who saw no need to be quick, or hot, or restless.

But this world was made for quick, hot, restless things; not like the quiet Halls of the Dead. With a sigh, Nancy abandoned her stillness and turned to open her suitcase. Then she froze again, this time out of shock and dismay. Her clothing—the diaphanous gowns and gauzy black shirts she had packed with such care—was gone, replaced by a welter of fabrics as colorful as the things strewn on Sumi's side of the room. There was an envelope on top of the pile. With shaking fingers, Nancy picked it up and opened it.

Nancy—

We're sorry to play such a mean trick on you, sweetheart, but you didn't leave us much of a choice. You're going to boarding school to get better, not to keep wallowing in what your kidnappers did to you. We want our real daughter back. These clothes were your favorites before you disappeared. You used to be our little rainbow! Do you remember that?

You've forgotten so much.

We love you. Your father and I, we love you more than anything, and we believe you can come back to us. Please forgive us for packing you a more suitable wardrobe, and know that we only did it because we want the best for you. We want you back.

Have a wonderful time at school, and we'll be waiting for you when you're ready to come home to stay.

The letter was signed in her mother's looping, unsteady hand. Nancy barely saw it. Her eyes filled with hot, hateful tears, and her hands were shaking, fingers cramping until they had crumpled the paper into an unreadable labyrinth of creases and folds. She sank to the floor, sitting with her knees bent to her chest and her eyes fixed on the open suitcase. How could she wear any of those things? Those were *daylight* colors, meant for people who moved in the sun, who were hot, and fast, and unwelcome in the Halls of the Dead.

"What are you doing?" The voice belonged to Sumi.

Nancy didn't turn. Her body was already betraying her by moving without her consent. The least she could do was refuse to move it voluntarily.

"It *looks* like you're sitting on the floor and crying, which everyone knows is dangerous, dangerous, don't-do-that dangerous; it makes it look like you're not holding it together, and you might shake apart altogether," said Sumi. She leaned close, so close that Nancy felt one of the other girl's pigtails brush her shoulder. "Why are you crying, ghostie girl? Did someone walk across your grave?"

"I never died, I just went to serve the Lord of the Dead

for a while, that's all, and I was going to stay forever, until he said I had to come back here long enough to be *sure*. Well, I was *sure* before I ever left, and I don't know why my door isn't here." The tears clinging to her cheeks were too hot. They felt like they were scalding her. Nancy allowed herself to move, reaching up and wiping them viciously away. "I'm crying because I'm angry, and I'm sad, and I want to go *home*."

"Stupid girl," said Sumi. She placed a sympathetic hand atop Nancy's head before smacking her—lightly, but still a hit—and leaping up onto her bed, crouching next to the open suitcase. "You don't mean home where your parents are, do you? Home to school and class and boys and blather, no, no, no, not for you anymore, all those things are for other people, people who aren't as special as you are. You mean the home where the man who bleached your hair lives. Or doesn't live, since you're a ghostie girl. A stupid ghostie girl. You can't go back. You have to know that by now."

Nancy raised her head and frowned at Sumi. "Why? Before I went through that doorway, I knew there was no such thing as a portal to another world. Now I know that if you open the right door at the right time, you might finally find a place where you belong. Why does that mean I can't go back? Maybe I'm just not finished being *sure*."

The Lord of the Dead wouldn't have lied to her, he *wouldn't*. He loved her.

He did.

"Because hope is a knife that can cut through the foundations of the world," said Sumi. Her voice was suddenly crystalline and clear, with none of her prior whimsy. She looked at Nancy with calm, steady eyes. "Hope *hurts*. That's what you need to learn, and fast, if you don't want it to cut you open from the inside out. Hope is bad. Hope means you keep on holding to things that won't ever be so again, and so you bleed an inch at a time until there's nothing left. Ely-Eleanor is always saying 'don't use this word' and 'don't use that word,' but she never bans the ones that are really *bad*. She never bans hope."

"I just want to go home," whispered Nancy.

"Silly ghost. That's all any of us want. That's why we're here," said Sumi. She turned to Nancy's suitcase and began poking through the clothes. "These are pretty. Too small for me. Why do you have to be so *narrow*? I can't steal things that won't fit, that would be silly, and I'm not getting any smaller here. No one ever does in this world. High Logic is no fun at all."

"I hate them," said Nancy. "Take them all. Cut them up and make streamers for your tree, I don't care, just get them away from me."

"Because they're the wrong colors, right? Somebody else's rainbow." Sumi bounced off the bed, slamming the suitcase shut and hauling it after her. "Get up, come on. We're going visiting."

"What?" Nancy looked after Sumi, bewildered and beaten down. "I'm sorry. I've just met you, and I really don't want to go anywhere with you."

"Then it's a good thing I don't care, isn't it?" Sumi beamed for a moment, bright as the hated, hated sun, and then she was gone, trotting out the door with Nancy's suitcase and all of Nancy's clothes.

Nancy didn't *want* those clothes, and for one tempting moment, she considered staying where she was. Then she sighed, and stood, and followed. She had little enough to cling to in this world. And she was eventually going to need clean underpants.

2 BEAUTIFUL BOYS AND GLAMOROUS GIRLS

SUMI WAS RESTLESS, in the way of the living, but even for the living, she was *fast*. She was halfway down the hall by the time Nancy emerged from the room. At the sound of Nancy's footsteps, she paused, looking back over her shoulder and scowling at the taller girl.

"Hurry, hurry, hurry," she scolded. "If dinner catches us without doing what needs done, we'll miss the scones and jam."

"Dinner *chases* you? And you have scones and jam for dinner if it doesn't catch you?" asked Nancy, bewildered.

"Not usually," said Sumi. "Not *often*. Okay, not ever, yet. But it could happen, if we wait long enough, and I don't want to miss out when it does! Dinners are mostly dull, awful things, all meat and potatoes and things to build healthy minds and bodies. *Boring.* I bet your dinners with the dead people were a lot more fun."

"Sometimes," admitted Nancy. There had been banquets, yes, feasts that lasted weeks, with the tables groaning under the weight of fruits and wines and dark, rich desserts. She had tasted unicorn at one of those feasts, and gone to her bed with a mouth that still tingled from the delicate venom of the horse-like creature's sweetened flesh. But mostly, there had been the silver cups of pomegranate juice, and the feeling of an empty stomach adding weight to her stillness. Hunger had died quickly in the Underworld. It was unnecessary, and a small price to pay for the quiet, and the peace, and the dances; for everything she'd so fervently enjoyed.

"See? Then you understand the importance of a good dinner," Sumi started walking again, keeping her steps short in deference to Nancy's slower stride. "Kade will get you fixed right up, right as rain, right as rabbits, you'll see. Kade knows where the best things are."

"Who is Kade? Please, you have to slow down." Nancy felt like she was running for her life as she tried to keep up with Sumi. The smaller girl's motions were too fast, too constant for Nancy's Underworld-adapted eyes to track them properly. It was like following a large hummingbird toward some unknown destination, and she was already exhausted.

"Kade has been here a very-very long time. Kade's parents don't want him back." Sumi looked over her shoulder and twinkled at Nancy. There was no other word to describe her expression, which was a strange combination of wrinkling her nose and tightening the skin around her eyes, all without visibly smiling. "My parents didn't want me back either, not unless I was willing to be their good little girl again and put all this nonsense about Nonsense aside. They sent me here, and then they died, and now they'll never want me at all. I'm going to live here always, until Ely-Eleanor has to let me have the attic for my own. I'll pull taffy in the rafters and give riddles to all the new girls."

They had reached a flight of stairs. Sumi began bounding up them. Nancy followed more sedately.

"Wouldn't you get spiders and splinters and stuff in the candy?" she asked.

Sumi rewarded her with a burst of laughter and an actual smile. "*Spi*ders and *splin*ters and *stu*ff!" she crowed. "You're alliterating already! Oh, maybe we *will* be friends, ghostie girl, and this won't be completely dreadful after all. Now come on. We've much to do, and time does insist on being linear here, because it's awful."

The flight of stairs ended with a landing and another flight of stairs, which Sumi promptly started up, leaving Nancy no choice but to follow. All those days of stillness had made her muscles strong, accustomed to supporting her weight for hours at a time. Some people thought only motion bred strength. Those people were wrong. The mountain was as powerful as the tide, just . . . in a different way. Nancy *felt* like a mountain as she chased Sumi higher and higher into the house, until her heart was

thundering in her chest and her breath was catching in her throat, until she feared that she would choke on it.

Sumi stopped in front of a plain white door marked only with a small, almost polite sign reading KEEP OUT. Grinning, she said, "If he meant that, he wouldn't say it. He knows that for anyone who's spent any time at all in Nonsense that, really, he's issuing an invitation."

"Why do people around here keep using that word like it's a place?" asked Nancy. She was starting to feel like she'd missed some essential introductory session about the school, one that would have answered all her questions and left her a little less lost.

"Because it is, and it isn't, and it doesn't matter," said Sumi, and knocked on the attic door before hollering, "We're coming in!" and shoving it open to reveal what looked like a cross between a used bookstore and a tailor's shop. Piles of books covered every available surface. The furniture, such as it was—a bed, a desk, a table—appeared to be made *from* the piles of books, all save for the bookshelves lining the walls. Those, at least, were made of wood, probably for the sake of stability. Bolts of fabric were piled atop the books. They ranged from cotton and muslin to velvet and the finest of thin, shimmering silks. At the center of it all, cross-legged atop a pedestal of paperbacks, sat the most beautiful boy Nancy had ever seen.

His skin was golden tan, his hair was black, and when he looked up—with evident irritation—from the book he was holding, she saw that his eyes were brown and his features were perfect. There was something timeless about him, like he could have stepped out of a painting and into the material world. Then he spoke.

"What'n the fuck are you doing in here again, Sumi?" he demanded, Oklahoma accent thick as peanut butter spread across a slice of toast. "I told you that you weren't welcome after the last time."

"You're just mad because I came up with a better filing system for your books than you could," said Sumi, sounding unruffled. "Anyway, you didn't mean it. I am the sunshine in your sky, and you'd miss me if I was gone."

"You organized them by color, and it took me weeks to figure out where anything was. I'm doing important research up here." Kade unfolded his legs and slid down from his pile of books. He knocked off a paperback in the process, catching it deftly before it could hit the ground. Then he turned to look at Nancy. "You're new. I hope she's not already leading you astray."

"So far, she's just led me to the attic," said Nancy inanely. Her cheeks reddened, and she said, "I mean, no. I'm not so easy to lead places, most of the time."

"She's more of a 'standing really still and hoping nothing eats her' sort of girl," said Sumi, and thrust the suitcase toward him. "Look what her parents did."

Kade raised his eyebrows as he took in the virulent pinkness of the plastic. "That's colorful," he said after a moment. "Paint could fix it."

"Outside, maybe. You can't paint underpants. Well, you *can,* but then they come out all stiff, and no one believes you didn't mess them." Sumi's expression sobered for a moment. When she spoke again, it was with a degree of clarity that was almost unnerving, coming from her. "Her parents swapped out her things before they sent her off to school. They knew she wouldn't like it, and they did it anyway. There was a note."

"Oh," said Kade, with sudden understanding. "One of those. All right. Is this going to be a straight exchange, then?"

"I'm sorry, I don't understand what's going on," said Nancy. "Sumi grabbed my suitcase and ran away with it. I don't want to bother anyone. . . ."

"You're not bothering me," said Kade. He took the suitcase from Sumi before turning toward Nancy. "Parents don't always like to admit that things have changed. They want the world to be exactly the way it was before their children went away on these life-changing adventures, and when the world doesn't oblige, they try to force it into the boxes they build for us. I'm Kade, by the way. Fairyland."

"I'm Nancy, and I'm sorry, I don't understand."

"I went to a Fairyland. I spent three years there, chasing rainbows and growing up by inches. I killed a Goblin King with his own sword, and he made me his heir with his dying breath, the Goblin Prince in Waiting." Kade walked off into the maze of books, still carrying Nancy's suitcase. His voice drifted back, betraying his location. "The King was my enemy, but he was the first adult to see me clearly in my entire life. The court of the Rainbow Princess was shocked, and they threw me down the next wishing well we passed. I woke up in a field in the middle of

Nebraska, back in my ten-year-old body, wearing the dress I'd had on when I first fell into the Prism." The way he said "Prism" left no question about what he meant: it was a proper name, the title of some strange passage, and his voice ached around that single syllable like flesh aches around a knife.

"I still don't understand," said Nancy.

Sumi sighed extravagantly. "He's *saying* he fell into a Fairyland, which is sort of like going to a Mirror, only they're really high Logic pretending to be high Nonsense, it's *quite* unfair, there's rules on rules on rules, and if you break one, wham"—she made a slicing gesture across her throat—"out you go, like last year's garbage. *They* thought they had snicker-snatched a little girl—fairies love taking little girls, it's like an addiction with them—and when they found out they had a little boy who just *looked* like a little girl on the outside, uh-oh, donesies. They threw him right back."

"Oh," said Nancy.

"Yeah," said Kade, emerging from the maze of books. He wasn't carrying Nancy's suitcase anymore. Instead, he had a wicker basket filled with fabric in reassuring shades of black and white and gray. "We had a girl here a few years ago who'd spent basically a decade living in a Hammer film. Black and white everything, flowy, lacy, super-Victorian. Seems like your style. I think I've guessed your size right, but if not, feel free to come and let me know that you need something bigger or smaller. I didn't take you for the corsetry type. Was I wrong?"

"What? Um." Nancy wrenched her gaze away from the basket. "No. Not really. The boning gets uncomfortable after a day or two. We were more, um, Grecian where I was, I guess. Or Pre-Raphaelite." She was lying, of course: she knew exactly what the styles had been in her Underworld, in those sweet and silent halls. When she'd gone looking for signs that someone else knew where to find a door, combing through Google and chasing links across Wikipedia, she had come across the works of a painter named Waterhouse, and she'd cried from the sheer relief of seeing people wearing clothes that didn't offend her eyes.

Kade nodded, understanding in his expression. "I manage the clothing swaps and inventory the wardrobes, but I do custom jobs too," he said. "You'll have to pay for those, since they're a lot more work on my part. I take information as well as cash. You could tell me about your door and where you went, and I could make you a few things that might fit you better."

Nancy's cheeks reddened. "I'd like that," she said.

"Cool. Now get out, both of you. We have dinner in a little while, and I want to finish my book." Kade's smile was fleeting. "I never did like to leave a story unfinished."

SUMI WATCHED NANCY as they walked down the stairs. The taller girl was holding tight to her basket of black and white clothing, cheeks still faintly touched with red. The color seemed almost obscene on her, like it had no business there.

"Do you want to fuck him?"

Nancy almost fell down the stairs.

After she had caught herself on the banister, she turned to Sumi, sputtering and blushing, and said, "*No!*"

"Are you sure? Because you looked like you did, and then you looked sort of upset, like you'd figured out you didn't want to after all. Jill—you'll meet her at dinner—wanted to fuck him until she found out he used to be a girl, and then she called him 'she' until Miss Ely said that we respect people's personal identities here, and then we all had to listen to this weird story about a girl who used to live in the attic who was really a rainbow who'd managed to offend the King of the Sky in one of the Fairylands and got herself kicked out." Sumi paused to take a breath and added, "That was sort of scary. You never think about people from *there* winding up *here,* only people from *here* winding up *there.* Maybe the walls are never as impermeable as we think they are."

"Yes," said Nancy, recovering her composure. She began walking again. "I'm quite sure I don't want to . . . have sexual relations with him, and I don't think his gender expression is any of my business." She was reasonably sure that was the right way to say things. She'd known the words once, before she left this world, and its problems, behind her. "That's between him and whoever he does, or doesn't, decide to get involved with."

"If you don't want to do the bing-bang with Kade, I guess I should tell you I'm taken," said Sumi breezily. "He's a candy corn farmer from the far reaches of the Kingdom and my one true love, and we're going to get married someday. Or we would have, if I hadn't gone and gotten myself exiled. Now he'll tend his fields alone, and I'll grow up and decide that he was just a dream, and maybe one day my daughter's daughter will visit his grave with licorice flowers and a prayer for the departed on her lips."

Her tone never wavered, not even as she was talking about the death of someone she called her one true love. Nancy gave her a sidelong look, trying to decide how serious she was. It was difficult to tell with Sumi.

They had reached the door to their shared room. Nancy reached a decision at the same time. "It doesn't matter whether you're taken or not," she said, opening the door and walking toward her bed. She put down the basket of clothing. She would need to go through it at more length, to check the fits and fabrics, but it was already an improvement over what she had left behind with Kade. "I don't do that. With anyone."

"You're celibate?"

"No. Celibacy is a choice. I'm asexual. I don't get those feelings." She would have thought her lack of sexual desire had been what had drawn her to the Underworld—so many people had called her a "cold fish" and said she was dead inside back when she'd been attending an ordinary high school, among ordinary teenagers, after all—except that none of the people she'd met in those gloriously haunted halls had shared her orientation. They lusted as hotly as the living did. The Lord of the Dead and the Lady of Shadows had spread their ardor throughout the palace, and all had been warmed by its light. Nancy smiled a little at the memory, until she realized Sumi was still watching her. She shook her head. "I just . . . I just don't. I can appreciate how beautiful someone is, and I can be attracted to them romantically, but that's as far as it goes with me."

"Huh," said Sumi, heading for her own side of the room. Then: "Well, okay. Is it going to bother you if I masturbate?"

"What, right *now*?" Nancy was unable to keep the horror from her voice. Not at the thought of masturbation—at the idea that this girl she had just met was going to drop her trousers and go to town.

"Um, ew," said Sumi, wrinkling her nose. "No, I meant in general. Like, late at night, when the lights are low and the moon-mantas are spreading their wings across the sky, and a girl's fingers might get the urge to go plowing in the fields."

"Please stop," said Nancy weakly. "No, I will not be upset if you masturbate. At night. In the dark. Without telling me about it. I have nothing against masturbation. I just don't want to watch."

"Neither did my last roommate," said Sumi, and that seemed to be the end of that, at least as far as she was concerned; she climbed out the window, leaving Nancy alone with her thoughts, the room, and her new wardrobe.

Nancy watched the empty window for almost a minute before she sank onto the bed and put her head in her hands. She'd expected boarding to school to be full of people like her, quiet and serious and eager to go back to the lands they'd left. Not . . . this. Not Sumi, and people slinging around technical terms for things she didn't understand.

She felt like she was trying to sail her way home without a map. She'd been sent back to the world of her birth to be *sure* . . . and she'd never been less sure in her life.

DINNER WAS HELD in the downstairs ballroom, a single, vast space made even larger by the polished marble floor and the vaulted cathedral ceiling. Nancy paused in the doorway, daunted by the scope of it, and by the sight of her classmates, who dotted the tables like so many knickknacks. There were seats for a hundred students, maybe more, but there were only forty or so in the room. They were so small, and the space was so big.

"It's rude and lewd to block the *food*," said Sumi, shoving past her. Nancy was knocked off balance and stumbled over the threshold into the ballroom. Silence fell as everyone turned to look at her. Nancy froze. It was the only defense mechanism she had learned from her time among the dead. When she was still, the ghosts couldn't see her to steal her life away. Stillness was the ultimate protection.

A hand settled on her shoulder. "Ah, Nancy, good," said Eleanor. "I was hoping I'd run into you before you reached a table. Be a good girl and escort an old woman to her seat."

Nancy turned her head. Eleanor had changed for dinner, trading electric orange trousers and rainbow sweater for a lovely sheath dress made from tie-dyed muslin. It was shockingly bright. Much like the sun, it hurt Nancy's eyes.

Still, she offered her arm to the older woman, unable to think of anything else that would fit the laws of propriety.

"How are you and Sumi getting on?" asked Eleanor, as they walked toward the tables.

"She's very . . . abrupt," said Nancy.

"She lived in high Nonsense for almost ten years subjective time, and much as you learned to be still, she learned never to stop," said Eleanor. "Stopping is what got people killed where she was. It was very close to where I was, you see, so I understand her better than most. She's a good girl. She won't steer you wrong."

"She took me to meet a boy named Kade," said Nancy.

"Oh? It's unusual for her to start making introductions that quickly—unless . . . Did you have trouble with your clothing? Was what you packed not what you found in your suitcase?"

Nancy didn't say anything. Her reddening cheeks and averted eyes said it all. Eleanor sighed.

"I'll write your parents and remind them that they agreed to allow me to guide your therapy. We should be able to have whatever they removed from your suitcase mailed here within the month. In the meantime, you can go back to Kade for whatever you need. The dear boy is a whiz with a needle. I really don't know how we got along without him."

"Sumi said he'd been to something called a 'high Logic world'? I still don't understand what any of those words mean. You throw them around like everyone knows them, but they're all new to me."

"I know, dear. You'll have therapy tonight and a proper orientation with Lundy tomorrow, and she'll explain everything." Eleanor straightened as they reached the tables, taking her hand from Nancy's arm. She clapped, twice. All conversation stopped. The students seated there—most with spaces between them, a few in tight conversational knots that left no visible way in—turned to look at her, faces expectant.

"Good evening, everyone," said Eleanor. "By now, some of you have doubtlessly heard that we have a new student with us. This is Nancy. She'll be rooming with Sumi until one of them attempts to murder the other. If you'd like to place a bet on who kills who, please talk to Kade."

Laughter from the girls—and they were *overwhelmingly* girls, Nancy realized. Apart from Kade, who was sitting by himself with his nose buried in a book, there were only three boys in the entire group. It seemed odd for a coed school to be so unbalanced. She didn't say anything. Eleanor had promised her an orientation, and maybe everything would be explained there, making questions unnecessary.

"Nancy is still adjusting to being back in this world after her travels, so please be gentle with her for the first few days, even as all of us were gentle with you, once upon a time." There was a thin line of steel in Eleanor's words. "When she's ready to join in with the hurly-burly and the cheerful malice, she'll let you know. Now, eat up, all of you, even though you may not want to. We are in a material place. Blood flows in your veins. Try to keep it there." She stepped away from Nancy, leaving her anchorless as she walked away.

Dinner was set up buffet-style along one wall. Nancy drifted over to it, recoiling from the braising dishes of meat and baked vegetables. They would sit like stones in her stomach, too heavy and unforgiving to tolerate. In the end, she filled a plate with grapes, slices of melon, and a scoop of cottage cheese. Picking up a glass of cranberry juice, she turned to consider the tables.

She'd been good at this, once. She'd never been one of the most popular girls in her high school, but she'd understood the game enough to play it, and play it well, to read the temperature of a room and find the safe shallows, where the currents of mean-girl intensity wouldn't wash her away, but where she wouldn't risk drowning in the brackish tide pools of the outcasts and the unwanted. She remembered a time when it had mattered so *much*. Sometimes she wished she knew how to get back to the girl who'd cared about such things. Other times, she was grateful beyond words that she couldn't.

The boys, except for Kade, were all sitting together, blowing bubbles in their milk and laughing. No; not them. One group had formed around a girl who was so dazzlingly beautiful that Nancy's eyes refused to focus on her face; another had formed around a punch bowl filled with candy-pink liquid from which they all furtively sipped. Neither looked welcoming. Nancy looked around until she found the only safe harbor she was likely to see, and started in that direction.

Sumi was sitting across from a pair of girls who couldn't have looked more different—or more alike. Her plate was piled high with no concern for what touched what. Gravy-covered melon slices cascaded into roast beef coated in jam. The sight of it made Nancy's stomach flip, but she still put her plate down next to Sumi's, cleared her throat, and asked the ritual question:

"Is this seat taken?"

"Sumi was just explaining how you're the most boring cardboard parody of a girl ever to walk this world or any other, and we should all feel sorry for you," said one of the strangers, adjusting her glasses as she turned to look at Nancy. "That makes you sound like my kind of person. Please, sit, and relieve some of the tedium of our table."

"Thank you," said Nancy, and settled.

The strangers wore the same face in remarkably different ways. It was amazing how a little eyeliner and a downcast expression, or a pair of wire-framed glasses and a steely gaze could transform what should have been identical into something distinct and individual. They both had long blonde hair, freckles across the bridges of their noses, and narrow shoulders. One was dressed in a white button-down shirt, jeans, and a black vest that managed to come across as old-fashioned and fashion-forward at the same time; her hair was tied back, no-nonsense and no frills. Her only adornment was a bow tie patterned with tiny biohazard symbols. The other wore a flowing pink dress with a low-cut bodice and a truly astonishing number of lace flourishes. Her hair hung in loose curls the size of soup cans, gathered at the back with a single pink ribbon. A matching ribbon was tied around her neck, like a makeshift choker. Both appeared to be in their late teens, with eyes that were much older.

"I'm Jack, short for Jacqueline," said the one in the glasses. She pointed to the one in pink. "This is Jill, short for Jillian, because our parents should never have been allowed to name their own children. You're Nancy."

"Yes," said Nancy, unsure of how else she was expected to respond. "It's nice to meet you both."

Jill, who otherwise had neither moved nor spoken since Nancy approached the table, turned her eyes toward Nancy's plate and said, "You aren't eating much. Are you on a diet?"

"No, not really. I just . . ." Nancy hesitated before shaking her head and saying, "My stomach's upset from the trip and the stress and everything."

"Am I the stress, or am I everything?" asked Sumi, picking up a jam-sticky piece of meat and popping it in her mouth. Around it, she continued, "I guess I could be both. I'm flexible."

"I'm on a diet," said Jill proudly. Her plate contained nothing but the rarest strips of roast, some of them so red and bloody that they were virtually raw. "I eat meat every other day and spinach the rest of the time. My blood is so iron-rich you could set a compass by it."

"That's, um, very nice," said Nancy, looking to Sumi for help. She'd known girls on diets her entire life. Iron-rich blood had rarely, if ever, been their goal. Most of them had been looking for smaller waists, clearer complexions, and richer boyfriends, spurred on by a deeply ingrained self-loathing that had been manufactured for them before they were old enough to understand the kind of quicksand they were sinking in.

Sumi swallowed. "Jack and Jill went up the hill, to watch a bit of slaughter, Jack fell down and broke her crown, and Jill came tumbling after."

Jack looked long-suffering. "I hate that rhyme."

"And that's not what happened at all," said Jill. She turned to beam at Nancy. "We went to a very nice place, where we met very nice people who loved us very much. But there was a little problem with the local constabulary, and we had to come back to this world for a while, for our own safety."

"What have I told you about abusing the word 'very'?" asked Jack. She sounded tired.

"Jack and Jill are more stupid, stupid girls," said Sumi. She stabbed a slice of melon with her fork, splashing gravy on the table. "They think they're going *back*, but they're *not*. Those doors are closed now. Can't go high Logic, high Wicked if you're not innocent. The Wicked doesn't want people it can't *spoil*."

"I don't understand anything you people say," said Nancy. "Logic? Nonsense? Wicked? What do those things even *mean*?"

"They're directions, or the next best thing," said Jack. She leaned forward, dragging her index finger through the wet ring left by the base of a glass and using the moisture to draw a cross on the table. "Here in the so-called 'real world,' you have north, south, east, and west, right? Those don't work for most of the portal worlds we've been able to catalog. So we use other words. Nonsense, Logic, Wickedness, and Virtue. There are smaller subdirections, little branches that may or may not go anywhere, but those four are the big ones. Most worlds are either high Nonsense *or* high Logic, and then they have some degree of Wickedness or Virtue built into their foundations from there. A surprising number of Nonsense worlds are Virtuous. It's like they can't work up the attention span necessary for anything more vicious than a little mild naughtiness."

Jill gave Nancy a sidelong look. "Did that help at all?"

"Not really," said Nancy. "I never thought that . . . You know, I read *Alice's Adventures in Wonderland* when I was a kid, and I never thought about what it would be like for Alice when she went back to where she'd started. I figured she'd just shrug and get over it. But I can't do that. Every time I close my eyes, I'm back in my real bed, in my real room, and all of this is the dream."

"It isn't home anymore, is it?" asked Jill gently. Nancy shook her head, blinking back tears. Jill reached across the table to pat her hand. "It gets better. It never gets easy, but it does start to hurt a little less. How long has it been for you?"

"Just under two months." Seven weeks, four days since the Lord of the Dead had told her she needed to be *sure*. Seven weeks, four days since the door to her chambers had opened on the basement she'd left behind so long before, in the house she thought she'd left behind forever. Seven weeks, four days since her screaming had alerted her parents to an intruder and they had come pounding down the steps, only to sweep her into an unwanted embrace, bawling about how upset they'd been when she had disappeared.

She'd been gone for six months, from their perspective. One month for each of the pomegranate seeds that Persephone had eaten, back at the beginning of things. Years for her, and months for them. They still thought she was dyeing her hair. They still thought she was eventually going to tell them where she'd been.

They still thought a lot of things.

"It gets better," repeated Jill. "It's been a year and a half, for us. But we don't lose hope. I keep my iron levels up. Jack has her experiments—"

Jack didn't say anything. She just stood and walked away from the table, leaving her half-eaten dinner behind.

"We're not cleaning up after you!" shouted Sumi, around a mouthful of food.

In the end, of course, they did. There was really no other option.

3 BIRDS OF A FEATHER

ACCORDING TO WHAT Nancy's parents had told her about the school, the mandatory group therapy had been one of the big selling points. What better way to bring their teenage daughter back from whatever strange hole she'd crawled into than having her sit and talk to people who'd suffered similar traumas, all under the watchful eye of a trained professional? As she sank into the embrace of a thickly padded armchair, surrounded by teens who twitched, chewed their hair, or stared moodily off into space without speaking, she had to wonder what they would have thought of the reality.

Then the eight-year-old walked into the room.

She was dressed like a middle-aged librarian, wearing a pencil skirt and a white blouse, both of which were much too old for her. Her hair was pulled back into a tight, no-nonsense bun. The overall effect was of a child playing dress-up in her mother's closet. Nancy sat up straighter. The school's brochures had mentioned an age range of twelve to nineteen, allowing both the precocious and those who needed a little time to catch up to attend. It hadn't said anything about children under the age of ten.

The girl stopped at the center of the room, turning to look at each of them in turn. One by one, the fidgeters became still; the hair chewers stopped chewing; even Sumi, who'd been doing an elaborate cat's cradle with a piece of yarn, lowered her hands and sat quietly. The girl smiled.

"For those of you who've been here for a while, welcome to Wednesday night group. We're going to be sharing with the high Wicked visitors tonight, but as always, the discussion is open to all." Her voice matched her body. Her tone was older, cadenced like an adult woman's, rendered high and strange by her prepubescent vocal cords. She looked at Nancy as she continued. "For those of you who are new here, my name is Lundy, and I am a fully licensed therapist with a specialization in child psychology. I'm going to be helping you through your recovery process."

Nancy stared. She couldn't think of anything else to do.

As Lundy walked over to the one remaining chair, Kade leaned over and murmured, "She's one of us, only she went to a high Logic, high Wicked world where they kicked visitors out on their eighteenth birthdays. She didn't want to leave, so she asked one of the local apothecaries to help her. This was the result. Eternal childhood."

"Not eternal, Mr. Bronson," said Lundy sharply. Kade

sat up and settled back in his own chair, shrugging unapologetically. Lundy sighed. "You would have gotten this at your orientation, Miss, ah . . . ?"

"Whitman," said Nancy.

"Miss Whitman," said Lundy. "As I was saying, you would have gotten this at your orientation, but: I'm not living out an eternal childhood. I'm aging in reverse, growing one week younger for every month that passes. I'll live a long, long time. Longer, maybe, than I would have had I continued aging in the usual way. But they threw me out anyway, because I had broken the rules. I'll never marry, or have a family of my own, and my daughters will never find their way to the door that once led me to the Goblin Market. So I suppose I've learnt the danger of making importune bargains with the fae, and can now serve as a warning to others. I am still, however, your therapist. It's amazing, the degrees you can get over the Internet these days."

"I'm sorry," whispered Nancy.

Lundy waved a hand as she sat, dismissing Nancy's apology. "It's no matter, honestly. Everyone finds out eventually. Now. Who wants to share first?"

Nancy sat in silence as the other students talked. Not all of them: slightly less than half seemed to have been to a world that fell on the "Wicked" side of the compass, or maybe that was just the number who felt like sharing. Jill recited an impassioned paean to the moors and wind-racked hills of the world she'd gone to with her sister, while Jack only muttered something about burning windmills and the importance of fire safety in laboratory settings.

A girl with hair the color of moonlight on wheat stared at her hands while she talked about boys made of glass whose kisses had cut her lips but whose hearts had been kind and true. The girl who was too beautiful to look at directly said something about Helen of Troy, and half the room laughed, but not because it was funny; because she was so beautiful that they wanted nothing more than they wanted her to like them.

Kade made a brief, bitter speech about how Wickedness and Virtue were just labels and didn't mean anything; the world he'd been to was labeled "Virtue" on all the maps, but it had still cast him out as soon as it realized what he was.

Finally, silence fell, and Nancy realized everyone was looking at her. She shrank back in her seat. "I don't know if the place I went was wicked or not," she said. "It never seemed wicked to me. It always seemed . . . kind, at the root of things. Yes, there were rules, and yes, there were punishments if you broke them, but they were never unfair, and the Lord of the Dead took good care of everyone who served in his halls. I don't think it was wicked at all."

"How can you be sure, though?" asked Sumi, and her voice was gentle, underneath her jeering tone. "You can't even say Wicked right. Maybe it was evil to the core, filled with wiggling worms and bad stuff, and you couldn't see it." She slanted a glance toward Jill, almost as if she were checking the other girl's reaction. Jill, whose eyes were fixed on Nancy, didn't appear to notice. "You shouldn't close doors just because you don't like what's on the other side."

"I know because I know," said Nancy doggedly. "I didn't go anyplace bad. I went *home*."

"That's the thing people forget when they start talking about things in terms of good and evil," said Jack, turning to look at Lundy. She adjusted her glasses as she continued, "For us, the places we went were home. We didn't care if they were good or evil or neutral or what. We cared about the fact that for the first time, we didn't have to pretend to be something we weren't. We just got to *be*. That made all the difference in the world."

"And on that note, I suppose we're done for the evening." Lundy stood. Nancy realized with a start that somewhere in the middle of the session, she'd started thinking of the little girl as an adult woman. It was the way she carried herself: too mature for the body she inhabited, too weary for the face she wore. "Thank you, everyone. Miss Whitman, I'll see you tomorrow morning for orientation. Everyone else, I'll see you tomorrow evening, when we'll be speaking to those who have traveled to the high Logic worlds. Remember, only by learning about the journeys of others can we truly understand our own."

"Oh, lovely," muttered Jack. "I do so love being in the hot seat two nights running."

Lundy ignored her, walking calmly out of the room. As soon as she was gone, Eleanor appeared in the doorway, all smiles.

"All right, my crumpets, it's time for good little girls and boys to go to bed," she said, and clapped her hands. "Off you go. Dream sweetly, try not to sleepwalk, and please don't wake me up at midnight trying to force a portal to manifest in the downstairs pantry. It isn't going to happen."

The students rose and scattered, some moving off in pairs, others going alone. Sumi went out the window, and no one commented on her disappearance.

Nancy walked back to her room, pleased to find it bathed in moonlight and filled with silence. She disrobed, garbed herself in a white nightgown from the pile Kade had given her, and stretched out on her bed, lying atop the covers. She closed her eyes, slowed her breathing, and slipped into sweet, motionless sleep, her first day done, and her future yet ahead of her.

ORIENTATION WITH LUNDY the next morning was odd, to say the least. It was held in a small room that had been a study once, before it had been filled with blackboards and the smell of chalk dust. Lundy stood at the center of it all, one hand resting on a wheeled stepladder, which she moved from blackboard to blackboard as the need to climb up and point to some complicated diagram arose. The need seemed to arise with dismaying frequency. Nancy sat very still in the room's single chair, her head spinning as she struggled to keep up.

Lundy's explanation of the cardinal directions of portals had been, if anything, less helpful than Jack's, and had involved a lot more diagrams, and some offhanded comments about minor directions, like Whimsy and Wild. Nancy had bitten her tongue to keep from asking any questions. She was deeply afraid that Lundy would attempt to answer them, and then her head might actually explode.

Finally, Lundy stopped and looked expectantly at Nancy. "Well?" she asked. "Do you have any questions, Miss Whitman?"

About a million, and all of them wanted to be asked at once, even the ones she didn't want to ask at all. Nancy took a deep breath and started with what seemed to be the easiest: "Why are there so many more girls here than boys?"

"Because 'boys will be boys' is a self-fulfilling prophecy," said Lundy. "They're too loud, on the whole, to be easily misplaced or overlooked; when they disappear from the home, parents send search parties to dredge them out of swamps and drag them away from frog ponds. It's not innate. It's learned. But it protects them from the doors, keeps them safe at home. Call it irony, if you like, but we spend so much time waiting for our boys to stray that they never have the opportunity. We notice the silence of men. We depend upon the silence of women."

"Oh," said Nancy. It made sense, in its terrible way. Most of the boys she'd known were noisy creatures, encouraged to be so by their parents and friends. Even when they were naturally quiet, they forced themselves to be loud, to avoid censure and mockery. How many of them could have slipped through an old wardrobe or into a rabbit's den and simply disappeared without sending up a thousand alarms? They would have been found and dragged back home before they reached the first enchanted mirror or climbed the first forbidden tower.

"We've always been open to male students; we just don't get many."

"Everyone here . . . everyone seems to want to go back." Nancy paused, struggling with the question that was trying to form. Finally, she asked, "How is it that *everyone* wants to go back? I thought people who went through this sort of thing mostly just wanted to go back to their old lives and forget that they'd ever known anything else."

"This isn't the only school, of course," said Lundy. She smiled at Nancy's surprise. "What, you thought Miss West could sweep up every child who'd ever stumbled into a painting and discovered a magical world on the other side? It happens all over the world, you know. The language barriers alone would make it impossible, as would the expense. There are two schools in North America, this campus and our sister school in Maine. That's where the students who hated their travels go, to learn how to move on. How to forget."

"So we're here to do . . . what?" asked Nancy. "Learn how to dwell? Eleanor dresses like she's still living on the other side of the mirror. Sumi is . . ." She didn't have the words for what Sumi was. She stopped speaking.

"Sumi is a classic example of someone who embraced life in a high Nonsense world," said Lundy. "She can't be blamed for what it made of her, any more than you can be blamed for the way you seem to stop breathing when no one's looking at you. She's going to need a lot of work before she's ready to face the world outside again, and she has to want to do it. That's what determines which school is better for you: the wanting. You want to go back, and so you hold on to the habits you learned while you were traveling, because it's better than admitting the journey's over. We don't teach you how to dwell. We also don't teach you how to forget. We teach you how to move on."

There was one more question that needed to be asked, a question bigger and more painful than all the questions before it. Nancy closed her eyes for a moment, allowing herself to sink into stillness. Then she opened them and asked, "How many of us have gone back?"

Lundy sighed. "Every student I've given this orientation to has asked that question. The answer is, we don't know. Some people, like Eleanor—like me—go back over and over again before we wind up staying in one world or the other for good. Others only take one trip in their lives. If your parents choose to withdraw you, or if you choose to withdraw yourself, we'll have no way of knowing what becomes of you. I know of three students who have returned to the worlds they left behind. Two were high Logic, both Fairylands. The third was high Nonsense. An Underworld, like the one you visited—although not the same, I'm afraid. That one was accessed by walking through a special mirror, under the full moon. The girl we lost to that world was home for the holidays when the door opened for her a second time. Her mother broke the glass after she went through. We learned later that the mother had also been there—it was a generational portal—and had wanted to spare her daughter the pain of returning."

"Oh," said Nancy, in a very small voice.

"The chances are, Miss Whitman, that you'll live out your days in this world. You may tell people of your adventures, when they're more distant, and when speaking of them hurts somewhat less. Many of our graduates have found that sort of sharing to be both cathartic and lucrative. People do so love a good fantasy." Lundy's expression was sorrowful but kind, like that of a doctor delivering a terminal diagnosis. "I won't stand here and say the door is closed forever, because there's no way of being sure. But I *will* tell you the odds were against you going in the first place, and that those same odds are against you now. They say lightning never strikes twice. Well, you're far more likely to be struck repeatedly by lightning than you are to find a second door."

"Oh," said Nancy again.

"I'm sorry." Then Lundy smiled, ridiculously bright. "Welcome to school, Miss Whitman. We hope that we can make you better."

PART II

WITH YOUR LOOKING-GLASS EYES

4 LIGHTNING TO KISS THE SKY

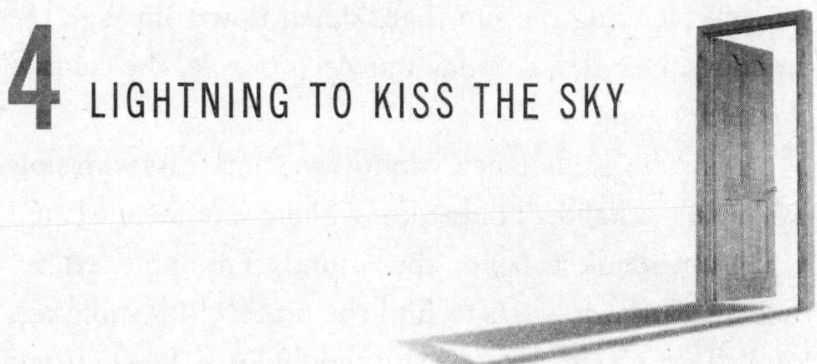

THE BUILDING WAS BIGGER than its population, filled with empty rooms and silent spaces. But all of them felt like they harbored the ghosts of the students who had tried—and failed—to find their way back to the worlds that had rejected them, and so Nancy fled to the outside. She hated to rush, but the sun burnt so badly that she actually *ran* for the deepest copse of trees she could find, shielding her eyes with her arm. She flung herself into the welcome shade of the grove, blinking back tears brought on as much by the light as by her dismay. Setting her back to an ancient oak, she sank to the ground, buried her face against her knees, and settled into perfect stillness as she wept.

"It's hard, isn't it?" The voice belonged to Jill, soft and wistful and filled with painful understanding. Nancy raised her head. The gossamer blonde was perched on a tree root, her pale lavender gown arranged to drape just so around her slender frame, a parasol resting against her left shoulder and blocking the sun that filtered down through the branches. Her choker today was deep purple, the color of elderberry wine.

"I'm sorry," said Nancy, wiping away her tears with slow swipes of her hand. "I didn't know there was anyone here."

"It's the shadiest spot on the grounds. I'm impressed, actually. It took me *weeks* to find the place." Jill's smile was kind. "I wasn't trying to say you should leave. I just meant, well, it's hard being here, surrounded by all these people who went to their pastel dream worlds full of sunshine and rainbows. They don't understand us."

"Um," said Nancy, glancing at Jill's pastel gown.

Jill laughed. "I don't wear these because I want to remember where I've been. I wear them because the Master liked it when I dressed in pale colors. They showed the blood better. Isn't that why you wear white? Because your Master liked to see you that way?"

"I . . ." Nancy stopped. "He wasn't my master, he was my Lord, and my teacher, and he loved me. I wear black and white because color is reserved for the Lady of Shadows and her entourage. I'd like to join them someday, if I can prove myself, but until then, I'm supposed to serve as a statue, and statues should blend in. Standing out is for people who've earned it." She touched the pomegranate ribbon in her hair—and one piece of color she *had* earned—before asking, "You had a . . . master?"

"Yes." Jill's smile was bright enough to replace the

blocked-away sun. "He was good to me. Gave me treats and trinkets and told me I was beautiful, even when I wasn't feeling well. *Jack* spent all her time locked away with her precious doctor, learning things that weren't ladylike or appropriate in the least, but I stayed in the high towers with the Master, and he taught me so many beautiful things. So many beautiful, wonderful things."

"I'm sorry you wound up back here," said Nancy.

Jill's smile died. She flapped a hand like she was trying to wave Nancy's words away, and said, "This isn't forever. The Master wanted to be rid of Jack. She didn't deserve what we had. So he arranged things so a door would open back to our world, and I stumbled and fell through after her. He'll find a way to open a door back to me. You'll see." She stood, spinning her parasol. "Excuse me. I have to go." Then she turned, not waiting for Nancy to say goodbye, and walked briskly away.

"And that, children, is why sometimes we don't let the Addams twins out into the general population," said a voice. Nancy looked up. Kade, who was seated on one of the tree's higher branches, waved sardonically down at her. "Hello, Nancy out of Wonderland. If you were looking for a private place to cry, you chose poorly."

"I didn't think anyone would be out here," she said.

"Because back at home, the other kids were more likely to hide in their rooms than they were to go running for the outdoors, right?" Kade closed his book. "The trouble is, you're at a school for people who never learned how to make the logical choice. So we go running for the tallest trees and the deepest holes whenever we want to be alone, and since there's a limited number of those, we wind up spending a lot of time together. I take it from the crying that your orientation didn't go well. Let me guess. Lundy told you about lightning striking twice."

Nancy nodded. She didn't speak. She no longer trusted her voice.

"She has a point, if your world kicked you out."

"It didn't kick me out," protested Nancy. She could still speak, after all, when she really needed to. "I was sent back to learn something, that's all. I'm going back."

Kade looked at her sympathetically and didn't contradict her. "Prism is never taking me back," he said instead. "That's not a nonstarter, that's a never-gonna-happen. I violated their rules when I wasn't what they wanted me to be, and the people who run that particular circus are *very* picky about rules. But Eleanor went back a bunch of times. Her door's still open."

"How . . . I mean, why . . ." Nancy shook her head. "Why did she stop? If her door is still open, why is she *here,* with us, and not there, where she *belongs*?"

Kade swung his legs around so they were braced on the same side of the branch. Then he dropped down from the tree, landing easily in front of Nancy. He straightened, saying, "This was a long time ago, and her parents were still alive. She thought she could have it all, go back and forth, spend as much time as possible in her real home without breaking her father's heart. But she forgot that adults don't thrive in Nonsense, even when they're raised to it. Every time she came back *here,* she got a little older. Until one day she went back *there,* and it nearly broke her. Can you imagine what that must have been like? It would be like opening the door that was supposed to take you home and discovering you couldn't breathe the air anymore."

"That sounds horrible," said Nancy.

"I guess it was." Kade sank down to sit, cross-legged, across from her. "Of course, she'd already spent enough time in Nonsense for it to have changed her. It slowed her aging—that's probably why she was able to keep going for as long as she did. Jack checked the record books the last time we had an excursion to town, and she found out Eleanor was almost a hundred. I always figured she was in her sixties. I asked her about it, and you know what she told me?"

"What?" asked Nancy, fascinated and horrified at the same time. Had the Underworld changed more than just her hair? Was she going to stay the same, immortal and unchanging, while everything around her withered and died?

"She said she's just waiting to get senile, like her mother and father did, because once her mind slips enough, she'll be able to tolerate the Nonsense again. She's going to run this school until she forgets why she isn't going back, and then, when she *does* go back, she'll be able to stay." He shook his head. "I can't decide if it's genius or madness."

"Maybe it's a little bit of both," said Nancy. "I'd do anything to go home."

"Most of the students here would," said Kade bitterly.

Nancy hesitated before she said, "Lundy said there was a sister school for people who *didn't* want to go back. People who wanted to forget. Why are you enrolled here, instead of there? You might be happier."

"But you see, I don't want to forget," said Kade. "I'm the loophole kid. I want to remember Prism more than anything. The way the air tasted, and the way the music sounded. Everyone played these funky pipes there, even little kids. Lessons started when you were, like, two, and it was another way of communicating. You could have whole conversations without putting down your pipes. I grew *up* there, even if I wound up getting tossed out and forced to do it all over again. I figured out who I was there. I kissed a girl with hair the color of cabbages and eyes the color of moth-wings, and she kissed me back, and it was wonderful. Just because I wouldn't go back if you paid me, that doesn't mean I want to forget a *second* of what happened to me. I wouldn't be who I am if I hadn't gone to Prism."

"Oh," said Nancy. It made sense, of course, it was just an angle she hadn't considered. She shook her head. "This is all so much more complicated than I ever expected it to be."

"Tell me about it, princess." Kade stood, offering her his hand. "Come on. I'll walk you back to school."

Nancy hesitated before reaching up and taking the offered hand, letting Kade pull her to her feet. "All right," she said.

"You're pretty when you smile," said Kade as he led her out of the trees, back toward the main building. Nancy couldn't think of anything to say in response to that, and so she didn't say anything at all.

CORE CLASSES WERE SURPRISINGLY dull, taught as they were by an assortment of adults who drove in from the town, Lundy, and Miss Eleanor herself. Nancy got the distinct feeling that someone had a chart showing exactly what was required by the state and that they were all receiving the educational equivalent of a balanced meal.

The electives were slightly better, including music, art, and something called "A Traveler's History of the Great Compass," which Nancy guessed had something to do with the various portal worlds and their relations to one another. After hesitantly considering her options, she had signed up. Maybe something in the syllabus would tell her more about where her Underworld fell.

After reading the introductory chapters of her home-printed textbook, she was still confused. The most common directions were Nonsense, usually paired with Virtue, and Logic, usually paired with Wicked. Sumi's madhouse of a world was high Nonsense. Kade's Prism was high Logic. With those as her touchstones, Nancy had decided that her Underworld was likely to have been Logic; it had consistent rules and expected them to be followed. But she couldn't see why it should really be considered Wicked just because it was ruled by the Lord of the Dead. Virtue seemed more likely. Her first actual class was scheduled for two days' time. It was too long to wait. It was no time at all.

By the end of her first day, she was exhausted, and her head felt like it had been stuffed well beyond any reasonable capacity, spinning with both mundane things like math and history, and with the ever-increasing vocabulary needed to talk to her fellow students. One, a shy girl with brown braids and thick glasses, had confessed that *her* world was at the nexus of two minor compass directions, being high Rhyme and high Linearity. Nancy hadn't known what to say to that, and so she hadn't said anything at all. Increasingly, that felt like the safest option she had.

Sumi was sitting on her bed, braiding bits of bright ribbon into her hair, when Nancy slipped into the room. "Tired as a titmouse at a bacchanal, little ghostie?" she asked.

"I don't know what you mean, so I'm going to assume you want to be taken at face value," said Nancy. "Yes. I am very tired. I'm going to bed."

"Ely-Eleanor thought you might be tired," said Sumi. "New girls always are. She said you can skip group tonight, but you can't make a habit of it. Words are an important part of the healing process. Words, words, words." She wrinkled her nose. "She asked me to remember so many of them, and all in the order she gave, and all for *you*. You're not Nonsense at all, are you, ghostie? You wouldn't want so many words if you were."

"I'm sorry," said Nancy. "I never said I was from . . . a place like you went to visit."

"Assumptions will be the death of all, and you're better than most of the roommates she's tried to give me; I'll keep you," said Sumi wearily. She stood, walking toward the door. "Sleep well, ghostie. I'll see you in the morning."

"Wait!" Nancy hadn't intended to speak; the word had simply escaped her lips, like a runaway calf. The thought horrified her. Her stillness was eroding, and if she stayed in this dreadful, motile world too long, she would never be able to get it back again.

Sumi turned to face her, cocking her head. "What do you want *now*?"

"I just wanted to know—I mean, I was just wondering—how old are you?"

"Ah." Sumi turned again, finishing her walk toward the door. Then, facing into the hall, she said, "Older than I look, younger than I ought to be. My skin is a riddle not to be solved, and even letting go of everything I love won't offer me the answer. My window is closing, if that's what you're asking. Every day I wake up a little more linear, a little less lost, and one day I'll be one of the women who says 'I had the most charming dream,' and I'll mean it. Old enough to know what I'm losing in the process of being found. Is that what you wanted to know?"

"No," said Nancy.

"Too bad," said Sumi, and left the room. She closed the door behind herself.

Nancy undressed alone, letting her clothes fall to the floor, until she stood naked in front of the room's single silver mirror. The electric light was harsh against her skin. She flipped the switch, and smiled to see her reflection transmuted into the purest marble, becoming unyielding, unbending stone. She stood there, frozen, for almost an hour before she finally felt like she could sleep, and slid, still naked, between her sheets.

She woke to a room full of sunlight and the sound of screaming.

Screams had not been not uncommon in the Halls of the Dead. There was an art to decoding their meaning: screams of pleasure, screams of pain, screams of sheer boredom in the face of an uncaring eternity. These were screams of panic and fear. Nancy rolled out of her bed in an instant, grabbing her nightgown from where it lay discarded at the foot of the bed and yanking it on over her head. She didn't feel like running into potential danger while completely exposed. She didn't feel like *running* anywhere, but the screams were still happening, and it seemed like the appropriate thing to do.

Sumi's bed was empty. The thought that Sumi could be the screamer crossed Nancy's mind as she ran, but was quickly dismissed. Sumi was not a screamer. Sumi was a reason for *other* people to scream.

Half a dozen girls were clustered in the hallway, forming an unbreakable wall of flannel and silk. Nancy pushed her way into their midst and stopped, freezing in place. It was a stillness so absolute, so profound, that she would have been proud of herself under any other circumstances. As it was, this felt less like proper stillness and more like the freeze of a rabbit when faced with the promise of a snake.

Sumi was the cause of the screaming: that much was clear. She was slumped limply against the base of the wall, eyes closed. She wasn't breathing, and her hands—her clever, never-still hands—were gone, severed at the wrists. She would never tie another knot or weave another cat's cradle out of yarn. Someone had stolen that from her. Someone had stolen *everything* from her.

"Oh," whispered Nancy, and the sound was like a stone dropped into a still pool: small, but creating ripples that touched everything in their path. One of the girls whirled and ran, shouting for Miss Eleanor. Another began to sob, pressing her back to the wall and sinking down to the floor until she looked like a cruel parody of Sumi. Nancy thought about telling her to get up and decided against it. What did she know of grief in the face of death? All the dead people she'd ever met had been perfectly pleasant and not overly inconvenienced by the fact that they no longer had material bodies. Maybe Sumi would find her way to the Underworld and be able to tell the Lord of the Dead that Nancy was still trying to be sure, so that she could come back. He would be pleased, Nancy was sure, to hear that she was trying.

Belatedly, Nancy realized that it might look suspicious, her roommate dying when she had just arrived from the Underworld—maybe they would assume she preferred the dead to the living, or that Eleanor's comments about them killing each other had been warnings—but since she hadn't touched Sumi, she decided not to worry about it. There were better things to worry about, like Eleanor, now hurrying along the hall, flanked by the girl who'd run to fetch her on one side and by Lundy on the other. Lundy was wearing a grandmotherly flannel nightgown, with curlers in her hair. It should have looked ridiculous. Somehow, it just looked sad.

The girls parted to let Eleanor through. She stopped a few feet from Sumi, pressing one hand over her mouth, her eyes filling with tears. "Oh, my poor girl," she murmured, kneeling to press her fingers to the side of Sumi's neck. It was just a formality: she had clearly been dead for quite some time. "Who did this to you? Who could have done this to you?"

Nancy was somehow unsurprised when several of the girls turned to look at her. She was new; she had been touched by the dead. She didn't protest her innocence. She just held up her hands, showing them the pale, unblemished skin. There was no way she could have washed the blood away so completely in one of their shared bathrooms, not without being seen. Even in the middle of the night, the amount of scrubbing required to get the blood from under her fingernails would have attracted attention, and she would have been undone.

"Leave poor Nancy alone; she didn't do this," said Eleanor. She wiped her eyes before offering her arm to Lundy, who helped her up. "No daughter of the Underworld would kill someone who hadn't earned their place in those hallowed halls, isn't that right, Nancy? She might be a murderess someday, but not on the basis of two days' acquaintance." Her tone was leaden with sorrow but perfectly matter-of-fact at the same time, as if the idea that Nancy might someday start mowing her friends down like wheat was of no real concern.

In the here and now, Nancy supposed that it wasn't. She watched dully as Lundy produced a sheet from somewhere—linen closets, there had to be linen closets in a house this large—and covered Sumi's body. The blood from Sumi's stumps soaked through the fabric almost instantly, but it was still a little bit better than looking at the motionless girl with the ribbons in her hair.

"What happened?"

Nancy glanced to the side. Jack had appeared next to her, the collar of her shirt open and her bow tie hanging untied on the left. She looked unfinished. "If you don't know what happened, why are you here?" It occurred to Nancy that she didn't know where Jack's room was, and she amended, "Unless this is your hall."

"No, Jill and I sleep in the basement. It's more comfortable for us, all things considered." She adjusted her glasses, squinting at the red blotches on the sheet. "That's blood. Who's under the sheet?"

The girl with the brown braids from the Rhyme and Linearity world turned to glare at Jack. There was pure hatred in her gaze, enough that Nancy took an involuntary step backward. "Like you don't know, you *murderer*," she spat. "You did this, didn't you? This is just like what happened to Angela's guinea pig. You can't keep your hands or your scalpels to yourself."

"I told you, it was a cultural mix-up," said Jack. "The

guinea pig was in a common area, and I thought it was supposed to be for anyone who wanted it."

"It was a *pet,*" snapped the girl.

Jack shrugged helplessly. "I offered to put it back together. Angela declined."

"New girl." The voice was Kade's. Nancy looked over to see him nodding toward her room. "Why don't you take that Addams and show her your room? I'll try to intercept the other one before she can show up and start trouble."

"Anything to avoid another angry mob with torches," said Jack, seizing Nancy's hand. "Show me your room."

It sounded like a command rather than a request. Nancy didn't argue. Under the circumstances, getting Jack out of sight and hence hopefully out of mind seemed much more important than forcing the other girl to ask nicely. She turned and hauled Jack to her door, still ajar after her hurried exit, and then inside.

Jack let go of Nancy's hand as soon as they were inside, producing a handkerchief from her pocket and wiping her fingers. Her cheeks reddened when she saw Nancy's startled look. "Difficult as it may be to believe, none of us escaped our travels unscathed, not even me," she said. "I am perhaps a bit *too* aware of the natural world and its many wonders. A lot of those wonders would like nothing more than to melt the skin off your body. All those people in their creepy labs hooking dead bodies up to funky wires? There's a reason they usually wear gloves."

"I don't really understand what the world you traveled to was *like,*" said Nancy. "Sumi's world was all about candy and not making any sense at all, and Kade went to a war or something, but the world you describe and the world Jill describes barely seem to match up."

"That's because the worlds we experienced barely seemed to match up, despite being the same place," said Jack. "Our parents were . . . let's go with 'overbearing.' The sort who always wanted to put things in boxes. I think they hated us being identical twins more than we did."

"But your names—"

Jack shrugged broadly, tucking the handkerchief back into her pocket. "They weren't so upset that they were willing to pass up the chance to make our lives a living hell. Parents are special that way. For some reason, they'd expected fraternal twins, maybe even that holy grail of the instant nuclear family, a boy and a girl. Instead, they got us. Ever watch a pair of perfectionists try to decide which of their identical children is the 'smart one' versus the 'pretty one'? It would have been funny, if our lives hadn't been the prize they were trying to win."

Nancy frowned. "You look just like your sister. How could they think she was the pretty one instead of seeing that you were both lovely?"

"Oh, *Jill* wasn't the pretty one. Jill got to be the smart one, with expectations and standards she was supposed to live up to. *I* was the pretty one." Jack's smile was quick, lopsided, and wry. "If we both asked for Lego, she got scientists and dinosaurs, and I got a flower shop. If we both asked for shoes, she got sneakers, and I got ballet flats. They never asked us, naturally. My hair was easier to brush one day when we were toddlers—probably because she had jam in hers—and bam, the roles were set. We couldn't get away from them. Until one day we opened an old trunk and found a set of stairs inside."

Jack's voice had gone distant. Nancy held herself in perfect stillness, not speaking, barely daring to breathe. If she wanted to hear this story, she couldn't interrupt it. Something about the way Jack was glaring at the wall told her she was only going to get one chance.

"We went down the mysterious stairs that couldn't possibly be there, of course. Who *wouldn't* go down an impossible staircase in the bottom of a trunk? We were twelve. We were curious, and angry with our parents, and angry with each other." Jack tied her bow tie with quick, furious jerks. "We went down, and at the bottom there was a door, and on the door there was a sign. Two words. BE SURE. Sure of what? We were *twelve,* we weren't sure of *anything.* So we went through. We came out on this moor that seemed to go on forever, between the mountains and the angry sea. And that sky! I'd never seen so many stars before, or such a red, red moon. The door slammed shut behind us. We couldn't have gone back if we'd wanted to—and we didn't want to. *We were twelve.* We were going to have an adventure if it killed us."

"Did you?" asked Nancy. "Have an adventure, I mean?"

"Sure," said Jack bleakly. "It didn't even kill us. Not permanently, anyway. But it changed everything. I finally got to be the smart one. Dr. Bleak taught me everything he knew about the human body, the ways of recombining and reanimating tissue. He said I was the best pupil he'd ever had. That I had incredibly talented hands." She looked at her fingers like she was seeing them for the first time. "Jill went in a different direction. The world we went to, it was . . . feudal, almost, divided into villages and moors and protectorates, with a master or mistress holding sway over each of them. Our Master was a bloodsucker, centuries old, with a fondness for little girls—not like that! Not in any sort of inappropriate way. Even Dr. Bleak was a child to him, and the Master wasn't the sort of man who thought about children like that. But he did need blood to live. He made Jill a lot of promises. He told her she could be his daughter one day and rule alongside him. I guess that's why it was so important we be taken care of. When the villagers marched on the castle, he sent my sister to hide with me in the laboratory. Dr. Bleak said . . . he, uh, said it was too dangerous for us to stay, and he opened a doorway. Neither of us wanted to go, but I understood the necessity. I promised I would stay a scientist, no matter what else happened, and that one day, I'd find a way back to him. Jill—he had to sedate her before she would go through. We found ourselves back in that old trunk, the lid half closed and the stairway gone. I've been looking for the formula to unlock the way back for the both of us ever since."

"Oh," said Nancy, in a hushed voice.

Jack smiled that wry smile again. "Spending five years apprenticed to a mad scientist sort of changes your outlook on the world. I know Kade hates the fact that he had to go through puberty twice—he thinks it was unfair, and I guess for him, it was. Gender dysphoria is a form of torture. But I wish we'd gotten the same deal. We were twelve when we went into that trunk. We were seventeen when we came out. Maybe we would have been able to adapt to this stupid, colorful, narrow-minded world if we'd woken from a shared dream and been thrown straight into middle school. Instead, we staggered down the stairs and found our parents having dinner with our four-year-old brother, who'd been told for his entire life that we were dead. Not missing. That would have been *messy*. God forbid that we should ever make a *mess*."

"How long have you been here?" asked Nancy.

"Almost a year," said Jack. "Dearest Mommy and Daddy had us on the bus to boarding school within a month of our coming home. They couldn't stand to have us under the same roof as their precious boy, who didn't tell crazy stories about watching lightning snake down from the heavens and shock a beautiful corpse back into the land of the living." Her eyes went soft and dreamy. "I think the rules were different there. It was all about science, but the science was magical. It didn't care about whether something *could* be done. It was about whether it *should* be done, and the answer was always, always *yes*."

There was a knock at the door. Nancy and Jack both turned to see Kade stick his head inside.

"The crowd has mostly dissipated, but I have to ask: Jack, did you kill Sumi?"

"I'm not offended that you'd suspect me, but I'm offended that you think I'd kill for a pair of hands," said

Jack. She sniffed, squaring her shoulders. She looked suddenly imperious, and Nancy realized how much of Jack's superior attitude was just a put-on, something to keep the world a little more removed. "If *I* had killed Sumi, there would have been no body to find. I would have put every scrap of her to good use, and people would be wondering for years whether she'd finally managed to pry open the door that would take her back to Candyland. Alas, I didn't kill her."

"She called it Confection, not Candyland, but point taken." Kade stepped into the room. "Seraphina and Loriel have taken Jill someplace quiet while we wait for everyone to calm down. We're supposed to stay in our rooms and out of sight while Eleanor summons the city coroner."

Nancy stiffened. "What's going to happen to us now?" she asked. "They're not going to send us away, are they?" She couldn't go back. Her parents loved her, there was no question of that, but their love was the sort that filled her suitcase with colors and kept trying to set her up on dates with local boys. Their love wanted to *fix* her, and refused to see that she wasn't broken.

"Eleanor's been here for a long time," said Kade. He shut the door. "Sumi was her ward, so there are no parents to involve, and the local authorities know what's what. They'll do their best to make sure this doesn't shut us down."

"It would have been better had she not called at all," sniffed Jack. "An unreported death is just a disappearance in its Sunday clothes."

"See, it's things like that that explain why you don't have many friends," said Kade.

"But Sumi was among them," said Jack. She turned to look at Sumi's side of the room. "If she has no family, what are we supposed to do about her things?"

"There's storage space in the attic," said Kade.

"So we box them up," said Nancy firmly. "Where can we get some boxes?"

"The basement," said Jack.

"I'll go with you," said Kade. "Nancy, you stay here. If anyone asks, we'll be right back."

"All right," said Nancy, and held herself perfectly still as the others walked away. There was nothing left to do but wait. There was peace in stillness, a serenity that couldn't be found anywhere else in this hot, fast, often terrible world. Nancy closed her eyes and breathed down into her toes, letting her stillness become the only thing that mattered. Flashes of Sumi kept breaking her concentration, making it difficult to keep her knees from shaking or her fingers from twitching. She forced the images away and kept breathing, looking for serenity.

She still hadn't managed to find it when the others returned, the door banging open to Kade's declaration of "We are ready to box the world!"

Nancy opened her eyes and turned toward him, somehow mustering a smile. "All right," she said. "Let's get to work."

Sumi's things were as tangled and chaotic as Sumi had been. There was neither rhyme nor reason to the way they were piled around her bed and dresser. A pile of books on candy making was tied together with a pair of training bras. A bouquet of roses folded out of playing cards was shoved under the bed, next to a frilly blue dress that didn't look like something Sumi would ever have worn and a roast beef sandwich about a month past its "best by" date. Jack, who had put on gloves before they got to work, disposed of all the soiled or biologically questionable material without complaint: apparently, her squeamishness extended only as far as her bare skin. Kade sorted through Sumi's clothing, folding it neatly before boxing it up. Nancy was fairly sure it would all wind up back in the big group wardrobe. She was okay with that. Sumi wouldn't mind other people wearing her clothes. She probably wouldn't have minded while she was alive; she certainly wasn't going to object now that she was dead.

Nancy found herself tasked with handling the rest, the things that were neither trash nor fabric. She dug boxes of origami paper and embroidery floss from under the bed—Sumi had apparently always been good with her hands—and pushed them to one side, still digging. Her questing hands found a shoebox. She pulled it out and sat, removing the lid. Photos spilled onto the floor. Some showed Sumi as she'd been during their too-short acquaintance, mismatched clothing and tousled pigtails. Others showed a solemn, sad-eyed girl in a school uniform, sometimes holding a violin, other times empty-handed. It was plain, just from the still images, that this had been a girl who understood the virtue of being overlooked, of being a statue, but not because she had chosen stillness as Nancy had; it had been thrust upon her, until one day she'd discovered a door that could lead her to a world where she had a prayer of being happy.

Nancy realized that Sumi's granddaughter was never going to visit the candy corn farmer's grave, and it took everything she had not to weep for what had been irrevocably lost. Sumi might go to the Halls of the Dead, might even be happy there, but all the things she would have done among the living were gone now, rendered impossible when her heart stopped beating. Death was precious. That didn't change the fact that life was limited.

"Poor kid." Kade leaned over and took the picture from Nancy's motionless fingers, looking at it for a moment before he tucked it into his shirt. "Let's get this stuff out of here. You shouldn't have to look at it, not with her gone."

"Thank you," said Nancy, more earnestly than she would have believed before she'd seen that picture. Sumi was over, and it wasn't fair.

Working together, it took the three of them less than an hour to transfer all of Sumi's possessions to the attic, tucking the boxes away on unused shelves and in dusty corners, of which there seemed to be more than the usual number. When they were done, Jack removed her gloves and began meticulously wiping her fingers on a fresh handkerchief. Kade pulled the picture out of his shirt and tacked it up on a bulletin board, next to a picture of Sumi as Nancy had known her, all bright eyes and brighter smile, hands slightly blurred, as if she'd been photographed in motion.

"I'll stay with you tonight, if you don't mind," said Kade. "It doesn't seem safe for you to sleep in there alone."

"I won't stay with you tonight, whether you mind or not," said Jack. "That room gets too much sun, and Jill has a tendency to sleepwalk when I'm not with her."

"You shouldn't leave her alone," said Kade. "Watch yourself, okay? A lot of people are looking for someone to blame, and you're the best scapegoat in the school."

"I always wanted to be best at something," said Jack philosophically.

"Great," said Kade. "Now let's be best at getting to class before we get a lecture from Lundy on punctuality."

They filed out of the attic. Nancy looked back at Sumi's pictures on the bulletin board, so quiet, so still. Then she turned off the light and closed the door.

5 SURVIVORS, FOR A TIME

MORNING CLASSES HAD BEEN canceled; they resumed after lunch. Maybe it was rushing things, but there was nothing else to do with an entire school's worth of anxious, uneasy students: routine would keep them from wandering off and frightening themselves to death in the aftermath of Sumi's murder. Even so, it was a strained routine. Homework was forgotten, questions written on chalkboards went unanswered, and even the teachers clearly wanted to be elsewhere. Going back to normal after someone had died was never easy. When that someone had been brutally killed, all bets were off.

Dinner was worse. Nancy was sitting across from Jack and Jill when the girl with the brown braids walked up to the table and dumped her soup over Jack's head. "Oops," she said, flatly. "I slipped."

Jack sat rigidly unmoving, soup dripping down her forehead and running down her nose. Jill gasped, leaping to her feet. "Loriel!" she shrieked, the sound of her voice bringing all other conversation in the dining hall grinding to a halt. "How *could* you?"

"It was an accident," said Loriel. "Just like your sister there 'accidentally' took apart Angela's guinea pig, and 'accidentally' murdered Sumi. She's going to get caught, you know. This would all go a lot faster if she'd confess."

"Loriel sneezed in that before she poured it on you," said the girl's companion to Jack, a look of fake concern on her face. "Just thought you'd want to know."

Jack began to tremble. Then, still dripping soup, she jerked away from the table and bolted for the door, leaving Jill to run after her. Half the students burst out laughing. The other half stared after her in mute satisfaction, clearly condoning anything that made Jack miserable. She had already been tried and found guilty by a jury of her peers. All that remained was for the law to catch up.

"You're horrible," said a voice. Nancy was only a little surprised to realize that it was hers. She pushed back her chair, leaving her own dinner of grapes and cottage cheese relatively untouched, and glared at the two. "You're horrible people. I'm *glad* we didn't go through the same door, because I would hate to have traveled to a world that didn't teach its tourists any manners." She turned and stalked away, head held high, following the trail of soup out of the dining room and down the hall to the basement stairs.

"You walk slow, but you move fast. How do you *do*

that?" said Kade, catching up with her at the top of the stairs. He followed her gaze down into the darkness. "That's where the Addams twins live. They were in your room for a while, until the kid who had the basement before them graduated."

"Had he been to the same world?"

"No, he visited a race of mole people. I think he realized he enjoyed sunshine and bathing, and sort of gave up on the idea of going back."

"Oh." Nancy took a tentative step down. "Is she going to be all right?"

"Jack doesn't like being messy. They have their own bathroom. She'll be all cleaned up and back in tip-top faintly morbid shape before group is over." Kade shook his head. "I just hope this is as bad as it gets. Jack can handle a little soup, and she worked for a mad scientist; for her, the wrath of the locals is all part of a day's work. But if people want to get violent, she'll fight back, and that'll just prove that they were in the right to accuse her."

"This is awful," said Nancy. "I let my parents send me here because Miss West said she understood what had happened to me and could help me learn how to live with it."

"And because you were hoping that if you understood it, you'd be able to do it again," said Kade. Nancy didn't say anything. He laughed ruefully. "Hey, it's okay. I understand. Most of us are here because we want to be able to open our doors at will, at least at first. Sometimes the desire goes away. Sometimes the door comes back. Sometimes we just have to learn to deal with being exiles in our home countries."

"What if we can't?" asked Nancy. "What happens to us then?"

Kade was silent for a long moment. Then he shrugged, and said, "I guess we open schools for people who still have what we want most in the world. Hope."

"Sumi said 'hope' was a bad word."

"Sumi wasn't wrong. Now come on. Let's get to group before we get in trouble."

They walked silently through the halls, and they saw no one moving in the rooms around them. The idea that sticking together was the only way to be safe seemed to have taken root with preternatural speed. Nancy found herself matching her steps to Kade's, hurrying to keep up with his longer stride. She didn't like hurrying. It was indecorous and would have resulted in a scolding back ho—back in the Underworld. Here, however, it was necessary, even encouraged, and there was no reason to feel guilty about it. She tried to hold to that thought as she and Kade stepped into the room where group was being held.

Everyone turned to look at them. Loriel actually sneered. "Couldn't get the little killer out of her basement?"

"That's quite enough, Miss Youngers," said Lundy sharply. "We have already agreed to stop speculating about who may have harmed Sumi."

She gets a name now, not a title and surname, thought Nancy. *That's not right. The dead deserve more dignity, not less. Dignity is all the dead possess.* Aloud, she said nothing, only made her way to an open chair and sat. She was gratified when Kade took the seat next to her. Loriel's glare intensified. Apparently Nancy wasn't the only one who found Kade beautiful, although she would have been willing to bet she was the only one who found his beauty more aesthetic than romantic.

"*You* agreed," said Loriel. "The rest of us are scared. Who would kill her like that? And mutilating the body afterward? That's just sick. We have a right to want to know what's going on, and how to keep ourselves safe!"

"I'm reasonably sure she bled out from her injuries, given the mess; corpses don't bleed as much," said Jack. Everyone in the room turned to see the twins, freshly scrubbed and wearing clean clothes, as they made their entrance. Jack looked more the old-fashioned professor than ever, wearing a tweed vest over a long-sleeved white shirt that buttoned at the wrists. Jill was wearing a cream-colored gown that Nancy would have considered sleepwear, not something to wear to group therapy. "Whoever killed her was no scientist."

"What do you mean?" asked one of the few boys, a tall Latino kid who was spinning a long piece of wood carved to resemble an ulna between his fingers. Nancy felt an odd kinship when she looked at him. Perhaps he'd been to someplace like her Underworld, filled with shadows, secrets, and safety. Perhaps he would understand if she went to him and spoke of stillness and respect for the dead.

But this was not the time. Jack met the question with a haughty sniff, and a too-calm, "I saw her body, like the rest of you. I know some of you have decided that I'm responsible for her death. I know further that those of you who believe my guilt will probably refuse to believe anything else. Draw on what you know of me. If I had decided to start killing my classmates, would I have left a body?"

The boy with the bone raised an eyebrow. "She makes a good point," he said.

"Making a good point doesn't mean she's not a killer," said Loriel, but the heat was gone; her accusations had been met with reality, and they didn't have anyplace else to go. She crossed her arms and slouched back in her chair. "I'm keeping an eye on her."

"Good," said Lundy. "We all need to be keeping our eyes on each other right now. We don't know who hurt Sumi. Eleanor is working with the authorities, and we should know more soon, but in the meantime, we need to be watching out for one another. No one goes anywhere alone—yes, Miss Youngers?"

Loriel lowered her hand as the attention of the group switched back to her. "What if one of us finds our door before the killer's caught?" she asked. "I can't take someone through with me just because we're not supposed to go anywhere alone, and I am *not* missing the passage back over this. I'm *not*."

"I think we can all agree that if someone happens to find their door while we're still staying together, the person whose door has been found will go, and the person who is left behind will find another buddy," said Lundy, with deliberate precision. Nancy realized with a start that Lundy didn't think any of them were going to find their doors. Not soon; maybe not ever. Lundy had given up on them. It was clear by her tone and by the way she chose her words. And maybe that made sense. Lundy's doors were closed, no matter where things went from here. Lundy needed to adapt to the idea that this was the world where she was going to die.

"Try for groups of three," said the boy with the bone. "If you can't manage that, try not to find your door."

Some of the students laughed. Others looked pained. Loriel was among the latter.

"Tell us about your door, Miss Youngers," urged Lundy.

"I almost didn't see it," said Loriel. Her voice turned distant. "It was so small. This perfect little door, carved into the lintel below the porch light. Like a door for moths. I just wanted to see what it was, that was all, so I got up really close, and I knocked with the tip of my pinkie finger. The world went all twisty and strange, and then I was standing in the hall on the other side of the door, looking back on this impossibly huge porch. I didn't go through. It pulled me. That was how bad the Webworld wanted me."

Loriel's story was grand and sprawling, a majestic, epic tale of spider princesses and tiny dynasties. Her eyes had always been keen, but after spending a year in service to the smallest, they had sharpened so much that she had to wear lenses made of carnival glass to keep the world from being so magnified that it was painful to behold. She had fought and she had triumphed, she had loved and she had lost, until finally the Queen of Dust had asked if she would become a princess of the land and stay forever.

"I said I wanted nothing more, but that I had to go home and tell my parents before I could accept," said Loriel, sniffling. The tears had started to fall somewhere around the death of her beloved Wasp Prince, and seemed set to continue for the foreseeable future. "She told me it would be hard to find the door again. That I would have to look harder than I had ever looked in my life. I said I could do it. That was almost two years ago. I've looked everywhere, but I haven't seen my door."

"Some doors open only once," said Lundy. There was a murmur of agreement from the room. Nancy frowned and sank deeper into her seat. It seemed cruel to dredge up everyone's pasts like this, pin them quivering to the floor, and then say things like that. Loriel surely knew by now that she probably wasn't going back through her tiny door to her even tinier world. She was smart enough to have figured it out for herself. What was the point in saying it?

If this was the school for those who wanted to come to peace with their voyages and remember them fondly, she would have hated to see the other campus.

"She said I could come back," said Loriel. "She promised me. Queens keep their promises. I just have to look more closely. Once I find the door, I'm gone."

"And your parents? Are they prepared for this inevitable disappearance?"

Loriel snorted. "I told them where I'd been—a year for

me, twelve days for them—and they said I'd clearly been through some trauma and couldn't be trusted. They sent me here so I'd stop being crazy. But there's nothing *wrong* with me. I went on a journey. That's all."

"A journey to a documented world, even," said Eleanor. She was standing in the doorway, new lines of exhaustion graven in the soft skin around her mouth and eyes. She looked like she had aged a decade in a day. "There have been five children pulled into the Webworld since I began seeking you all out. Two of them found their way back again after returning home. So you see, there *is* hope. For Loriel, and for all of us. Our doors are hidden, but by looking closely enough, we can find them."

"Eleanor." Lundy stood. "You're supposed to be resting."

"I've had rest enough to last a lifetime, and only a lifetime for the rest of what's to be done," said Eleanor. She moved away from the door. Several students rose to help her to an open chair. She smiled, patting at their cheeks. "Good children, all of you—yes, even you, Lundy. You're all children to me, and I your teacher, the only one who refuses to lie to you. So listen to me now, because it sounds like you're doing a fine job of confusing and upsetting yourselves.

"You will not all find your doors again. Some doors really do appear only once, the consequence of some strange convergence that we can't predict or re-create. They're drawn by need and by sympathy. Not the emotion—the resonance of one thing to another. There's a reason you were all pulled into worlds that suited you so well. Imagine, for a moment, if you'd fallen into the world described by your neighbor instead."

Nancy glanced at Jack and Jill, uneasily imagining what her life would have been like if she'd found their door instead of her own. The Moors didn't seem to care about stillness, only obedience and blood. Neither of those things were strong suits of hers. All around her, other students exchanged equally uncomfortable glances, making their own connections and finding them just as unpleasant as she did.

"Sumi had Nonsense in her heart, and so a door opened that would take her to a world where she could wear it proudly, not hide it away. That was her real story. Finding a place where she could be free. That's your story, too, every one of you." Eleanor tipped her chin up. Her eyes were clear. "You found freedom, if only for a moment, and when you lost it, you came here, hoping it could be found again. I hope the same, for each of you. I want to make excuses to your parents when you disappear, to tell them that runaways will always run again if they have half the chance. I want to see the back of you more than I want almost anything in this world."

What she wanted most didn't need to be spoken, for they shared her hunger, her brutal, unforgiving desire: what she wanted most was a door, and the things that waited on its other side. But unlike the rest of them, she knew where her door was. It was simply closed to her for the time being, until she could find her way back to childhood.

The boy with the wooden bone put his hand up. "Eleanor?"

"Yes, Christopher?"

"Why did your door stay, while all ours disappeared?" He bit his lip before adding, "It doesn't seem fair for it to work like that. We should have been able to go back."

"Stable doors like Miss West's are less common than the temporary kind," said Lundy, back on familiar ground. "Most children who go through them don't come back, either on their first trip or after making a short return to their original world. So while we have records of several, the chances of finding a stable door that resonates with the story you need are slim."

"What about, like, Narnia?" asked Christopher. "Those kids went through all sorts of different doors, and they always wound up back with the big talking lion."

"That's because Narnia was a Christian allegory pretending to be a fantasy series, you asshole," said one of the other boys. "C. S. Lewis never went through any doors. He didn't know how it worked. He wanted to tell a story, and he'd probably heard about kids like us, and he made shit up. That's what all those authors did. They made shit up, and people made them famous. We tell the truth, and our parents throw us into this glorified loony bin."

"We don't use terms like that here," said Eleanor. There was steel in her tone. "This is not an asylum, and you are not mad—and so what if you were? This world is unforgiving and cruel to those it judges as even the slightest bit outside the norm. If anyone should be kind, understanding, accepting, loving to their fellow outcasts, it's you. All of you. You are the guardians of the secrets of the universe, beloved of worlds that most will never dream of, much less see . . . can't you see where you owe it to yourselves to be *kind*? To care for one another? No one outside this room will ever understand what you've been through the way the people around you right now understand. This is not your home. I know that better than most. But this is your way station and your sanctuary, and you will treat those around you with respect."

Both boys wilted under her glare. Christopher looked down. The other boy mumbled, "Sorry."

"It's all right. It's late, and we're all tired." Eleanor stood. "Get some sleep, all of you. I know it won't be easy. Nancy, can you—"

"I already said I'd room with her tonight," said Kade. A wave of relief washed over Nancy. She'd been afraid she would have to go to another room, and while she hadn't been there long, she was already attached to the familiarity of her own bed.

Eleanor looked at Kade thoughtfully. "Are you sure? I was going to suggest she room with someone on her hall, and that you lock your door tonight. This is a great imposition."

"No, it's fine. I volunteered." Kade flashed a quick smile. "I like Nancy, and she was Sumi's friend. I figure a little stability will do her good, and that makes any inconvenience to me completely beside the point. I want to help. This is my home." He looked slowly around the room. "My *forever* home. I turned eighteen last month, my parents don't want me, and the Prism wouldn't have me back even if I wanted to go. So it's important to me that we take care of this place, because it's been taking care of all of us since the day we got here."

"Go to bed, my darlings," said Eleanor. "This will all look better in the morning."

THE BODY LAY in the front yard, covered in a thin sheen of dew, face turned up toward the uncaring sky. The dead were capable of sight, as Nancy would have been quick to point out had she been asked, but this body saw nothing, for it had no eyes, only black and blood-rimmed holes where eyes had once been. Its hands were folded neatly on its chest, glasses clutched in cooling fingers. Loriel Youngers would never find her door (which had been waiting for her all this time, tucked into a corner of her bedroom at home, half an inch high and held in place by the most complicated magics the Queen of Dust, her adopted mother, could conceive; it would linger another six months before the spells were released and the Queen took to her chambers for a year of mourning). She would never have another grand adventure or save another world. Her part in the story was over.

She lay there, unmoving, as the sun rose and the stars winked out. A crow landed on the grass near her leg, watching her warily. When she still didn't move, it hopped on her knee, waiting for the trap to spring. When she *still* didn't move, it launched itself into the air and flew the few short feet to her head, where it promptly buried its beak in the bloody hole that had been her left eye.

Angela—she of the dissected guinea pig, whose enchanted sneakers had once allowed her to run on rainbows—was just stepping out onto the porch, rubbing the sleep from her eyes and intending to scold her roommate for sneaking out when they were supposed to stay together. Sometimes Loriel couldn't keep her eyes closed long enough to fall asleep, and then she had a tendency to roam the grounds, looking for her missing door. It wasn't unusual to find her dozing on the lawn. At first, Angela's mind refused to register Loriel's motionless body as anything unusual.

Then the crow pulled its bloody beak out of her eye socket and cawed at Angela, angrily protesting the interruption of its breakfast.

Angela's scream sent the crow flapping off into the morning sky. It didn't wake Loriel.

6 THE BODIES WE HAVE BURIED

ALL THE STUDENTS had been gathered in the dining hall, most dragged from their beds by either Angela's shrieks or the staff pounding on their doors. Nancy had been jerked awake by Kade shaking her shoulder, leaning so close that she could see the delicate filigree pattern of lines in his irises. She had jerked away, blushing and clutching the sheets around herself. Kade had only laughed, turning his back like a gentleman while she got up and put her clothes on.

Now, sitting at a table with a plate of scrambled eggs getting cold in front of her, Nancy found herself clinging to the memory of his laughter. She had the feeling that no one was going to be laughing here for quite some time. Maybe not ever again.

"Loriel Youngers was found dead this morning on the

front lawn," said Lundy, standing ramrod straight in front of them, her hands folded in front of her. She looked like a porcelain doll on the verge of shattering. "I was against telling you anything more than that. I don't feel that such morbid things are appropriate for the ears of young people. But this is Miss West's school, and she felt your knowing what had happened might make you take her request that you stay together more seriously. Miss Youngers was found without her eyes. They had been . . . removed. We thought at first that it might have been predation by local wildlife, but a closer study of the body showed that they had been removed with a sharp object."

No one asked what kind of sharp object. Not even Jack, although Nancy could see that she was practically vibrating from keeping her questions contained. Jill, in contrast, seemed perfectly serene, and was one of the few students who was actually eating. Spending a few years in a horror movie must have done a great deal to harden her sensibilities.

"Unlike Sumi, Loriel's parents were still involved with her care, and we have not yet contacted the authorities." There was a catch in Lundy's voice. "Eleanor is in her chambers, deciding what to do. Please, finish your breakfasts and then return to your rooms. Do not go anywhere alone, not even the restrooms. The school is not safe." She turned, not waiting for them to respond to her, and walked quickly to the exit.

When she was gone, Jack finally frowned and let one of her questions out. "Eleanor sat there last night and said she was looking forward to lying to our parents about what happened to us," she said. "Why can't she just make Loriel disappear, and tell that lie?"

"Not everyone is as comfortable as you are with the idea of getting rid of bodies," said Angela through her tears. She had been crying since finding Loriel's body. It didn't look like she was ever intending to stop.

"It's not a bad question," said Christopher. He touched his bone nervously as he spoke. For the first time, Nancy wondered if it might be real, instead of wood as she had first assumed. "Miss West already has a system in place for making it look like we ran away when we really went home. Why shouldn't she lie to Loriel's family? They lost her either way. At least a lie means we can all stay here, instead of going back."

"Going back" had two distinct meanings at the school, depending on how it was said. It was the best thing in the world. It was also the worst thing that could happen to anybody. It was returning to a place that understood you so well that it had reached across realities to find you, claiming you as its own and only; it was being sent to a family that wanted to love you, wanted to keep you safe and sound, but didn't know you well enough to do anything but hurt you. The duality of the phrase was like the duality of the doors: they changed lives, and they destroyed them, all with the same, simple invitation. *Come through, and see.*

"I don't want to stay in a place where we just make bodies go away," said Angela. "That isn't why I came here."

"Get off your high horse," snapped Jack. "Bodies are a consequence of life. Or do you truly mean for us to believe that when you were running along rainbows, you never saw anyone fall? Someone plummets out of the sky, they're not going to get up and walk away from it. They're going to die. And unless they fell into a place like the Moors, they're going to stay dead. Someone disposed of those bodies. One slip, and they'd have been disposing of yours."

Angela stared at Jack, eyes wide and horrified. "I never thought about it," she said. "I saw . . . I saw people fall. The rainbows were slippery. Even with the right shoes, you could fall through if you slowed down too much."

"Someone disposed of those bodies," said Jack. "Ashes to ashes, right? If we call Loriel's parents, if we tell them what happened, that's it, we're done. Anyone who's under eighteen gets taken home by their loving parents. Half of you will be on antipsychotic drugs you don't need before the end of the year, but hey, at least you'll have someone to remind you to eat while you're busy contemplating the walls. The rest of us will be out on the streets. No high school degrees, no way of coping with this world, which doesn't want us back."

"At least you have prospects," said Christopher, giving his bone another spin. "How many colleges you been accepted to?"

"Every one that I've applied to, but they're all assuming I'll graduate before I come knocking," said Jack. "And of course, I've Jill to consider. I can't go running out into the world without making provisions for my sister."

"I can take care of myself," said Jill.

"You won't have to," said Eleanor. She walked wearily into the room, looked toward Jack and Kade, and said, "Make her go away, darlings. Put her someplace where I'll never find her, not if I look for a thousand years. We'll have a memorial service. We'll honor her as best we can. But I can't endanger us all because of one lost life. I almost wish I could. I would feel less like a monster, and more like the child who danced with foxes under the slow October moon. I simply cannot bring myself to do it."

"Of course," said Jack, and started to stand.

Angela was on her feet first. "She *killed* her, and now you're going to let her have the body?" she shrilled, pointing at Jack. Her face was a mask of outrage. "She's a murderess! Loriel knew it, I know it, and I can't believe that *you* don't know it!"

"Points for knowing the feminine form of 'murderer,' although I'm a little insulted that you feel the need to put a lacy bow on the crime before you can believe I committed it," said Jack. "What would I do with a pair of eyes, Angela? I don't care about the visual sciences. I'm sure there were some fascinating adaptations to her cones and rods, but I don't have the facilities or equipment here to study them. If I were going to kill her for her eyes, I would have done it in ten years, after I was nicely established as the head of research and development for a biotech firm big enough to make murder charges just go away. Killing her now benefits me not at all."

"Can we stop pointing fingers at each other and *deal*

with this? Please?" Kade stood. "We already have one body on our hands. I don't want any more."

"I can help," said Nancy. The others turned toward her. She reddened slightly, but pushed on, saying, "I can make sure nothing is done that's not respectful toward the dead. The flesh they leave behind when they depart doesn't bother me."

"You're a creepy girl," said Christopher approvingly. He stood, tucking his bone into his pocket. "I'll help as well. The Skeleton Girl would never forgive me if I didn't."

"I won't," said Jill. "It would ruin my dress."

"Thank you, all of you," said Eleanor. "Classes have been canceled for the rest of the morning. We'll see you after lunch, once you've had time to put yourselves together again."

"Bad choice of words," said Jack—but she looked thoughtful, almost pensive, as she turned her face away and led Kade and Nancy out of the room. Christopher brought up the rear, his bone sticking out of his back pocket like an upthrust middle finger. The door swung closed behind him.

Together, they walked out to the porch. Loriel was still on the lawn, covered by a sheet, and for a moment, all Nancy could think was that if this didn't stop soon, they were going to run out of bedclothes. Nancy, Christopher, and Jack kept walking. Kade stopped.

"I'm sorry," he said. "I can't. I just . . . I *can't.* This was never my job." Because he'd been a princess in Prism, before they'd learned that he was really a prince; because unlike the rest of them, he had never been responsible for tending to the dead. He'd killed people, sure. That was what had earned him the title of Goblin Prince. But his part in their deaths had ended on the blade of his sword.

"It's all right," said Nancy gently, looking back over her shoulder at him. "The dead are much more understanding than the living. Let us take care of her. You keep watch."

"I can do that," said Kade, relieved.

Nancy, Jack, and Christopher made their way to the body. They came from very different traditions. For Nancy, the entire experience of death was revered. For Christopher, the flesh was temporary, but the bones were eternal and deserved to be treated as such. For Jack, death was an inconvenience to be conquered, and a corpse was a Pandora's box of beautiful possibilities. But all of them shared a love for those who had passed, and as they lifted Loriel from the ground, they did so with gentle, compassionate hands.

"If we take her to the basement, I can mix up something to strip the flesh from her bones," said Jack. "The skeleton will still appear fresh to any forensics tests, but it's a start."

"Once she's a skeleton, I might be able to find out what happened to her," said Christopher, sounding almost shy.

There was a pause. Finally, dubiously, Jack said, "I'm sorry, but it sounded like you just confessed to being able to talk to bones. Why have we never heard this before?"

"Because I was there when you said you could raise the dead. I saw how everybody reacted, and I enjoy having a social life at this school," said Christopher. "It's not like I can go hang out at the pizza parlor in town if the other kids stop talking to me. And don't say you and your sister would have talked to me. The two of you don't talk to *anybody*."

"He's got you there," called Kade from the porch.

Nancy frowned. "They talked to me."

"Because Sumi made them, and because you went to a world full of ghosts," said Christopher. "I guess that was close enough to living in a horror movie that they were cool with you. And they talked to Sumi because she didn't give them a *choice*. Sumi was like a small tornado. When she sucked you up, you just tightened your grip and went along for the ride."

"We keep to ourselves for good reason," said Jack stiffly, adjusting her grasp on Loriel's shoulders. "Most of you got unicorns and misty meadows. We got the Moors, and if there was a unicorn out there, it probably ate human flesh. We learned quickly that sharing our experiences with others just drove them away, and most of the social connections at this place are based on those shared experiences. On the doors, and on what happened when we went through them."

"I went to a country of happy, dancing skeletons who said that one day I'd come back to them and marry their Skeleton Girl," said Christopher. "So pretty sunshiny, but sort of sunshine by way of Día de los Muertos."

"Maybe we should have talked to you a long time ago," said Jack. "Let's get Loriel to the basement."

They carried her around the side of the manor, walking until they found the ground-level doors that had once been used by tradesmen delivering coal or food to the house above. Their hands were full, and so Nancy twisted to look over her shoulder as she called, "Kade? We need you."

"This I can do," said Kade. He jogged past them and opened the cellar doors, releasing a rush of cool, sepulchral air. He held the doors until the others were through, and then he followed them, closing the doors with a final-sounding *clank* that left them in near darkness. Nancy had dwelt in the Halls of the Dead, where the lights were never turned above twilight, for fear of hurting sensitive eyes. Christopher had learnt to navigate a world of skeletons, none of whom *had* eyes anymore, and many of whom had long since forgotten about the squishy living and their need for constant illumination. Jack could see by the light of a single storm. Only Kade stumbled, managing not to fall as the group made their way to the base of the stairs.

"Can you hold her up without me for a second?" asked Jack. "I should turn the lights on before one of you buffoons trips and damages something valuable."

"See, that's the other reason no one talks to you," said Christopher. "You're sort of mean, like, all the time. Even when you don't have any real reason to be. You could just say 'please.' "

"*Please* can you hold her up without me for a second, so that we don't knock over the jug of acid I was planning to use to dissolve her flesh," said Jack. "I enjoy having non-skeletal feet. Perhaps you do as well."

"For now," said Christopher. He shifted his grip around Loriel's torso, getting his arms locked. "All right, I think I have her."

"Excellent. I'll be right back." The body seemed to grow heavier in Nancy's and Christopher's arms as Jack let go. They heard her moving away, steps light on the concrete floor of the basement. Then, calmly, she said, "You may want to close your eyes."

They tensed, expecting a blazing surgical light. Instead, when she flipped the switch, a soft orange glow bathed the room, revealing metal racks filled with jars and lab equipment, dressers bulging with wispy lace and ribbons, and a stainless-steel autopsy table. There was only one bed.

Nancy made a small sound of dismay as she realized what this meant. "You sleep on the autopsy table?" she asked.

Jack touched the smooth metal with one hand. "Not much call for pillows or blankets in the lab," she said. "Jill got the canopy beds and the cushions. I learned how to sleep on stone floors. Turns out that sort of thing is hard to unlearn. Sleeping in a real bed is like trying to sleep in a cloud. I'm afraid I'll sink right through and fall to my death." She sighed, taking her hand off the autopsy table. "Put her here. I want to look at her before we dissolve her."

"Is this a creepy perv thing?" asked Christopher, as he and Nancy maneuvered the body through the lab. "I'm not sure I can stay to help if it's a creepy perv thing."

"I don't like corpses in that way unless they've been reanimated," said Jack. "Corpses are incapable of offering informed consent, and are hence no better than vibrators."

"I wish that didn't make so much sense," said Christopher. Together, he and Nancy boosted Loriel up onto the autopsy table. He let go and stepped away. Nancy remained, taking a moment to straighten the body's limbs and smooth out its hair. There was nothing she could do for the pits that had been Loriel's eyes—she couldn't even close them. In the end, she simply folded Loriel's hands over her chest and backed away.

Jack moved into the position Nancy had vacated. Unlike the other girl, she didn't shy away from the damage to Loriel's face. She leaned in close, studying the striations in the flesh, the way it had been torn and opened. Pulling on a pair of rubber gloves, she reached out and carefully rolled Loriel's head to the side, probing her skull with quick, careful motions. Nancy and Christopher watched closely, but nothing Jack was doing was disrespectful: if anything, she was showing more respect to Loriel now that she was dead than she ever had when the other girl was among the living.

Jack grimaced. "Her skull's been cracked," she said. "Someone hit her from behind hard enough to knock her down and disorient her. I can't say for sure whether it knocked her out. Knocking someone out is harder than most people guess. It was a blitz attack; she didn't have a chance to defend herself or scream for help before she was down. But it wouldn't have killed her right away. And there's quite a lot of blood in her sockets."

"Jack . . ." Kade's voice was low and horrified. "Please tell me you're not saying what I think you're saying."

"Hmm?" Jack looked up. "I'm not *psychic,* Kade, I don't even believe that psychics *exist.* There is no possible way I could read your mind and know what you think I'm saying. I'm simply talking about the manner in which Loriel's eyes were extracted."

"You mean removed?" asked Christopher.

"No, I mean extracted," said Jack. "I'd need to open her skull to be sure, and I don't have a proper bone saw, which makes that a difficult task, but it appears that her eyes were fully extracted, all the way along the optic nerve. Whoever assaulted her didn't just pluck them out like grapes. They used some sort of blade to separate the eye from the muscles holding it in place, and once that was done, they—"

"Do you know who did it?" asked Kade.

"No."

"Then please, stop telling us how it was done. I can't take it anymore."

Jack looked at him solemnly, and said, "I haven't gotten to the important part yet."

"Then please, get there, before the rest of us throw up on the floor."

"Based on the damage to the skull and the amount of bleeding, she was alive when her eyes were taken," said Jack. Silence greeted her proclamation. Even Nancy put a hand over her mouth. "Whoever did this subdued her, removed her eyes, and let the shock kill her. I'm not even sure her death was the goal. Just getting her eyes."

"Why?" asked Christopher.

Jack hesitated before shaking her head and saying, "I don't know. Come on. Let's prepare her for burial."

Kade retreated back to the far side of the basement and

stayed there as the others got to work. Nancy undressed Loriel, folding each piece of clothing with care before setting it aside. She somehow doubted that these clothes were going to make it into the general supply. They would probably need to be destroyed along with Loriel's body, just for the sake of safety.

While Nancy worked, Jack and Christopher pulled an old claw-footed bathtub out of a corner of the basement and into the center of the room. Jack uncorked several large glass jugs and poured their greenish, fizzing contents into the tub. Kade watched this with dismay.

"Why does Eleanor let you have that much acid?" he asked. "Why would you *want* that much acid? You don't need that much acid."

"Except that it appears I do, since I have just enough to dissolve a human body, and we have a human body in need of dissolving," said Jack. "Everything happens for a reason. And Eleanor didn't 'let' me have this much acid. I sort of collected it on my own. For a rainy day."

"What were you expecting it to rain?" asked Christopher. "Bears?"

"There was always a chance we'd get lucky," said Jack. She pulled several plastic aprons off a shelf and held them out to the others. "You're going to want to put one of these on, and a pair of the gloves that go with them. Acid is not a fun exfoliator unless you come from Christopher's world."

Wordlessly, Nancy and Christopher donned their plastic aprons, rubber gloves, and goggles. Jack did the same, and together they lowered Loriel into the fizzing green liquid.

Kade turned his face away. The smell was surprisingly pleasant, not meaty at all: it smelled like cleaning fluid, faintly citrus, with a minty undertone. The bubbles increased as Loriel disappeared beneath the surface, until the liquid was completely opaque, obscuring her from view. Jack turned away.

"It'll take about an hour to reduce her to a skeletal state," she said. "I'll neutralize the acid and drain it off when she's done. Christopher, do you think you can handle her from there?"

"She'll dance for me." Christopher touched the bone in his pocket. Nancy realized there were small indentations in the surface. Not holes, not quite, and yet it still managed to suggest a flute. The tunes he played on that instrument wouldn't be audible to the living. That didn't mean they wouldn't be real. "All skeletons dance for me. It's my honor to play for them."

"All right, clearly the two of you"—Jack gestured to Nancy as she stripped off her gloves—"were meant to be together. If you can't find your doors, you should get married and breed the next generation of creepy world-traveling children."

Christopher's cheeks turned red. Nancy's didn't. It was a pleasant change.

"Maybe we should figure out why people are dying before we start trying to set up a breeding program," said Kade mildly. "Besides, I met Nancy first. I get asking-out dibs."

"Sometimes I suspect you learned all your hallmarks of

masculinity from a Neanderthal," said Jack. She removed her apron, hanging it on a nearby hook. "Everyone please take off the gear you borrowed. That stuff is expensive, and I only get to place three orders a year."

"Do I get a say in this?" asked Nancy, shooting an amused look over at Kade. She didn't mind flirting. Flirting was safe, flirting was fun; flirting was a way of interacting with her peers without anyone realizing that there was anything strange about her. She could have flirted forever. It was just the things that came after flirting that she had no interest in.

"Maybe later," said Jack. "Right now, we need to get out of here. The acid will do some off-gassing as it breaks down her tissues, and I don't want to fill my lungs with Loriel. Besides, I shouldn't leave Jill alone for too long." She sounded uneasy.

"I'm sure no one will hurt your sister," said Nancy. "She can take care of herself."

"That's what I'm worried about," said Jack. "When you spend years with a vampire, all those lessons about 'don't bite the other children' sort of go out the window. If they corner her because they've decided I'm guilty, she's liable to hurt someone just so she can get away. I'd rather not get expelled right after I've disposed of a body. Seems like a waste of good acid."

"All right," said Nancy, pulling her apron off over her head. "Let's go."

Since they were no longer trying to spare their fellow students the sight of Loriel's body, the foursome walked up the interior stairs, emerging into the deserted hallway. Kade looked in both directions before turning to Jack and asking, "Where would she go?"

"How would I know?" asked Jack. She sighed when the others stared at her. "I'm her *twin*. I'm not her keeper. I'm not even her friend. We mostly stick together out of self-defense. The other girls think she's weird, and they think I'm weirder. At least when we present a united front, they're less likely to do things to us."

"Things?" asked Nancy blankly.

Jack fixed her with a look that was equal parts pitying and envious. "You didn't get a hazing phase. That's the real reason Eleanor put you in with Sumi. Once Sumi liked you—or at least tolerated you—no one else was going to cross the line, because everyone knew better than to mess with Sumi. She was vicious. Nonsense girls always are. Jill and I . . ."

"I remember when you got here," said Christopher. "I thought your sister was hot, you know? So I offered to show her around the school, figured maybe I could get in good before one of the other guys showed up and started talking about his magic sword and how he'd saved the universe or whatever. I'm a dude with a flute no one can hear. I have to be persistent."

"She laughed at you, didn't she?" Most people would have been surprised by the gentleness of Jack's tone. She wasn't the sort of person who seemed inclined to gentleness.

Christopher nodded. "She said I was a cute little boy,

but that she couldn't lower herself to be seen with me. Like, that was her opening statement. Not 'thanks, no thanks,' not 'my name's Jill.' Just straight to 'you're a cute little boy.' I stopped trying after that."

"She was trying to save you, in her way," said Jack. "Her Master was the jealous sort. She used to try to make friends with the kids from the village below his castle. Jill liked having a lot of friends around. Believe it or not, she used to be the gregarious one, even if it was a nerdy sort of friendly. She'd run you to ground to tell you about the latest episode of *Doctor Who*. This was early on, before she'd embraced the lacy dresses and the iron-rich diet. Back then, she thought we were just having an adventure. She was the one who thought we were going to go home someday and wanted to learn as much as she could."

"And you?" asked Kade.

"I gave up on wanting to go home the second Dr. Bleak put a bone saw in my hand and told me he would teach me anything I wanted to know," said Jack. "For a while, Jill was opening doors and looking for a road home, and I was the one who never wanted to leave."

"What happened to the kids from the village?" asked Christopher. "The ones she tried to make friends with?"

Jack's expression went blank. It wasn't coldness, exactly, more a means of *distancing* herself from what she was about to say. "We lived in the grace and at the sufferance of a vampire lord. What do you *think* happened to the kids from the village? Her Master didn't want her talking to anyone he couldn't control. I think he only spared me because

Dr. Bleak begged, and because he pointed out the wisdom in keeping a self-replenishing source of blood transfusions for Jill. We're twins. If anything happened to her, I could be used for spare parts."

Nancy's mouth dropped open. "That's *horrible,*" she squeaked.

"That was the Moors." Jack shook her head. "It was cruel and cold and brutal and beautiful, and I would give anything to go back there. Maybe it broke me in some deep, intrinsic way that I am incapable of seeing, just like Jill can't understand that she's not a normal girl anymore. I don't care. It was my home, and it finally let me be myself, and I hate it here."

"We pretty much all hate it here," said Kade. "Even me. That's why we're at this school. Now think. Your sister isn't in the basement, so where would she go?"

"She might still be in the dining hall, since it's harder to pick on her when there's supervision around," said Jack. "Or she could have gone out to sit in the trees and pretend that she's back at home. We spent a lot of time outside there, for one reason or another."

"We saw her there yesterday," said Kade. "Nancy and I will go check the trees; you and Christopher check the dining hall. We'll meet back at the attic no matter what we find."

"Why the attic?" asked Christopher.

But Jack was nodding. "Good call. We can go through your books while Loriel finishes stewing. Maybe there's something in there about why someone would be harvesting parts from world-walkers. It's a long shot. At this point, I'll take it. Come on, bone boy." She turned and strode down the hall, every inch the confident mad scientist's protégée once again. Any vulnerability she had shown was gone, tamped down and covered over by the mask she wore.

"Thanks for sticking me with the scary girl," said Christopher to Kade, and ran after her, pulling the bone flute from his pocket.

"You're welcome," Kade called after him. He offered his arm to Nancy, grinning. "C'mon. Let's go see if we can't find ourselves an Addams." His drawl grew thicker, dripping from his words like sweet and tempting honey.

Nancy set her hand in the crook of his elbow, feeling the traitorous red creeping back into her cheeks. This was always the difficult part, back when she'd been at her old school: explaining that "asexual" and "aromantic" were different things. She *liked* holding hands and trading kisses. She'd had several boyfriends in elementary school, just like most of the other girls, and she had always found those practice relationships completely satisfying. It wasn't until puberty had come along and changed the rules that she'd started pulling away in confusion and disinterest. Kade was possibly the most beautiful boy she'd ever seen. She wanted to spend hours sitting with him and talking about pointless things. She wanted to feel his hand against her skin, to know that his presence was absolute and focused entirely on her. The trouble was, it never seemed to end there, and that was as far as she was willing to go.

Kade must have read her discomfort, because he flashed

her a smile and said, "I promise I'm a gentleman. You're as safe with me as you are with anyone who's not the murderer."

"And see, I was just trying to decide whether I thought you might be the killer," said Nancy. "I'm really relieved to hear that you're not. I'm not either, just for the record."

"That's good to know," said Kade.

They walked together through the deserted manor. Whispers sometimes drifted from the rooms they passed, indicating the presence of their fellow students. They didn't stop. Everyone had their own concerns, and Nancy had an uneasy feeling that by helping Jack destroy Loriel's body, she had just placed herself firmly in the "enemy" camp for anyone who had been a friend of Loriel's when she was alive. Nancy had never made so many enemies before, or so quickly. She didn't like it. She just didn't see a way to undo it.

There was no one outside. The lawn was empty as she and Kade walked toward the trees; even the crows had flown away, off to look for some richer pickings. Everything was silent, eerily so.

Jill wasn't in the trees. That was almost a disappointment: Nancy had been fully expecting to step into the sheltered grove and see the other girl sitting on a root, posed like something out of a gothic novel, with her parasol blocking out any stray sunbeams that had dared to come too close. Instead, the sun shone down undisturbed, and Nancy and Kade were alone.

"Well, that's one down," said Nancy, suddenly nervous.

What if Kade wanted to kiss her? What if Kade didn't want to kiss her? There was no good answer, and so she did what she always did when she was confused or frightened: she froze, becoming a girl-shaped statue.

"Whoa," said Kade. He sounded genuinely impressed. "That's some trick. Do you actually turn into stone, or does it only seem like you do?" He prodded her gently in the arm with one finger. "Nope, still flesh. You're holding really, really still, but you're not inanimate. How are you doing that? Are you even breathing? I can't do that."

"The Lady of Shadows required that everyone who served her be able to hold properly still," said Nancy, releasing her pose. Her cheeks reddened again. This was all going so *wrong*. "I'm sorry. I tend to freeze up when I get nervous."

"Don't worry, you're safe with me," said Kade. "Whoever the killer is, they're only striking when people are alone. We'll stick together, and we'll be fine."

But you're what I'm nervous about, thought Nancy. She forced a wan smile. "If you really think so," she said. "Jill isn't here. We should get back to the attic before Jack and Christopher start to worry about us."

They walked side by side back the way that they had come, Nancy's fingers resting on Kade's arm and her eyes scanning the grassy expanse of the lawn, looking for some clue as to what had happened. There had to be *something* that would bring all this together, that would force it to make sense. They couldn't just be at the mercy of an unseen killer, who slaughtered them for no apparent reason.

“Hands,” she murmured.

“What’s that?” asked Kade.

“I was just thinking about Sumi’s hands,” she said. “She was really good with her hands, you know? Like they were the most important thing about her. Maybe someone is trying to take away the things we treasure the most. I don’t know why, though, or how they’d know.”

“It makes sense,” said Kade. They had reached the porch steps. As they started up, he said, “Most of the students lost the things that were most precious to them when their doors closed. Maybe someone’s so heartbroken that they’re trying to make sure nobody gets to be happy. If they have to be miserable, so does everyone else.”

“But you’re not miserable when you’re dead,” said Nancy.

“I sure do hope not,” said Kade, and reached for the doorknob.

The door opened before he touched it.

7 COCOA

LUNDY STOOD IN the doorway, eyeing the pair suspiciously. "Where were you?"

"Morning to you, too, ma'am," said Kade. "We got Loriel sorted, just like Miss Eleanor asked us to, and then we went to find Jill. Jack and Christopher are looking inside; we went to look outside. Since she's not out here, do you mind if we come back in?"

"She shouldn't be alone," said Lundy, stepping to the side and holding the door wider to let them pass. "Why didn't you take her with you?"

"Getting blood out of her dress would have been really hard," said Nancy, without thinking about it. Lundy turned a startled, offended look on her, and she winced. "Um, sorry. It's true, though. You can't get blood out of taffeta, no matter how much you scrub."

"What fascinating life lessons you have to share," said Lundy. "Both of you need to get back inside. It's not safe out here." Her eyes stayed on Nancy, cold and judgmental.

Nancy shivered, trying not to let her unhappiness show. Her hand still bore down involuntarily on Kade's arm, tightening. "All right," she said. "We'll see you at lunch."

They walked past Lundy, past the gleaming chandelier with its dusting of frozen tears, and up the stairway to the attic. Only when they were standing outside the door did Nancy allow her fingers to unclench and the shaking that had been threatening to overwhelm her to take over. She sank to the floor, pressing her back to the wall and pulling her knees up against her chest.

Be still, she thought. *Be still, be still, be still.* But the shaking continued as her traitorous body betrayed her, trembling like a leaf in a hard wind.

"Nancy?" Kade sounded alarmed. He knelt next to her, putting his hand on her shoulder. "Nancy, what's wrong? Are you all right?"

"She thinks I did it." Her voice came out thin and reedy, but audible. She drew in a deep breath, forced her head away from her knees, and looked at Kade as she said, "Lundy thinks I did it. She thinks I'm the one who killed Sumi and Loriel. I come from a world full of ghosts. I'm closer to Jack and Jill than I am to anyone else here, and they've been here forever without killing anybody. But I show up, and people start dropping dead. Suspecting the new girl only makes sense. When the new girl doesn't mind helping with the bodies, it becomes almost too easy. She thinks I did it, because anything else would be complicated and hard."

"Lundy thinks in stories," said Kade, rubbing Nancy's back soothingly. "She spent too long in the Goblin Market before she made her bargain. She has stories in her blood. You're right about being the most logical suspect—new girl, no strong ties, came from an Underworld. You're probably right about Lundy suspecting you. But you're wrong if you think that Eleanor will let her hurt you. Eleanor knows you didn't do it, just like I do. Now come on. I have a hot plate and a teapot in the attic. I can make you something hot to drink, soothe your nerves."

"Actually, I already made cocoa," said Jack, opening the door and poking her head out. "Did you find my sister?"

"No, didn't you?" Kade looked over his shoulder and frowned. "I figured if we didn't find her, you would. Did you check the dining hall?"

"Yes, *and* the library, *and* the classroom we're supposed to be in this time of day, just in case she'd been so absorbed in thinking about her hair that she hadn't paid attention to what we were told to do," said Jack. Her frustration seemed only skin-deep, a cover for her all-too-real concern. "She wasn't in any of the places we looked. I was hoping you'd find her."

"Sorry." Kade stood, offering Nancy his hand. "We looked, we didn't find, we got a scolding from Lundy, and Nancy—"

"Had a little cry when she realized Lundy suspected her," finished Nancy, taking Kade's hand and pulling herself to her feet. "I'm better now. As long as Eleanor doesn't suspect me, I probably won't be expelled. Let's just stick together so that none of us gets hurt, and we'll ride this thing out as a group."

"Huh," said Jack, looking wistful. "I haven't been part of a group since we left our old school. Now come on. Like I said, I made hot chocolate, and Christopher will drink it all if we leave him alone too long."

"I heard that!" called Christopher. Jack snorted and withdrew into the attic.

Kade shot Nancy a worried look, which she answered with a smile and a reassuring squeeze of his hand before she let go and stepped into the attic ahead of him. As promised, the air smelled like hot chocolate. Christopher was sitting on one of the heaps of books, a mustache of whipped cream on his lip and a mug cupped in his hands. Jack was at the hot plate, fixing three more mugs. Kade raised an eyebrow.

"Where did you find the whipped cream?" he asked.

"You had milk, I had science," said Jack. "It's amazing how much of culinary achievement can be summarized by that sentence. Cheese making, for example. The perfect intersection of milk, science, and foolish disregard for the laws of nature."

"How did the laws of nature come into this?" asked Nancy, walking over to claim one of the mugs. The smell was alluring. She took a sip, and her eyes widened. "This tastes like . . ."

"Pomegranate, I know," said Jack. "Yours was made with

pomegranate molasses. Christopher's has a pinch of cinnamon, and Kade's contains clotted cream fudge, which I stole from Miss Eleanor's private supply. She'll never notice. She has the stuff shipped over from England by the pound, and her next delivery is due in three days."

"What's in yours?" asked Nancy.

Jack smiled, holding her mug up in a silent toast. "Three drops of warm saline solution and a pinch of wolfsbane. Not enough to be dangerous to me—I'm human, despite what Angela might say to the contrary—but enough to make it taste like tears, and like the way the wind smells when it sweeps along the moor at midnight. If I knew the taste of the sound of screaming, I'd add that as well, and never drink anything again, as long as I chanced to live."

Christopher swallowed a mouthful of cocoa, shook his head, and said, "You know, sometimes I almost forget how *creepy* you are, and then you go and say something like that."

"It's best if you remember my nature at all times," said Jack, and offered Kade his mug.

"Thank you," he said, taking it from her and wrapping his long fingers around it.

"Say nothing of it," said Jack. Somehow, coming from her, it wasn't politeness: it was a plea. *Let this momentary kindness be forgotten,* it said. *Don't let it linger, lest it be seen as weakness.* Outwardly, all she did was twitch one corner of her mouth in a transitory smile. Then she turned, hands cupping her own mug, and moved to find a seat on the piles of books.

“Isn’t this cozy?” Kade returned to what seemed to be his customary perch, leaving Nancy standing awkward and alone next to the hot plate. She looked around before heading for one of the few actual pieces of furniture, an old-fashioned, velvet-covered chair that was being encroached upon by the books, but hadn’t been swallowed yet. She sank down into its embrace, tucking her feet underneath her, hands still cupped around her mug.

“I like it,” said Christopher, after it became apparent that no one else was going to say anything. He shrugged before he added, “The guys—uh, the other guys, I mean, not you, Kade—put up with me because there’re so few of us here, but they all went to sparkly worlds. They all sort of think where I went was weird, so I can’t talk to them about it much. They start insulting the Skeleton Girl and then I have to punch them in their stupid mouths until they stop. Not the best way to make friends.”

“No, I suppose not,” said Jack. She looked down at her cocoa. “I had similar issues when I attempted to make friends with my fellow students. I gave up trying before Jill did. All they ever wanted to do was talk about how strange the Moors must have been, and how inferior to their own cotton-candy wonderlands. Honestly, I don’t blame them for thinking I could be a killer. I blame them for thinking I would have waited this long.”

“And bonding just got creepy again,” said Christopher cheerfully, before taking a gulp of his hot chocolate. “Luckily for you, I’ll forgive anything for cocoa this good.”

"Like I said, cooking is a form of science, and I am a scientist," said Jack.

"We do need to figure out what's going on," said Kade. "I don't know about the rest of you, but I'm not so well-equipped to go back to my old life. My parents still think they're somehow magically going to get back the little girl they lost. They haven't let me come home for five years. No, maybe that's unfair—or too fair. They won't let *me* come home. If I want to put on a skirt and tell them to call me 'Katie,' they'll welcome me with open arms. Pretty sure that if the school closes down, I'm homeless."

"My folks would let me come back," said Christopher. "They think this is all some complicated breakdown triggered by the things that happened after I 'ran away.' Mom genuinely believes the Skeleton Girl is some girl I fell for who died of anorexia. Like, she asks me on the regular whether I can remember her 'real name' yet, so they can track down her parents and tell them what happened to her. It's really sad, because they care so damn much, and they're so completely wrong about everything, you know? The Skeleton Girl is real, and she isn't dead, and she was never alive the way that people are here."

"Skeleton people generally aren't," said Jack, setting her cocoa aside. "If they were, I would expect them to die instantly, due to their lack of functional respiration or circulatory systems. The lack of tendons alone—"

"You must be a lot of fun at parties," said Christopher.

Jack smirked. "It depends on the kind of party. If there

are shovels involved, I'm the life, death, and resurrection of the place."

"I can't go home," said Nancy. She looked down at her cocoa. "My parents . . . they're like Christopher's, I guess. They love me. But they didn't understand me *before* I went away, and now, I might as well be from another planet. They keep trying to get me to wear colors and eat every day, and go on dates with boys like nothing ever happened. Like everything is just the way it used to be. But I didn't want to go on dates with boys before I went to the Underworld, and I don't want to do it now. I won't. I *can't*."

Kade looked a little hurt. "No one is going to make you do anything you don't want to do," he said, and his tone was stiff and wounded.

Nancy shook her head. "That's not what I mean. I don't want to go on dates with girls, either. I don't want to go on dates with *anyone*. People are pretty, sure, and I like to look at pretty things, but I don't want to go on a date with a painting."

"Oh," said Kade, understanding replacing stiffness. He smiled a little. Nancy, glancing up from her cocoa, smiled back. "Well, looks like we've all got good reason to keep this school open. We've had two deaths. Sumi and Loriel. What did they have in common?"

"Nothing," said Christopher. "Sumi went to a Mirror, Loriel went to a Fairyland. High Nonsense and high Logic. They didn't hang out together, they didn't have friends in common, they didn't do any of the same things for fun. Sumi liked origami and making friendship bracelets, Loriel did puzzles and paint-by-numbers. They only overlapped in class and during meals, and I'm pretty sure they would have stopped doing that if they'd been able to. They weren't enemies. They were just . . . disinterested."

"Nancy said something before about Sumi's hands being the most important things about her," said Kade.

Jack sat up straighter. "Why, Nancy, how callous and odd of you."

Nancy reddened. "I'm sorry. I just . . . I just thought . . ."

"Oh, that wasn't a complaint. It's just that usually, if someone around here is going to be callous and odd, it's me." Jack frowned thoughtfully. "You may be onto something there. Each of us has some attribute that attracted the attention of our door in the first place, some inherent point of sympathy that made it possible for us to be happy on the other side. It's an assumption, I know, built on seeing only the survivors—maybe most of those who go through the doors never return, and so what we see is only ever the best-case scenario. Either way, we'd need to have *something* to get us through the story alive. And for many people, that intangible *something* seems to have been concentrated in a certain part of the body."

"Like Loriel's eyes," said Kade.

Jack nodded. "Yes, or Nancy's incredibly robust musculature—don't look at me like that, you need very strong muscles to stand without collapsing for the sort of times you've described—or Angela's legs, or Seraphina's beauty. The girl's a rancid bucket of leeches on the inside, but she has a face that could move angels to murder. I've seen pictures from before she went traveling. She was always pretty. She was no Helen of Troy, until she traveled."

"How have you seen pictures from before she went traveling?" asked Kade.

"I have the Internet, and her Facebook password is the name of her cat, which she has a picture of above her bed." Jack snorted. "I am a genius of infinite potential and highly limited patience. People shouldn't try me so."

"I'll keep that in mind the next time I'm trying to keep a secret," said Kade. "What are you saying?"

"I'm saying that back when I worked for Dr. Bleak, sometimes he wanted me to gather things for him," said Jack. "Only the best would do, which was absolutely right and fair: he was a genius, too, a greater genius than I can ever dream of being. So he'd say 'I need six bats,' and I would spend days with a net out on the moor, catching the very best, biggest bats, and bring him the finest specimens for his work. Or he might say 'I need a golden carp without a single silver scale,' and I'd spend a week by the river, netting fish after fish, until I had something perfect. Those were the easy jobs. Other times he'd say 'I need a perfect dog, but you're never going to *find* a perfect dog, so go out and find the parts I need.' Head and haunches, tail and toes, I'd have to gather them wherever they were found, and bring them back to him."

"Okay, first, that's gross," said Christopher. "Second, that's inhumane. Third, what are you saying? That some mad scientist is trying to build a perfect girl out of the best parts of us?"

"I'm the only mad scientist at this school, and I'm not killing people," said Jack. "Apart from that? Yes. I'm saying that sometimes, murder isn't about the bodies, or the dead. Those are the things that are left behind. Sometimes, murder is about what's *missing*."

There was a knock at the attic door. Everyone jumped, even Jack. Cocoa slopped over the side of Nancy's cup. Jack sat up straight, putting her cup down and tensing, like a snake getting ready to strike. Kade cleared his throat.

"Who is it?" he called.

"Jill." The doorknob turned. The door swung open. Jill stepped inside. She looked curiously around before announcing, "I looked for you, and when I didn't find you, I decided to come here, since it was the highest point in the house and the closest to the sun, which made it the least likely place for you to be. Now there you are, and here I am. Why did you run off and leave me alone for so long?"

"I was disposing of the body, as I had been asked." Jack slid off her perch, straightening her vest with a quick tug, and said, "Speaking of the body, the acid should be finished with Loriel's soft tissues by this point. Christopher, did you want to come help me with her bones?"

"Sure," said Christopher, sounding bemused. He stood, setting his cocoa aside, and followed Jack out of the attic.

Jill didn't say anything as her sister walked away and left her. She just turned a bright, guileless smile on Kade, and asked, "Is there any more of that cocoa?"

8 HER SKELETON, IN RAINBOWS CLAD

JACK DESCENDED THE STAIRS as if they had personally challenged her, taking them two and three at a time, until Christopher had to jog to keep pace. Throughout her flight, she never seemed to be working: she remained perfectly serene, cold-eyed and thin-lipped, not breathing hard or struggling in the slightest. She didn't speak. Christopher was worried, but also grateful. He wasn't sure he would have been able to answer her without gasping.

"Do we need to clean the bones before you call them?" she asked, as they walked the last length of hallway between the last stretch of stairs and the basement. There were no students there. They hadn't seen any students since leaving the attic. The campus would have seemed deserted, if not for the whispers still drifting from behind closed doors. "Acid is pretty, but it's not a good thing to dress a dancer."

"No," said Christopher, taking the bone flute from his pocket and wrapping his fingers around it, as much for reassurance as for anything else. "She'll rise up clean and lovely. Back in the Country of the Bones, we would free new citizens by—" He stopped midsentence, like he'd just realized he was about to say something horrible.

Jack looked back at him as she opened the basement door. "All right, now I'm genuinely curious. You have to tell me. Don't worry about upsetting me, I once removed a man's lungs from his chest while he was still alive, awake, and trying to talk."

"Why would you do something like that?"

"Why wouldn't I?" Jack shrugged and started down the stairs.

Christopher stared after her for a moment before he started moving again. When he caught up, he said defiantly, "We freed new citizens by cutting through their flesh. Big, deep cuts, all the way down to the bone. That way the skeletons within could rise up without having to struggle and risk fracturing themselves. Bones heal slow, even outside the body."

"The fact that the bones healed at all is the strange thing to me," said Jack. Her voice was quiet. "The rules were so *different* there. For all of us."

"Yeah," agreed Christopher, looking at the reddish liquid filling the tub. A few chunks floated on the surface. He didn't want to think about them too hard.

"You shouldn't tell anyone what you just told me. The petty-minded fools here think surgery and butchery are the same thing. Look at the way they look at me. Right now, you're still one of them, but don't make the mistake of thinking that can't change." Jack walked across the room to the wardrobe. "Everything changes."

"I know," said Christopher, and raised his flute to his lips, and began to play.

There was no sound, not that the living could hear: there was only the *idea* of sound, the sudden, overwhelming sensation that something was being overlooked, something small and subtle and hidden between the molecules of silence. Jack opened the wardrobe and took out a cravat, listening as hard as she could as she removed her bow tie. She heard her own breathing. She heard Christopher's fingers brushing across bone. She heard a splash.

She turned around.

Christopher was still playing, and Loriel was sitting up, a polished bone sculpture. Her scapulae were delicate wings; her skull was a psalm to the elegant dancer waiting beneath the flesh of all who walked the earth. There was a pearlescent sheen to her, like opal, and Jack wondered idly whether that was the acid or the magic of Christopher's flute at work. It was a pity she would probably never know. The school, pleasant as it was, didn't exactly go out of its way to provide her with bodies to examine.

Slowly, gingerly, Loriel's bones stood, wobbling slightly, and climbed out of the tub. A single drop of acid rolled from her elbow and fell to the floor, where it hissed as it ate a pit in the stone. She stopped, rocking from side to side, her empty eye sockets fixed on Christopher.

"That's amazing," said Jack, taking a step forward. "Can she see you? Is she *aware*? Or is this just magic animating her bones? Does it work on any skeleton, or just those who died violently? Can you—you can't answer any of my questions unless you stop playing, can you?"

Christopher shook his head and gestured with an elbow toward the stairs that would lead to the old servant's door. Jack nodded.

"I'll get it open," she said, and trotted off, tying the cravat as she went. Her fingers, while not as nimble as Sumi's, were quick, and the knot was a familiar one; by the time she reached the door and shoved it open, she was once more impeccably dressed. Of all the skills she'd learned from Dr. Bleak, the ability to groom herself while running for her life seemed the most likely to continue to serve her well in this strange, often confusing world she presently called "home."

Christopher followed her more sedately, playing his silent flute all the way. Loriel trailed after him, her toes tapping on the stairs, making a sound that was virtually indistinguishable from the clatter of dried branches on a windowpane. Jack stood and watched as the pair walked outside, and then she followed, closing the door.

"Are we looking for a place to bury her where she won't be found?" she asked. Christopher nodded. "Follow me, then."

Together, they walked across the property, the girl, the boy, and the dancing skeleton wrapped in rainbows. Neither of those who still possessed tissue and tongue spoke.

This was the closest thing Loriel would have to a funeral; it would have been inappropriate to make light of it. They walked until they came to the place where the landscaping dropped away, replaced by tangle and weed, and the hard stretch of stony earth that had never been farmed or claimed as anything other than wilderness. Eleanor West owned it all, of course: her family had owned the countryside for miles around, and now that she was the last, every inch of it belonged to her. She had simply refused to sell or allow development on any of the lots surrounding her school. The local conservationists considered her a hero. The local capitalists considered her an enemy. Some of her greatest detractors said she acted like a woman with something to hide, and they were right, in their way; she was a woman with something to protect. That made her more dangerous than they could ever have suspected.

"Wait," said Jack, when they reached the waste. She turned to Loriel, and said, "If you can hear me, if you can understand me, nod. Please. I know you didn't like me when you were alive, and I didn't like you either, but there are lives on the line. Save them. Answer me."

Christopher kept playing. Slowly, Loriel's skull dipped toward her sternum, moving in the absence of muscles or tendons to command it. Jack blew out a breath.

"See, this could be a Ouija situation, where any answers I get from you are just the things Christopher wants me to hear, but I don't think that's the case," she said. "Maybe it would have been a week ago, but Nancy's at the school now, and ghosts want to be near her. I think you're still Loriel, on some level, deep down. So please, if you can, tell me. Who killed you?"

Loriel was still for several seconds. Then, slowly, as if every move were an impossible effort, she raised her right arm and pointed her index finger at the space next to Jack. Jack turned to look at the empty air. Then she sighed.

"I suppose that was too much to ask," she said. "Christopher?"

He nodded, and moved his fingers on the flute. Loriel's skeleton walked down the short hill into the waste—and kept walking downward, her steps carrying her into and through the ground, as if she were walking on an unseen stairway. In less than a minute, she was gone, the crown of her head vanishing below the soil. Christopher lowered his flute.

"She was so beautiful," he said.

"I'd find that less creepy if I thought you were talking about her with the skin on," said Jack. "Come on. Let's get back to the others. It's not safe to be alone." She turned, and Christopher followed her, and they trudged together across the wide green lawn.

9 THE BROKEN BIRDS OF AVALON

LUNCH WAS A STILTED affair, with no one talking and few students actually eating. For once, Nancy's preference for sipping fruit juice and pushing the solid food around her plate without tasting it didn't come across as strange; if anything, the strange part was her willingness to ingest anything at all. She found herself scanning the other students, trying to guess at their stories, their hidden worlds, to figure out what, if anything, would drive them to kill. Maybe if she had been there longer, if they hadn't been such strangers to her, she would have been able to find the answers she needed. As it was, it felt like she wasn't able to find anything but questions.

After lunch there was an assembly in the library, where Miss Eleanor praised everyone for their calm and their compassion, and thanked Jack, Nancy, and the others for disposing of Loriel's body. Nancy reddened and sank lower in her seat, trying to avoid the eyes that were turning toward her. *She* was a stranger, as far as they were concerned, and as such, her willingness to be intimate with the dead had to be suspicious.

Eleanor took a deep breath and looked out upon the room—her students, her charges—with a somber expression on her face. "As you all know, my door is still open," she said. "My world is a Nonsense world, with high Virtue and moderate Rhyme as its crosswise directions. Many of you wouldn't be able to survive there. The lack of logic and reason would destroy you. But for those of you who thrive in Nonsense, I am willing to open the door and let you go through. You can hide there, for a time."

A gasp ran through the room, accompanied by a few quick, choked-off sobs. A girl with bright blue hair bent double, burying her face against her knees and starting to rock back and forth, like she could soothe her distress away. One of the boys got up and went to the corner, turning his back on everyone. Worse were the ones who simply sat and wept, tears running down their faces, hands folded tightly in their laps.

Nancy looked blankly at Kade. He sighed and leaned closer to her.

"Miss Eleanor is very protective of her door. Doors can be fickle, and she's waited so long to go back that every time she lets someone through, she risks being replaced. Now she's offering to put all the students who can thrive in Nonsense through. That means she's scared, and she's doing what she can to take care of us." He kept his voice low. The students around them didn't seem to notice. Most were too busy crying. On the other side of the room, even Jill was weeping, propped against her sister for support. Only Jack's eyes were dry. "Trouble is, Nonsense is one of the two big directions—she can save half the students, at best, and not everyone who's been to a Nonsense world is suited for *every* Nonsense world. They're all so different. Maybe a quarter of the kids she's just offered to save will be able to go through."

"Oh," said Nancy softly. She understood a few things about false hope, however well-intentioned the offer might have been. Eleanor was trying to save her beloved charges in the only way she knew. She was hurting them in the process.

At the head of the room, Eleanor took a shaky breath. "As always, my darlings, attendance at this school is purely voluntary. If any of you want to call your parents and ask them to take you home, I will refund the rest of the fees for the semester, and I won't try to stop you. I only ask that, for the sake of the students who remain, you don't tell them why you want to withdraw. We'll find a way to fix this."

"Oh, yeah?" asked Angela bitterly. "Can you fix it for Loriel?"

Eleanor looked away. "Get to class," she said. Her voice was soft, and suddenly old.

She stood there, head bowed, as the students rose and filed out. Some were still crying. She would seek out the Nonsense children soon, tap them on their shoulders and lead them to her door. Some would be able to go through, she was sure. There were always a few for whom her world was close enough. Still not home, not the checkerboard sky or mirrored sea that they were dreaming of, but . . . close enough. Close enough for them to be happy, for them to start to live again. And who knew? Doors opened everywhere. Maybe one day, the children of this world who had gone to that world to save themselves would see a door that didn't fit right with the walls around it, something with a doorknob made of a moon, or a knocker that winked. Maybe they could still go home.

A hand touched her shoulder. She turned to find Kade behind her, a worried expression on his face. She glanced toward the seats, and there was Nancy, retreated once more into stillness. It didn't matter. There were too many secrets here to be shy about revealing them. Eleanor turned to Kade once more and buried her face against his chest, weeping.

"It's all right, Aunt Ely, it's all right," said Kade, stroking her back with one hand. "We're going to figure this out."

"My students are *dying,* Kade," she said. "They're dying, and I can get so few of them out of harm's way. I can't save you. When you found your door, I thought—"

"I know," he said. "It's too bad for all of us that I have a Logical heart." He kept stroking her back. "It'll be okay. You'll see. We'll figure this out, we'll find a way, and we'll keep the doors open, no matter what."

Eleanor sighed, pulling away. "You're a good boy, Kade. Your parents don't know what they're missing."

His smile in response was sad. "That's the trouble, Auntie.

They know exactly what they're missing, and since she's never going to be found again, they don't know what to do with me."

"Silly child," said Eleanor. "Now get to class."

"Getting," he said, and walked toward the door. Nancy shook off her statue stillness and followed him.

She waited until they were halfway down the hall before she said, "Eleanor is your . . . ?"

"Great-great-great-aunt," said Kade. "She never married or had children. Her sister, on the other hand, had six. Since my great-great-great-grandma had a husband to take care of her, Eleanor inherited the entire estate. I'm the first of her nieces or nephews to find a door of my own. She was so happy thinking that I'd traveled into Nonsense that it took me almost a month to admit she was typing me wrong, and I'd been in a world of pure Logic. She loves me anyway. Someday, all this"—he gestured to the walls around them—"will be mine, and the school will stay open for another few decades. Assuming we don't close in the next week."

"I'm sure we won't," said Nancy. "We'll figure this out."

"Before the authorities get involved?"

Nancy didn't have an answer to that.

CLASSES WERE PERFUNCTORY and distracted, taught by instructors who could sense that the campus was uneasy, even if they didn't—except for Lundy—know why. Dinner was equally rushed, the beef overcooked and dry, the fruit sliced so haphazardly that bits of peel and rind stuck to the outside when it was served. Students went off in threes and fours, arranging impromptu sleepovers with their friends. Nancy didn't bat an eye when Kade and Christopher showed up at her room clutching sleeping bags and flipped a coin for the use of Sumi's bed. Kade won and settled on the mattress, while Christopher rolled his bedding out on the floor. All three of them closed their eyes and pretended to sleep—a pretense that, for Nancy, became reality sometime after midnight.

She dreamt of ghosts, and silent halls where the dead walked, untroubled.

Christopher dreamt of dancing skeletons that gleamed like opals, and the unchanging, ever-welcoming smile of the Skeleton Girl.

Kade dreamt a world in all the colors of the rainbow, a prism of a country, shattering itself into a thousand shards of light. He dreamt himself home and welcomed as he was, not as they had wanted him to be, and of the three, he was the one who cried into his pillow and woke, cheeks wet, to the sound of screaming.

It was a far-off sound, coming from somewhere outside the window; Nancy and Christopher were still asleep, which only made sense. They had come from worlds where screams were more common, and less dangerous, than they were here. Kade sat up, wiping the sleep from his eyes, and waited for the screams to come again. They did not. He hesitated.

Should he wake them, take them with him when he went to investigate? Nancy was already under suspicion by most of her peers, and Christopher would be too, if he kept getting involved. Kade could go alone. Most of the students liked him, since he was the one who kept the wardrobe in order, and they would forgive him for finding another body. But then he'd be alone, and if either Nancy or Christopher woke before he got back, they would worry. He didn't want to worry them.

Kade knelt and shook Christopher by the shoulder. The other boy groaned before opening his eyes and squinting up at Kade. "What is it?" he asked, voice heavy with sleep.

"Somebody just screamed out near the trees," said Kade. "We need to go see why."

Christopher sat up, seeming instantly awake. "Are we taking Nancy?"

"Yes," said Nancy, sliding out of her bed. Screams hadn't been enough to wake her, but speech had: in the Halls of the Dead, no one spoke unless they wanted to be listened to. "I don't want to stay here alone."

Neither of the boys argued. All of them shared the same fear of being left alone in this suddenly haunted house, where the ghosts were nothing they could understand.

They walked quietly, but they didn't creep, all of them secretly hoping someone would wake, come out of their room, and join the small processional. Instead, the doors stayed shut, and the trio found themselves walking alone toward the shadowy grove where Nancy and Jill had sought shelter from the unforgiving sun. There was no sunlight now: only the moon, looking down from between the patches in the clouds.

Then they stepped into the trees, and the moonlight became too much to bear, for the moonlight was enough to show Lundy, lying small and silent on the ground, her eyes open and staring into the leaves. *She* still had her eyes and her hands, and seemed to have everything else. Her clothes were unbloodied, her limbs intact.

"Lundy," said Kade, and moved to kneel beside her, reaching for a pulse. The motion caused her head to roll to the side, revealing what had been taken.

Kade scrabbled away, shambling to his feet, before running to the other side of the clearing and vomiting noisily into the bushes. Nancy and Christopher, who were less disturbed by gore, looked at the empty bowl of Lundy's skull and stepped a little closer together, shivering despite the warmth of the night.

"Why would someone take her *brain*?" asked Nancy.

"I was about to ask you the same question," snarled Angela.

Nancy and Christopher turned. Angela was standing at the edge of the grove, a flashlight in her hand and several shadow-draped students behind her. Shining the light directly in Nancy's eyes, she demanded, "Where is Seraphina?"

"Who's Seraphina?" asked Nancy, raising a hand to shade her eyes. She heard footsteps a moment before Kade's hand settled on her shoulder. She took a half step back, letting him shelter her. "We came out here because we heard screaming."

"You came out here to hide the body," snapped Angela. "Where is she?"

"Seraphina is the prettiest girl in school, Nancy—you've seen her. She traveled to a Nonsense world, high Wicked, high Rhyme," said Kade. "Pretty as a sunrise, mean as a snake. She ain't here, Angela." His Oklahoma accent was suddenly strong, dominating his words. "Go back to your room. I have to go wake Miss Eleanor. Odds are good she's let Seraphina through her door."

"If she hasn't, you better give her back," said Angela. "If you hurt her, I will kill you."

"We don't have her," said Christopher. "We were asleep up until five minutes ago."

"Who's that with you?" asked Kade. "Have you just been roaming the campus looking for someone to accuse? You're out here as much as we are. This could be your handiwork."

"We went to good, respectable worlds," said Angela. "Moonbeams and rainbows and unicorn tears, not . . . not skeletons and dead people and deciding to be boys when we're really girls!"

Sudden silence fell over the grove. Even Angela's supporters seemed stunned by her words. Angela paled.

"I didn't mean that," she said.

"Oh, but I believe you did," said Eleanor. She stepped around Angela and the others, walking slowly to where Lundy was sprawled in the dirt. She was leaning on a cane. That was new, as were some of the lines in her cheeks. She seemed to be aging by the day. "Ah, my poor Lundy. I suppose this may have been a kinder death than the one you were looking forward to, but I still wish you hadn't gone."

"Ma'am—" began Kade.

"All of you, go back to your rooms," said Eleanor. "Angela, we'll speak in the morning. For now, stay together and try to survive the night." She braced both hands on her cane and stayed where she was, looking down at Lundy's body. "My poor girl."

"But—"

"I am still headmistress here, at least until I'm dead," said Eleanor. "Go."

They went.

Their tiny group managed to stay together until they had reached the front steps. Then Angela turned on Kade, and said, "I meant what I said. It's sick, how you pretend like you're something you're not."

"I was about to say the same thing to you," said Christopher. "I mean, you always did a pretty good job of pretending to be a decent human being. You had me fooled."

Angela gaped at him. Then she turned and stormed up the stairs, with her friends at her heels. Nancy turned to Kade, who shook his head.

"It's all right," he said. "Let's go back to bed."

"I would prefer if you didn't," said Jack.

The three of them turned. The usually dapper mad scientist was standing by the corner of the house, drenched in blood, clutching her left shoulder with her right hand. Blood trickled from between her fingers, bright enough to be visible in the gloom. Her tie was undone. Somehow, that was the worst part of all.

"I seem to need assistance," she said, and pitched forward in a dead faint.

10 BE STILL AS STONE, AND YOU MAY LIVE

KADE AND CHRISTOPHER gathered Jack up; Kade and Christopher carried Jack away, while Nancy stood, frozen and temporarily forgotten, in the shadows on the porch. She knew, in an academic way, that she should hurry after them—that she shouldn't stand out here alone, where anything could happen to her. But that seemed hasty, and dangerous. Stillness was safer. Stillness had saved her before, and it would save her now.

She had forgotten how much like pomegranate juice a bloodstain could look, in the right light.

She had forgotten how beautiful it was.

So now: stand still, so still that she became one with the background, that she could feel her heart slowing, five beats becoming four, becoming three, until there was no more than one beat per minute, until she barely had to breathe.

Maybe Jack was right; maybe her ability to be still was preternaturally honed. It didn't feel like anything special. It just felt *correct,* as if this was what she should have been all the time, always.

Her parents worried because she didn't eat enough, and maybe that was something they needed to worry about when she was moving like a hot, fast thing, but they didn't understand. She wasn't going to stay here, in their hot, fast world. She *wasn't.* And when she slowed her body down like this, when she was *still,* she didn't need to eat any more than she already did. She could survive for a century on a spoonful of juice, a crumb of cake, and consider herself well-nourished. She didn't have an eating disorder. She knew what she needed, and what she needed was to be still.

Nancy breathed deeper into her stillness and felt her heart stop for the span of a minute, becoming as motionless as the rest of her, like a pomegranate seed nestled safe at the center of a fruit. She was preparing to take another breath, to let her heart enjoy another beat, when someone stepped around the corner of the house. Nancy would have said that she couldn't become any more motionless. In that moment, she proved herself wrong. In that moment, she was as still and as inconsequential as stone.

Jill walked past the porch, bloodstains on her hands and a parasol slung over one shoulder, blocking out any errant rays of moonlight that might dare caress her skin. There was a drop of blood at the corner of her mouth, like a spot of jam that her napkin had missed. As Nancy watched, motionless, Jill's little pink tongue flicked out and wiped the blood away. Jill kept walking. Nancy didn't move.

Please, she thought. *Please, my Lord, keep my heart from beating. Please, don't let her see me.*

Nancy's heart did not beat.

Jill walked around the far corner of the house and was gone.

Nancy breathed in. Her lungs ached at the invasion of air; her heart protested as it started to pound, going from stillness to a race in under a second. It took a few seconds more for the blood to resume circulating through her body, and then she spun and ran for the house, following the drops of blood on the floor until she reached the heretofore unseen kitchen and burst through the door.

Kade whirled, a carving knife in his hand. Christopher stepped in front of Eleanor. Jack was lying motionless on the butcher block in the middle of the room, her shirt cut away and makeshift bandages covering the stab wound in her arm.

"Nancy?" Kade lowered the knife. "What happened?"

"I *saw* her," gasped Nancy. "I saw Jill. She did this."

"Yes," said Jack wearily. "She did."

11 YOU CAN NEVER GO HOME

JACK'S EYES WERE OPEN and fixed on the ceiling. Slowly, she used her uninjured arm to push herself upright. When Christopher stepped forward as if to help, she waved him off, muttering an irritated, "I am injured, not an invalid. Some things I must do myself." He backed away. She finished sitting and held that position for a moment, head bowed, fighting to get her breath back.

No one moved. Finally, Jack said, "I should have seen it sooner. I suppose I did, on some level, but I didn't *want* to, so I refused it as best I could. She makes it out like it was my fault we had to leave the Moors, like the work I was doing with Dr. Bleak riled up the villagers. That's not true. Dr. Bleak and I never killed anyone—not on purpose—and most of the locals left us their bodies when they died, because they knew we could use the bits they'd left behind to save lives. We were *doctors*. She's the one who went and became beloved of a monster. She's the one who wanted to be just. Like. Him."

"Jack . . . ?" said Kade, warily.

Nancy, who remembered the moonlight glittering off a speck of blood like jam, said nothing.

"She would have made a beautiful monster, if she'd been a little smarter," said Jack quietly. "She certainly had the appetite for it. Eventually, I suppose she would have learnt subtlety. But she didn't learn fast enough, and they found out what she was doing, and they took up their torches and they marched, and Dr. Bleak knew she'd never be forgiven. He drugged her. He opened the door and went to throw her through. I couldn't let her go alone. She's my *sister*. I just didn't know how *hard* it would be."

"Sweetheart, what are you saying?" asked Eleanor.

Nancy, who remembered the way Jill had smiled when she talked about her Master, and how far she'd been willing to go to please him, said nothing.

"It's my sister." Jack looked at Kade rather than Eleanor, like it was easier for her to say this to a peer. "She killed them all. She's trying to build herself a key. We have to stop her." She slid off the butcher block, only wincing a little when the impact of her feet hitting the floor traveled up through her bad arm. "Seraphina is still alive."

"That's why Loriel pointed next to you, but not at you," said Christopher.

Jack nodded. "I didn't kill her. She knew it. Jill did."

"I saw her outside," said Nancy. "She was walking like there was no hurry. Where would she go?"

"She stabbed me in the basement, but she'll be heading for the attic," said Jack. She grimaced. "The skylights . . . it's easier when there's a storm. I tried to stop her. I tried."

"It's all right," said Kade. "We've got it from here."

"You're not going without me," said Jack. "She's my sister."

"Can you keep up?"

Jack's smile was thin and strained. "Try to stop me."

Kade glanced to Eleanor, expression questioning. She closed her eyes.

"Jack can keep up, but I can't," she said. "Don't go if you're not sure that you'll come back to me."

They went.

The four students ran through the house, fleet and angry. Jack was surprisingly steady on her feet, given the amount of blood she had lost. Nancy brought up the rear. Stillness and speed were diametrically opposed. But she did the best she could, and they all reached the attic door at roughly the same time. Kade slammed the door open.

Jill was standing in an ocean of books with a knife in her hand. The table she had swept clear was now occupied by Seraphina—the most beautiful girl in the world—and an assortment of jars, each with its own, terrible burden. Jill raised her head as the door opened, and sighed. "Go *away,*" she said peevishly. "This is delicate work. I don't have time for you."

Kade was the first to step into the room, his hands held out in front of him. "You don't want to do this."

"I think I do," Jill countered. "You don't know me. None of you know me. Not even her." She jerked her chin at Jack. "I'm going *home*. I'm going back to my Master. I figured out the way, and no one can stop me. If you try, they'll have all died in vain, and I'll just do it again. I'm going to build my skeleton key."

Seraphina whimpered behind the gag that covered her mouth, eyes rolling wildly as she looked for a way out. She wasn't finding one.

"The door home is locked for a reason," said Jack. "You can't get around that."

"But I can, dear sister, *I can,*" said Jill. "Everyone here has something special about them, something that called the doors. I'm building the perfect girl. The girl who has everything. The smartest, prettiest, fastest, strongest girl. Every door will open for her. Every world will want her. And when I get to the Moors, I'll kill her, and I'll be allowed to stay forever. I just want to go home. Surely you can appreciate that."

"We all do," said Christopher. "This isn't the way."

"There isn't any other," said Jill.

"The dead aren't tools," said Nancy, stepping past Kade with her hands held loosely at her sides. "Please. You're hurting them. You're stealing the things that make them important because you want a skeleton key, but they can't move on to their afterlives until you give those things back." She didn't know that her words were true, but they felt so *right* that she didn't question them. "Why is your happy-ever-after the only one that matters?"

"Because I'm the one who's willing to take it," snapped Jill. "Back off, or she dies, and I tell everyone it was you. Who are they going to believe? The ingénue, or the girl who talks to ghosts? Even your supporters are weird. I'll come out smelling like a rose, just you watch."

Jill's eyes were fixed on Nancy. She didn't see Jack move away from the others, making her slow way around the edge of the attic. Christopher and Kade were silent.

"You know this is wrong, Jill," said Nancy. "You know the dead are angry with you."

Jack continued to move, slow and easy and quiet as a prayer. She picked up a pair of scissors.

"I don't care about the dead," said Jill. "I care about going *home*. I care about my Master. I care about my*self*, and the rest of you can hang, as far as I'm—" She stopped in the middle of her sentence, making a small choking sound. She looked down as blood began to spread through the front of her lacy peignoir. Then, gracelessly, she collapsed, revealing the scissors sticking out of her back.

Jack looked down at her fallen sister for a moment. Her eyes were dry when she raised her head and looked at the others. "I'm sorry," she said. "I should have understood faster. I should have seen it. I didn't. I apologize."

"You killed your sister." Nancy sounded puzzled. "Did you have to . . . ?"

"Murder trials are so messy, aren't they? And death isn't forever if you know what you're doing. Jill was the one

Dr. Bleak locked the door against, not me. I've always been welcome at home, if I was willing to leave her behind . . . or change her. Her Master won't want her now. Once you've died and been resurrected, you can't be a vampire." Jack bent to pull the scissors from Jill's back. They came up dripping red. She grimaced as the blood oozed onto her fingers. "If you'll forgive me, we must be going. So much to do, and resurrections always work better when they're performed quickly. I can bring her back. She'll still be my sister."

She slashed the bloody scissors through the air. They cut lines in the nothingness, until a rectangle hung open next to her, showing a dark, wind-racked field. In the distance, a castle, with a village at its base. Jack's face softened, becoming suffused with unspeakable longing.

"Home," she breathed. She bent, sliding her arms under Jill—grunting slightly as the motion reopened the slash in her left shoulder—and lifting her sister's body in a bridal carry. She stepped through the door. She didn't look back.

The last any of them saw of the sisters was Jack, suddenly distant and so small on that vast, empty plain, walking through the darkness toward the castle lights. Then the rectangle faded, leaving them alone in the attic once again.

Seraphina whimpered behind her gag. Time resumed.

Time had a way of doing that.

AND THEY ALL LIVED

WITHOUT JACK TO HELP, disposing of Lundy's body was more difficult: no one really wanted to go into the basement save for Christopher and Nancy, and they didn't know enough about chemicals to dissolve her safely. In the end, she was laid to rest in the grove where she'd been killed, buried deep among the tree roots. Sumi's hands and Loriel's eyes were buried with her. The police pursued a few false leads looking for Sumi's killer, but eventually they admitted that the trail had gone cold, and the case was closed.

Eleanor was slow to recover her vitality; she still walked with a cane, although she was sturdy enough to run the school without her right-hand woman and best friend. Kade began stepping up to fill the void Lundy had left. More and more, it was obvious that one day, the school would be his—and that he would do a good job. Eleanor's legacy would be protected, as it always should have been.

Nancy moved into the basement, once it had been thoroughly cleaned out. Seraphina had repeated the story of her rescue often enough that the other students no longer blamed Nancy or her friends for the deaths; while they might not be friends, at least they weren't enemies.

The rest of the semester passed like a dream. Nancy was packing to go home when she heard footsteps on the stairs and turned to see Kade standing there, a familiar flowered suitcase in his hand.

"Hey," he said.

"Hey," she replied.

"Heard you were going home for the holidays."

Nancy nodded. "My parents insisted." They had begged, they had pleaded with her over the phone, and every word had solidified her determination not to do anything that would give them an excuse to pull her out of school. She didn't want to stay here, where it was bright and colorful and fast, but she would take a thousand school days over a single day in the presence of her parents, who would never understand.

She couldn't even be excited at the thought of seeing them again. During her days among the dead, she had wondered what her family was doing, whether they missed her; now she just wondered if they'd ever let her go.

"I thought you might want to take this"—he held out the suitcase—"so they wouldn't think we'd been encouraging your weirdness."

"That's very kind of you." Nancy smiled as she walked over to take the case from him. "Will you be all right without me?"

"Oh, always," he said. "Christopher and I are working on a new map for worlds connected to the dead. I'm starting to think that maybe Vitus and Mortis are minor directions. That might explain a few things."

"I'll look forward to seeing your work," said Nancy gravely.

"Cool." Kade took a step back up the stairs. "Have a good vacation, okay?"

"I will," said Nancy. She watched him walk away. When the door shut behind him, she closed her eyes and allowed herself a few seconds of stillness, centering her thoughts.

So this was the world. This was the place she'd come from—and more, this was the place where she came closest to belonging *in* this world. She could stay at the school until she graduated, and after. She could be Kade's Lundy, once Eleanor was gone, to Nonsense or to the grave; she could be the woman who stood beside him and helped to keep things going. She'd do a better job, she thought, of telling the students about their futures without making those futures seem like life sentences. She could learn to be happy here, if she had to. But never completely. That would be too much to ask.

She opened her eyes and looked at the suitcase in her hands before she walked over and set it on Jack's old autopsy table, now blunted with a plain white sheet. The latches resisted a little as she pressed them open and revealed the welter of brightly colored clothes that her parents had packed for her all those months ago.

There was an envelope on top of the tangled blouses and skirts and undergarments. Carefully, Nancy picked it up and opened it, pulling out the note inside.

> *You're nobody's rainbow.*
>
> *You're nobody's princess.*
>
> *You're nobody's doorway but your own, and the only one who gets to tell you how your story ends is you.*

Sumi's name wasn't signed: it was scrawled, in big, jagged letters that took up half the page. Nancy laughed, the sound turning into something like a sob. Sumi must have written it that first day, just in case Nancy couldn't handle it; in case she became less sure, and started trying to forget.

Nobody gets to tell me how my story ends but me, she thought, and the words were true enough that she repeated them aloud: "Nobody gets to tell me how my story ends but me."

The air in the room seemed to shift.

The letter still in her hand, Nancy turned. The stairs were gone. There was a doorway in their place, solid oak and so familiar. Slowly, as in a dream, she walked toward it, Sumi's letter falling from her hand and drifting to the floor.

At first, the knob refused to turn. She closed her eyes again, hoping as hard as she could, and felt it give beneath her hand. This time, when she opened her eyes and twisted, the door swung open, and she found herself looking at a grove of pomegranate trees.

The air smelled so sweet, and the sky was black velvet, spangled with diamond stars. Nancy was shaking as she stepped through. The grass was wet with dew, tickling her ankles. She bent to untie her shoes, stepping out of them and leaving them where they lay. The dew coated her toes as she reached up to pluck a pomegranate from the nearest branch. It was so ripe that it had split down the middle, revealing a row of ruby seeds.

The juice was bitter on her lips. It tasted like heaven.

Nancy began walking down the path between the trees, never looking back. The door was gone long before she broke into a run. It wasn't needed anymore. Like a key that finds its keyhole, Nancy was finally home.

DOWN AMONG THE STICKS AND BONES

FOR MEG

I think the rules were different there. It was all about sciencc, but the science was magical. It didn't care about whether something *could* be done. It was about whether it *should* be done, and the answer was always, always *yes*.

—JACK WOLCOTT

PART I

JACK AND JILL LIVE UP THE HILL

1 THE DANGEROUS ALLURE OF OTHER PEOPLE'S CHILDREN

PEOPLE WHO KNEW Chester and Serena Wolcott socially would have placed money on the idea that the couple would never choose to have children. They were not the parenting kind, by any reasonable estimation. Chester enjoyed silence and solitude when he was working in his home office, and viewed the slightest deviation from routine as an enormous, unforgiveable disruption. Children would be more than a slight deviation from routine. Children would be the nuclear option where routine was concerned. Serena enjoyed gardening and sitting on the board of various tidy, elegant nonprofits, and paying other people to maintain her home in a spotless state. Children were messes walking. They were trampled petunias and baseballs through picture windows, and they had no place in the carefully ordered world the Wolcotts inhabited.

What those people didn't see was the way the partners at Chester's law firm brought their sons to work, handsome little clones of their fathers in age-appropriate menswear, future kings of the world in their perfectly shined shoes, with their perfectly modulated voices. He watched, increasingly envious, as junior partners brought in pictures of their own sleeping sons and were lauded, and for what? Reproducing! Something so simple that any beast in the field could do it.

At night, he started dreaming of perfectly polite little boys with his hair and Serena's eyes, their blazers buttoned just *so,* the partners beaming beneficently at this proof of what a family man he was.

What those people didn't see was the way some of the women on Serena's boards would occasionally bring their daughters with them, making apologies about incompetent nannies or unwell babysitters, all while secretly gloating as everyone rushed to *ooh* and *ahh* over their beautiful baby girls. They were a garden in their own right, those privileged daughters in their gowns of lace and taffeta, and they would spend meetings and tea parties playing peacefully on the edge of the rug, cuddling their stuffed toys and feeding imaginary cookies to their dollies. Everyone she knew was quick to compliment those women for their sacrifices, and for what? Having a baby! Something so easy that people had been doing it since time began.

At night, she started dreaming of beautifully composed little girls with her mouth and Chester's nose, their dresses explosions of fripperies and frills, the ladies falling over themselves to be the first to tell her how wonderful her daughter was.

This, you see, is the true danger of children: they are

ambushes, each and every one of them. A person may look at someone else's child and see only the surface, the shiny shoes or the perfect curls. They do not see the tears and the tantrums, the late nights, the sleepless hours, the worry. They do not even see the love, not really. It can be easy, when looking at children from the outside, to believe that they are things, dolls designed and programmed by their parents to behave in one manner, following one set of rules. It can be easy, when standing on the lofty shores of adulthood, not to remember that every adult was once a child, with ideas and ambitions of their own.

It can be easy, in the end, to forget that children are people, and that people will do what people will do, the consequences be damned.

It was right after Christmas—round after round of interminable office parties and charity events—when Chester turned to Serena and said, "I have something I would like to discuss with you."

"I want to have a baby," she replied.

Chester paused. He was an orderly man with an orderly wife, living in an ordinary, orderly life. He wasn't used to her being quite so open with her desires or, indeed, having desires at all. It was dismaying . . . and a trifle exciting, if he were being honest.

Finally, he smiled, and said, "That was what I wanted to talk to you about."

There are people in this world—good, honest, hardworking people—who want nothing more than to have a baby, and who try for years to conceive one without the slightest success. There are people who must see doctors in small, sterile rooms, hearing terrifying proclamations about how much it will cost to even begin hoping. There are people who must go on quests, chasing down the north wind to ask for directions to the House of the Moon, where wishes can be granted, if the hour is right and the need is great enough. There are people who will try, and try, and try, and receive nothing for their efforts but a broken heart.

Chester and Serena went upstairs to their room, to the bed they shared, and Chester did not put on a condom, and Serena did not remind him, and that was that. The next morning, she stopped taking her birth control pills. Three weeks later, she missed her period, which had been as orderly and on-time as the rest of her life since she was twelve years old. Two weeks after that, she sat in a small white room while a kindly man in a long white coat told her that she was going to be a mother.

"How long before we can get a picture of the baby?" asked Chester, already imagining himself showing it to the men at the office, jaw strong, gaze distant, like he was lost in dreams of playing catch with his son-to-be.

"Yes, how long?" asked Serena. The women she worked with always shrieked and fawned when someone arrived with a new sonogram to pass around the group. How nice it would be, to finally be the center of attention!

The doctor, who had dealt with his share of eager parents, smiled. "You're about five weeks along," he said. "I don't recommend an ultrasound before twelve weeks, under normal circumstances. Now, this is your first pregnancy.

You may want to wait before telling anyone that you're pregnant. Everything seems normal now, but it's early days yet, and it will be easier if you don't have to take back an announcement."

Serena looked bemused. Chester fumed. To even *suggest* that his wife might be so bad at being pregnant—something so simple that any fool off the street could do it—was offensive in ways he didn't even have words for. But Dr. Tozer had been recommended by one of the partners at his firm, with a knowing twinkle in his eye, and Chester simply couldn't see a way to change doctors without offending someone too important to offend.

"Twelve weeks, then," said Chester. "What do we do until then?"

Dr. Tozer told them. Vitamins and nutrition and reading, so much reading. It was like the man expected their baby to be the most difficult in the history of the world, with all the reading that he assigned. But they did it, dutifully, like they were following the steps of a magical spell that would summon the perfect child straight into their arms. They never discussed whether they were hoping for a boy or a girl; both of them knew, so completely, what they were going to have that it seemed unnecessary. So Chester went to bed each night dreaming of his son, while Serena dreamt of her daughter, and for a time, they both believed that parenthood was perfect.

They didn't listen to Dr. Tozer's advice about keeping the pregnancy a secret, of course. When something was this good, it needed to be shared. Their friends, who had never seen them as the parenting type, were confused but supportive. Their colleagues, who didn't know them well enough to understand what a bad idea this was, were enthusiastic. Chester and Serena shook their heads and made lofty comments about learning who their "real" friends were.

Serena went to her board meetings and smiled contently as the other women told her that she was beautiful, that she was glowing, that motherhood "suited her."

Chester went to his office and found that several of the partners were dropping by "just to chat" about his impending fatherhood, offering advice, offering camaraderie.

Everything was perfect.

They went to their first ultrasound appointment together, and Serena held Chester's hand as the technician rubbed blueish slime over her belly and rolled the wand across it. The picture began developing. For the first time, Serena felt a pang of concern. What if there was something wrong with the baby? What if Dr. Tozer had been right, and the pregnancy should have remained a secret, at least for a little while?

"Well?" asked Chester.

"You wanted to know the baby's gender, yes?" asked the technician.

He nodded.

"You have a perfect baby girl," said the technician.

Serena laughed in vindicated delight, the sound dying when she saw the scowl on Chester's face. Suddenly, the things they hadn't discussed seemed large enough to fill the room.

The technician gasped. "I have a second heartbeat," she said.

They both turned to look at her.

"Twins," she said.

"Is the second baby a boy or a girl?" asked Chester.

The technician hesitated. "The first baby is blocking our view," she hedged. "It's difficult to say for sure—"

"Guess," said Chester.

"I'm afraid it would not be ethical for me to guess at this stage," said the technician. "I'll make you another appointment, for two weeks from now. Babies move around in the womb. We should be able to get a better view then."

They did not get a better view. The first infant remained stubbornly in front, and the second infant remained stubbornly in back, and the Wolcotts made it all the way to the delivery room—for a scheduled induction, of course, the date chosen by mutual agreement and circled in their day planners—hoping quietly that they were about to become the proud parents of both son and daughter, completing their nuclear family on the first try. Both of them were slightly smug about the idea. It smacked of efficiency, of tailoring the perfect solution right out the gate.

(The thought that babies would become children, and children would become *people,* never occurred to them. The concept that perhaps biology was not destiny, and that not all little girls would be pretty princesses, and not all little boys would be brave soldiers, also never occurred to them. Things might have been easier if those ideas had ever slithered into their heads, unwanted but undeniably important. Alas, their minds were made up, and left no room for such revolutionary opinions.)

The labor took longer than planned. Serena did not want a C-section if she could help it, did not want the scarring and the mess, and so she pushed when she was told to push, and rested when she was told to rest, and gave birth to her first child at five minutes to midnight on September fifteenth. The doctor passed the baby to a waiting nurse, announced, “It’s a girl,” and bent back over his patient.

Chester, who had been holding out hope that the reticent boy-child would push his way forward and claim the vaunted position of firstborn, said nothing as he held his wife’s hand and listened to her straining to expel their second child. Her face was red, and the sounds she was making were nothing short of animal. It was horrifying. He couldn’t imagine a circumstance under which he would touch her ever again. No; it was good that they were having both their children at once. This way, it would be over and done with.

A slap; a wail; and the doctor’s voice proudly proclaiming, “It’s another healthy baby girl!”

Serena fainted.

Chester envied her.

LATER, WHEN SERENA WAS tucked safe in her private room with Chester beside her and the nurses asked if they wanted to meet their daughters, they said yes, of course. How could they have said anything different? They were parents now, and parenthood came with expectations. Parenthood came with *rules.* If they failed to meet those expectations, they would be labeled unfit in the eyes of everyone they knew, and the consequences of *that,* well . . .

They were unthinkable.

The nurses returned with two pink-faced, hairless things that looked more like grubs or goblins than anything human. "One for each of you," twinkled a nurse, and handed Chester a tight-swaddled baby like it was the most ordinary thing in the world.

"Have you thought about names?" asked another, handing Serena the second infant.

"My mother's name was Jacqueline," said Serena cautiously, glancing at Chester. They had discussed names, naturally, one for a girl, one for a boy. They had never considered the need to name two girls.

"Our head partner's wife is named Jillian," said Chester. He could claim it was his mother's name if he needed to. No one would know. No one would ever know.

"Jack and Jill," said the first nurse, with a smile. "Cute."

"Jacqueline and Jillian," corrected Chester frostily. "No daughter of mine will go by something as base and undignified as a nickname."

The nurse's smile faded. "Of course not," she said, when what she really meant was "of course they will," and "you'll see soon enough."

Serena and Chester Wolcott had fallen prey to the dangerous allure of other people's children. They would learn the error of their ways soon enough. People like them always did.

2 PRACTICALLY PERFECT IN VIRTUALLY NO WAYS

THE WOLCOTTS LIVED in a house at the top of a hill in the middle of a fashionable neighborhood where every house looked alike. The homeowner's association allowed for three colors of exterior paint (two colors too many, in the minds of many of the residents), a strict variety of fence and hedge styles around the front lawn, and small, relatively quiet dogs from a very short list of breeds. Most residents elected not to have dogs, rather than deal with the complicated process of filling out the permits and applications required to own one.

All of this conformity was designed not to strangle but to comfort, allowing the people who lived there to relax into a perfectly ordered world. At night, the air was quiet. Safe. Secure.

Save, of course, for the Wolcott home, where the silence was split by healthy wails from two sets of developing lungs. Serena sat in the dining room, staring blankly at the two screaming babies.

"You've had a bottle," she informed them. "You've been changed. You've been walked around the house while I bounced you and sang that dreadful song about the spider. Why are you still *crying*?"

Jacqueline and Jillian, who were crying for some of the many reasons that babies cry—they were cold, they were distressed, they were offended by the existence of gravity—continued to wail. Serena stared at them in dismay. No one had told her that babies would *cry* all the time. Oh, there had been comments about it in the books she'd read, but she had assumed that they were simply referring to bad parents who failed to take a properly firm hand with their offspring.

"Can't you shut them up?" demanded Chester from behind her. She didn't have to turn to know that he was standing in the doorway in his dressing gown, scowling at all three of them—as if it were somehow *her* fault that babies seemed designed to scream without cease! He had been complicit in the creation of their daughters, but now that they were here, he wanted virtually nothing to do with them.

"I've been trying," she said. "I don't know what they want, and they can't tell me. I don't . . . I don't know what to do."

Chester had not slept properly in three days. He was starting to fear the moment when it would impact his work and catch the attention of the partners, painting him and his parenting abilities in a poor light. Perhaps it was desperation, or perhaps it was a moment of rare and impossible clarity.

"I'm calling my mother," he said.

Chester Wolcott was the youngest of three children: by the time he had come along, the mistakes had been made, the lessons had been learned, and his parents had been comfortable with the process of parenting. His mother was an unforgivably soppy, impractical woman, but she knew how to burp a baby, and perhaps by inviting her now, while Jacqueline and Jillian were too young to be influenced by her ideas about the world, they could avoid inviting her later, when she might actually do some damage.

Serena would normally have objected to the idea of her mother-in-law invading her home, setting everything out of order. With the babies screaming and the house already in disarray, all she could do was nod.

Chester made the call first thing in the morning.

Louise Wolcott arrived on the train eight hours later.

By the standards of anyone save for her ruthlessly regimented son, Louise was a disciplined, orderly woman. She liked the world to make sense and follow the rules. By the standards of her son, she was a hopeless dreamer. She thought the world was capable of kindness; she thought people were essentially good and only waiting for an opportunity to show it.

She took a taxi from the train station to the house, because of course picking her up would have been a disruption to an already-disrupted schedule. She rang the bell, because of course giving her a key would have made no sense at all. Her eyes lit up when Serena answered the door, a baby in each arm, and she didn't even notice that her daughter-in-law's hair was uncombed, or that there were stains on the collar of her blouse. The things Serena thought were most important in the world held no relevance to Louise. Her attention was focused entirely on the babies.

"*There* they are," she said, as if the twins had been the subject of a global manhunt spanning years. She slipped in through the open door without waiting for an invitation, putting her suitcases down next to the umbrella stand (where they did *not* compliment the décor) before holding out her arms. "Come to Grandma," she said.

Serena would normally have argued. Serena would normally have insisted on offering coffee, tea, a place to put her bags where no one would have to see them. Serena, like her husband, had not slept a full night since coming home from the hospital.

"Welcome to our home," she said, and dumped both babies unceremoniously into Louise's arms before turning and walking up the stairs. The slam of the bedroom door followed a second later.

Louise blinked. She looked down at the babies. They had left off crying for the moment and were looking at her with wide, curious eyes. Their world was as yet fairly limited, and everything about it was new. Their grandmother was the newest thing of all. Louise smiled.

"Hello, darlings," she said. "I'm here now."

She would not leave for another five years.

THE WOLCOTT HOUSE had been too big for Serena and Chester alone: they had rattled around in it like two teeth in a jar, only brushing against each other every so often. With two growing children and Chester's mother in the mix, the same house seemed suddenly too small.

Chester told the people at his work that Louise was a nanny, hired from a reputable firm to assist Serena, who had been overwhelmed by the difficulty of meeting the needs of twins. He spun her not as an inexperienced first-time mother but as a doting parent who had simply needed an extra pair of hands to meet the needs of her children. (The idea that he might have been that extra pair of hands never seemed to arise.)

Serena told the people on her boards that Louise was her husband's invalid mother, looking for a way to be useful while she recovered from her various non-contagious ailments. The twins were perfect angels, of course, she couldn't wish for better or more tractable children, but Louise needed *something* to do, and so it only made sense to let her play babysitter for a short while. (The idea of telling the truth was simply untenable. It would be tantamount to admitting failure, and Wolcotts did not *fail*.)

Louise told stories to Jacqueline and Jillian, told them they were clever, they were strong, they were miracles. She told them to sleep well and dry their eyes, and as they grew older, she told them to eat their vegetables and pick up their rooms, and always, always, she told them that she loved them. She told them that they were perfect exactly as they were, and that they would never need to change for anyone. She told them that they were going to change the world.

Gradually, Chester and Serena learned to tell their own daughters apart. Jacqueline had been the first born, and that seemed to have taken up all of her bravery; she was the more delicate of the two, hanging back and allowing her sister to go ahead of her. She was the first to learn to be afraid of the dark and start demanding a nightlight. She was the last to be weaned off the bottle, and she continued sucking her thumb long after Jillian had stopped.

Jillian, on the other hand, seemed to have been born with a deficit of common sense. There was no risk she wouldn't throw herself bodily against, from the stairs to the stove to the basement door. She had started walking with the abruptness of some children, going through none of the warning stages, and Louise had spent an afternoon chasing her around the house, padding the corners of the furniture, while Jacqueline had been lying comfortably in a sunbeam, oblivious to the danger her sister was courting.

(Serena and Chester had been furious when they came home from their daily distractions to find that all of their elegant, carefully chosen furniture now bore soft, spongy corners. It had taken Louise asking how many eyes they would like their daughters to have between them to convince them they should allow the childproofing to remain in place, at least for the time being.)

Unfortunately, with recognition came relegation. Identical twins were unsettling to much of the population: dressing them in matching outfits and treating them as one interchangeable being might seem appealing while they were young enough, but as they aged, they would start to unnerve people. Girls, especially, were subject to being viewed as alien or wrong when they seemed too alike. Blame science fiction, blame John Wyndham and Stephen King and Ira Levin. The fact remained that they needed to distinguish their daughters.

Jillian was quicker, wilder, more rough-and-tumble. Serena took her to the salon and brought her home with a pixie cut. Chester took her to the department store and brought her home with designer jeans, running shoes, and a puffy jacket that seemed almost bulkier than she was. Jillian, who was on the verge of turning four and idolized her often-distant parents as only a child could, modeled her new clothes for her wide-eyed, envious sister, and didn't think about what it meant for them to finally look different to people who weren't each other, or Gemma Lou, who had been able to tell them apart from the first day that she held them in her arms.

Jacqueline was slower, tamer, more cautious. Chester gave Serena his credit card, and she took their daughter to a store straight out of a fairy tale, where every dress was layered like a wedding cake and covered in cascades of lace and bows and glittering buttons, where every shoe was patent leather, and how they *shone.* Jacqueline, who was smart enough to know when something was wrong, came home dressed like a storybook, and clung to her sister, and cried.

"What a little tomboy she is!" people gushed when they saw Jillian—and because Jillian was young enough for being a tomboy to be cute, and endearing, and desirable, rather than something to judge, Chester beamed with pride. He might not have a son, but there were soccer leagues for girls. There were ways for her to impress the partners. A tough daughter was better than a weak son any day.

"What a little princess she is!" people gushed when they saw Jacqueline—and because that was all she had ever wanted from a daughter, Serena demurred and hid her smile behind her hand, soaking in the praise. Jacqueline was perfect. She would grow up just like the little girls that had inspired Serena to want one of her own, only better, because they would make none of the errors that other, lesser parents made.

(The idea that perhaps she and Chester hadn't made any errors in parenting because they hadn't really been parenting at all never occurred to her. She was their mother. Louise was a nanny at best, and a bad influence at worst. Yes, things had been difficult before Louise arrived, but that was just because she was recovering from childbirth. She would have picked up the necessary tricks of the trade quickly, if not for Louise hogging all the glory. She would.)

The twins began attending a half-day preschool when they were four and a half. Old enough to behave themselves in public; old enough to begin making the right friends, establishing the right connections. Jillian, who was brave within the familiar confines of her home and terrified of everything outside it, cried when Louise got them ready for their first day. Jacqueline, who had an endlessly curious mind and hungered for more to learn than one house could contain, did not. She stood silent and stoic in her frilly pink dress with the matching shoes, watching as Gemma Lou soothed her sister.

The idea of being jealous didn't occur to her. Jillian was getting more attention now, but she knew that meant that later, Gemma Lou would find an excuse to do something with just Jacqueline, something that would be just between them. Gemma Lou always knew when one twin was being left out, and she always made an effort to make up for it, to prevent gaps from forming. "There will come a day when you're all either of you has" was what she always said when one of them fussed about the other getting something. "Hold to that."

So they went off to preschool, and they held to each other until Jillian's fears were soothed away by the teacher, who had a pretty skirt and a pretty smile and smelled like vanilla. Then Jillian let go and ran off to play with a bunch of boys who had found a red rubber ball, while Jacqueline drifted into the corner occupied by girls whose pretty dresses were too tight to let them do more than stand around and admire one another.

They were all young. They were all shy. They stood in the corner like a flock of bright birds, and looked at each other out of the corners of their eyes, and watched as the louder, freer children rolled and tumbled on the floor, and if they were jealous, none of them said so.

But that night when she got home, Jacqueline kicked her dress under the bed, where it wouldn't be found until long after she had outgrown it, while Jillian sat in the corner with her arms full of dolls and refused to speak to anyone, not even Gemma Lou. The world was changing. They didn't like it.

They didn't know how to make it stop.

ON JACQUELINE AND JILLIAN'S fifth birthday, they had a cake with three tiers, covered in pink and purple roses and edible glitter. They had a party in the backyard with a bouncy castle and a table covered in gifts, and all the kids from their preschool were invited, along with all the children whose parents worked at Chester's firm, or served on one of Serena's boards. Many of them were older than the twins and formed their own little knots in corners of the yard or even inside, where they wouldn't have to listen to the younger children screaming.

Jillian loved having all her friends in her very own yard, where she knew the topography of the lawn and the location of all the sprinkler heads. She raced around like a wild thing, laughing and shrieking, and they raced with her, because that was how her friends had learned to play. Most of them were boys, too young to have learned about cooties and "no girls allowed." Louise watched from the back porch, frowning a little. She knew how cruel children could be, and she knew how much of Jillian's role was being forced upon her by her parents. In a year or two, the flow of things was going to change, and Jillian was going to find herself marooned.

Jacqueline held back, sticking close to Gemma, wary of getting dirt on her pretty dress, which had been chosen specifically for this event, and which she was under strict instructions to keep as clean as possible. She wasn't sure why—Jillian got covered in mud all the time, and it always washed out, so why couldn't they wash her dresses?—but she was sure there was a reason. There was always a reason, and it was never one her parents could explain to her.

Chester manned the barbecue, demonstrating his skill as a chef and a provider. Several of the partners were nearby, nursing beers and chatting about work. His chest felt like it was going to burst with pride. Here he was, the father in his own home, and there they were, the people he worked for, seeing how impressive his family was. He and Serena should have had children much sooner!

"Your daughter's a real scrapper, eh, Wolcott?"

"She is indeed," said Chester, flipping a burger. (The fact that he called people who did this for a living "burger-flippers" and looked down his nose at them was entirely lost on him, as it was on everyone around him.) "She's going to be a spitfire when she gets a little older. We're already looking into peewee soccer leagues. She'll be an athlete when she grows up, just you wait and see."

"My wife would kill me if I tried to put our daughter in a pair of pants and send her off to play with the boys," said another partner, a wry chuckle in his voice. "You're a lucky man. Having two at once was the way to go."

"Absolutely," said Chester, as if they had planned this all along.

"Who's the old lady with your other daughter?" asked the first partner, nodding toward Louise. "Is that your nanny? She seems a little, well. Don't you think she's going to get tired, chasing two growing girls around all the time?"

"She's doing very well with them so far," said Chester.

"Well, keep an eye on her. You know what they say about old ladies: blink, and you'll be taking care of her instead of her taking care of your kids."

Chester flipped another burger, and said nothing at all.

On the other side of the yard, near the elegant, sugar-dusted cake, Serena moved in the center of a swarm of cooing society wives, and she had never felt more at home, or more like she was finally taking her proper place in the world. This had been the answer: children. Jacqueline and Jillian were unlocking the last of the doors that had stood between Serena and true social success—mostly Jacqueline, she felt, who was everything a young lady should be, quiet and sweet and increasingly polite with every year that passed. Why, some days she even forgot that Jillian was a girl, the contrast between them was so strong!

Some of the women she worked with were uncomfortable with the way she enforced Jacqueline's boundaries—usually the women who called her daughter "Jack" and encouraged her to do things like hunt for eggs on wet grass, or pet strange dogs that would shed on her dresses, dirtying them. Serena sniffed at them and calmly, quietly began moving their names down the various guest lists she controlled, until some of them had dropped off entirely. Those who remained had caught on quickly, after that, and stopped saying anything that smacked of criticism. What good was an opinion if it meant losing your place in society? No.

Better to keep your mouth closed and your options open, that was what Serena always said.

She looked around the yard, searching for Jacqueline. Jillian was easy to find: as always, she was at the center of the largest degree of distasteful chaos. Jacqueline was harder. Finally, Serena spotted her in Louise's shadow, sticking close to her grandmother, as if the woman were the only person she trusted to protect her. Serena frowned.

The party was a success, as such things are reckoned: cake was eaten, presents were opened, bounces were bounced, two knees were skinned (belonging to two separate children), one dress was ruined, and one overexcited child failed to reach the bathroom before vomiting strawberry ice cream and vanilla cake all over the hall. When night fell, Jacqueline and Jillian were safely tucked in their room and Louise was in the kitchen, preparing herself a cup of tea. She heard footsteps behind her. She stopped, and turned, and frowned.

"Out with it," she said. "You know how Jill fusses if I'm not in my room when she comes looking for midnight kisses."

"Her name is Jillian, Mother, not Jill," said Chester.

"So you say," said Louise.

He sighed. "Please don't make this more difficult than it has to be."

"What, exactly?"

"We want to thank you for all the time you've spent helping with our children," said Chester. "They were a handful in the beginning. But I think we have things under control now."

Five is not where handfuls end, my boy, thought Louise. Aloud, she said, "Is that so?"

"Yes," said Serena. "Thank you so much, for everything you've done. Don't you think you deserve the chance to rest?"

"There's nothing tiring about caring for children you love like your own," said Louise, but she had already lost, and she knew it. She had done her best. She had tried to encourage both girls to be themselves, and not to adhere to the rigid roles their parents were sketching a little more elaborately with every year. She had tried to make sure they knew that there were a hundred, a thousand, a million different ways to be a girl, and that all of them were valid, and that neither of them was doing anything wrong. She had tried.

Whether she had succeeded or not was virtually beside the point, because here were her son and his wife, and now she was going to leave those precious children in the hands of people who had never taken the time to learn anything about them beyond the most narrow, superficial things. They didn't know that Jillian was brave because she knew Jacqueline was always somewhere behind her with a careful plan for any situation that might arise. They didn't know that Jacqueline was timid because she was amused by watching the world deal with her sister, and thought the view was better from outside the splash radius.

(They also didn't know that Jacqueline was developing a slow terror of getting her hands dirty, thanks to them and their constant admonishments about protecting her dresses, which were too fancy by far for a child her age. They wouldn't have cared if she'd told them.)

"Mother, please," said Chester, and that was it: she'd lost.

Louise sighed. "When would you like me to go?" she asked.

"It would be best if you were gone when they woke up," said Serena, and that was that.

Louise Wolcott slipped out of her granddaughters' lives as easily as she had slipped into them, becoming a distant name that sent birthday cards and the occasional gift (most confiscated by her son and daughter-in-law), and was one more piece of final, irrefutable proof that adults, in the end, were not and never to be trusted. There were worse lessons for the girls to learn.

This one, at least, might have a chance to save their lives.

3 THEY GROW UP SO FAST

AGE SIX WAS KINDERGARTEN, where Jacqueline learned that little girls who wore frilly dresses every day were goody-goodies, not to be trusted, and Jillian learned that little girls who wore pants and ran around with the boys were weirdos and worse.

Age seven was first grade, where Jillian learned that she had cooties and smelled and no one wanted to play with her anyway, and Jacqueline learned that if she wanted people to like her, all she had to do was smile at them and say she liked their shoes.

Age eight was second grade, where Jacqueline learned that no one expected her to be smart if she was going to be pretty, and Jillian learned that everything about her was wrong, from the clothes she wore to the shows she watched.

"It must be *awful* to have such a dorky sister," said the girls in their class to Jacqueline, who felt like she should defend her sister, but didn't know how. Her parents had never given her the tools for loyalty, for sticking up or standing up or even sitting down (sitting down might muss her dress). So she hated Jillian a little, for being weird, for making things harder than they had to be, and she ignored the fact that it had been their parents all along, making their choices for them.

"It must be amazing to have such a pretty sister," said the boys in their class to Jillian (the ones who were still speaking to her, at least; the ones who had managed to get their cootie shots, and were starting to realize that girls were decorative, if nothing else). Jillian twisted in on herself, trying to figure out how she and her sister could share a face and a bedroom and a life, and still one of them was "the pretty one," and the other one was just Jillian, unwanted and ignored and increasingly being pushed from the role of "tomboy" and into the role of "nerd."

At night, they lay in their narrow, side-by-side beds and hated each other with the hot passion that could only exist between siblings, each of them wanting what the other had. Jacqueline wanted to run, to play, to be free. Jillian wanted to be liked, to be pretty, to be allowed to watch and listen, instead of always being forced to move. Each of them wanted people to *see* them, not an idea of them that someone else had come up with.

(A floor below them, Chester and Serena slept peacefully, untroubled by their choices. They had two daughters: they had two girls to mold into whatever they desired. The thought that they might be harming them by forcing them into narrow ideas of what a girl—of what a *person*—should be had never crossed their minds.)

By the time the girls turned twelve, it was easy for the people who met them to form swift, incorrect ideas of who they were as people. Jacqueline—*never* Jack; Jack was a knife of a name, short and sharp and cutting, without sufficient frills and flourishes for a girl like her—was quick-tongued and short-tempered, surrounded by sycophants who flocked to her from all sides of the school, eager to bask in the transitory warmth of her good graces. Most of the teachers thought that she was smarter than she let on, but virtually none of them could get her to show it. She was too afraid of getting dirty, of pencil smudges on her fingers and chalk dust on her cashmere sweaters. It was almost like she was afraid her mind was like a dress that couldn't be washed, and she didn't want to dirty it with facts she might not approve of later.

(The women on Serena's boards told her how lucky she was, how fortunate, and went home with their own daughters, and traded their party dresses for jeans, and never considered that Jacqueline Wolcott might not have the option.)

Jillian was quick-witted and slow-tempered, eager to please, constantly aching from rejection after rejection after rejection. The other girls wanted nothing to do with her, said that she was dirty from spending so much time playing with the boys, said that she wanted to be a boy herself, and that was why she didn't wear dresses, that was why she hacked off all her hair. The boys, standing on the precipice of puberty and besieged on all sides by their own sets of conflicting expectations, wanted nothing to do with her either. She wasn't pretty enough to be worth kissing (although a few of them had questioned how that could be, when she looked exactly like the prettiest girl in school), but she was still a girl, and their parents said that they shouldn't play with girls. So they'd cut her off, one by one, leaving her alone and puzzled and frightened of the world to come.

(The partners at Chester's firm told him how lucky he was, how fortunate, and went home to their own daughters, and watched them race around the backyard playing games of their own choosing, and never considered that Jillian Wolcott might not have any say in her own activities.)

The girls still shared a room; the girls were still friends, for all that the space between them was a minefield of resentment and resignation, always primed to explode. Every year, it got harder to remember that once they had been a closed unit, that neither of them had chosen the pattern of their life. Everything had been assigned. That didn't matter. Like bonsai being trained into shape by an assiduous gardener, they were growing into the geometry of their parents' desires, and it was pushing them further and further away from one another. One day, perhaps, one of them would reach across the gulf and find that there was no one there.

Neither of them was sure what they would do when that happened.

On the day our story truly starts—for surely none of

that seemed like the beginning! Surely all of that was background, was explanation and justification for what's to come, as unavoidably as thunder follows lightning—it was raining. No: not raining. It was pouring, bucketing water from the sky like an incipient flood. Jacqueline and Jillian sat in their room, on their respective beds, and the room was so full of anger and of silence that it screamed.

Jacqueline was reading a book about fashionable girls having fashionable adventures at a fashionable school, and she thought that she couldn't possibly have been more bored. She occasionally cast narrow-eyed glances at the window, glaring at the rain. If the sky had been clear, she could have walked down the street to her friend Brooke's house. They could have painted each other's nails and talked about boys, a topic that Jacqueline found alternately fascinating and dull as dishwater, but which Brooke always approached with the same unflagging enthusiasm. It would have been *something.*

Jillian, who had been intending to spend the day at soccer practice, sat on the floor next to her bed and moped so vigorously that it was like a gray cloud spreading across her side of the room. She couldn't go downstairs to watch television—no TV before four o'clock, not even on weekends, not even on rainy days—and she didn't have any books to read that she hadn't read five times already. She'd tried taking a look at one of Jacqueline's fashionable girl books, and had quickly found herself baffled at the number of ways the author found to describe everyone's hair. Maybe some things were worse than boredom after all.

When Jillian sighed for the fifth time in fifteen minutes, Jacqueline lowered her book and glowered at her across the room. "What *is* it?" she demanded.

"I'm bored," said Jillian mournfully.

"Read a book."

"I don't have any books I haven't read already."

"Read one of my books."

"I don't like your books."

"Go watch television."

"I'm not allowed for another hour."

"Play with your Lego."

"I don't feel like it." Jillian sighed heavily, letting her head loll backward until it was resting against the edge of the bed. "I'm *bored*. I'm very *very* bored."

"You shouldn't say 'very' so much," said Jacqueline, parroting their mother. "It's a nonsense word. You don't need it."

"But it's true. I'm *very* very *very* bored."

Jacqueline hesitated. Sometimes the right thing to do with Jillian was wait her out: she would get distracted by something and peace would resume. Other times, the only way to handle her was to provide her with something to do. If something wasn't provided, she would *find* something, and it would usually be loud, and messy, and destructive.

"What do you want to do?" she asked finally.

Jillian gave her a sidelong, hopeful look. The days when her sister would willingly spend hours playing with her were long gone, as lost as the baseball cap she'd worn when she went to ride the carnival Scrambler with her father the summer before. The wind had taken the cap, and time had taken her sister's willingness to play hide-and-seek, or make-believe, or anything else their mother said was untidy.

"We could go play in the attic," she said finally, shyly, trying to keep herself from sounding like she hoped her sister would say yes. Hope only got you hurt. Hope was her least favorite thing, of all the things.

"There might be spiders," said Jacqueline. She wrinkled her nose, less out of actual distaste and more out of the knowledge that she was *supposed* to find spiders distasteful. She really found them rather endearing. They were sleek and clean and elegant, and when their webs got messed up, they ripped them down and started over again. People could learn a lot from spiders.

"I'll protect you, if there are," said Jill.

"We could get in trouble."

"I'll give you my desserts for three days," said Jill. Seeing that Jacqueline wasn't sold, she added, "And I'll do your dishes for a week."

Jacqueline *hated* doing the dishes. Of all the chores they were sometimes assigned, that was the worst. The dishes were bad enough, but the dishwater . . . it was like making her own personal swamp and then *playing* in it. "Deal," she said, and put her book primly aside, and slid off the bed.

Jillian managed not to clap in delight as she rose, grabbed her sister's hand, and hauled her out of the room. It was time for an adventure.

She had no idea how big an adventure it was going to be.

THE WOLCOTT HOME WAS still far too large for the number of people it contained: large enough that Jacqueline and Jillian could each have had their own room, if they had wanted to, and never seen each other except for at the dinner table. They had started to worry, over the past year, that that would be their next birthday present: separate rooms, one pink and one blue, perfectly tailored to the children their parents wanted and not to the children that they had. They had been growing apart for years, following the paths that had been charted for them. Sometimes they hated each other and sometimes they loved each other, and both of them knew, deep down to the bone, that separate rooms would be the killing blow. They would always be twins. They would always be siblings. They might never be friends again.

Up the stairs they went, hand in hand, Jillian dragging Jacqueline, as had always been their way, Jacqueline making note of everything around them, ready to pull her sister back if danger loomed. The idea of being safe in their home had never occurred to either one of them. If they were seen—if their parents emerged from their room and saw the two of them moving through the house together—they would be separated, Jillian sent off to play in the puddles out back, Jacqueline returned to their room to read her books and sit quietly, not disturbing anything.

They were starting to feel, in a vague, unformed way, as if their parents were doing something wrong. Both of them knew kids who were the way they were supposed to be, girls who loved pretty dresses and sitting still, or who loved mud and shouting and kicking a ball. But they also knew girls who wore dresses while they terrorized the tetherball courts, and girls who wore sneakers and jeans and came to school with backpacks full of dolls in gowns of glittering gauze. They knew boys who liked to stay clean, or who liked to sit and color, or who joined the girls with the backpacks full of dolls in their corners. Other children were allowed to be mixed up, dirty *and* clean, noisy *and* polite, while they each had to be just one thing, no matter how hard it was, no matter how much they wanted to be something else.

It was an uncomfortable thing, feeling like their parents weren't doing what was best for them; like this house, this vast, perfectly organized house, with its clean, artfully decorated rooms, was pressing the life out of them one inch at a time. If they didn't find a way out, they were going to become paper dolls, flat and faceless and ready to be dressed however their parents wanted them to be.

At the top of the stairs there was a door that they weren't supposed to go through, leading to a room that they weren't supposed to remember. Gemma Lou had lived there when they were little, before they got to be too much trouble and she forgot how to love them. (That was what their mother said, anyway, and Jillian believed it, because Jillian knew that love was always conditional; that there was always, always a catch. Jacqueline, who was quieter and hence saw more that she wasn't supposed to see, wasn't so sure.) The door was always locked, but the key had been thrown into the kitchen junk drawer after Gemma Lou left, and Jacqueline had quietly stolen it on their seventh birthday, when she had finally felt strong enough to remember the grandmother who hadn't loved them enough to stay.

Since then, when they needed a place to hide from their parents, a place where Chester and Serena wouldn't think to look, they had retreated to Gemma Lou's room. There was still a bed there, and the drawers of the dresser smelled like her perfume when they were opened, and she had left an old steamer trunk in the closet, filled with clothes and costume jewelry that she had been putting aside for her granddaughters, waiting for the day when they'd be old enough to play make-believe and fashion show with her as their appreciative audience. It was that trunk that had convinced them both that Gemma Lou hadn't always intended to leave. Maybe she'd forgotten how to love them and maybe she hadn't, but once upon a time, she had been planning to stay. That anyone would ever have planned to stay for their sake meant the world.

Jacqueline unlocked the door and tucked the key into her pocket, where it would be secure, because she never lost anything. Jillian opened the door and took the first step into the room, making sure their parents weren't lurking for them there, because she was always the first one past the threshold. Then the door was closed behind them, and they were finally safe, truly safe, with no roles to play except for the ones they chose for themselves.

"I call dibs on the pirate sword," said Jacqueline excitedly, and ran for the closet, grabbing the lid of the trunk and shoving it upward. Then she stopped, elation fading into confusion. "Where did the clothes go?"

"What?" Jillian crowded in next to her sister, peering into the trunk. The dress-up clothes and accessories were gone, all of them, replaced by a winding wooden staircase that descended down, down, down into the darkness.

Had Gemma Lou been allowed to stay with them, they might have read more fairy tales, might have heard more stories about children who opened doors to one place and found themselves stepping through into another. Had they been allowed to grow according to their own paths, to follow their own interests, they might have met Alice, and Peter, and Dorothy, all the children who had strayed from the path and found themselves lost in someone else's fairyland. But fairy tales had been too bloody and violent for Serena's tastes, and children's books had been too soft and whimsical for Chester's tastes, and so somehow, unbelievable as it might seem, Jacqueline and Jillian had never been exposed to the question of what might be lurking behind a door that wasn't supposed to be there.

The two of them looked at the impossible stairway and were too baffled and excited to be afraid.

"Those weren't there last time," said Jillian.

"Maybe they were, and the dresses were just all on top of them," said Jacqueline.

"The dresses would have fallen," said Jillian.

"Don't be stupid," said Jacqueline—but it was a fair

point, wasn't it? If there had always been stairs in the trunk, then all the things Gemma Lou had left for them would have fallen. Unless . . . "There's a lid here," she said. "Maybe there's a lid on the bottom, too, and it came open, and everything fell down the stairs."

"Oh," said Jillian. "What should we do?"

Dimly, Jacqueline was beginning to realize that this wasn't just a mystery: it was an *opportunity*. Their parents didn't know there was a stairway hidden in Gemma Lou's old closet. They couldn't know. If they *had* known, they would have put the key somewhere much harder to find than the kitchen junk drawer. The stairs looked dusty, like no one had walked on them in years and years, and Serena *hated* dust, which meant she didn't know that the stairs existed. If Jacqueline and Jillian went down those stairs, why, they would be walking into something secret. Something new. Something their parents had maybe never seen and couldn't fence in with inexplicable adult rules.

"We should go and find all our dress-up clothes and put them away, so that we're not making a mess in Gemma Lou's room," said Jacqueline, as if it were the most reasonable thing in the world.

Jillian frowned. There was something in her sister's logic that didn't sit right with her. She was fine with sneaking into their grandmother's room, because they had been welcome there before Gemma Lou had stopped loving them and gone away; this was their place as much as it had been hers. The stairs in the trunk, on the other hand . . . those were something new and strange and alien. Those belonged to someone other than Gemma Lou, and someone other than them.

"I don't know . . ." she said warily.

Perhaps, if the sisters had been encouraged to love each other more, to trust each other more, to view each other as something other than competition for the limited supplies of their parents' love, they would have closed the trunk and gone to find an adult. When they had led their puzzled parents back to Gemma Lou's room, opening the trunk again would have revealed no secrets, no stairs, just a mess of dress-up clothes, and the confusion that always follows when something magical disappears. Perhaps.

But that hadn't been their childhood: that hadn't been their life. They were competitors as much as they were companions, and the thought of telling their parents would never have occurred to them.

"Well, *I'm* going," said Jacqueline, with a prim sniff, and slung her leg over the edge of the trunk.

It was easier than she had expected it to be. It was like the trunk *wanted* her to step inside, like the stairs *wanted* her to descend them. She climbed through the opening and went down several steps before smoothing her dress with the heels of her hands, looking back over her shoulder, and asking, "Well?"

Jillian was not as brave as everyone had always assumed she was. She was not as wild as everyone had always wanted her to be. But she had spent her life so far being told that she was both those things, and more, that her sister was neither of them; if there was an adventure to be had, she simply could not allow Jacqueline to have it without her. She hoisted herself over the edge of the trunk, tumbling in her hurry, and came to a stop a step above where Jacqueline was waiting.

"I'm coming with you," she said, picking herself up without bothering to dust herself off.

Jacqueline, who had been expecting this outcome, nodded and offered her hand to her sister.

"So neither one of us gets lost," she said.

Jillian nodded, and took her sister's hand, and together they walked down, down, down into the dark.

The trunk waited until they were too far down to hear before it swung closed, shutting them in, shutting the old world out. Neither of the girls noticed. They just kept on descending.

SOME ADVENTURES BEGIN EASILY. It is not *hard,* after all, to be sucked up by a tornado or pushed through a particularly porous mirror; there is no skill involved in being swept away by a great wave or pulled down a rabbit hole. Some adventures require nothing more than a willing heart and the ability to trip over the cracks in the world.

Other adventures must be committed to before they have even properly begun. How else will they know the worthy from the unworthy, if they do not require a certain amount of effort on the part of the ones who would undertake them? Some adventures are cruel, because it is the only way they know to be kind.

Jacqueline and Jillian descended the stairs until their legs ached and their knees knocked and their mouths were dry as deserts. An adult in their place might have turned around and gone back the way they had come, choosing to retreat to the land of familiar things, of faucets that ran wet with water, of safe, flat surfaces. But they were children, and the logic of children said that it was easier to go down than it was to go up. The logic of children ignored the fact that one day, they would have to climb back up, into the light, if they wanted to go home.

When they were halfway down (although they didn't know it; each step was like the last), Jillian slipped and fell, her hand wrenched out of Jacqueline's. She cried out, sharp and wordless, as she tumbled down, and Jacqueline chased after her, until they huddled together, bruised and slightly stunned, on one of the infrequent landings.

"I want to go back," sniffled Jillian.

"Why?" asked Jacqueline. There was no good answer, and so they resumed their descent, down, down, down, down past earthen walls thick with tree roots and, later, with the great white bones of beasts that had walked the Earth so long ago that it might as well have been a fairy tale.

Down, down, down they went, two little girls who couldn't have been more different, or more the same. They wore the same face; they viewed the world through the same eyes, blue as the sky after a storm. They had the same hair, white-blonde, pale enough to seem to glow in the dim light of the stairway, although Jacqueline's hung in long corkscrew curls, while Jillian's was cut short, exposing her ears and the elegant line of her neck. They both stood, and moved, cautiously, as if expecting correction to come at any moment.

Down, down, down they went, until they stepped off the final stair, into a small, round room with bones and roots embedded in the walls, with dim white lights on strings hanging around the edges of it, like Christmas had been declared early. Jacqueline looked at them and thought of mining lights, of dark places underground. Jillian looked at them and thought of haunted houses, of places that took more than they gave. Both girls shivered, stepping closer together.

There was a door. It was small, and plain, and made of rough, untreated pine. A sign hung at adult eye level. BE SURE, it said, in letters that looked like they had been branded into the wood.

"Be sure of what?" asked Jillian.

"Be sure that we want to see what's on the other side, I guess," said Jacqueline. "There isn't any other way to go."

"We could go back up."

Jacqueline looked flatly at her sister. "My legs hurt," she said. "Besides, I thought you wanted an adventure. 'We found a door, but we didn't like it, so we went back without seeing what was on the other side' isn't an adventure. It's . . . it's running away."

"I don't run away," said Jillian.

"Good," said Jacqueline, and reached for the doorknob.

It turned before she could grab it, and the door swung

open, revealing the most impossible place either girl had ever seen in their life.

It was a field. A big field, so big that it seemed like it went on just shy of forever—and the only reason it didn't go on farther was because it ran up against the edge of what looked like an ocean, slate-gray and dashing itself against a rocky, unforgiving shore. Neither girl knew the word for "moor," but if they had, they would have both agreed in an instant that this was a moor. This was *the* moor, the single platonic ideal from which all other moors had been derived. The ground was rich with a mixture of low-growing shrubs and bright-petaled flowers, growing blue and orange and purple, a riot of impossible color. Jillian stepped forward with a small sound of amazement and delight. Jacqueline, not wanting to be left behind, followed her.

The door slammed shut behind them. Neither girl noticed, not yet. They were busy running through the flowers, laughing, under the eye of the vast and bloody moon.

Their story had finally begun.

PART II

JILL AND JACK INTO THE BLACK

4 TO MARKET, TO MARKET, TO BUY A FAT HEN

JILLIAN AND JACQUELINE ran through the flowers like wild things—and in that moment, that brief and shining moment, with their parents far away and unaware of what their daughters were doing, with no one who dwelt in the Moors yet aware of their existence, they *were* wild things, free to do whatever they wanted, and what they wanted to do was *run*.

Jacqueline ran like she had been saving all her running for this moment, for this place where no one could see her, or scold her, or tell her that ladies didn't behave that way, sit down, slow down, you'll rip your dress, you'll stain your tights, be *good*. She was getting grass stains on her knees and mud under her fingernails, and she knew she'd regret both those things later, but in the moment, she didn't care. She was finally running. She was finally free.

Jillian ran more slowly, careful not to trample the flowers, slowing down whenever she felt like it to look around herself in wide-eyed wonder. No one was telling her to go faster, to run harder, to keep her eyes on the ball; no one wanted this to be a competition. For the first time in years, she was running solely for the joy of running, and when she tripped and fell into the flowers, she went down laughing.

Then she rolled onto her back and the laughter stopped, drying up in her throat as she stared, wide-eyed, at the vast ruby eye of the moon.

Now, those of you who have seen the moon may think you know what Jillian saw: may think that you can picture it, shining in the sky above her. The moon is the friendliest of the celestial bodies, after all, glowing warm and white and welcoming, like a friend who wants only to know that all of us are safe in our narrow worlds, our narrow yards, our narrow, well-considered lives. The moon worries. We may not know how we know that, but we know it all the same: that the moon watches, and the moon worries, and the moon will always love us, no matter what.

This moon watched, but that was where the resemblance to the clean and comfortable moon that had watched over the twins all the days of their lives ended. This moon was huge, and red as a ruby somehow set into the night sky, surrounded by the gleaming points of a million stars. Jillian had never in her life seen so many stars. She stared at them as much as at the moon, which seemed to be *looking* at her with a focus and intensity that she had never noticed before.

Gradually, Jacqueline tired of running, and moved to sit down next to her sister in the flowers. Jillian pointed mutely upward. Jacqueline looked, and frowned, suddenly uneasy.

"The moon is wrong," she said.

"It's red," said Jillian.

"No," said Jacqueline—who had, after all, been encouraged to sit quietly, to read books rather than play noisy games, to *watch*. No one had ever thought to ask her to be smart, which was good, in the grand scheme of things: her mother would have been much more likely to ask her to be a little foolish, because foolish girls were more tractable than stubbornly clever ones. Cleverness was a boy's attribute, and would only get in the way of sitting quietly and being mindful.

Jacqueline had found cleverness all on her own, teasing it out of the silences she found herself marooned in, using it to fill the gaps naturally created by a life lived being good, and still, and patient. She was only twelve years old. There were limits to the things she knew. And yet . . .

"The moon shouldn't be that big," she said. "It's too far away to be that big. It would have to be so close that it would mess up all the tides and pull the world apart, because gravity."

"Gravity can do that?" asked Jillian, horrified.

"It could, if the moon were that close," said Jacqueline. She stood, leaning down to pull her sister along with her. "We shouldn't be here." The moon was wrong, and there were mountains in the distance. *Mountains*. Somehow, she didn't have a problem with the idea that there was a field and an ocean below the basement, but mountains? That was a step too far.

"The door's gone," said Jillian. She had a sprig of some

woody purple plant in her hair, like a barrette. It was pretty. Jacqueline couldn't think of the last time she'd seen her sister wearing something just because it was pretty. "How are we supposed to go home if the door's gone?"

"If the moon can be wrong, the door can move," said Jacqueline, with what she hoped would sound like certainty. "We just need to find it."

"Where?"

Jacqueline hesitated. The ocean was in front of them, big and furious and stormy. The waves would carry them away in an instant, if they got too close. The mountains were behind them, tall and craggy and foreboding. Shapes that looked like castles perched on the highest peaks. Even if they could climb that far, there was no guarantee that the people who lived in castles like grasping hands, high up the slope of a mountain, would ever be friendly toward two lost little girls.

"We can go left or we can go right," said Jacqueline finally. "You choose."

Jillian lit up. She couldn't remember the last time her sister had asked her to choose something, had trusted her not to lead them straight into a mud puddle or other small disaster. "Left," she said, and grabbed her sister's hand, and hauled her away across the vast and menacing moor.

IT IS IMPORTANT to understand the world in which Jacqueline and Jillian found themselves marooned, even if they would not understand it fully for some time, if ever. And so, the Moors:

There are worlds built on rainbows and worlds built on rain. There are worlds of pure mathematics, where every number chimes like crystal as it rolls into reality. There are worlds of light and worlds of darkness, worlds of rhyme and worlds of reason, and worlds where the only thing that matters is the goodness in a hero's heart. The Moors are none of those things. The Moors exist in eternal twilight, in the pause between the lightning strike and the resurrection. They are a place of endless scientific experimentation, of monstrous beauty, and of terrible consequences.

Had the girls turned toward the mountains, they would have found themselves in a world washed in snow and pine, where the howls of wolves split the night, and where the lords of eternal winter ruled with an unforgiving hand.

Had the girls turned toward the sea, they would have found themselves in a world caught forever at the moment of drowning, where the songs of sirens lured the unwary to their deaths, and where the lords of half-sunken manors never forgot, or forgave, those who trespassed against them.

But they did neither of those things. Instead, they walked through brush and bracken, pausing occasionally to gather flowers that they had never seen before, flowers that bloomed white as bone, or yellow as bile, or with the soft suggestion of a woman's face tucked into the center of their petals. They walked until they could walk no more, and when they curled together in their exhaustion, the undergrowth made a lovely mattress, while the overgrowth shielded them from casual view.

The moon set. The sun rose, bringing storm clouds with it. It hid behind them all through the day, so that the sky was never any brighter than it had been when they arrived. Wolves came down from the mountains and unspeakable things came up from the sea, all gathering around the sleeping children and watching them dream the hours away. None made a move to touch the girls. They had made their choice: they had chosen the Moors. Their fate, and their future, was set.

When the moon rose again the beasts of mountain and sea slipped away, leaving Jacqueline and Jillian to wake to a lonely, silent world.

Jillian was the first to open her eyes. She looked up at the red moon hanging above them, and was surprised twice in the span of a second: first by how close the moon still looked, and second by her lack of surprise at their location. Of course this was all real. She had had her share of wild and beautiful dreams, but never anything like this. And if she hadn't dreamed it, it had to be real, and if it was real, of course they were still there. Real places didn't go away just because you'd had a nap.

Beside her, Jacqueline stirred. Jillian turned to her sister, and grimaced at the sight of a slug making its slow way along the curve of Jacqueline's ear. They were having an adventure, and it would all be spoiled if Jacqueline started to panic over getting dirty. Careful as anything, Jillian reached over and plucked the slug from her sister's ear, flicking it into the brush.

When she looked back, Jacqueline's eyes were open. "We're still here," she said.

"Yes," said Jillian.

Jacqueline stood, scowling at the grass stains on her knees, the mud on the hem of her dress. It was a good thing she couldn't see her own hair, thought Jillian; she would probably have started crying if she could.

"We need to find a door," said Jacqueline.

"Yes," said Jillian, and she didn't mean it, and when Jacqueline offered her hand, she took it anyway, because they were together, the two of them, really *together,* and even if that couldn't last, it was still novel and miraculous. When people heard that she had a twin, they were always quick to say how nice that had to be, having a best friend from birth. She had never been able to figure out how to tell them how wrong they were. Having a twin meant always having someone to be compared to and fall short of, someone who was under no obligation to like you—and wouldn't, most of the time, because emotional attachments were dangerous.

(Had she been able to articulate how she felt about her home life, had she been able to tell an adult, Jillian might have been surprised by the way things could change. But ah, if she had done that, she and her sister would never have become the bundle of resentments and contradictions necessary to summon a door to the Moors. Every choice feeds every choice that comes after, whether we want those choices or no.)

Jacqueline and Jillian walked across the moorland hand in hand. They didn't talk, because they didn't know what there was to talk about: the easy conversation of sisters had stopped coming easily to them almost as soon as they had learned to speak. But they took comfort in being together, in the knowledge that neither one of them was making this journey alone. They took comfort in proximity. After their semi-shared childhood, that was the closest they could come to enjoying one another's company.

The ground was uneven, as rocky heaths and moorlands often are. They had been climbing for a little while, coming to the end of the flat plain. At the crest of the hill Jacqueline's foot hit a dip in the soil, and she fell, tumbling down the other side of the hill with a speed as surprising as it was bruising. Jillian shouted her sister's name, lunging for her hand, and found herself falling as well, two little girls rolling end over end, like stars tumbling out of an overcrowded sky.

In places like the Moors, when the red moon is looking down from the sky and making choices about the story, when the travelers have made their decisions about which way to go, distance is sometimes more of an idea than an enforceable law. The girls tumbled to a stop, Jacqueline landing on her front and Jillian landing on her back, both with queasy stomachs and heads full of spangles. They sat up, reaching for each other, brushing the heath out of their eyes, and gaped in open-mouthed amazement at the wall that had suddenly appeared in front of them.

A word must be said, about the wall.

Those of us who make our homes in the modern world, where there are very few monsters roaming the fens, very few werewolves howling in the night, think we understand the nature of walls. They are dividing lines between one room and another, more of a courtesy than anything else. Some people have chosen to do away with them altogether, living life in what they call an "open floor plan." Privacy and protection are ideas, not necessities, and a wall outside is better called a fence.

This was no fence. This was a *wall,* in the oldest, truest sense of the word. Entire trees had been cut down, sharpened into stakes and driven into the ground. They were bound together with iron and with hand-woven ropes, the spaces between them sealed with concrete that glittered oddly in the moonlight, like it was made of something more than simply stone. An army could have run aground against that wall, unable to go any farther.

There was a gate in the wall, closed against the night, as vast and intimidating as the scrubland around it. Looking at that gate, it was difficult to believe that it would ever open, or that it *could* ever open. It seemed more like a decorative flourish than a functional thing.

"Whoa," said Jillian.

Jacqueline was cold. She was bruised. Worst of all, she was *dirty.* She had, quite simply, Had Enough. And so she marched forward, out of the bracken, onto the hard-packed dirt surrounding the wall, and she knocked as hard on the gate as her soft child's hands would allow. Jillian gasped, grabbing her arm and dragging her back.

But the damage, such as it was, had been done. The gate creaked open, splitting down the middle to reveal a medieval-looking courtyard. There was a fountain in the center, a bronze-and-steel statue of a man in a long cloak, his pensive gaze fixed upon the high mountains. No one stirred. It was a deserted place, an abandoned place, and looking at it filled Jillian's heart with dread.

"We shouldn't be here," she murmured.

"Indeed, you probably should not," said a man's voice. Both girls screamed and jumped, whirling around to find the man from the fountain standing behind them, looking at them like they were a strange new species of insect found crawling around his garden.

"But you *are* here," he continued. "That means, I suppose, that I'll have to deal with you."

Jacqueline reached for Jillian's hand, found it, and held fast, both of them staring in mute fear at the stranger.

He was a tall man, taller than their father, who had always been the tallest point in their world. He was a handsome man, like something out of a movie (although Jacqueline wasn't sure she'd ever seen a movie star so pale, or so seemingly sculpted out of some cold white substance). His hair was very black, and his eyes were orange, like jack-o'-lanterns. Most surprising of all was his red, red mouth, which looked like it had been painted, like he was wearing lipstick.

The lining of his cloak was the same red color as his mouth, and his suit was as black as his hair, and he held himself so perfectly still that he didn't seem human.

"Please, sir, we didn't mean to go anywhere we aren't supposed to be," said Jillian, who had, after all, spent years pretending she knew how to be brave. She tried so hard that sometimes she forgot that she was lying. "We thought we were still in our house."

The man tilted his head, like he was looking at a very interesting bug, and asked, "Does your house normally include an entire world? It must be quite large. You must spend a great deal of time dusting."

"There was a door," said Jacqueline, coming to her sister's defense.

"Was there? And was there, by any chance, a sign on the door? An instruction, perhaps?"

"It said . . . it said 'be sure,' " said Jacqueline.

"Mmm." The man inclined his head. It wasn't a nod; more a form of acknowledgment that someone else had spoken. "And were you?"

"Were we what?" asked Jillian.

"Sure," he said.

The girls stepped a little closer together, suddenly cold. They were tired and they were hungry and their feet hurt, and nothing this man said was making any sense.

"No," they said, in unison.

The man actually smiled. "Thank you," he said, and his voice was not unkind.

Maybe that was what gave Jillian the courage to ask, "For what?"

"For not lying to me," he said. "What are your names?"

"Jacqueline," said Jacqueline, and "Jillian," said Jillian,

and the man, who had seen his share of children come walking through those hills, come knocking at those gates, smiled.

"Jack and Jill came down the hill," he said. "You must be hungry. Come with me."

The girls exchanged a look, uneasy, although they could not have said why. But they were only twelve, and the habits of obedience were strong in them.

"All right," they said, and when he walked through the gates into the empty square, they followed him, and the gates swung shut behind them, shutting out the scrubland. They could not shut out the disapproving red eye of the moon, which watched, and judged, and said nothing.

5 THE ROLES WE CHOOSE OURSELVES

THE MAN LED THEM through the silent town beyond the wall. Jill kept her eyes on him as she walked, trusting that if anything were to happen, it would begin with the only person they had seen since climbing into the bottom of their grandmother's trunk. Jack, who was more used to silence, and stillness, and found it less distracting, watched the windows. She saw the flicker of candles as they were moved hastily out of view; she saw the curtains sway, as if they had just been released by an unseen hand.

They were not alone there, and the people they shared the evening with were all in hiding. But why? Surely two little girls and a man who wore a cape couldn't be *that* frightening. And she was hungry, and cold, and tired, and so she kept her mouth closed and followed along until they came to a barred iron door in a gray stone wall. The man turned to look at them, his expression grave.

"This is your first night in the Moors, and the law says I must extend to you the hospitality of my home for the duration of three moonrises," he said solemnly. "During that time, you will be as safe under my roof as I am. No one will harm you. No one will hex you. No one will draw upon your blood. When that time is done, you will be subject to the laws of this land, and will pay for what you take as would anyone. Do you understand?"

"What?" said Jill.

"No," said Jack. "That doesn't . . . What do you mean, 'draw upon our blood'? Why would you be doing anything with our blood?"

"What?" said Jill.

"We're not even going to *be* here in three days. We just need to find a door, and then we're going to go home. Our parents are worried about us." It was the first lie Jack had told since coming to the Moors, and it stuck in her throat like a stone.

"What?" said Jill, for the third time.

The man smiled. His teeth were as white as his lips were red, and for the first time, the contrast seemed to put some color into his skin. "Oh, this will be fun," he said, and opened the iron door.

On the other side was a hall. It was a perfectly normal hall, as subterranean castle halls went: the walls were stone, the floor was carpeted in faded red and black filigree, and the chandeliers that hung from the ceiling were rich with spider webs, tangled perilously close to the burning candles. The man stepped through. Jack and Jill, lacking any better options, followed him.

See them now as they were then, two golden-haired little

girls in torn and muddy clothes, following a spotless stranger through the castle. See how he moves, as fluid as a hunting cat, his feet barely seeming to brush the ground, and how the children hurry to keep up with him, almost tripping over themselves in their eagerness to not be left behind! They are still holding each other's hands, our lost little girls, but already Jack is beginning to lag a little, suspicious of their host, wary of what happens when the three days are done.

They are not twins who have been taught the importance of cleaving to each other, and the cracks between them are already beginning to show. It will not be long before they are separated.

But ah, that is the future, and this is the present. The man walked and Jack and Jill followed, already wearing their shortened names like the armor that they would eventually become. Jack had always been "Jacqueline," avoiding the short, sharp, masculine sound of "Jack" (and her mother had asked, more than once, whether there was a way to trade the names between the girls, to make Jacqueline Jillian, to let Jillian be Jack). Jill had always been "Jillian," clinging to the narrow blade of femininity that she had been allowed, refusing to be truncated (and her father had looked into the question of name changes, only to dismiss it as overly complicated, for insufficient gain). Jill dogged their guide's heels and Jack hung back as much as their joined hands allowed, and when they reached a flight of stairs, narrower than the one that had brought them there, made of stone instead of dusty wood, they both stopped for a moment, looking at the steps in silence.

The man paused to look at them, a smile toying with the corner of his mouth. "This is not the way home for you, little foundlings," he said. "I'm afraid that will be more difficult to find than the stairs that connect my village to my dining room."

"*Your* village?" asked Jack, forgetting to be afraid in her awe. "The whole thing? You own the whole thing?"

"Every stick and every bone," said the man. "Why? Does that impress you?"

"A bit," she admitted.

The man's smile grew. She was very lovely, after all, with hair like sunlight and the sort of smooth skin that spoke of days spent mostly indoors, away from the weather. She would be tractable; she would be sweet. She might do.

"I have many impressive things," he said, and started up the stairs, leaving the girls with little choice but to follow him unless they wanted to be left behind.

Up they went, up and up and up until it felt like they must have climbed all the way back to the bottom of Gemma Lou's trunk, back into the familiar confines of their own house. Instead, they emerged from the stairwell and into a beautiful dining room. The long mahogany table was set for one. The maid standing near the far wall looked alarmed when the man stepped into the room, trailed by two little girls. She started to step forward, only to stop herself and stand there, wringing her hands.

"Peace, Mary, peace," said the man. "They're travelers—

foundlings. They came through a door, and this is their first night of three."

The woman didn't look reassured. If anything, she looked more concerned. "They're quite dirty," she said. "Best give them to me, so's I can give them a bath, and they don't disturb your dinner."

"Don't be silly," he said. "They're eating with me. Notify the kitchen that I'll require two plates of whatever it is that children eat."

"Yes, m'lord," said Mary, bobbing a quick and anxious curtsey. She was not old, but she was not young either; she looked like one of the neighborhood women who were sometimes hired to watch Jack and Jill during the summer, when their parents had to work. Camp was too messy and loud for Jack, and summer enrichment programs could only fill so many hours of the day. Childcare, distasteful as it was, was sometimes the only option.

(Age was the only thing Mary had in common with those poised and perfect ladies, who always came with credentials and references and carpetbags filled with activities for them to share. Mary's hair was brown and curly and looked as likely to steal a hairbrush as it was to yield before it. Her eyes were the cloudy gray of used dishwater, and she stood at the sort of rigid attention that spoke of bone-deep exhaustion. Had she shown up on the doorstep seeking work, Serena Wolcott would have turned her away on sight. Jack trusted her instantly. Jill did not.)

Mary gave the girls one last anxious look before heading for the door on the other side of the room. She was almost there when the man cleared his throat, stopping her dead in her tracks.

"Tell Ivan to send for Dr. Bleak," he said. "I haven't forgotten our agreement."

"Yes, m'lord," she said, and she was gone.

The man turned to Jack and Jill, smiling when he saw how intently they were watching him. "Dinner will be ready soon, and I'm sure that you will find it to your liking," he said. "Don't let Mary frighten you. Three days I promised, and three days you'll have, before you need to fear anything within these walls."

"What happens when the three days are over?" asked Jill, who had long since learned that games had rules, and that rules needed to be followed.

"Come," said the man. "Sit."

He walked to the head of the table, where he settled at the place that had been set for him. Jill sat on his left. Jack moved to sit beside her, and he shook his head, indicating the place on his right.

"If I'm to have a matching pair for three days, I may as well enjoy it," he said. "Don't worry. There's nothing to fear from me." The word *yet* seemed to hang, unspoken but implied, over the three of them.

But ah, Jack had seen very few horror movies in her day, and Jill, who might have been better prepared to interpret the signs, was exhausted and overwhelmed and still dizzy with the novelty of spending a day in the company of her sister without fighting. They sat where they were told, and they were still sitting there when Mary returned, followed by two silent, hollow-cheeked men in black tailcoats that hung almost to their knees. Each of the men was carrying a silver-domed plate.

"Ah, good," said the man. "How were these prepared?"

"The kitchen-witch conjured things that are pleasing to children," said Mary, voice stiff, chin raised. "She promises their satisfaction."

"Excellent," said the man. "Girls? Which will you have?"

"The left, please," said Jill, remembering every scrap of manners she had ever possessed. Her stomach rumbled loudly, and the man laughed, and everything felt like it was going to be all right. They were safe. There were walls around them, and food was being put in front of them, and the watching eye of the bloody moon was far away, watching the scrubland instead of the sisters.

The men set their trays down in front of the sisters, whisking the silver domes away. In front of Jack, half a rabbit, roasted and served over an assortment of vegetables: plain food, peasant food, the sort of thing she might, given time, have learned to prepare for herself. There was a slice of bread and a square of cheese, and she had been raised to be polite, even when she didn't want to be; she did not complain about the strange shape of her meat, or the rough skins of the vegetables, which had been cooked perfectly, but in a more rustic manner than she was accustomed to.

In front of Jill, three slices of red roast beef, so rare that it was bleeding into the mashed potatoes and the spinach that surrounded it. No bread, no cheese, but a silver goblet full of fresh milk. The metal was covered in fine drops of condensation, like dew.

"Please," said the man. "Eat." Mary reached over and took the silver dome from his food, revealing a plate that looked very much like Jill's. His goblet matched hers as well, although the contents were darker; wine, perhaps. It looked like the wine their father sometimes drank with dinner.

Jack hoped that it was wine.

Jill began to eat immediately, falling on her food like a starving thing. She might have wrinkled her nose at meat that rare at home, but she hadn't eaten in more than a day; she would have eaten meat raw if it meant that she was eating *something*. Jack wanted to be more cautious. She wanted to see whether this stranger drugged her sister, or something worse, before she let her guard down. But she was so hungry, and the food smelled so good, and the man had said they'd be safe in his house for three days. Everything was strange, and they still didn't know his name—

She stopped in the act of reaching for her fork, turning to look at him with wide eyes while she frantically tried to kick Jill under the table. Her legs were too short and the table was too wide; she missed by more than a foot. "We don't know your name," she said, voice a little shrill. "That means you're a stranger. We're not even supposed to *talk* to strangers."

Mary paled, which Jack would have thought was impossible; the woman had almost no color in her to start with. The two silent servers took a step backward, putting their backs to the wall. And the man, the strange, nameless man in his red-lined cloak, looked amused.

"You don't know my name because you haven't earned it, little foundling," he said. "Most call me 'Master,' here. You may call me the same."

Jack stared at him and held her tongue, unsure of what she could possibly say; unsure of what would be *safe* to say. It was plain as the moon in the sky that the people who worked for this man were afraid of him. She just didn't know why, and until she knew why, she didn't want to say anything at all.

"You should eat," said the man, not unkindly. "Unless you'd prefer what your sister is having?"

Jack mutely shook her head. Jill, who had been eating throughout the exchange, continued to shovel meat and potato and spinach into her mouth, seemingly content with the world.

Heavy footsteps echoed up the stairs, loudly enough to catch the attention of everyone at the table, even Jill, who chewed and swallowed as she turned to look toward the sound. The man grimaced, an expression of distaste which only deepened as another stranger walked into the room.

This man was solid, built like a windmill, sturdy and strong and aching to burn. His clothing was practical, denim trousers and a homespun shirt, both protected by a leather apron. He had a chin that could have been used to split logs, and bright, assessing eyes below the heavy slope of his brow. Most fascinating of all was the scar that ran all the way along the circumference of his neck, heavy and white and frayed like a piece of twine, like whatever had cut him had made no effort whatsoever to do it cleanly.

"Dr. Bleak," said the first man, and sneered. "I wasn't sure you would deign to come. Certainly not so quickly. Don't you have some act of terrible butchery to commit?"

"Always," said Dr. Bleak. His voice was a rumble of thunder in the distant mountains, and Jack loved it at once. He sounded like a man who had shouted his way into understanding the universe. "But we had an arrangement, you and I. Or have you forgotten?"

The first man grimaced. "I sent for you, didn't I? I told Ivan to tell you that I remembered."

"The things Ivan says and the things you say are sometimes dissimilar." Dr. Bleak finally turned to look at Jack and Jill.

Jill had stopped eating. Both of them were sitting very, very still.

Dr. Bleak frowned at the red-stained potatoes on Jill's plate. The meat was long since gone, but the signs of it remained. "I see you've already made your choice," he said. "*That* was not a part of the arrangement."

"I allowed the girls to select their own meals," said the first man, sounding affronted. "It's not my fault if she prefers her meat rare."

"Mmm," said Dr. Bleak noncommittally. He focused on Jill. "What's your name, child? Don't be afraid. I'm not here to harm you."

"Jillian," whispered Jill, in a squeak of a voice.

"Dr. Bleak lives outside the village," said the first man.

"He has a hovel. Rats and spiders and the like. It's nothing compared to a castle."

Dr. Bleak rolled his eyes. "Really? *Really?* You're going to resort to petty insults? I haven't even made my choice yet."

"But as you're clearly going for the one I'd be inclined to favor, I feel no shame in pleading my case," said the first man. "Besides, *look* at them. A matched set! How could you begrudge me the desire to keep them both?"

"Wait," said Jack. "What do you mean, 'keep' us? We're not stray dogs. We're very sorry we trespassed in your big creepy field, but we're not *staying* here. As soon as we find a door, we're going home."

The first man smirked. Dr. Bleak actually looked . . . well, almost sad.

"The doors appear when they will," he said. "You could be here for a very long time."

Jack and Jill bore identical expressions of alarm. Jill spoke first.

"I have soccer practice," she said. "I can't miss it. They'll cut me from the team, and then Daddy will be furious with me."

"I'm not supposed to go outside," said Jack. "My mother's going to be so mad when she finds out that I did. We can't be here for a very long time. We just *can't*."

"But you will," said the first man. "For three days as guests in my home, and then as treasured residents, for as long as it takes to find a door back to your world. If you ever do. Not all foundlings return to the places that they ran away from, do they, Mary?"

"No, m'lord," said Mary, in a dull, dead voice.

"The last foundling to come stumbling into the Moors was a boy with hair like fire and eyes like a winter morning," said the first man. "Dr. Bleak and I argued over who should have his care and feeding—because we both love children, you see. They're so lively, so energetic. They can make a house feel like a home. In the end, I won, and I promised Dr. Bleak that, in order to keep the peace, he would have the next foundling to pass through. Imagine my surprise when there were two of you! Truly the Moon provides."

"Where is he now?" asked Jack warily.

"He found his door home," said Dr. Bleak. "He took it." He glared down the length of the table at the first man, like he was daring him to say something.

Instead, the first man simply laughed, shaking his head. "So dramatic! Always so dramatic. Sit down, Michel. Let me feed you. Enjoy the hospitality of my home for an evening, and perhaps you'll see the wisdom of letting these pretty sisters stay together."

"If you're so set on keeping them as a matched set, honor the spirit of our agreement and let them both come home with me," said Dr. Bleak. His next words were directed at the girls. "I can't keep you in luxury. I have no servants, and you'll be expected to work for your keep. But I'll teach you how the world works, and you'll go home wiser, if wearier. You will never be intentionally harmed beneath my roof."

The word "never" seemed to leap out at Jack. The first

man had only promised them three days. She looked across the table at Jill and found her sister sulky-eyed and pouting.

"Will you eat, Michel?" asked the first man.

"I suppose I should," said Dr. Bleak, and dropped himself into a chair like an avalanche coming finally to rest. He looked to Mary. His eyes were kind. "Meat and bread and beer, if you would be so kind, Mary."

"Yes, sir," said Mary, and actually smiled as she fled the room.

The first man—the Master—raised his goblet in a mocking toast. "To the future," he said. "It's on its way now, whether we're prepared or not."

"I suppose that's true," said Dr. Bleak, to him, and "Eat," he said, to Jack and Jill. "You'll need your strength for what's to come.

"We all will."

6 THE FIRST NIGHT OF SAFETY

JACK AND JILL were tucked away in the same round tower room, in two small beds shaped like teardrops, with their heads at the widest point and their feet pointed toward the tapering end. The windows were barred. The door was locked. "For your protection," Mary had said, before turning the key and sealing them in for the evening.

Many children would have railed at their confinement, would have gone looking for clever ways to pull the bars from the windows or break the latch on the door. Many children had been raised to believe that they were allowed to rail against unnecessary rules, that getting out of bed to use the bathroom or get a glass of water was not only allowed but encouraged, since taking care of their needs was more important than an eight-hour stretch spent perfectly in bed. Not Jack and Jill. They had been raised to obey, to behave, and so they stayed where they were.

(It is, perhaps, important to note that while blindly following rules can be a dangerous habit, it can also mean salvation. The ground below the tower window was white with old bones from children who had tried to make clever ropes out of braided sheets, only to find them too short and fall to their deaths. Some rules exist to preserve life.)

"We can't stay here," whispered Jack.

"We have to stay *somewhere,*" whispered Jill. "If we have to wait for a door, why not wait here? It's nice here. I like it."

"That man wants us to call him '*master.*' "

"The other man wants us to call him 'doctor.' How is that different?"

Jack didn't know how to explain that those things were different; she just knew that they were, that one was a title that *said* something about the person who used it, while the other said how much that person knew, how much they understood about the world. One was a threat and the other was a reassurance.

"It just is," she said finally. "I want to go with Dr. Bleak. If we have to go with somebody, I want it to be him."

"Well, *I* want to stay here," said Jill. She scowled at her sister across the gap between their beds. "I don't see why we always have to do what you want to do."

There had never in their lives been a time when Jack was allowed to decide their actions. Their parents had always set the course for them, even down to their school days, where they had played out the roles set for them with the fervency of actors who knew the show would be cancelled if they made a single mistake. Jack was silent, stung, wondering how her sister could have read the world so very wrong.

Finally, in a soft voice, she said, "We don't have to stay together."

Jill had been enjoying spending time with her sister. It was . . . nice. It was nice to feel like they were together, like they were united, like they actually *agreed* on something. But she liked it there, in the big, fancy castle with the silver plates and the smiling man in the long black cloak. She liked feeling like she was safe behind thick walls, where that big red moon couldn't get her. She would have been happy to share being there with Jack, but she wasn't going to give it up because her sister liked some smelly, dirty doctor better.

"No, we don't," she said, and rolled over, and pretended to go to sleep.

Jack rolled onto her back and stared at the ceiling, and didn't pretend anything at all.

They were both tired, confused children with full stomachs, tucked into warm beds. Eventually, they both fell asleep, dreaming tangled dreams until the sound of the door being unbolted woke them. They sat up, still in the same dirty, increasingly tattered clothing they'd been wearing since their adventure began, and watched as the door swung open. Mary held it for the two men who had served them dinner the night before. Each carried a tray, setting them down next to the girls before whisking the lids away to reveal scrambled eggs, buttered toast, and slices of thick, greasy ham.

"The Master expects you to eat quickly," said Mary, as the men retreated to stand behind her. "He understands that you are in no position to clean yourselves up, and will forgive you for your untidiness. I'll wait in the hall until you're done and ready to see him."

"Wait," said Jack, feeling suddenly grimy and uncomfortable. She had almost forgotten how filthy she was. "Can we have a bath?"

"Not yet," said Mary, stepping out of the room. Again, the two men followed her; the last one out shut the door behind himself.

"Why can't we have a bath?" asked Jack plaintively.

"I don't need a bath," said Jill, who very much did. She grabbed her knife and fork, beginning to cut her ham into small squares.

Jack, who had never in her life been allowed to stay dirty for more than a few minutes, shuddered. She looked at her food, and saw only butter, grease, and other things that would add to the mess she was already wearing. She slid out of the bed, leaving the food where it was.

Jill frowned. "Aren't you going to eat?"

"I'm not hungry."

"*I'm* going to eat."

"That's okay. I can wait."

"Well, you shouldn't." Jill pointed to the door. "Tell Mary you're done, and maybe she'll let you get a bath. Or she'll let you talk to your new doctor friend. You'd like that, wouldn't you?"

"I'd like the bath more," said Jack. "You're sure you don't mind?"

"I'm going to steal all your toast," said Jill serenely, and Jack realized two very important things: first, that her sister still thought this was an adventure, something that would only last until she was tired of it and would then go mercifully away, and second, that she needed to leave as soon as possible. The Master—how she hated that she was starting to think of him that way!—struck her as the sort of person who wanted little girls to be decorative and pretty, toys lined up on a shelf. He hadn't talked about keeping them together because sisters needed to be together; he'd talked about keeping them together so he'd have a matching set.

If she couldn't get Jill out of there, she couldn't stay, because if she stayed, she would be better at being decorative. She would show Jill up. They wouldn't match, no matter how much they tried. And the Master . . .

She didn't know how she knew, but she knew that he wouldn't like that. He would be displeased. She didn't think either she or Jill would enjoy his displeasure.

Her dress was stiff and her tights stuck to her legs like bandages as she stepped out into the hall. Mary was waiting there, as she had promised, along with the two serving men.

"All done?" she asked.

Jack nodded. "Jill's still eating," she said. "I can wait here with you until she's done."

"No need," said Mary. "The Master doesn't care for dawdling. If you want him to choose you, you'd be well served by heading down now."

"What if I don't want him to choose me?"

Mary paused. She looked at the two dead-eyed men, assessing. Then she looked around the hall as a whole, seeming to search every crack and corner. Finally, when she was sure that they were alone, she returned her attention to Jack.

"If you don't want to be chosen, you run, girl. You go down to that throne room—"

"Throne room?" squeaked Jack.

"—and you tell Dr. Bleak you want to go with him, and you *run*. The Master likes your sister's appetite, but he likes the way you hold yourself. He likes the way you sit. He'll toy with her until the three days are up, and then he'll choose you and break her heart. He'll say that Dr. Bleak could leave you both here, but he knows Dr. Bleak would never do that. When he can save a foundling, he does. I wish to God that he'd saved me." There was fire in Mary's eyes, bright and burning like a candle. "Your sister will be safer if you're gone. He'll have to make her into a lady before he can make her into a daughter, and who knows? You may find your door before that happens."

"Were you . . ." Jack stopped, unsure of how to finish the question.

Mary nodded. "I was. But I never wanted to be his child, and when he asked me to let him be my father, I said no. So he kept me as a reminder to other foundlings that there are more places in a noble household than the ones set at the head of the table. He'll never harm her without her invitation: you don't need to worry about that. Men like him, they can't come in unless you invite them. You'll have time."

"Time for what?"

"Time to figure out why you were called to the Moors; time to decide whether or not you want to stay." Mary straightened, the fire seeming to go out as she turned to the nearest of the dead-eyed men. "Take her down to see the Master. Go quickly now. You'll need to be back up here before the second child is ready to descend."

The man nodded but did not speak. He beckoned for Jack to follow him, and he started down the stairs. Jack looked at Mary. Mary shook her head and said nothing. The time for words between them was done, it seemed; what Jack did from here was up to her. Jack hesitated. Jack looked at the door to the room where her sister sat, enjoying her breakfast.

Jack went down the stairs.

The dead-eyed man had predicted her recalcitrance; he was waiting on the first landing, as silent and impassive as ever. When she reached him, he started walking again, leaving her to trail along behind. His stride was long enough to force her to hurry, until it felt as if her feet were barely touching the ground, like she was going to tumble down the stairs and land at the bottom in a heap.

But that didn't happen. They reached the bottom and stepped back into the grand dining hall. The Master and Dr. Bleak were seated at opposite ends of the table, watching each other warily. Dr. Bleak had a plate of food in front of him, which he was not touching. The Master had another goblet of thick red wine. The dead-eyed man walked silently. Jack did not, and the Master and Dr. Bleak turned toward the sound of her arrival.

The Master looked at the stains on her dress, the tangles in her hair, and smiled. "So eager," he said, voice practically a purr. "Have you made your choice, then? It's clear you want first pick of guardians." *It's clear you're choosing me,* said the silence that followed.

"I have," said Jack. She stood as straight as she could, trying not to let her shoulders shake or her knees knock. The choice had seemed difficult when she was alone with her sister. Now, with both men looking at her, it felt impossible.

Still, her feet moved, somehow, and carried her down the length of the room to stand next to a startled Dr. Bleak.

"I'd like to come and work for you, please," she said. "I'd like to learn."

Dr. Bleak looked at her soft hands and her frilly, lacy dress, and frowned. "It won't be easy," he said. "The work will be hard. You'll blister, and bleed, and leave something of yourself behind if you ever leave me."

"You told us that last night," said Jack.

"I don't have time for fripperies or finery. If you want those things, you should stay here."

Jack frowned, eyes narrowing. "Last night you wanted us both, even if you wanted my sister more," she said. "Now you seem like you don't want me at all. Why?"

Dr. Bleak opened his mouth to answer. Then he stopped,

and cocked his head to the side, and said, "Honestly, I don't know. A willing apprentice is always better than an unwilling one. Shall I return for you in two days?"

"I'd rather go with you today," said Jack. She had a feeling that if she lingered, she would never leave, and again, that would go poorly for her sister—Jill, who had always been the strong one, always been the smart one, but who had never been expected to be the *clever* one. Jill trusted too easily, and got hurt even easier.

Jack had to go *now*.

If Dr. Bleak was surprised, he didn't show it. He simply nodded, said, "As you like," and stood, offering a shallow bow to the Master. "Thank you for honoring our agreement. As mine has chosen me, the second constitutes your turn; the next foundling to enter the Moors is mine by right."

"As yours has chosen you, and slighted me, what's to stop me killing her where she stands?" The Master sounded bored. That didn't stop the fear from coiling through Jack's heart, where it lay, heavy and waiting, like a serpent preparing to strike. "She forsook the protection of my house when she rejected me."

"She's more useful alive," said Dr. Bleak. "She's her sister's mirror. If something should . . . happen, to the first, you could draw upon the second to guarantee her survival. And if you killed her, you would break our bargain. Do you really want to risk a fight between us? Do you think this is the time?"

The Master scowled but did not rise. "As you like, Michel," he said, sounding almost bored. His eyes went to Jack, as calm as if he hadn't just threatened her. "If you tire of living in squalor, little girl, feel free to return. My doors are always open to one as lovely as you."

Jack, who had long since tired of being viewed as simply "lovely," and who had not forgotten the threat, even if the Master had, said nothing. She nodded, and stepped a little closer to Dr. Bleak, and when he rose and walked out of the room, she followed him.

BUT THAT IS ENOUGH of Jack for now: this is a story about two children, even if it is sometimes necessary to follow one at the exclusion of the other. That is often the way. Give children the opportunity and they will scatter, forcing choices to be made, forcing the one who seeks them to run down all manner of dark corridors. And so:

Jill ate her breakfast, and when she was done, she ate Jack's breakfast, glaring all the while at her sister's empty bed. Stupid Jack. They were finally in a place where someone *liked* their shared face, their shared reflection, and now Jack was just going to walk away and leave her. She should have known that Jack wouldn't want to start being a twin now. Not when she'd spent so many years avoiding it.

(It did not occur to Jill that Jack's avoidance, like her own, had been born purely of parental desire and never of a sincere wanting. Their parents had done everything they could to blur the lines of twinhood, leaving Jack and Jill stuck in the middle. But Jack was gone and Jill was not, and in the moment, that was all that mattered.)

When the last scrap of toast had been used to mop up the last smear of egg, Jill finally got out of bed and walked to the door. Mary was waiting there, and she curtseyed when Jill emerged.

"Miss," she said. "Was breakfast to your liking?"

Jill, who had never been treated like she *mattered* before—especially not by an adult—beamed. "It was fine," she said grandly. "Did you see to my sister?"

"I'm sorry, miss, I believe she's already gone with Dr. Bleak. He doesn't often stay away from his laboratory long."

Jill's face fell. "Oh," she said. Until that moment, she hadn't realized how much she was hoping Jack would have changed her mind; would be waiting, penitent and hungry, on the stairs.

Let Jack throw away the chance to be a princess and live in a castle. Jack already knew what it was to be treated like royalty, to have the pretty dress and the shining tiara and the love of everyone around her. She'd realize her mistake and come crawling back, and would Jill forgive her?

Probably. It would be nice, to share this adventure with her sister.

"The Master is waiting, miss," said Mary. "Are you ready to see him?"

"Yes," said Jill, and *no* said something deep inside her, a still, small voice that understood the danger they were in, even if that danger was shadowy and ill defined. Jill stood up a little straighter, raised her chin the way she'd seen Jack do when she was showing off a new dress to their mother's friends, and swallowed the fear as deep as it would go. "I want to tell him that I'll stay."

"You haven't a choice now, miss," said Mary. Her tone was cautioning, almost apologetic. "Once your sister chose to go, you were set to stay."

Jill frowned, the still, small voice that had been counseling caution instantly silenced in the face of this new affront. "Because *she* chose, I don't get to?"

"Yes, miss. I don't mean to speak out of turn, but you may wish to approach the Master with deference. He doesn't like being selected second."

Neither did Jill, and she had been selected second all her life. In that instant, hot, fierce love for the nameless man in the lonely castle washed over her, wiping any remnants of caution away. The Master was second-best for no good reason, just like she was. Well, she would make him understand that it wasn't true. She'd chosen him before Jack had even known her stupid Dr. Bleak existed. They were going to be happy together until the door home opened, and they were never going to be second-best again. Never.

"I chose him first. Jacqueline skipped breakfast so she could look like the star," said Jill, all bitterness and cold anger. "I'll tell him so."

Mary had seen many foundlings come and go since her

own arrival in the Moors. She looked at Jill, and for the first time, she felt as if, perhaps, the Master might be pleased. This one might live long enough to leave, assuming the door home ever opened at all.

"Follow me, miss," she said, and turned, and walked down the stairs to where the Master waited, still and silent as he always was when he saw no need for motion.

(How the children who tumbled through the occasional doors between the Moors and elsewhere couldn't see that he was a predator, she didn't understand. Mary had known him for a predator the second she'd seen him. It had been a familiar danger: the family she had been fleeing from had been equally predatory, even if their predations had been of a more mundane nature. She had been comfortable in his care because she had known him, and when he had revealed himself fully to her, it had come as no surprise. That was rare. Most of the children she walked through these halls were terribly, terribly surprised when their time came, no matter how often they'd been warned. There would never be warning enough.)

The Master was sitting at the table when they stepped back into the dining hall, sipping moodily from a silver goblet. He looked at Mary—and hence, at Jill—with narrow, disinterested eyes. He lowered his drink.

"I suppose we're stuck together," he said, looking at Jill.

"I chose you," said Jill.

The Master lifted his eyebrows. "Did you, now? I don't remember seeing you in front of me before your foolish sister left with that filthy doctor. I seem to recall sitting here alone, no foundling by my side, as she came down those stairs and declared her intent to go with him."

"She said she didn't want to stay," said Jill. "I thought it would be better if I ate my breakfast and let her go. That way, I'd be ready for whatever you wanted me to do today. Skipping meals isn't healthy."

"No, it's not," said the Master, with a flicker of what might have been amusement. "You swear you chose me before she chose him?"

"I chose you as soon as I saw you," said Jill earnestly.

"I don't care for liars."

"I don't lie."

The Master tilted his head, looking at her with new eyes. Finally, he said, "You will need to be washed and dressed, prepared to live here with me. My household has certain standards. Mary will assist you in meeting them. You will be expected to present yourself when I want you, and to otherwise stay out from underfoot. I will arrange for tutors and for tailors; you will want for nothing. All I ask in exchange are your loyalty, your devotion, and your obedience."

"Unless her door comes," said Mary.

The Master shot a sharp, narrow-eyed glance in her direction. She stood straight and met his eyes without flinching. In the end, astonishingly, it was the Master who looked away.

"You will always be free to take the door back to your original home," he said. "I am bound by a compact as old as the Moors to let you go, if that's truly your desire. But I hope that when that door eventually opens, you might find that you prefer my company."

Jill smiled. The Master smiled back, and his teeth were very sharp, and very white.

Both girls, through different routes, down different roads, had come home.

7 TO FETCH A PAIL OF WATER

DR. BLEAK LIVED OUTSIDE the castle, outside the village; outside the seemingly safe bulk of the wall. The gates opened when he approached them, and he strode through, never looking back to see whether Jack was following him. She was—of course she was—but her life had been defined by sitting quietly and being decorative, allowing interesting things to come to her, rather than chasing them through bracken and briar. Her chest felt like it was too tight. Her heart thudded and her side ached, making speech impossible.

Once, only once, she stumbled to a stop and stood, swaying, eyes fixed on her feet as she tried to get her breath back. Dr. Bleak continued onward for a few more steps before he stopped in turn. Still, he did not look back.

"You are not Eurydice, but I won't risk losing you to something so trivial," he said. "You need to be stronger."

Jack, who could not breathe, said nothing.

"We'll have time to improve what can be improved, and

compensate for what can't," he said. "But night comes quickly here. Recover, and resume."

Jack took a vast, shaky breath, following it with a step, and then with another. Dr. Bleak waited until he heard her take the third step. Then he resumed his forward progress, trusting Jack to keep pace.

She did. Of course she did. There was no other choice remaining. And if she thought longingly of the soft bed where she'd spent the night, or the comfortable dining hall where the Master had served them delicate things on silver trays, well. She was twelve years old; she had never worked for anything in her life. It was only reasonable that she should yearn for something that felt like a close cousin to the familiar, even if she knew, all the way down to her bones, that she did not, should not, *would* not want it for her own.

Dr. Bleak led her through the bracken and brush, up the sloping side of a hill, until the shape of a windmill appeared in the distance. It seemed very close, and then, as they walked on and on without reaching it, she realized that it was, instead, very large; it was a windmill meant to harness the entire sky. Jack stared. Dr. Bleak walked, and she followed, until the brush under their feet gave way to a packed-earth trail, and they began the final ascent toward the windmill. The last part of the hill was steeper than the rest, ending some ten feet before the door. The ground all around the foundation had been cleared and covered in raised planter beds that grew green with plants Jack had never seen before.

"Touch nothing until you know what it is," said Dr. Bleak, not unkindly. "No honest question will go unanswered, but many of the things here are dangerous to the unprepared. Do you understand?"

"I think so," said Jack. "Can I ask a question now?"

"Yes."

"What did you mean before, about drawing on me to save Jill?"

"I meant blood, little girl. Everything comes down to blood here, one way or another. Do you understand?"

Jack hesitated before shaking her head.

"You will," said Dr. Bleak, and pulled a large iron key out of the pocket of his apron, and unlocked the windmill door.

The room on the other side was vast, large enough to seem cavernous, bounded on all sides by the curving windmill walls, and yet no less intimidating for its limitations. The ceiling was more than twenty feet overhead, covered with dangling things the likes of which Jack had never seen before: stuffed reptiles and birds and something that looked like a pterodactyl, leathery wings spread wide and frozen for eternity. Racks of tools and shelves laden with strange bottles and stranger implements lined the walls.

There was a large oaken table near the smallest of the room's three fireplaces, and what looked like a surgical table at the very center of the room, well away from any source of heat. There were unknowable machines, and jars filled with terrible biological specimens that seemed to track her with their lifeless eyes. Jack walked slowly into the

very center of the room, where she could turn, taking everything in.

A spiral stairway occupied the center of the room, winding down into the basement and up into the heights of the structure, where there must be other rooms, other horrifying wonders. It seemed strange, that a windmill should have a basement. It was something she had never considered before.

Dr. Bleak watched her, the door still open behind him. If the girl was going to flee screaming into the night, it was going to happen now. He had been expecting the other one to come with him, the one with the short hair and the fingernails that had been worn down and dirtied by playing in the yard. He knew more than most that appearances could be deceiving, but he had found that certain markers were often true. This girl looked cosseted, sheltered; girls like her did not often thrive in places like this.

She stopped looking. She turned back to him. She plucked at the stained and increasingly stiff skirt of her dress.

"I think this will get caught on things," she said. "Is there something else that I could wear?"

Dr. Bleak lifted his eyebrows. "That's your only question?"

"I don't know what most of these things are, but you said you were going to teach me," said Jack. "I don't know what questions I'm supposed to *ask,* so I guess I'm going to let you give me the answers, and then I can match them up with the questions. I can't do that if I'm getting snagged on everything all the time."

Dr. Bleak gave her an assessing look, closing the door. Somehow, he no longer worried that she was going to run. "I warned you that you'd work if you came with me. I'll put calluses on your hands and bruises on your knees."

"I don't mind working," said Jack. "I haven't done it much, but I'm tired of sitting still."

"Very well." Dr. Bleak walked across the room to one of the high shelves. He reached up and lifted down a trunk, as lightly as if it were made of cobwebs and air. Setting it down on the floor, he said, "Take what you like. Everything is clean; nothing is ever put away here without being cleaned first."

Jack heard that for the instruction that it was, and nodded before walking carefully over to the trunk and kneeling to open it. It was full of clothing—children's clothing, some of it in styles she had never seen before. Much of it seemed old-fashioned, like something out of an old black-and-white movie. Some was made of shimmering, almost futuristic fabric, or cut to fit bodies she couldn't quite envision, torsos as long as legs, or with three arms, or with no hole for the head.

In the end, she selected a white cotton shirt with starched cuffs and collar, and a knee-length black skirt made of what felt like canvas. It would be sturdy enough to stand up to learning how to work, unlikely to snag or stop her in her tracks. The thought of wearing someone else's underthings was unsettling, no matter how many times they'd been bleached, but in the end, she also selected a pair of white shorts, her cheeks burning with the indignity of it all.

Dr. Bleak, who had watched her make her selections (all save for the shorts; when he'd realized what she was looking for, he had turned politely aside), did not smile; smiling was not his way. But he nodded approvingly, and said, "Up the stairs, you will find several empty rooms. One of them will be yours, to keep your things in, to use when you need to be alone. You will not have many opportunities for idleness. I suggest you enjoy them when you can."

Jack hesitated.

"Yes?" asked Dr. Bleak.

"I'm . . . it's not just my dress that's filthy," said Jack, grimacing a little, like she had never admitted to dirtiness in her life. Which perhaps she hadn't: perhaps she had never been given the opportunity. "Is there any chance I could have a bath?"

"You will have to haul the water yourself, and heat it, but if that is all you desire, yes." Dr. Bleak closed the trunk, lifting it back onto the shelf where it belonged. Then he took down a vast tin bucket from a hook that dangled from the ceiling. It was shallow enough that Jack thought she could crawl into it if she needed to, almost as large as the bathtub at home.

Her eyes widened. The bathtub at home. This and that were the same, separated by centuries of technological advancement, but serving an identical purpose.

Dr. Bleak set the bucket down in front of the largest of the three fires before lifting a kettle down from the shelf and handing it to Jack. "The well is outside," he said. "I will be back in two hours. Figure out how to clean yourself." Then he was gone, striding back to the door and stepping out onto the Moors, leaving Jack to gape after him, the kettle in her hands, utterly bemused.

"THE MASTER WANTS YOU cleaned and smartened up," said Mary, dragging a brush through the tangled strands of Jill's hair. Jill ground her teeth, trying not to flinch away from the bristles. She was used to brushing her own hair, and sometimes she allowed knots to form for weeks, until they had to be cut out with scissors.

The room she'd been removed to was small and smelled of talcum powder and sharp copper. The walls were papered in the palest pink, and a vanity much like her mother's took up one entire wall. There was no mirror. That was the only truly odd thing about the room, which was otherwise queasily familiar to Jill, the sort of feminine stronghold that she had always been denied admission to. Her sister was the one who should have been sitting on this stool, having her hair brushed, ready to be "smartened up."

"It's a shame it's so short," said Mary, seemingly unaware of Jill's discomfort. "Ah, well. Hair will grow, and at least this way, he'll be able to decide what length he likes best without cutting off something that's already there."

"I get to grow my hair out?" asked Jill, suddenly hopeful.

"Long enough to cover your throat," said Mary, and her tone was dire, and Jill missed it entirely. She was too busy thinking of what she'd look like with long hair, how it would feel against the back of her neck; wondering whether adults on the street would smile at her the way they smiled at Jack, like she was something special, something *beautiful,* and not just another tomboy.

The trouble with denying children the freedom to be themselves—with forcing them into an idea of what they should be, not allowing them to choose their own paths—is that all too often, the one drawing the design knows nothing of the desires of their model. Children are not formless clay, to be shaped according to the sculptor's whim, nor are they blank but identical dolls, waiting to be slipped into the mode that suits them best. Give ten children a toy box, and watch them select ten different toys, regardless of gender or religion or parental expectations. Children have *preferences.* The danger comes when they, as with any human, are denied those preferences for too long.

Jill had always wanted to know what it was like to be allowed to wear her hair long, to put on a pretty skirt, to sit next to her sister and hear people cooing over what a lovely matched pair they were. She liked sports, yes, and she liked reading her books; she liked *knowing* things. She would probably have been a soccer player even if her father hadn't insisted, would definitely have watched spaceships on TV and superheroes in the movies, because the core of who *Jill* was had nothing to do with the desires of her parents and everything to do with the desires of her heart. But she would have done some of those things in a dress. Having half of everything she wanted denied to her for so long had left her vulnerable to them: they were the forbidden fruit, and like all forbidden things, even the promise of them was delicious.

"Your hair will take time," said Mary, seeing that her warnings had gone unheard. "Your clothing, we can fix right away—in time for your lunch. A bath has been drawn for you." She set the brush aside, motioning for Jill to get off the chair. "I'll have your new attire ready when you get out."

Jill stood, all eyes and anticipation. "Where do I go?"

"There," said Mary, and indicated a door that hadn't been there a moment before.

Jill hesitated. Doors were dangerous things. The Master (and that dreadful Dr. Bleak) had talked about doors that would take her home again, and she wasn't *ready* to go home. She wanted to stay here, to enjoy her adventure in a world where she was allowed to have long hair and wear skirts and be whoever she wanted to be.

Mary saw the hesitation and sighed, shaking her head. "This is not your doorway home," she said. "The Master's castle is malleable, and matches to our needs. Go. Clean yourself up. It doesn't do to keep him waiting."

Mary's warnings might have gone unnoticed, but Jill

had grown up surrounded by adults who said one thing and did another, adults who were so consumed with *wanting* that it never occurred to them to wonder whether children might not know about wanting too. She knew better than to disappoint if she could help it.

"All right," she said, and opened the door, and stepped into a mermaid's grotto, into a drowned girl's sanctuary. The walls were tiled in glittering blue and silver, like scales, arching together to form the high, pointed dome of the roof. It was a flower frozen in the moment before it could open; it was a teardrop turned to crystal before it could fall. Little nooks were set into the walls, filled with candles, which cast a dancing light over everything they touched.

The floor was a narrow lip, no more than two feet at its widest point, circling the outside of the room. The rest was given over to a basin filled with sweetly scented water, dotted with frothing mounds of bubbles. Everything smelled of roses and vanilla. Jill stopped and stared. This was . . . this was amazing, this was incredible, and it was *all for her*.

A small dart of smug delight wedged itself in her heart. Jack wasn't here. Jack wasn't standing in this room, looking at a bath fit for a fairy-tale princess. This was hers, and hers alone. She was the princess in this story.

(Would she have felt bad about her smugness if she had known that, at that very moment, Jack was puzzling her way through the process of getting water from well to kettle to tin tub without scalding or freezing herself? Or would it have delighted her to think of her poised and pampered sister sitting in lukewarm water to her hips, marinating in her own dirt, scrubbing the worst of it away with brittle yellow sponges that had once been living things, and were now remembered only by their bones? How quickly they grow apart, when there is something to be superior about.)

Jill removed her stained and filthy clothing and stepped into the bath. The temperature was perfect, and the water was silky-smooth with perfumes and oils. She sank down to her chin and closed her eyes, enjoying the heat, enjoying the feeling that soon, she would be *clean*.

Some untold time later, there was a knock at the door, and Mary's voice said, briskly, "Time to come out, miss. Your clothes are ready, and it's nearly time for lunch."

Jill snapped out of her daze, opening her mouth to protest—it couldn't be time for lunch, they'd just eaten breakfast—before her stomach gave a loud growl. The water was still warm, but maybe that didn't matter in a magic room inside a magic castle.

"Coming!" she called, and waded through the water toward the place where she'd left her clothes. They were gone, a towel and robe in their place. Understanding what was expected of her, Jill dried her body with the towel and covered it with the robe, which was soft and white and felt almost like the bubbles from her bath. There was no towel rack or hamper. She folded the used towel as carefully as she could and put it down against the base of the wall, hoping that would be tidy enough, *good* enough, for her host. Then she let herself out of the room, to where Mary waited.

The maid gave her a thoughtful once-over before saying, in a faintly surprised tone, "I suppose you'll do. Here." She picked up a bundle of pale fabric—purple and blue and white, like a bruise in the process of healing—and thrust it at the girl. "Get dressed. If you need help with the buttons, I'll be here. The Master is waiting."

Jill nodded silently as she took the clothes, and was unsurprised to see that a screen had appeared on the far side of the room. She slipped behind it, setting the clothes down on the waiting stool before untying her robe and beginning to dress herself.

She was relieved to find that the undergarments were ones she recognized, panties and a slip-chemise that was halfway to being a thin tank top. The dress, though . . . oh, the dress.

It was an ocean of cascading silk, a sea of draped fabric. It was not an adult dress, meant to grace an adult figure; it was a fantasy gown intended for a child, one that made her look as much like an inverted orchid as she did a girl. It took her three tries to figure out which hole was for her head and which were for her arms, and when she was done, the whole thing seemed to slouch around her, unwilling to fit properly.

"Mary?" she said, hopefully.

The maid appeared around the corner of the screen, clucking her tongue when she saw the state Jill was in. "You have to fasten it if you want it to fit you," she said, and began doing up buttons and ties and snaps, so many that Jill's head spun just watching Mary's fingers move.

But when Mary was done, the dress fit Jill like it had been tailored for her. Looking down, Jill could see her bare toes peeping out from beneath the cascading skirts, and she was grateful, because without that one small flaw, it would have all been too perfect to be real. She looked up. Mary was holding a purple choker with a small pearl-and-amethyst pendant dangling from its center. Her expression was grave.

"You are a member of the Master's household now," she said. "You must always, always wear your choker when you're in the company of anyone other than the servants. That includes the Master. Do you understand me?"

"Why?" asked Jill.

Mary shook her head. "You'll understand soon enough," she said. Leaning forward, she tied the choker around Jill's neck. It was tight, but not so tight as to be uncomfortable; Jill thought she would be able to get used to it. And it was beautiful. She didn't get to wear beautiful things very often.

"There," said Mary, stepping back and looking at her frankly. "You're as good as you're going to get without more time, and time's a thing we don't have right now. You're to sit quietly. Speak when spoken to. Think before you agree to anything. Do you understand?"

No, Jill thought, and "Yes," Jill said, and that was that: there was no saving her.

Mary, who had not spoken the word "vampire" aloud in over twenty years, who knew all too well the limitations that they labored under, only sighed and offered her hand to the girl. "All right," she said. "It's time."

WHEN DR. BLEAK RETURNED from his errands with an armful of firewood and a bundle of herbs, it was to find Jack in the front yard, carefully wiping the last of the grime from the sides of the tin tub. She looked up at the sound of his footsteps. He stopped where he was and looked at her like he was seeing her for the first time.

It had taken her six trips to the well and three turns with the kettle, but she had washed the grime from her body and hair, using a thick, caustic soap that she'd found next to the sponges. Her hair was braided sensibly back, and the only things that remained of her old attire were her shoes, patent leather and wiped as clean as the rest of her. She still looked too delicate to be a proper lab assistant, but appearances can be deceiving, and she had not balked from what he'd asked of her.

"What's for dinner?" asked Dr. Bleak.

"I have no idea, and you wouldn't want to eat it if I did," said Jack. "I don't know how to cook. But I'm willing to learn."

"Willing to learn, but not to lie?"

Jack shrugged. "You would have caught me."

"I suppose that's true," said Dr. Bleak. "Are you truly willing to learn?"

Jack nodded.

"All right, then," said Dr. Bleak. "Come inside." He walked across the yard with great, ground-eating steps, and when he stepped through the open door, Jack followed without hesitation.

She closed the door behind herself.

PART III

JACK AND JILL WITH TIME TO KILL

8 THE SKIES TO SHAKE, THE STONES TO BLEED

IT WOULD BECOME QUICKLY dull, recounting every moment, every hour the two girls spent, one in the castle and one in the windmill, one in riches and one in artfully mended rags: it would become quickly dull, and so it shall not be our focus, for we are not here for dullness, are we? No. We are here for a story, whether it be wild adventure or cautionary tale, and we do not have the time to waste on mundane things. And yet.

And yet.

And yet look to the castle on the bluffs, the castle near to the sea, which sits atop a crumbling cliff in the belly of the lowlands. Look to the castle where the golden-haired girl walks the battlements at dusk and dawn in her dresses like dreams, with her throat concealed from prying eyes, with the wind tying beautiful knots in the long curtain of her hair. She waxes and wanes like the moon, now pale as milk, now healthy and pink as any village girl. There are those in the village below who whisper that she is the

Master's daughter, sired on a princess from a far-away land and finally returned to her father when he howled her name to the western winds.

(There are those in the village who whisper darker things, who speak of disappearing children and lips stained red as roses. She is not a vampire yet, they say, and "yet" is such a powerful, unforgiving word that there is no questioning its truth, and no hiding from its promises.)

And yet look to the windmill in the hills, the windmill on the Moors, which stands higher than anything around it, inviting lightning, tempting disaster. Look to the windmill where the golden-haired girl works in the soil at all hours of the day and night, with her hands protected from the soil by heavy leather gloves and from everything else by gloves of the finest suede. She toils without cease, burns her sleeves on smoking machinery, strains her eyes peering into the finest workings of the universe. There are those in the village near the cliffs who smile to see her coming, dogging at the doctor's heels, her shoes becoming sturdier and more sensible with every passing season. She is learning, they say; she is finding her way.

(There are those in the village who whisper darker things, who point out the similarities between her and the Master's daughter, who recognize that a single body can only contain so much blood, can only take so much damage. She is not called to service yet, but when the Master and Dr. Bleak clash, there is never any question of the winner.)

Look at them, growing up, growing into the new shapes

that have been offered to them, growing into girls their parents would not recognize, would turn their noses up at. Look at them finding themselves in this wind-racked place, where even the moon is not always safe to look upon.

Look at them in their solitary beds, in their solitary lives, growing further and further apart from one another, unable to entirely let go. Look at the girl in the gossamer gowns standing on the battlements, yearning for a glimpse of her sister; look at the girl in the dirty apron sitting atop the windmill, looking toward the distant walls of the town. They have so much, and so little, in common.

Someone with sharp enough eyes might see the instant where one wounded heart begins to rot while the other starts to heal. Time marches on.

There are moments in the years that we are skipping over, moments that are stories in and of themselves. Jack and Jill begin their menses on the same day (a word that comes from the village women and from Mary, who came from a different time, and Jack finds it charming in its antiquity, and Jill finds it terrifying in its strangeness). Jack packs her underpants with rags and begins trying to find a better way. It is unsafe, on the Moors, to smell of blood. Dr. Bleak calls the village women to help her. They bring their old clothes and their sewing needles; she rampages through his herbs and simples, testing chemical combinations until she strikes upon the right one. Together, she and the village women make something stronger and safer, which holds the smell of blood from prying noses. It keeps them safe when they have cause to venture out of their homes. It keeps monsters and the Master from noticing them.

They learn to love her, at least a little, on that day.

While all this is happening, Jill sinks deeper and deeper into her perfumed baths, bleeding into the water, emerging only to eat plates of chopped beef and spinach, her head spinning with the strangeness of it all. And when her period passes, the Master comes to her, and finally shows her his teeth, which she has been dreaming of for so long. He talks to her all night, almost until the sunrise, making sure that she's comfortable, making sure she *understands*.

He is not so different from the boys she had been dreading meeting when she started her high school career. Like them, he wants her for her body. Like them, he is bigger than her, stronger than her, more powerful than her in a thousand ways. But unlike them, he tells her no lies, puts no veils before his intentions; he is hungry, and she is meat for his table, she is wine for his cup. He promises to love her until the stars burn out. He promises to make her like him, when she is old enough, so that she will never need to leave the Moors. And when he asks her for her answer, she unties the choker that has circled her neck for the last two years, lets it fall away, and exposes the soft white curve of her neck.

There are moments that change everything.

A year after Jill becomes the Master's child in everything but name, Jack stands next to Dr. Bleak on the top floor of their shared windmill. The roof has been opened, and the storm that stains the sky is black as ink, writhing and lit from within by flashes of lightning. A village girl lies stretched on the stone slab between them, her body covered by a sheet, her hands strapped tight around two metal rods. She is only a year older than Jack, found dead when the sun rose, with a streak of white in her hair that spoke to a heart stopped when some phantom lover kissed her too deeply. Hearts that have been stopped without being damaged can sometimes start again, under the right circumstances. When the right circumstances cannot be arranged, lightning can make a surprisingly good substitute.

Dr. Bleak howls orders and Jack hurries to fulfill them, until lightning snakes down from the sky and strikes their array of clever machines. Jack is thrown across the room by the impact; she will taste pennies in the back of her throat for three days. Everything is silence.

The girl on the slab opens her eyes.

There are moments that change everything, mired in the mass of more ordinary time like insects caught in amber. Without them, life would be a tame, predictable thing. But with them, ah. With them, life does as it will, like lightning, like the wind that blows across the castle battlements, and none may stop it, and none may tell it "no." Jack helps the girl off the slab, and everything is different, and nothing will ever be the same.

The girl has eyes as blue as the heather that grows on the hill, and her hair, where it is not white, is the golden color of drying bracken, and she is beautiful in ways Jack fumbles to find the words for, ways that seem to defy the laws of nature and the laws of science in the same breath.

Her name is Alexis, and it is a crime that she was ever dead, even for a second, because the world is darker when she's gone.

(Jack hadn't noticed the darkness, but that doesn't matter. A man who has lived his entire life in a cave does not mourn the sun until he sees it, and once he has, he can never go back underground.)

When Alexis kisses her for the first time, out behind the windmill, Jack realizes that she and Jill have one thing in common: she never, *never* wants to go back to the world she came from. Not when she could have this world, with its lightning and its blue-eyed, beautiful girls, instead.

There are moments that change everything, and once things have been changed, they do not change back. The butterfly may never again become a caterpillar. The vampire's daughter, the mad scientist's apprentice, they will never again be the innocent, untouched children who wandered down a stairway, who went through a door.

They have been changed.

The story changes with them.

"JACK!" DR. BLEAK'S VOICE was sharp, commanding, and impossible to ignore. Not that Jack was in the habit of ignoring it. Her first season with the doctor had been more than sufficient to teach her that when he said "jump," her correct response wasn't to ask "how high?" It was to run for the nearest cliff and trust that gravity would sort things out.

Still, sometimes he had the *worst* timing. She untangled

herself from Alexis's arms, grabbing her gloves from the shelf where they had been discarded, and yanked them on while shouting, "Coming!"

Alexis sighed as she sat up and pulled her shift back into position. "What does he want *now*?" she asked. "Papa expects me back before nightfall." Days on the Moors were short, precious things. Sometimes the sun didn't come entirely out from behind the clouds for weeks at a time, allowing careful vampires and careless werewolves to run free even when it shouldn't have been their time. Alexis's family ran an inn. They didn't have to worry about farming or hunting during the scarce hours of daylight. That didn't mean they were in any hurry to offer their child a second funeral.

(Those who had died once and been resurrected couldn't become vampires: whatever strange mechanism the undead used to reproduce themselves was magic, and it shied away from the science of lightning and the wheel. Alexis was safe from the Master's whims, no matter how pretty she became as she aged. But the Master wasn't the only monster on the Moors, and most wouldn't care about Alexis's medical history. They would simply devour her.)

"I'll find out," said Jack, hastily buttoning her own vest. She stopped to look at Alexis, taking in the soft white curves of her body, the rounded flesh of her shoulder and breast. "Just . . . just stay right where you are, all right? I'll be back as soon as I can. If you don't move, we won't have to take another bath."

"I won't move," said Alexis, with a lazy smile, before

lying back on the bed and staring at the taxidermy-studded ceiling.

After four years with Dr. Bleak, Jack had grown stronger than she ever could have expected, capable of hoisting dead bodies and bushels of potatoes over her shoulders with equal ease. She had grown like a weed, shooting up more than a foot, necessitating multiple trips to the village to buy new cloth to mend her trousers. The contents of Dr. Bleak's wardrobe trunk had stopped fitting her properly by the time she was fourteen, all long limbs and budding breasts and unpredictable temper. (Much of that year had been spent shouting at Dr. Bleak for reasons she could neither understand nor explain. To his credit, the doctor had borne up admirably under her unpredictable tempers. He was, after all, somewhat unpredictably tempered himself.)

After the third pair of badly patched trousers had split down the middle, Jack had learnt to tailor her own clothes, and had started buying fabric by the bolt, cutting and shaping it into the forms she desired. Her work was never going to make her the toast of some fashionable vampire's court, but it covered her limbs and provided her with the necessary protection from the elements. Dr. Bleak had nodded in quiet understanding as her attire became more and more like his, with cuffs that went to her wrists and buttoned tight, and cravats tied at her throat, seemingly for fashion but really to prevent anything getting past the fine weave of her armor. She was not denying her femininity by wearing men's clothing; rather, she was protecting it from caustic chemicals and other, less mundane compounds.

She was still thin, for while her belly was generally full, she did not have the luxury of second helpings or sweet puddings with her tea; she was still fair, for daylight was rare on the Moors. Her hair was still long, a tight blonde braid hanging down the center of her back, picked free and retied every morning. Alexis said that it was like butter, and sometimes cajoled Jack into letting her unbraid it so that she could run her fingers through the kinked strands, smoothing and soothing them. But it was never loose for long. Like everything else about Jack, it had grown into something precise and organized, always bent to its place in the world.

The newest things about her were her glasses, the lenses milled and shaped in Dr. Bleak's lab, set into bent wire frames. Without them, the world was slightly fuzzy around the edges—not a terrible thing, given how brutal this world could sometimes be, but not the best of attributes in a scientist. So she wore her glasses, and she saw things as they were, sharp and bright and unforgiving.

She found Dr. Bleak inside the windmill, a large brown bat spread out on the autopsy table with nails driven through the soft webbing of its wings. Its mouth was stuffed full of garlic and wild rose petals, just as a precaution. There was nothing about the bat to *prove* that it was a visiting vampire, but there was nothing to prove that it *wasn't,* either.

"I need you to go to the village," he said, not looking up. An elaborate loupe covered his left eye, bringing the internal organs of the bat into terrible magnification. "We're running low on aconite, arsenic, and chocolate biscuits."

"I still don't understand how we even have chocolate here," said Jack. "Cocoa trees grow in tropical climates. This is not a tropical climate."

"The terrible things that dwell beneath the bay scavenge it from the ships they wreck and trade it to the villagers for vodka," said Dr. Bleak. "That's also where we get rum, tea, and the occasional cursed idol."

"But where do the ships *come* from?"

"Far away." Dr. Bleak finally looked up, making no effort to conceal his irritation. "As you cannot dissect, resurrect, or otherwise scientifically trouble the sea, leave it *alone,* apprentice."

"Yes, sir," said Jack. The rest of Dr. Bleak's words finally caught up with her. Her eyes widened. "The village, sir?"

"Has your time with your buxom friend destroyed what little sense you had? I'm of no mood to take a new apprentice, not when you're finally becoming trained enough to be useful. Yes, Jack, the village. We need things. You are the apprentice. You fetch things."

"But sir . . ." Jack glanced to the window. The sun, such as it was, hung dangerously low in the sky. "Night is coming."

"Which is why you'll be purchasing aconite, to ward off werewolves. The gargoyles of the waste won't trouble you. They're still grateful for the repair job we did last month on their leader. As for vampires, well. You haven't much to worry about in that regard."

Jack wanted to argue. She opened her mouth to argue.

Then she closed it again, recognizing a losing proposition when she saw one. "May I walk Alexis home?" she asked.

"As long as it doesn't make you late for the shops, I don't care what you do," said Dr. Bleak. "Give my regards to her family."

"Yes, sir," said Jack. Giving Dr. Bleak's regards to Alexis's family would probably mean coming home with a pot of stew and a loaf of bread, at the very least. They knew that he had given back their daughter, and more, they knew that Alexis was beautiful: her death and resurrection had probably protected her from an eternity of vampirism. For that alone, they would be grateful until the stars blew out.

Jack picked up the basket from beside the door, and counted out twenty small gold coins stamped with the Master's face from the jar that held their spending money. Then, shoulders slightly slumped, she went to tell Alexis that they were leaving.

Dr. Bleak waited until she was gone before he sighed, shaking his head, and reached for another scalpel. Jack was an excellent apprentice, eager to learn, obedient enough to be worth training, rebellious enough to be worth caring about. She would make a good doctor someday, if the Moors chose to keep her long enough. And that was the problem.

There were very few people born to the Moors. Alexis, with her calm native acceptance that this was the way the world was intended to work, was more of an aberration than a normalcy. Unlike some worlds, which maintained their own healthy populations, the Moors were too inimical to human life for that to be easily accomplished. So they sent doors to other places, to collect children who might be able to thrive there, and then they let what would happen naturally . . . happen.

Dr. Bleak had not been born to the Moors. Neither, truth be told, had the Master. The Master had been there for centuries; Dr. Bleak, for decades. Long enough to train under his own teacher, the bone-handed Dr. Ghast, who had trained under her own teacher, once upon a time. He knew that one day, he would die, and the lightning would not be enough to call him back. Some days, he thought he might even welcome that final period of rest, when he would no longer be called upon to play the lesser villain of the piece—who was, by comparison, the unwitting hero. He had not been born to the Moors, but he had been there for long enough to recognize the shape of things.

The Master had taken Jill as his latest daughter. She walked the battlements nightly, smiling and humming to herself; her regard for human life dwindled by the day. She was not yet a vampire, nor would be for several years, but it was . . . troubling . . . that a door should open and deposit two so well matched, yet so suited for opposing roles, into the Moors.

Did the Moon, all-seeing and all-judging, tire of the Master, as She had tired of so many vampire lords before him? Jill would make a truly brutal replacement, once the last of her human softness was stripped away. Dr. Bleak could see the story stretching out from the moment of Jill's transformation. Jack, for all that she had little to do with her sister anymore, preferring to avoid the cloying glories of the Master's regard whenever possible, was still of the same blood. She wouldn't forgive the Master for taking her sister away from her. A determined mad scientist was a match for any monster—they were the human side of the essential balance between the feudal houses that ruled these shores—and he could easily see the Master destroyed, while his bright new child ascended, callous and cruel, to his throne.

Jack and Jill were a story becoming real in front of him, and he didn't know how to stop it. So yes, he was trying to force Jack to see her sister. He needed Jill to remember that Jack existed, that Jack was human, and that logic said Jill must be human as well.

It might be the only thing that saved them.

ALEXIS SAT UP AGAIN when she heard Jack approach, and frowned at the expression on her face. "That doesn't look like 'everything's fixed, now kiss me more,' " she said.

"Because it's not," said Jack. "Dr. Bleak wants me to go into the village for supplies."

"Now?" Alexis made no effort to conceal her distress. "But I've only been here for an hour!" Which meant that—after the bath, and the physical exam, and the cleansing of her teeth, and the gargling with sharp, herbal disinfectant, to make sure that no bacteria had been knocked loose when she flossed—she had only been clean enough,

by Jack's standards, for about five minutes before they'd been interrupted.

"I know," said Jack, kicking the floor in frustration. "I don't know why he's so set on my doing this now. I'm sorry. At least I can walk you home?"

Alexis heaved a put-upon sigh. "At least there's that," she agreed. "My mother will try to feed you dinner."

"Which I will gratefully accept, because your mother boils everything to within an inch of its life," said Jack. "If she asks why I don't remove my gloves, I'll tell her I've cut my hand and don't want to risk the wound cracking open, bleeding, and attracting the undead."

"That's what you told her last time."

"It's a valid concern. She should be pleased that you're stepping out with such a conscientious young apprentice, instead of one of those village oafs." Jack offered Alexis her gloved hand.

With another sigh, Alexis took it and slid off the bed. "Those 'village oafs,' as you like to call them, will have houses and trades of their own one day. You'll have a windmill."

"A very *clean* windmill," said Jack.

"They'd be able to give me children. That's what Mother says."

"I could give you children," said Jack, sounding faintly affronted. "You'd have to tell me how many heads you wanted them to have, and what species you'd like them to be, but what's the point of having all these graveyards if I can't give you children when you ask for them?"

Alexis laughed and punched her in the shoulder, and Jack smiled, knowing that all was forgiven.

They made an odd pair, strolling across the Moors, neither of them looking like they had a care in the world. Alexis was soft where Jack was spare, the daughter of wealthy parents who made sure she never went to bed hungry, trusting her to know her own body and its needs. (And if the local vampire favored willowy girls who would die if left outside in the slightest frost, well, loosen your belt and pass the potatoes; we'll keep our darling daughters safe at home.) Jack's hair was tightly braided where Alexis's was loose, and her hands were gloved where Alexis's were bare. But those hands were joined as tightly together as any lover's knot had ever been, and they walked in smooth, matched steps, never turning their ankles, never forcing the other to rush.

Occasionally, Jack would stop, produce a pair of bone-handled scissors from her pocket, and snip off a piece of some bush or weed. Alexis always stopped and watched indulgently as Jack made the vegetation vanish into her basket.

When they resumed, she said lightly, teasing, "You can touch every filthy plant in the world, but you can't touch me without a bucket of boiling water on hand?"

"I don't touch them," said Jack. "My scissors touch them, and my gloves touch them, but *I* don't touch them. I don't touch much of anything."

"I wish you could."

"So do I," said Jack, and smiled, a wry twist of a thing.

"Sometimes I think about what my mother would say if she could see me now. She was the one who first told me that I should be afraid of getting dirty."

"My mother told me the same thing," said Alexis.

"Your mother is a reasonable terror of a woman who frightens me more than all the vampires in all the castles in the world, but she has nothing on my mother when there was a chance one of the neighbors might see me with dirt on my dress," said Jack darkly. "I learned to be afraid of dirt before I learned how to spell my own name."

"I can't imagine you in a dress," said Alexis. "You'd look . . ." She stopped herself, but it was too late: the damage was done.

"Like my sister, yes," said Jack. "We would be two peas in a terrible pod. I don't think I'd make a good vampire, though. They never seem to have a napkin on hand when the spurting starts." She shuddered theatrically. "Can you imagine me covered in all that *mess*? And they haven't reflections. I'd be unable to tell whether I'd wiped my face clean. The only solution would be dipping myself nightly in bleach."

"Hard on the hair," said Alexis.

"Hard on the heart," said Jack. She gave Alexis's fingers a squeeze. "I am what I am, and there's much about me that won't be changed with any amount of wishing or wanting. I'm sorry for that. I'd trade a great deal to share an afternoon in the hay with you, dust in the air and sweat on our skins and neither of us caring. But I'm afraid the experience would drive me mad. I am a creature of sterile environments. It's too late for me to change."

"You say that, and yet I've seen you leap into an open grave like it was nothing."

"Only with the proper footwear, I assure you."

Alexis laughed and stepped a little closer to Jack, hugging her arm as they walked toward the looming wall of the village. She rested her head against Jack's shoulder. Jack inhaled, breathing in the salty smell of her lover's hair, and thought that there was something to be said for worlds of blood and moonlight, where the only threat more terrible than the things that dwelt in the sea were the things that lived on the shore. Beauty was all the brighter against a background of briars.

The walk was too short, or maybe their legs had just become too long: both of them were still so haunted by the ghosts of childhood that they had yet to learn the fine art of dawdling, of stretching things out until they lasted as long as they would ask them to. In what seemed like no time at all, they were standing in front of the great wall.

Alexis let go of Jack's hand. Cupping her hands around her mouth, she called, "Alexis Chopper, returning home," to the sentry.

"Jacqueline Wolcott, apprentice to Dr. Bleak, escorting Miss Chopper and purchasing supplies," called Jack. Residents always spoke first—to give them the opportunity to scream for help if they felt that it was needed, she supposed. The "help" would probably take the form of scalding oil,

or possibly a rain of arrows, but at least the residents would die knowing that they'd protected the rest of the village.

It was fascinating, how frightened people who lived in a vampire's backyard could be of the rest of the world. Just because something was unfamiliar, that didn't mean it had sharper teeth or crueler claws than the monster they already knew. But Dr. Bleak said that conducting psychological experiments on the neighbors never ended well, and he was in charge, so Jack kept her thoughts to herself.

"Watch the gate!" called the sentry. There was a lot of shouting and creaking of wood, and then the gate swung open, heavy and slow and supposedly secure.

Alexis, who had been born behind that gate, knowing that the Master watched her every step, walked through serenely. The fact that she was willingly strolling into a vampire's hunting ground didn't seem to trouble her—and maybe it didn't. On the few occasions when Jack had tried to speak to her about it, she had spoken darkly of the werewolves in the mountains, of the Drowned Gods under the sea, of all the terrible dangers that the Moors had to offer. Apparently, being a prey animal living under the auspices of a predator was better.

Maybe it was. Jack had only spent a single night under the Master's roof, and while she was sometimes sad that she hadn't been able to save her sister, she was never sorry that she'd gotten out. Jill had made her own choice.

Jack chuckled to herself. Alexis glanced at her.

"Something funny?"

"Everything," said Jack, as the doors swung shut behind

them. She offered Alexis her hand. "Let's go see your parents."

THE SUN, ALTHOUGH FADING, was still in the sky; the Master was deep inside his castle, resting up for the night that was to come. Jill was not allowed in his presence for another two days. It was always like that after a feeding. He said she needed to reach a certain age before he could stop her heart in her chest, preserving it forever. He said she would be happier facing the unending night as an adult, with an adult's position and privilege.

Jill thought it was really because he was afraid. No one had ever heard of a foundling going back to their own world after their eighteenth birthday: if you came of age in the Moors, you stayed there until you died. Or undied, as the case might be. She was only sixteen. She still had two years to wait, two years of him leaving her alone for three days every two weeks, two years of walking the battlements alone, feeling the cruel kiss of the sun on her skin. The Master insisted. He wanted the people to grow used to her, and he wanted her to fully accept what she was giving up.

Nonsense. It was all nonsense. As if anyone could be offered an eternity of privilege and power and refuse it on a whim. Anyone who walked away from the Master would have to be a fool, or worse—

There was a flicker of motion down in the square. Two people had entered via the mountainside gate. The fat girl from the inn, and a skinny figure in a black vest. Light glinted off Jack's glasses when she turned her head. Jill felt her hated, hated heart clench in her chest. Her sister, here.

This could not be allowed to stand.

9 SOMEONE'S COMING TO DINNER

THE INN OWNED by Alexis's parents was small and cozy and reasonably clean, as such things went. Jack could be in it for hours before she started wanting to scratch her own skin off, which was remarkable for anyplace outside of the lab.

(Alexis had remarked once, after a particularly tense visit, that it was odd how Jack could handle working in the garden for Dr. Bleak, but not the idea of sitting on a seat that another human had used without first scrubbing it to a mirror sheen. Jack had attempted, not very well, to explain that dirt was dirt; dirt was capable of being clean, if it was in its native environment. It was the mixture of dirt and other things—like sweat and skin and the humors of the human body—that became a problem. It was the recipe, not the ingredients.)

Alexis's mother looked like her, but older, and when she smiled, it was like someone had lit a jack-o'-lantern fire in the space behind her eyes. Jack thought she could endure any amount of dirt for the warmth of Ms. Chopper's smile.

She had searched her memory over and over again, and never found anything that even implied her own mother had been capable of such a smile.

Alexis's father had been a woodcutter before he'd settled into the innkeeper's life: hence the family name and the axe that hung above the fire. He was a mountain of a man, and Jack thought he might be the only human in the Moors who would stand a chance against Dr. Bleak in a physical contest. (The werewolves would win, no contest. Fortunately, werewolves were less interested in wrestling and axe-hurling than they were in mauling people and fetching sticks.)

As always at the Sign of the Hind and Hare, the food was simple and plentiful, and reminded Jack uncomfortably of the rabbit and root vegetables she'd eaten on her one night with the Master. He took what he wanted from the village stores for the people who lived under his roof: she had no doubt that her very first meal had been prepared by Ms. Chopper's loving hand. Maybe Alexis had eaten the same thing that night. Maybe they had started her tenure in the Moors by sharing a meal, all unaware of what lay ahead of them.

She hoped so. It made the bread taste better, and the milk seem sweeter, to think they'd been eating together for as long as that.

Ms. Chopper was passing the potatoes around the table one more time when the kitchen door blew open, shuddering in its frame like it had been caught in a heavy wind. Alexis jumped. Mr. Chopper tensed, hand going to his side like he expected to find his axe hanging there, ready to be swung. Ms. Chopper froze, her hands clenching around the edges of her tray.

Jack sat quietly, her eyes on her food, trying to look as if she thought stewed mushrooms and roast rabbit was the most fascinating thing in the entire world.

"You could at least say hello, *sister*," hissed Jill, and her voice was poisonously sweet, like something that had been allowed to sit too long in the sun and had spoiled from the heat.

"Oh, I'm sorry." Jack raised her head, reaching up to adjust her glasses as she did. "I thought it was a stray dog knocking the door open. Where I come from, people knock."

"You come from the same place I do," said Jill.

"Yes, and people knocked."

Jill glared at her. Jack looked impassively back.

Their faces were identical: there was no denying that. All the time in the world wouldn't change the shape of their lips or the angle of their eyes. They could dye their hair, style themselves entirely differently, but they would always be cast from the same mold. But that was where the resemblance ended.

Jill was dressed in a gown of purple so pale that it might as well have been white, if not set against the pallor of her skin and the icy blonde of her hair. It was cut straight across her chest in a style that was modest now, although it wouldn't be for much longer; it was a little girl's dress, and she, like Jack, was well on her way to womanhood. Her skirt was long enough to trail on the ground. The bottom six inches or so were gray with dirt. Jack shuddered slightly, hoping her sister wouldn't see.

No such luck. While Jack had been living in a windmill, learning the secrets of science and how to raise the dead, Jill had been living in a castle, learning the secrets of survival and how to serve the dead. Her eyes saw all. Slowly, she smiled.

"Aw, I'm sorry, sister," she said. "Am I dirty? Does that bother you, that I'm a dirty girl? The Master doesn't mind if I spoil my dresses. I can always get another."

"How nice for you," said Jack, through gritted teeth. "Why are you here?"

"I saw you come through the gates. I thought surely you *must* be coming up to the castle to see me, since I'm your sister, after all, and it's been so long since you last came to visit. Imagine my surprise when you followed your little fat girl to the inn to stuff your face." Jill's nose wrinkled. "Really, it's bestial. Is this the way you want to spend your youth? With pigs and peasants?"

Jack started to stand. Alexis grabbed her wrist, pulling her back down.

"It's not worth it," she said, voice low. "Please, it's not worth it."

Jill laughed. "See? Everyone here knows their place except for you. Is it because you're jealous? Because you could have had what I have, and you didn't move fast enough? Or is it because you miss me?"

"I never knew my sister well enough to miss her, and with the way you behave, I'm not sure I'd want you for my sister," said Jack. "As for having what you have . . . you have a dress that shows every speck of dust that lands on it. You have hands so pale that they can never look clean. I don't want what you have. What you have is terrible. Leave me alone."

"Is that any way to talk to your family? Blood of your blood?"

Jack sneered. "Last time I checked, you were planning to get rid of your blood as soon as the Master was willing to take it. Or did you change your mind? Are you going to stick around and try living for a little while? I recommend it. Maybe get some more sun. You're clearly vitamin D–deficient."

"Jack, please," whispered Alexis.

Jill was still smiling. Jack went cold.

The Sign of the Hind and Hare was the only inn the village had. That didn't make it indispensable. If something should happen to it—if it burned to the ground in the middle of the night, say, or if its owners were found with all the blood drained from their bodies—well, that would just be too bad. Another inn would open before the next full moon, equipped with a new family, eager to serve without breaking the rules.

Like everyone who lived under the grace of the Master, the Choppers obeyed his rules. They did as they were told. They went where they were bid. And they didn't fight, ever, not with him, and not with the girl he'd chosen as his heir.

Jack swallowed. Jack smoothed her vest with the heels

of her gloved hands and stood, leaving her plate behind. Alexis let go of her arm. The moment of absence, when the pressure of Alexis's hand was first removed, was somehow worse than the surrender.

"I'm . . . so sorry, Jillian," said Jack, in a careful, measured voice. "I was hungry. You know how cranky I get when I'm hungry."

Jill giggled. "You're the *worst* when you haven't eaten. So did you come to visit me, really?"

"Yes. Absolutely." Jack didn't need to turn to know that Alexis was trembling, or that her parents were fighting not to rush to her. They hadn't been expecting her to bring danger to their door. They should have been. They should have known. *She* should have known. She'd been a fool, and now they were paying the price. "Dr. Bleak expects me back by midnight, but I have shopping to do in the square before then. Would you like to come with me? I think I have enough coin that I could buy you something nice. Candied ginger, or a ribbon for your hair."

Jill's gaze sharpened. "If you'd really come to see me, you'd know whether you had enough coin to get me a present."

"Dr. Bleak controls the money. I'm just his apprentice." Jack spread her hands, trying to look contrite without seeming overly eager. Jill seemed to believe her—or maybe Jill just didn't care, as long as she got her own way in the end. *We're strangers now,* she thought, and mourned. "I'm learning a lot, but that doesn't mean he trusts me with more than he has to."

"The Master trusts me with *everything,*" said Jill, and skipped—skipped!—across the room to slide her arm through Jack's. "I suppose we can shop before you buy me a present. If Dr. Bleak cast you out, you'd have to live in the barn with the pigs, and you'd be filthy all the time. That would be awful, wouldn't it?"

Jack, who already felt like she needed a bath from just that short contact with her sister, suppressed a shudder. "Awful," she agreed, and grabbed her basket, and let Jill lead her out into the night.

The door slammed shut behind them. Ms. Chopper dropped the tray of potatoes in her hurry to fling her arms around her daughter, and the three of them huddled together, shaking and crying, and suddenly all too aware of the dark outside.

JILL STEPPED LIGHTLY, like she was dancing her way across the muddy cobblestones in the village square. She never stopped talking, words spilling over each other like eager puppies as she recounted everything that had happened to her in the months since she'd last seen her sister. Jack realized, with a dull, distant sort of guilt, that Jill was lonely: she might have servants in that great pile of a castle, and she might have the love, or at least the fondness, of her Master, but she didn't have *friends.*

(That was probably a good thing. Jack could remember Dr. Bleak returning from trips to the village shortly after she'd gone to live with him, a dire expression on his face and his big black medical bag in his hands. There had been deaths among the village children. That was all he'd been willing to tell her, when she pressed. It hadn't been until years later, when Alexis started coming around, that she'd learned that all the children who'd died had been seen playing with Jill around the fountain. The Master was a jealous man. He didn't want her to have anything in her life except for him, and he was happy to do whatever he deemed necessary to make sure that he remained the center of her world. Friends were a nuisance to be dealt with. Friends were expendable.)

Jack was accustomed to doing her shopping alone, or in the company of Dr. Bleak. It was surprising how often people forgot that Jill was her sister, or felt no need to guard their tongues in her presence. She was used to jokes and gossip, and even the occasional sly barb about the Master's policies.

As she walked through the shops on Jill's arm, the real surprise was the silence. People who knew her as Dr. Bleak's apprentice went quiet when she approached side by side with the Master's daughter, and some of them looked at her face like she was a riddle that had just been unexpectedly solved. Jack had to fight not to grimace. It would take her months, maybe years, to rebuild the ground she was losing with every person who saw her in Jill's company. Suddenly, she was the enemy again. It was not a comfortable prospect.

Several of the merchants tried to give her deeper discounts than they usually did, or could afford. When possible, she paid the normal amount anyway, shaking her head to silence them. Unfortunately, if Jill caught her, she would snatch the coins from the merchant's hand, rolling her eyes.

"We only *pay* as a courtesy," she would say. "We *pay* as a symbol, to show that we're part of this village, not just the beating heart that sustains it in a world of wolves. If they want to make the symbol even more symbolic, you're to let them. You promised me a present."

"Yes, sister," Jack would reply, and on they would go to the next merchant, while the hole in the pit of her stomach got bigger and bigger, until it felt like it was going to swallow the entire world.

She'd have to tell Dr. Bleak about this. If she didn't, the villagers would, the next time he came for supplies or to check on someone's ailing mother. They would talk about his apprentice and the Master's daughter walking arm in arm, and he would wonder why she'd hid it from him, and everything would be ruined. Even more ruined than it already was.

The basket over her arm was heavy with the things she'd been sent to buy, and with an occasional extra that Jill had picked up and simply placed among everything else. A jug of heavy cream; a jar of honey. Luxuries that were nice, in their way, but which had never been considered necessary in the windmill up on the hill. Finally, it was time for Jill to choose her gift.

The stallholder, a slender village maiden who shook and shivered like a reed dancing in the wind, stood with her hands clasped tight against her apron, like by refusing to let them flutter, she could somehow conceal the rest of her anxiety. And maybe she could: Jill didn't appear to notice. She was busy running her fingers through the ribbons, cooing and twittering about the feel of the fabric against her skin.

Jack tried to make eye contact with the stallholder. She looked away, refusing to let Jack look into her eyes. Jack felt the hole in her stomach grow greater still. Most of the villagers were superstitious, if it could be called that when the vampire was *right there,* when there were werewolves in the mountains and terrible things with tentacles in the sea. They knew that the Master could influence their minds by meeting their eyes. None of them had looked directly at Jill without being ordered to in years, even though she wouldn't have her own power over the human heart until she was transformed. Now, it seemed, some of that superstition was transferring to Jack.

"Do you like this one?" asked Jill, holding up a length of shimmering gray silk that looked like it had been sliced out of the mist on the moor. "I have a dress it would look perfect with."

"It's beautiful," said Jack. "You should get that one."

Jill pouted prettily. "But there are so *many* of them," she protested. "I haven't seen more than half."

"I know," said Jack, trying to sound soothing, or at least, trying not to sound frustrated. "Dr. Bleak expects me back by midnight, remember? I can't disobey my master any more than you can disobey yours."

It was a calculated risk. Jill knew what it was to be obedient, to bend her desires to another's. She also had a tendency to fly into a towering rage at the slightest implication that *her* Master was not the only master in the Moors, as if having a capital letter on his name somehow gave him a monopoly on shouting orders.

Jill wound the ribbon around her finger and said, "The Master would be happy to have you still, if you wanted to come home. You're very unsuitable now, you know. You'd have to be reeducated. I'd have to teach you how to be a *lady*. But you could come home."

The thought of calling the castle "home" was enough to make Jack woozy with terror. She damped it down and shook her head, saying, "I appreciate the offer. I have work to do with Dr. Bleak. I *like* what we do together. I like what I'm learning." An old memory stirred, of her mother in a pink pantsuit, telling her how to refuse an invitation. "Thank you so much for thinking of me."

Jill sighed. "You'll come home one day," she said, and grabbed a fistful of ribbons, so many of them that they trailed between her fingers like a rainbow of worms. "I'll take these," she informed the stallholder. "My sister will pay you." Then she was gone, turning on her heel and flouncing back toward the castle gates. Ribbons fell unnoticed from her fist as she walked, leaving a trail behind her in the dust.

Jack turned back to the stallholder, reaching for the coins at the bottom of her basket. "I'm so sorry," she said, voice pitched low and urgent. "I didn't mean to bring her to you. She forced my hand. I may not have enough to pay you, but I promise, I'll return with the rest, only tell me what I owe."

"Nothing," said the stallholder. She still wasn't looking at Jack.

"But—"

"I said, nothing." The stallholder moved to start smoothing the remaining ribbons, trying to restore order to the chaos Jill had made. "She never pays anyway. The Master will send someone with gold, will overpay for the next dress he orders in her name. She didn't threaten me this time. She didn't show me her teeth or ask if I wanted to look at the skin under her choker. You made her better, not worse."

"I'm so sorry."

"Leave." The stallholder finally looked up, finally focused on Jack. When she spoke again, her voice was so soft that it was barely audible. "Everyone knows that children who talk to the Master's daughter disappear, because he can't stand to share her. But not you. Because even though you're not his child, you're still her sister, and *she* gets jealous of the people who talk to *you*. Get away from me before she decides you're my friend."

Jack took a step backward. The stallholder went back to sorting through her ribbons, expression grim. She did not speak again, and so Jack turned and walked through the silent village. The sun was down. The huge red moon hung ominously close to the horizon, like it might descend and begin crushing everything in its path.

The door of the inn was closed. A single candle burned in the window. Jack looked at it and kept on walking, out of the village, through the gates, and onto the wild and lonely moor.

THE LIGHT IN THE windmill window made it seem more like a lighthouse, something perfect and pure, calling the lost souls home. Jack started to walk a little faster when she realized that she was almost home. That wasn't enough. She broke into a run, and would have slammed straight into the door if Dr. Bleak hadn't opened it a split second before she could. She ran into the hard flesh of his midsection instead, the rough leather of his apron grinding against her cheek.

She dropped the basket, scattering supplies and her small remaining store of coins at her feet.

"Jack, what's wrong?" asked Dr. Bleak, and his voice was a rope thrown to a drowning girl, his voice was the solid foundation of her world, and she clung to him, pressing her face against his chest, for once not caring about the dirt, and cried and cried, under the eye of the unforgiving moon.

PART IV

JILL AND JACK WILL NOT COME BACK

10 AND FROM HER GRAVE, A RED, RED ROSE . . .

TIME PASSED. JACK STAYED away from the village, electing to do extra chores at home rather than accompanying Dr. Bleak to town on shopping trips. She began to make plans for the future, for the time when she would have her own garden, her own windmill, and be able to provide for a household of her own.

Alexis continued to visit, cautiously at first, and then more and more brazenly as nothing terrible happened to her family.

Jill walked the battlements, and counted down the days until their eighteenth birthday. She was nestled snug in her bed, dreaming of rivers of beautiful red, when sunlight flooded the room and slapped her out of sleep. She sat bolt upright, shocked and bewildered, and blinked against the terrible brightness.

"Miss," said Mary, voice polite, deferential. She had been using that tone with Jill for two years, since the day Jill had thrown a fit and demanded she be spoken to with respect, lest Mary find herself thrown over the battlements. "The Master requested I wake you."

"Why?" demanded Jill. She dug at her eyes with the heels of her hands, rubbing until the sting of the sunlight faded. When she lowered her hands, blinking rapidly, she realized that Mary was holding a large vase filled with red, red roses. Jill's eyes widened. She reached out her hands, making small wanting motions.

"Give them to me," said Jill.

"Yes, miss." Mary did not hand the vase to Jill. Rather, she walked a few steps along the length of the bed and set them on the table next to the headboard, where Jill could breathe in their fragrance and admire their beauty without pricking herself on the thorns. If she were responsible for the Master's precious girl bleeding when he was not in the room, her head would be the one hitting the floor.

"From the Master?" demanded Jill.

"Yes, miss."

"They're *beautiful.*" Jill's expression went soft, her eyes growing wet with grateful tears. "Do you see how beautiful they are? He loves me so much. He's so good to me."

"Yes, miss," said Mary, who was well acquainted with the shape of a vampire's love. She thought sometimes that Jill had utterly forgotten that she had been a foundling too, long ago; that Jill was not the first girl to wear a pale dress and a choker around her throat.

"Did he tell you why?" Jill turned a hopeful face toward Mary. "Is he coming to see me today? I know it's only been two days, but—"

"Do you really not know, miss?" Of course she didn't. Vampires cared about time only as it impacted other people, and Jill, while still human, was already thinking like a vampire. Mary forced herself to smile. "Today is the fifth anniversary of your arrival in the Moors."

Jill's eyes widened. "I'm seventeen?"

"Yes, miss." Time in the Moors was not precisely like time in the world Jack and Jill had originally come from: it followed a different set of natural rules and did not map precisely to any other calendar. But a year was a year. Even if their precise birthday was impossible to mark, the date of their arrival was clear.

Jill tumbled out of bed in an avalanche of blankets and fluffy nightgown. "I was almost twelve and a half when we arrived here," she said excitedly, starting to shovel her covers back onto the mattress. "That makes me practically eighteen. Does he want me? Tonight? Is it finally time?"

"Practically eighteen is not the same as actually eighteen, miss," said Mary, fighting to keep the precise balance of kindness and deference she needed when speaking to Jill. "He knew you would ask about this. He said to tell you that because we do not know your precise birthday, he will err on the side of caution; things will continue as they are until the Drowned Abbey rings the bells for the change of seasons."

"But that's *forever*!" protested Jill. "Why so long? I've done nothing wrong! I've been so good! Everything he's asked me to be, I've become!" She dropped her armload of pillows and straightened, waving her hands to indicate the elegant lace of her nightgown, the carefully arrayed curl of her hair. She had long since mastered the art of sleeping motionlessly, so as to rise perfectly coifed and ready to face whatever the night might hold.

"Everything except an adult," said Mary gently. "The door could still open for you. The world of your birth could still pull you back."

"That's a bedtime story to frighten children," snapped Jill. "Doors don't come back when they're not wanted."

"You knew what a vampire was when you came here," said Mary. "Didn't you wonder why that was? The rules we have exist because mistakes have been made in the past. Things have gone wrong." Newly made vampires, things of anger and appetite, stumbling through magical doors and back into worlds that had no defenses against them . . .

Mary suppressed the urge to shiver. The Moors knew how to live with vampires. The Moors were equipped to survive alongside their own monsters.

"Had you gone to the mountains and the care of the werewolf lord, he would tell you the same," she said. "Or down to the sea. The Drowned Gods change no one young enough to go back to where they came from. We must be careful, lest we attract the attention of whatever force creates the doors. If they stopped, the Moors would be lost."

"The Moon makes the doors," said Jill in a waspish tone. "Everyone knows that."

"There are other theories."

"Those theories are wrong." Jill glared at her. "The door we used said 'Be Sure' on it, and I'm sure. I'm sure I want to be a vampire. I want to be strong and beautiful and *forever*. I want to know that no one can ever, ever take all this away from me. Why can't I have that?"

"You will," said Mary. "When the bells of the Drowned Abbey ring, you will. The Master will take you to the highest tower, and he'll make you ruthless, and he'll make you swift, and most of all, he'll make you his. But you must wait for the bells to ring, miss, you must. I know it's difficult. I know you don't want to wait. But—"

"What do *you* know, Mary?" snapped Jill. "You were a foundling. This could have been yours. You refused him. Why?"

"Because I didn't want to be ruthless, miss." It had all seemed like a game at first, her and the vampire in the high castle, him offering her whatever she wanted, while she laughed and refused everything but what she needed. It had seemed like a *game*.

And then he had asked to be her new father, and asked her to be his child, to rule alongside him forever in fury and in blood.

And then he had raged at her refusal. Her friends from the village kept disappearing, and at first that had seemed like a game too, a vast conspiracy of hide-and-seek . . . until the day he'd dragged little Bela in front of her and said "This is what becomes of those who oppose me," and ripped the boy's throat out with his teeth. Sometimes Mary thought she could still feel the blood on her face.

But Jill had never seen that side of him. Jill had been his precious little princess from the start. Jill walked on clouds and dreamt of vampirism like it was a wonderful game, still a wonderful game, and there was no way Mary could convince her otherwise.

Jill's face hardened. "I can be ruthless," she said. "I'll show him that I can be ruthless, and then he'll see that we don't have to wait. I can be his daughter right now."

"Yes, miss," said Mary. "Do you want breakfast?"

"Don't be stupid," said Jill, which meant "yes." In that regard, at least, the girl was already a vampire: she was always hungry.

"Thank you, miss," said Mary, and made her exit as quickly and gracefully as possible.

Jill watched her go, face still hard. Once she was sure the other woman would not be coming back she turned and walked to her wardrobe, pulling it open to reveal a rainbow of pastel dresses. She selected the palest of them, a cream silk gown that brought out the gold in her hair and the ivory in her skin. It was the next best thing to white, to a wedding gown. She would show him that she didn't need to wait.

She would show him that she already understood what it was to be ruthless.

TODAY WAS THE ANNIVERSARY of their arrival. The Master would no doubt host a party in her honor when the sun went down, something decadent and grand. He might even invite the other vampires to come and coo over his protégée, how far she'd come, how beautiful she was. Yes: it would be a lovely affair, and the only way it could be better was if it ended with her glorious demise and even more glorious rebirth.

Waiting was pointless. Even if a door opened, she wouldn't go through it. She would never leave her beloved Master like that. All she needed to do was prove to him that she was serious, that she was ruthless enough to be his child, and everything would be perfect.

If there was to be a party in her honor, something glorious and befitting a vampire's child, that dreadful Dr. Bleak would be doing something for Jack as well. He had to. Everyone knew that being a mad scientist's apprentice wasn't as good as being the Master's daughter, and that meant that Dr. Bleak couldn't afford to miss any opportunity to bind Jack's loyalty more tightly to him. There would be a party.

And if there was a party, Alexis would be attending.

Jack's unnatural fondness for the innkeeper's daughter had not faded with time; if anything, it had grown more intense. Jill had seen them together many times. Jack laughed when she was with Alexis. *Laughed,* like she wasn't making them both look bad by wandering around the Moors in ugly vests and cravats, acting like a lady had any place in a nasty old mad scientist's lab. It wasn't right. It wasn't proper.

Jill could fix everything. She could set her sister on the right path and show the Master that she was ruthless enough to be his child in truth, not just in name. One single act would make it all better.

She wrinkled her nose in distaste before taking a heavy brown cloak down from its peg inside the wardrobe and fastening it over her beautiful gown. She hated dull, ordinary colors, but it was necessary. She knew how much she stood out when she didn't take steps to hide herself.

Mary was still downstairs, seeing to breakfast. Jill slipped through the secret door on the landing—every good castle had secret doors—and started down the stairs. She had made this walk so many times that she could do it with her eyes closed, and so she let her mind drift, thinking about how wonderful it would be when the Master took her in his arms and showed her all the mysteries that death had to offer.

Soon. So soon.

She emerged from a small door at the base of the castle wall, secluded and mostly concealed by a fold in the architecture. Pulling her hood up over her head, she walked into the village, keeping her cloak closed, attracting no attention to herself. Mysterious cloaked figures were a common enough occurrence in the Moors that no one gave her a second look. It was best not to interfere with people who might be carrying secret messages for the Master, or looking for sacrifices to carry back to the Drowned Gods.

The village looked different by day. Smaller, meaner, *filthier*. Jill walked through the streets, imagining the way people would shy away if they knew who she was. It almost made up for the dirt that stained her hem, turning it from cream to muddy brown. She didn't mind mess the way Jack did, but it wasn't *elegant*. Hard to strike a terrifying figure when it looked as if she'd forgotten to do the laundry.

The villagers were surprisingly noisy when not watching their tongues in the presence of the Master's daughter. People laughed and shouted to one another, bargaining, talking about the harvest. Jill frowned under the safety of her hood. They sounded *happy*. But they lived short, brutish lives, protected only by the grace of the Master. They wallowed in dirt and worked their fingers to the bone just to keep a roof over their heads. How could they be *happy*?

It was a train of thought that might have led her to some unpleasant conclusions had it been allowed to continue; this story might have ended differently. A single revelation does not change a life. It is a start. But alas, the inn door opened; the innkeeper's daughter emerged, dressed in what passed among the villagers for finery. Her dress was green, her bodice was blue, and her skirts were hiked daringly high enough to show her ankles. There was a basket over one arm, laden with bread and wine and fresh-picked apples.

Her mother, coming to the threshold, said something. The girl laughed, and leaned in to kiss her mother's cheek. Then she turned and started for the gate, walking like she hadn't a care in the world.

On silent feet, Jill followed.

Jill rarely left the safety of the castle and village, where the Master's word was absolute law and no one would dare to raise a hand against her. The moor outside the walls was his as well, of course, but the territories could get murky out in the open. Those who walked too carelessly were always at risk of werewolf attack, or being selected as a sacrifice for the Drowned Gods. The walk into the bracken was thus tainted with a giddy wickedness, like she was getting away with something. Surely this would prove how serious she was!

The innkeeper's daughter walked surprisingly fast. Jill stayed just far enough behind her to go unnoticed.

Alexis had grown up in the shadow of the castle, hearing the werewolves howl at night and the ringing of the bells in the Drowned Abbey. She was a survivor. But she knew that her status as one of the resurrected made her unappealing to many of the monsters she had grown up fearing, and she knew that neither gargoyles nor phantom hounds prowled during the day, and besides, she was going to see the woman she loved. She was relaxed. She was daydreaming. She was careless.

A hand touched her shoulder. Alexis stiffened and turned, preparing for the worst. She relaxed when she saw the face peeping at her from beneath the concealing hood.

"Jack," she said warmly. "I thought you had chores all morning."

Jill frowned. Alexis, finally realizing that the woman behind her wasn't wearing glasses, took a stumbling step backward.

"You're not Jack," she said. "What are you doing here?"

"Being sure," said Jill. She unfastened her cloak, letting

it fall into the bracken as she drew the knife from inside her bodice, and leapt.

We will leave them there. There are some things that do not need to be seen to be understood; things that can be encompassed by a single sharp scream, and by a spray of blood painting the heather, red as roses, red as apples, red as the lips of the vampire's only child.

There is nothing here for us now.

11 . . . AND FROM HIS GRAVE, A BRIAR

"SHE SHOULD *BE* HERE by now," said Jack, putting aside the bone saw she had been carefully sharpening. Her eyes went to the open door, and to the moor beyond. Alexis did not appear. "I told her we were going to have supper at nightfall."

Alexis had been granted permission to stay the night at the windmill. It would have been considered improper, but with Dr. Bleak to serve as a chaperone, there was no question of her virtue being imperiled. (Not that her parents had any illusions about her virtue, or about Jack's intentions toward their daughter. Despite Alexis's status as one of the resurrected, they were both relieved to know that she had found someone who would care for her when they were gone.)

Dr. Bleak looked up from his own workbench. "Perhaps she stopped to pick flowers."

"On the moor?" Jack stood, grabbing her jacket from the back of the chair. "I'm going to go find her."

"Patience, Jack—"

"Is an essential tool of the scientific mind; raise no corpse before its time. I know, sir. But I also know that this isn't like Alexis. She's never late." Jack looked at her mentor, expression pleading.

Dr. Bleak sighed. "Ah, for the energy of the young," he said. "Yes, you may go and find her. But be quick about it. The festivities will not begin until you finish your chores."

"Yes, sir," said Jack. She yanked on her gloves, and then she was off, running for the door and down the garden path. Dr. Bleak watched her until she had dwindled to almost nothing in the distance. Only then did he close his eyes. He had lived in the Moors for a very long time. He knew, even better than Jack did, that lateness was rarely, if ever, as innocent as it seemed.

"Let her be alive," he whispered, and recognized his words for the useless things they were as soon as he heard them. He sat still, waiting. The truth would come clear soon enough.

IT WAS THE RED that caught Jack's attention first.

The Moors were far more complex than they had seemed to her on that first night, when she had been young and innocent and unaware of her own future. They were brown, yes, riddled with dead and dying vegetation. Every shade of brown that there was could be found on the Moors. They were also bright with growing green and mellow gold, and with the rainbow pops of flowers—yellow marigold and blue heather and purple wolf's bane. Hemlock bloomed white as clouds. Foxglove spanned the spectrum of sunset. The Moors were beautiful in their own way, and if their beauty was the quiet sort that required time and introspection to be seen, well, there was nothing wrong with that. The best beauty was the sort that took some seeking.

But nothing red grew on the Moors. Not even strawberries, or poisonous mushrooms. Those were found only on the outskirts of the forest held by the werewolves, or in private gardens, like Dr. Bleak's. The Moors were neutral territory, of a sort, divided between so many monsters that they could not bear to bleed. Red was an anomaly. Red was aftermath.

Jack began to walk faster.

The closer she got, the clearer the red became. It was like it had exploded outward from a single source, shed with wanton delight by whoever held the knife. There was a body at the center of it, a softly curving body, lush of breast and generous of hip. A body . . . a body . . .

Jack stopped dead, eyes fixed not on the body but on the basket that had fallen at the very edge of the carnage. It had landed on its side. Some of the bread was splattered with blood, but the apples had already been red; there was no way of telling whether they were clean. No way in the world.

Slowly, Jack sank to her knees in the bracken, for once utterly heedless of the possibility of mud or grass stains. Her eyes bulged as she stared at the basket, never looking any further than that; never looking at the things she didn't want to see.

Red. So much red.

When she began to howl, it was the senseless keen of someone who has been pushed past their breaking point and taken refuge in the comforting caverns of their own mind. In the village, people gathered their children close, shivering, and closed the windows. In the castle, the Master stirred in his sleep, troubled for reasons he could not name.

In the windmill, Dr. Bleak rose, sorrow etched into his features, and reached for his bag. Things from here would continue as they would. It was too late to control or prevent them. All he could do was hope that they'd survive.

JACK WAS STILL ON her knees in the bracken when Dr. Bleak walked up behind her, his boots crunching dry stalks underfoot. He made no effort to soften the sound of his footsteps; he wanted her to hear him coming.

She didn't react. Her eyes were fixed on the apples. So red. So red.

"The blood should get darker as it dries," she said, voice dull. "I'll be able to tell which ones are dirty, then. I'll be able to tell which ones can be saved."

"I'm sorry, Jack," said Dr. Bleak softly. He didn't share her squeamishness—understandable, given her youth, and how much she had cared for Alexis. He allowed his eyes to travel the length of the dead girl's body, noting the deep cuts, the blood loss, the places where it looked as if the flesh had been roughly hacked away.

Second resurrections were always difficult, even when the body was in perfect condition. Alexis . . . She was so damaged that he wasn't sure he could succeed, or that she would still be herself if he did. Sometimes, the twice-dead came back wrong, unstoppable monstrosities of science.

"I will, if you ask me to," he said abruptly. "You know I will. But I will expect you to help me if it goes wrong."

Jack raised her head, slowly turning to look at her mentor. "I don't care if it goes wrong," she said. "I just . . . It can't end this way."

"Then follow the blood, Jack. If a beast has taken her heart, I'll want it intact. The more of the original flesh we have to work with, the higher our chances will be of bringing her back whole." That was true, but it was also a convenient distraction. Dr. Bleak knew enough about bodies to know that Alexis would reveal more injuries when she was lifted. The dead always did. If he could spare Jack the sight . . .

Sparing Jack had never been his goal. If the girl was to survive in the Moors, she needed to understand the world into which she had fallen. But there was preparing her for the future, and then there was being cruel. He was perfectly happy to do the former. He would never do the latter. Not if he could help it.

"Yes, sir," said Jack, and staggered to her feet, beginning to follow the drips and drops of blood across the open ground. She had spent so many years looking for the slightest hint of a mess that she had absolutely no trouble following a blood trail. She was so focused on her feet that she didn't hear Dr. Bleak grunt as he hoisted Alexis's body up and onto his shoulders, turning to carry her back toward the distant shadow of the windmill.

Jack walked, on and on, until she reached the village wall. The gate was open. The gate was often open during the high part of the day. The sound of raised voices from inside was more unusual. It sounded like people were shouting.

She stepped through the gate. The noise took on form, meaning:

"Beast!"

"Monster! *Monster!*"

"Kill the witch!"

Jack stopped where she was, frowning as she tried to make sense of the scene. What looked like half the village was standing in the square, fists raised in anger. Some of them held knives or pitchforks; one enterprising soul had even stopped to find himself a torch. She would have admired the can-do spirit, if not for the figure at the center of their mob:

Jill, a confused expression on her face, blood gluing her gauzy dress to her body, so that she looked like she had just gone for a swim. Her arms were red to the elbow; her hands were terrors, slathered so thickly in red that it was as if they were gloved.

Ms. Chopper pushed her way through the throng, shrieking, "*Demon!*" before she flung an egg at Jill. It hit the front of her dress and burst, adding a smear of yellow to the red.

Jill's eyes widened. "You can't do that," she said, in a

surprisingly childish voice. "I'm the Master's daughter. You can't do that to me. It's not *allowed*."

"You're not his daughter yet, you foolish girl," snapped a new voice—a familiar one. Both Jack and Jill turned in unconscious unison to see Mary standing at the edge of the crowd, blocking Jill from the castle. "I told you to be patient. I told you that your time would come. You just had to rush things, didn't you? I told him he did you no favors by cosseting you."

"You told me to be ruthless!" protested Jill, balling her bloody hands into fists. "You said that he needed me to be ruthless!"

"The Master feeds from the village, but he protects them as well," said Mary coldly. "You have killed without his permission and without his blessing, and you are no vampire; you had no right." She lifted her chin slightly, shifting her attention to the crowd. "The Master has revoked the protection of his household. Do with her as you will."

A low, dangerous rumble spread through the crowd. It was the sound a beast made immediately before it attacked.

Perhaps Jack could have been forgiven if she had turned her back on her bewildered sister, still dressed in her lover's blood; if she had walked away. These were extraordinary circumstances, after all, and while Jack was an extraordinary girl, she was only seventeen. It would have been understandable of her to hold a grudge, even if she might have regretted it later.

She looked at Jill and remembered a twelve-year-old in blue jeans, short hair spiking up at the back, trying to talk her into having an adventure. She remembered how afraid she'd been to leave her sister behind, even if it had meant saving them both. She remembered Gemma Lou, when they were small—so small!—telling them to look out for each other, even when they were angry, because family was a thing that could never be replaced once it was thrown away.

She remembered loving her sister, once, a long, long time ago.

The crowd had been watching Jill for signs that she was preparing to run away. They hadn't been expecting Jack to push her way into the center of their ring, grab Jill's hand, and run. Surprise was enough to get the two girls to the edge of the crowd, Jack hauling her sister in her wake, struggling not to let the blood make her lose her grip. Jill was strangely pliant, not resisting Jack's efforts to pull her along. It was like she was in shock.

Becoming a murderer and getting disowned in the same day will do that, thought Jack dizzily, and kept on running, even as the first sounds of pursuit began behind them. All that mattered now was getting away. Everything else could happen later.

12 EVERYTHING YOU NEVER WANTED

SEE THEM NOW, two girls—almost women, but still not quite, not quite—running hand in hand across the vast and unforgiving moor. One wears a skirt that tangles and tears in the bracken. The other wears trousers, sturdy shoes, and gloves to protect her from the world around her. Both of them run like their lives depend on it.

Behind them, a river of anger, split into individual human bodies, running with the unstoppable fury of the crowd. More torches have been found and lit; more pitchforks have been liberated. In a place like this, under a sky like this, torches and pitchforks are the native trappings of the enraged. They appear without being asked for, and the more there are, the deeper the danger.

The crowd glitters like a starry sky with the individual flames of their ire. The danger is very real.

Jack runs and Jill follows. Both of them are weeping, the one for her lover blooming red as a rose in the empty moorland, the other for her adoptive father, who should have been so proud of her and has instead cast her aside. If our sympathy is more for the first of them, well, we are only human; we can only look on the scene with human eyes, and judge in our own ways.

They run, and the crowd pursues, and the rising moon observes, for the tale is almost ending.

DR. BLEAK COVERED ALEXIS with an oiled tarp when he heard footsteps pounding up the garden path. He turned, expecting to see Jack, and went still when he saw not only his apprentice but her bloody sister. Behind them, the furious body of the mob was gaining ground, outlined by the glow from their torches.

"Jack," he said. "What . . . ?"

"The Master revoked his protection when the villagers saw what she'd done to Alexis," said Jack, still running, pulling Jill into the windmill. Her voice was clear and cold: if he hadn't known her so well, he might not even have realized how badly it was shaking. "They're going to kill her."

Jill gave an almighty shriek and yanked her hand out of Jack's, letting the still-slippery blood work for her. "That's not true! He loves me!" she shouted, and whirled to run.

Dr. Bleak was somehow already there, a white rag in his hand. He clapped it over her nose and mouth, holding it in place. Jill made a desperate mewling sound, like a kitten protesting bedtime, and struggled for a few seconds before her knees folded and she fell, crumpling in on herself.

"Jack, quickly," he said, slamming the door. "There isn't much time."

Obedience had been the first thing Dr. Bleak drilled into her: failure to obey could result in nasty consequences, many of which would be fatal to a child like she had been. Jack rushed to Jill's side, gathering her unconscious sister in her arms. They were the same height, but Jill felt like she weighed nothing at all, like she was nothing but dust and down.

"We have to hide her," Jack said.

"Hiding her isn't good enough," Dr. Bleak replied. He grabbed a small machine from his workbench and moved toward the windmill's back door. "You've been an excellent apprentice, Jack. Quick-fingered, sharp-witted—you were everything I could have asked for. I'm sorry this has happened."

"What do you mean, sir?" Jack's stomach clenched in on itself. She was holding her sleeping sister, covered in the blood of her dead girlfriend, and the village was marching on the windmill with torches and pitchforks. She would have said this night couldn't get any worse. Suddenly, she was terribly sure that it could.

I've seen this movie before, she thought, almost nonsensically. *But we're not the ones who made the monster. The Master did that. We're just the ones who loved her.*

Only they weren't even that, were they? Dr. Bleak would have saved Jill instead of Jack, at the beginning, because he'd seen Jack as a more logical choice for a vampire lord. That didn't mean he'd known her or cared about her. Time is the alchemy that turns compassion into love, and Jill and Dr. Bleak had never had any time. If anyone in this room loved Jill, it was Jack, and the worst of it was, she wouldn't even have had that much if it hadn't been for Alexis. Their parents had never taught them how to love each other. Any connection they'd had had been despite the adults in their lives, not because of them.

Jill had run to the Master, and while she may have been the one who'd felt deserted, she was also the one who had never looked back. She had wanted to be a vampire's child, and vampires did not love what they were compelled to share. Jack had gone with Dr. Bleak, and he had cared for her, had taken care of her and taught her, but he had never encouraged her to *love*.

That was on Alexis. Alexis, who had walked with her in the village, introducing her to people who had only been passing faces before, telling her about their lives until she could no longer fail to recognize them as people. Alexis, who had cried with her and laughed with her and felt sorry for her sister, trapped and alone in the castle. It had been Alexis who put Jill back into a human context, and it had been seeing her sister terrified and abandoned that made Jack realize she still loved her.

Without Alexis, she might have forgotten how to love. Jill would still have killed—some villager or other, someone too slow to get out of her way—but Jack would not have saved her.

The worst of it was knowing that without Alexis, whoever played her role would have been properly avenged.

"I mean they'll kill her if they find her here, and they may kill you as well; you'd offer them a rare second chance to commit the same murder." He slapped his device onto the door, embedding its pointed "feet" in the wood, and began twisting dials. "The Master had to repudiate her to keep them from marching on the castle—even vampires fear fire—but he won't forgive them for killing his daughter. He'll burn the village to the ground. It's happened before. You did well in bringing her here. The only way to save them is to save her."

"Sir, what does that have to do with—"

"The doors are the greatest scientific mystery our world has to offer," said Dr. Bleak. He grabbed a jar of captive lightning and smashed it against the doorframe. Sparks filled the air. The device whirred into sudden life, dials spinning wildly. "Did you truly think I wouldn't find a way to harness them?"

Jack's eyes went wide. "We could have gone back anytime?" she demanded, in a voice that was barely more than a squeak.

"You could have gone back," he agreed. "But you would not have been going home."

Jack looked down at her silent, bloody sister, and sighed. "No," she said. "We wouldn't have been."

"Stay away at least a year, Jack. You have to. A year is all it takes for a mob to dissipate here; grudges are counter to survival." They could hear the shouting outside now. The flames would come next. "Blood will open the door, yours or hers, as long as it's on *your* hands. Leave her behind, or kill her and bring back her body, but she can't come here as she is. Do you understand? Do *not* bring your sister back here alive."

Jack's eyes widened further, until the muscles around them ached. "You're really sending me away? But I haven't done anything wrong!"

"You've denied the mob their kill. That, here, is more than enough. Go, stay gone, and come home if you still want to. This will always, always be your home." He looked at her sadly. "I'm going to miss you, apprentice."

"Yes, sir," whispered Jack, her lower lip shaking with the effort of keeping herself from bursting into tears. This wasn't fair. This wasn't *fair*. Jill had been the one to break the rules, and now Jack was the one on the cusp of losing everything.

Dr. Bleak opened the door. What should have been a view of the back garden was instead a wooden stairway, slowly winding upward into the dark.

Jack took a deep breath. "I'll be back," she promised.

"See that you are," he said.

She stepped through the door. He closed it behind her.

13 A THOUSAND MILES OF HARDSHIP BETWEEN HERE AND HOME

DESCENDING THE STAIRS as a twelve year-old had been tiring but achievable: the work of hours, the amusement of an afternoon.

Climbing the stairs as a seventeen year old, arms full of limp, slumbering sister, proved to be rather more difficult. Jack clumped up them methodically, trying to focus on all the repetitive, seemingly meaningless tasks Dr. Bleak had assigned her over the years. She had spent afternoons sorting frogspawn by minute gradations in color, or removing all the seeds from forest-grown strawberries, or sharpening all the thorns in a blackberry hedge. Every one of those chores had been infuriating when it was going on, but had left her better suited to her job. So: what did this leave her better suited to?

Betraying the girl who loved her, who was dead in the Moors, who might stay that way now that Dr. Bleak had no apprentice to assist him.

Carrying the sister who had cost her everything away from the damnation she had earned.

Giving up everything she had finally learned she wanted.

None of those were things she *wanted* to be suited to, but they were the answer all the same. Jack shook her head to dry her tears, and kept climbing.

The stairs were still old, still solid, still dusty; here and there, she thought she saw the ghosts of her own childish footprints, going down while she was coming up. It only made sense. There had been no foundlings in the Moors since she and Jill had arrived. Maybe there would be another now, since the position was no longer filled. Every breath had to be sucking in millions of dust particles. The thought was nauseating.

They were halfway up when Jill stirred, opening her eyes and staring upward at Jack in confusion. "Jack?" she squeaked.

"Can you walk?" Jack replied brusquely.

"I . . . Where are we?"

"On the stairs." Jack stopped walking and dropped Jill, unceremoniously, on her bottom. "If you can ask questions, you can walk. I'm tired of carrying you."

Jill blinked at her, eyes going wide and shocked. "The Master—"

"Isn't *here,* Jill. We're on the stairs. You remember the stairs?" Jack waved her arms, indicating everything around them. "The Moors kicked us out. We're going back."

"No! *No!*" Jill leapt to her feet, attempting to fling herself downward.

Jack was faster than she was. She hooked an arm around her sister's waist, jerking her back up and flinging her forward. "*Yes!*" she shouted.

Jill's head hit something hard. She stopped, rubbing it, and then turned, in slow confusion, to touch the air behind her. It lifted upward, like a trapdoor—like the lid of a trunk—and revealed a small, dusty room that still smelled, ever so faintly, of Gemma Lou's perfume.

"The stairs below me have gone," said Jack's voice, dull and unsurprised. "You'd best climb out before we're pushed out."

Jill climbed out. Jack followed.

The two stood there for a long moment, stepping unconsciously closer together as they looked at the room that had belonged to their first caretaker, that had once been so familiar, before both of them had changed. The trunk slammed shut. Jill gave a little shriek and dove for it, clawing it open. Jack watched almost indifferently.

Inside the trunk was a welter of old clothing and costume jewelry, the sort of things a loving grandmother would set aside for her grandchildren to amuse themselves with. No stairway. No secret door.

Jill plunged her bloody hands into the clothes, pawing them aside. Jack let her.

"It has to be here!" Jill wailed. "It *has* to be!"

It wasn't.

When Jill finally stopped digging and bowed her head to weep, Jack put a hand on her shoulder. Jill looked up, shaking, broken. She had never learned the art of thinking for herself.

I made the right choice, and I am so sorry I left you, thought Jack. Aloud, she said, "Come."

Jill stood. When Jack took her hand, she did not resist.

The door was locked. The key Jack carried in her pocket—the key she had been carrying for five long years—fit it perfectly. It turned, and the door opened, and they were, in the strictest and most academic of senses, home.

The house they had lived in for the first twelve years of their lives (not the house they had grown up in, no; they had aged there, but they had so rarely grown) was familiar and alien at the same time, like walking through a storybook. The carpet was too soft beneath feet accustomed to stone castle floors and hard-packed earth; the air smelled of sickly-sweetness, instead of fresh flowers or honest chemicals. By the time they reached the ground floor, they were walking so close together that it didn't matter if their hands never touched; they were still conjoined.

There was a light in the dining room. They followed it and found their parents sitting at the table, along with a small, impeccably groomed boy. They stopped in the doorway, both of them looking in bemusement at this small closed circle of a family.

Serena noticed them first. She shrieked, jumping from her chair. "Chester!"

Chester turned, opening his mouth to yell at the intruders. But one of the girls was covered in blood, and they both looked as if they had been crying, and something about them . . .

"Jacqueline?" he whispered. "Jillian?"

And the two girls clung to each other and wept, as outside the rain came down like a punishment, and nothing would ever be the same.

BENEATH THE SUGAR SKY

FOR MIDORI,
WHOSE DOORWAY IS WAITING

Sugar, flour, and cinnamon won't make a house a home,
So bake your walls of gingerbread and sweeten them with bone.
Eggs and milk and whipping cream, butter in the churn,
Bake our queen a castle in the hopes that she'll return.

—CHILDREN'S CLAPPING RHYME, CONFECTION

PART I

THE EMPTY SPACES

HOME AGAIN

CHILDREN HAVE ALWAYS tumbled down rabbit holes, fallen through mirrors, been swept away by unseasonal floods or carried off by tornadoes. Children have always *traveled,* and because they are young and bright and full of contradictions, they haven't always restricted their travel to the possible. Adulthood brings limitations like gravity and linear space and the idea that bedtime is a real thing, and not an artificially imposed curfew. Adults can still tumble down rabbit holes and into enchanted wardrobes, but it happens less and less with every year they live. Maybe this is a natural consequence of living in a world where being careful is a necessary survival trait, where logic wears away the potential for something bigger and better than the obvious. Childhood melts, and flights of fancy are replaced by rules. Tornadoes kill people: they don't carry them off to magical worlds. Talking foxes are a sign of fever, not guides sent to start some grand adventure.

But children, ah, children. Children follow the foxes, and open the wardrobes, and peek beneath the bridge. Children climb the walls and fall down the wells and run the razor's edge of possibility until sometimes, just sometimes, the possible surrenders and shows them the way to go home.

Becoming the savior of a world of wonder and magic before you turn fourteen does not exactly teach caution, in most cases, and many of the children who fall through the cracks in the world where they were born will one day find themselves opening the wrong door, peering through the wrong keyhole, and standing right back where they started. For some, this is a blessing. For some, it is easy to put the adventures and the impossibilities of the past behind them, choosing sanity and predictability and the world that they were born to be a part of. For others . . .

For others, the lure of a world where they *fit* is too great to escape, and they will spend the rest of their lives rattling at windows and peering at locks, trying to find the way home. Trying to find the one perfect door that can take them there, despite everything, despite the unlikeliness of it all.

They can be hard for their families to understand, those returned, used-up miracle children. They sound like liars to people who have never had a doorway of their own. They sound like dreamers. They sound . . . unwell, to the charitable, and simply sick to the cruel. Something must be done.

Something like admission to Eleanor West's Home for Wayward Children, a school for those who have gone, and come back, and hope to go again, when the wind is right, when the stars are bright, when the world remembers what it is to have mercy on the longing and the lost. There, they can be among their peers, if they can truly be said to have peers: they can be with people who understand what it is to have the door locked between themselves and home. The rules of the school are simple. Heal. Hope. And if you can, find your way back where you belong.

No solicitation. No visitors.

No quests.

1 ONE DOOR OPENS, ANOTHER IS BLOWN OFF ITS HINGES

AUTUMN HAD COME TO Eleanor West's Home for Wayward Children in the usual way, with changing leaves and browning grass and the constant smell of impending rain hanging heavy in the air, a seasonal promise yet to be fulfilled. The blackberry briars at the back of the field grew rich with fruit, and several students spent their afternoons with buckets in their hands, turning their fingers purple and soothing their own furious hearts.

Kade checked the seals on the windows one by one, running putty along the places where the moisture seemed likely to find a way inside, one eye on the library and the other on the sky.

Angela watched the sky too, waiting for a rainbow, ordinary shoes on her feet and enchanted shoes slung over her shoulder, laces tied in a careful, complicated knot. If the light and the water came together *just so,* if the rainbow touched down where she could reach it, she would be gone, off and running, running, running all the way home.

Christopher, whose door would open—if it ever opened for him again; if he ever got to find his way back home—on the Day of the Dead, sat in the grove of trees behind the house, playing ever more elaborate songs on his bone flute, trying to prepare for the moment of disappointment when the door failed to appear or of overwhelming elation when the Skeleton Girl called him back where he belonged.

So it was all across the school, each of the students preparing for the change of seasons in whatever way seemed the most appropriate, the most comforting, the most likely to get them through the winter. Girls who had gone to worlds defined by summer locked themselves in their rooms and wept, staring at the specter of another six months trapped in this homeland that had somehow, between one moment and the next, become a prison; others, whose worlds were places of eternal snow, of warm furs and hot fires and sweet mulled wine, rejoiced, seeing their own opportunity to find the way back opening like a flower in front of them.

Eleanor West herself, a spry ninety-seven-year-old who could pass for someone in her late sixties, and often did when she had to interact with people from outside the school, walked the halls with a carpenter's eye, watching the walls for signs of sagging, watching the ceilings for signs of rot. It was necessary to have contractors in every few years to keep things solid. She hated the disruption. The children disliked pretending to be ordinary delinquents, sent away by their parents for starting fires or breaking windows, when really they had been sent away for slaying dragons and refusing to say that they hadn't. The lies seemed petty and small, and she couldn't blame them for feeling that way, although she rather thought they would change their tune if she deferred the maintenance and someone got drywall dropped on their head.

Balancing the needs of her students with the needs of the

school itself was tiresome, and she yearned for the return to Nonsense and the carelessness she knew waited somewhere up ahead of her, in the golden country of the future. Like the children she called to her care, Eleanor West had been trying to go home for as long as she could remember. Unlike most of them, her struggle had been measured in decades, not months . . . and unlike most of them, she had watched dozens of travelers find their way back home while she was left standing in place, unable to follow, unable to do anything but weep.

She sometimes thought that might be the one piece of true magic this world possessed: so many children had found their way home while in her care, and yet not a single parent had accused her of wrongdoing, or attempted to launch an investigation into the disappearance of their beloved offspring. She knew their parents had loved them; she had listened to fathers weeping and held the hands of mothers who stared stoically into the shadows, unable to move, unable to process the size of their grief. But none of them had called her a killer, or demanded her school close its doors. They knew. On some level, they knew, and had known long before she came to them with the admission papers in her hands, that their children had only come back to them long enough to say goodbye.

One of the hallway doors opened, and a girl emerged, attention focused on her phone. Eleanor stopped. Collisions were unpleasant things, and should be avoided when possible. The girl turned toward her, still reading the display.

Eleanor tapped the point of her cane against the ground. The girl stopped and looked up, cheeks coloring blotchy red as she finally realized she was not alone.

"Er," she said. "Good morning, Miss West."

"Good morning, Cora," said Eleanor. "And please, it's Eleanor, if you don't mind. I may be old and getting older, but I was never a miss. More of a hit, in the places I usually roved."

Cora looked confused. That wasn't uncommon, with new students. They were still adapting to the idea of a place where people would believe them, where saying impossible things would earn them a shrug and a comment about something equally impossible, rather than a taunt or an accusation of insanity.

"Yes, ma'am," said Cora finally.

Eleanor swallowed a sigh. Cora would come around. If she didn't do it on her own, Kade would have a talk with her. He had become Eleanor's second-in-command since Lundy's death, and Eleanor would have felt bad about that—he was still only a boy, should still have been running in meadows and climbing trees, not filling out paperwork and designing curriculums—but Kade was a special case, and she couldn't deny needing the help. He would run this school one day. Better for him to start preparing now.

"How are you settling in, dear?" she asked.

Cora brightened. It was remarkable how pretty she became when she stopped looking dour and confused and a little lost. She was a short, round girl, made entirely of curves: the soft slope of breasts and belly, the gentle thickness of upper arms and thighs, the surprising delicacy of wrists and ankles. Her eyes were very blue, and her hair, long and once naturally brown, like the grass out in the yard, was now a dozen shades of green and blue, like some sort of tropical fish.

(It would turn brown again if she stayed here long enough, if she stayed dry. Eleanor had met other children who had traveled through Cora's door, and she knew, although she would never tell Cora, that on the day when the green and blue began to fade—whether that happened tomorrow or in a year—that would be when the door would be locked forever, and Cora would be shipwrecked forever on this now-foreign shore.)

"Everyone's been really nice," she said. "Kade says he knows where my world falls on the compass, and he's going to help me research other people who have gone there. Um, and Angela introduced me to all the other girls, and a few of them went to water worlds too, so we have lots to talk about."

"That's wonderful," said Eleanor, and meant it. "If there's anything you need, you'll let me know, won't you? I want all my students to be happy."

"Yes, ma'am," said Cora, the brightness fading. She bit her lip as she tucked her phone into her pocket, and said, "I have to go. Um, Nadya and I are going to the pond."

"Remind her to take a jacket, please. She gets cold easily." Eleanor stepped to the side, letting Cora hurry away. She couldn't keep up with the students anymore, and she supposed that was a good thing; the sooner she wore out, the sooner she could go home.

But oh, she was tired of getting old.

CORA HURRIED DOWN the stairs, shoulders hunched slightly inward, waiting for a sneer or insult that never came. In the six weeks since she had arrived at the school, no one had called her "fat" like it was another word for "monster," not even once. Kade, who served as the unofficial tailor and had a selection of clothing left behind by departing students that stretched back decades, had looked her up and down and said a number that had made her want to die a little bit inside, until she'd realized there was no judgement in his tone: he just wanted her clothes to fit.

The other students teased and fought and called each other names, but those names were always about things they'd done or places they'd gone, not about who they *were*. Nadya was missing her right arm at the elbow, and no one called her "gimp" or "cripple" or any of the other things Cora *knew* she would have been called if she'd gone to Cora's old school. It was like they had all learned to be a little kinder, or at least a little more careful about what they based their judgements on.

Cora had been fat her entire life. She had been a fat baby, and a fat toddler in swim classes, and a fat child in elementary school. Day after day, she had learned that "fat" was another way to say "worthless, ugly, waste of space, unwanted, disgusting." She had started to believe them by the time she was in third grade, because what else was she supposed to do?

Then she had fallen into the Trenches (don't think about how she got there don't think about how she might get back *don't do it*), and suddenly she'd been beautiful. Suddenly she'd been strong, insulated against the bitter chill of the water, able to dive deeper and swim further than anyone else in the school. Suddenly she'd been a hero, brave and bright and beloved. And on the day when she'd been sucked into that whirlpool and dropped into her own backyard, on dry land again, no gills in her neck or fins on her feet, she had wanted to die. She had thought she could never be beautiful again.

Maybe here, though . . . maybe here she could be. Maybe here she was allowed. Everyone else was fighting toward their own sense of safety, of beauty, of belonging. Maybe she could do that, too.

Nadya was waiting on the porch, examining the nails of her hand with the calm intensity of a dam getting ready to break. She looked up at the sound of the closing door. "You're late." The ghost of a Russian accent lingered in her words and wrapped itself like waterweeds around her vowels, pale and thin as tissue paper.

"Miss West was in the hall outside my room." Cora shook her head. "I didn't think she'd be there. She's so *quiet* for being so *old*."

"She's older than she looks," said Nadya. "Kade says she's almost a hundred."

Cora frowned. "That doesn't make sense."

"Says the girl whose hair grows in green and blue all over," said Nadya. "It's a miracle your parents got you here before the beauty companies snatched you up to try to figure out the mystery of the girl with the seaweed pubes."

"Hey!" yelped Cora.

Nadya laughed and started down the porch, taking the steps two at a time, like she didn't trust them to get her where she needed to go. "I only tell the truth, because I love you, and because one day you're going to be on the front of the supermarket magazines. Right next to Tom Cruise and the Scientology aliens."

"Only because you're going to turn me in," said Cora. "Miss West told me to remind you to bring a coat."

"Miss West can bring me a coat herself if she wants me to have one so bad," said Nadya. "I don't get cold."

"No, but you *catch* colds all the time, and I guess she's tired of listening to you hack up a lung."

Nadya waved her hand dismissively. "We must suffer for our chance to return home. Now come, come, hurry. Those turtles aren't going to tip themselves."

Cora shook her head, and hurried.

Nadya was one of the school's long-timers: five years so far, from the age of eleven to the age of sixteen. There had been no sign in those five years of her doorway appearing, or of her asking her adoptive parents to take her home. That was unusual. Everyone knew that parents could withdraw their children at any time; that all Nadya had to do was ask and she'd be able to return to the life she'd lived before . . . well, before everything.

According to everyone Cora had spoken to, most students chose to go back to their old lives after four years had passed without a doorway.

"That's when they give up," Kade had said, expression turning sad. "That's when they say, 'I can't live for a world that doesn't want me, so I guess I'd better learn to live in the world I have.' "

Not Nadya. She didn't belong to any clique or social circle, didn't have many close friends—or seem to want them—but she didn't leave, either. She went from classroom to turtle pond, from bathtub to bed, and she kept her hair perpetually wet, no matter how many colds she caught, and she never stopped watching the water for the bubbles that would mark her way back to Belyyreka, the Drowned World and the Land Beneath the Lake.

Nadya had walked up to Cora on her first day at the school, when she was standing frozen in the door of the dining hall, terrified to eat—what if they called her names?—and terrified to turn and run away—what if they made fun of her behind her back?

"You, new girl," she had said. "Angela tells me you were a mermaid. Is that so?"

Cora had sputtered and stammered and somehow signaled her agreement. Nadya had smirked and taken Cora's arm in hers.

"Good," she'd said. "I've been ordered to make more friends, and you seem to fit the bill. We damp girls have to stick together."

In the weeks since then, Nadya had been the best of friends and the worst of friends, prone to bursting into Cora's room without knocking, pestering her roommate and trying to convince Miss West to reassign one or both of them so they could room together. Miss West kept refusing, on the grounds that no one else in the school would be able to find a towel if the two girls who took the most baths were in the same place to egg each other on.

Cora had never had a friend like Nadya before. She thought she liked it. It was hard to say: the novelty of it all was still too overwhelming.

The turtle pond was a flat silver disk in the field, burnished by the sunlight, surface broken by the flat disks of the turtles themselves, sailing off to whatever strange turtle errands they had in the months before their hibernation. Nadya grabbed a stick off the ground and took off running, leaving Cora to trail behind her like a faithful balloon.

"Turtles!" Nadya howled. "Your queen returns!"

She didn't stop when she reached the edge of the pond, but plunged gleefully onward, splashing into the shallows, breaking the perfect smoothness of the surface. Cora stopped a few feet back from the water. She preferred the ocean, preferred saltwater and the slight sting of the waves against her skin. Fresh water wasn't enough.

"Come back, turtles!" shouted Nadya. "Come back and let me love you!"

That was when the girl fell out of the sky and landed in the middle of the turtle pond with an enormous splash, sending turtles skyward, and drenching both Cora and Nadya in a wave of muddy pond water.

2 GRAVITY HAPPENS TO THE BEST OF US

THE GIRL IN THE pond rose up sputtering, with algae in her hair and a very confused turtle snagged in the complicated draperies of her dress, which seemed to be the result of someone deciding to hybridize a ball gown with a wedding cake, after dycing both of them electric pink. It also seemed to be dissolving, running down her arms in streaks, coming apart at the seams. She was going to be naked soon.

The girl in the pond didn't seem to notice, or maybe she just didn't care. She wiped water and dissolving dress out of her eyes, flicking them to the side, and cast wildly about until she spotted Cora and Nadya standing on the shore, mouths open, gaping at her.

"You!" she yelled, pointing in their direction. "Take me to your leader!"

Cora's mouth shut with a snap. Nadya continued to gawk. Both of them had traveled to places where the rules were different—Cora to a world of beautiful Reason, Nadya to a world of impeccable Logic. None of this had prepared them for women who dropped out of the sky in a shower of turtles and started yelling, especially not here, in a world they both thought of as tragically predictable and dull.

Cora recovered first. "Do you mean Miss Eleanor?" she asked. Relief followed the question. Yes. The girl—she looked to be about seventeen—would want to talk to Miss Eleanor. Maybe she was a new student, and this was how admissions worked mid-term.

"No," said the girl sullenly, and crossed her arms, dislodging the turtle on her shoulder. It fell back to the pond with a resounding *plop*. "I mean my mother. She's in charge at home, so she must be in charge here. It's only"—her lip curled, and she spat out her next word like it tasted bad—"*logical*."

"What's your mother's name?" asked Cora.

"Onishi Sumi," said the girl.

Nadya finally shook off her shock. "That's not possible," she said, glaring at the girl. "Sumi's dead."

The girl stared at Nadya. The girl bent, reaching into the pond, and came up with a turtle, which she hurled as hard as she could at Nadya's head. Nadya ducked. The girl's dress, finally chewed to pieces by the water, fell off entirely, leaving her naked and covered with a pinkish slime. Cora put her hand over her eyes.

Maybe leaving her room today hadn't been the best idea after all.

MOST PEOPLE ASSUMED, upon meeting Cora, that being fat also meant she was lazy, or at least that she was unhealthy. It was true she had to wrap her knees and ankles before she did any heavy exercise—a few strips of tape now could save her from a lot of aching later—but that was as far as that assumption went. She had always been a runner. When she'd been little, her mother hadn't worried about her weight, because no one who watched Cora race around the yard could possibly believe there was anything wrong with her. She was chubby because she was preparing for a growth spurt, that was all.

The growth spurt, when it had come, hadn't been enough to consume Cora's reserves, but still she ran. She ran with the sort of speed that people thought should be reserved for girls like Nadya, girls who could cut through the wind like knives, instead of being borne along like living clouds, large and soft and swift.

She reached the front steps with feet pounding and arms pumping, so consumed by the act of running that she wasn't exactly looking where she was going, and slammed straight into Christopher, sending both of them sprawling. She yelped. Christopher shouted. They landed in a tangle of limbs at the base of the porch, him mostly under her.

"Uh," said Christopher.

"Ohfuck!" The exclamation came out as a single word, glued together by stress and terror. This was it: this was the moment where she stopped being the new student, and became the clumsy fat girl. She pushed herself away from him as fast as she could, overbalancing in the process, so that she rolled away rather than getting back to her feet. When she was far enough that they were no longer in physical contact, she shoved herself up onto her hands and knees, looking warily back at him. He was going to yell, and then she was going to cry, and meanwhile Nadya would be alone with the stranger who was asking for a dead person. And this day had started so *well*.

Christopher was staring back at her, looking equally wary, looking equally *wounded*. As she watched, he picked his bone flute out of the dust and said, in a hurt tone, "It's not contagious, you know."

"What's not contagious?"

"Going to a world that wasn't all unicorns and rainbows. It's not catching. Touching me doesn't change where you went."

Cora's cheeks flared red. "Oh, no!" she said, hands fluttering in front of her like captive parrotfish, trying to escape. "I didn't—I wasn't—I mean, I—"

"It's okay." Christopher stood. He was tall and lean, with brown skin and black hair, and a small, skull-shaped pin on his left lapel. He always wore a jacket, partially for the pockets, and partially for the readiness to run. Most of them were like that. They always had their shoes, their scissors, whatever talisman they wanted to have to hand when their doorways reappeared and they had to make the choice to stay or go. "You're not the first."

"I thought you were going to be mad at me for running into you and call me fat," blurted Cora.

Christopher's eyebrows rose. "I . . . okay, not what I expected. I, um. Not sure what to say to that."

"I *know* I'm fat, but it's all in how people say it," said Cora, hands finally drifting back to rest. "I thought you'd say it the bad way."

"I get it," said Christopher. "I'm Mexican American. It was gross, the number of people at my old school who thought it was funny to call me an anchor baby, or to ask, all fake concerned, if my parents were legal. It got to where I didn't want to say 'Mexican,' because it sounded like an insult in their mouths when it was really my culture, and my heritage, and my family. So I get it. I don't like it, but that's not your fault."

"Oh, good," said Cora, sighing her relief. Then she wrinkled her nose and said, "I have to go. I have to find Miss Eleanor."

"Is that why you were in such a hurry?"

"Uh-huh." She nodded quickly. "There's a strange girl in the turtle pond and she says she's the daughter of someone I've never heard of, but who Nadya says is dead, so I think we need an adult."

"If you need an adult, you should be looking for Kade, not Eleanor," said Christopher. He started toward the door. "Who's the dead person?"

"Someone named Sumi."

Christopher's fingers clamped down hard on his bone flute. "Walk faster," he said, and Cora did, following him up the steps and into the school.

The halls were cool and empty. There were no classes in session; the other students would be scattered across the campus, chatting in the kitchen, sleeping in their rooms. For a place that could explode with noise and life under the right circumstances, it was often surprisingly quiet.

"Sumi was a student before you got here," said Christopher. "She went to a world called Confection, where she pissed off the Countess of Candy Floss and got herself kicked out as a political exile."

"Did her parents take her away?"

"She was murdered."

Cora nodded solemnly. She had heard about the murders, about the girl named Jill who had decided the way to open her own door home was to cut away the doors of as many others as she deemed necessary. There was a certain amount of horror in those tales, and also a certain amount of shameful understanding. Many of them—not all, not even most, but many—would have done the same if they'd had the necessary skills. Some people even seemed to possess a certain grudging respect for what Jill had done. Sure, she'd killed people. In the end, it had been enough to take her home.

"The person who killed her wasn't a friend of mine, not really, but her sister kind of was. We were . . . Jack and Jill went to a world called the Moors, which was sort of horror movie–y, from the way they described it. A lot of people lumped me in with them, because of Mariposa."

"That's the world you went to?"

Christopher nodded. "Eleanor still can't decide whether it was a Fairyland or an Underworld or something new and in-between. That's why people shouldn't get too hung up on labels. Sometimes I think that's part of what we do wrong. We try to make things make sense, even when they're never going to."

Cora didn't say anything.

The hall ended at the closed door to Eleanor's studio. Christopher rapped his knuckles twice against the wood, then opened it without waiting to be asked.

Eleanor was inside, a paintbrush in her hand, layering oil paint onto a canvas that looked like it had already been subjected to more than a few layers. Kade was there as well, sitting in the window seat, a coffee mug cupped between his hands. Both of them looked at the open door, Eleanor with delight, Kade with slow confusion.

"Cora!" she said. "Have you come to paint with me, dear?

And Christopher. It's wonderful to see you making friends, after everything."

Christopher grimaced. "Yes, Miss Eleanor," he said. "We're not actually here for an art class. There's someone in the turtle pond."

"Is it Nadya?" asked Kade.

"Not this time," said Cora. "She fell out of the sky, and she has black hair, and her dress fell apart when it got wet, and she says—" She stopped, reaching a degree of impossibility past which even she, who had once fought the Serpent of Frozen Tears, could not proceed.

Luckily, Christopher had no such boundaries. "She says Sumi's her mother. Can someone please come to the turtle pond and figure out what the hell is going on?"

Kade sat up straight. "I'll go," he said.

"Go," said Eleanor. "I'll clean up here. Bring her to the office when you're finished."

Kade nodded and slid off his seat, leaving his mug behind as he hurried to collect Cora and Christopher and usher them both out the door. Eleanor watched the three of them go, silent. When the door was closed behind them, she put her head down in her hands.

Sumi's world, Confection, had been a Nonsense world, untethered to the normal laws that governed the order of things. There had been a prophecy of some sort, saying that Sumi would one day return, and overthrow the armies of the Queen of Cakes, establishing her own benevolent monarchy in its place. It wasn't unreasonable to think that the future had felt comfortable going about its business, once there was a prophecy. And now Sumi was dead, and the future, whatever it had once been, was falling apart.

Everything did, if left long enough to its own devices. Futures, pasts, it didn't matter. Everything fell apart.

3 DEAD WOMAN'S DAUGHTER

THE STRANGER WAS NO longer in the turtle pond. That was an improvement, of a sort, but only of a sort: without the water and the turtles to drape her, the stranger had no clothes remaining at all. She was standing naked in the mud, arms crossed, glowering at Nadya, who was trying to look at anything but her.

Christopher whistled as he came over the rise, walking to the left of Kade. Cora, who was on Kade's right, blushed red and turned her eyes away.

"She looks sort of like Sumi, if Sumi were older, and taller, and hotter," said Christopher. "Did someone place an order with a company that drops beautiful Japanese girls from the sky? Do they take special requests?"

"The only kind of girl you'd want dropped on you comes from a medical supply company," said Kade.

Christopher laughed. Cora blushed even harder.

Nadya, who had spotted the three of them, was waving her arms frantically over her head, signaling her distress. In case this wasn't enough, she shouted, "Over here! Next to the naked lady!"

"A cake's a cake, whether or not it's been frosted," said the stranger primly.

"You are not a cake, you are a *human being,* and I can see your *vagina,*" snapped Nadya.

The stranger shrugged. "It's a nice one. I'm not ashamed of it."

Kade walked a little faster.

Once he was close enough to speak without needing to shout, he said, "Hello. I'm Kade West. I'm the assistant headmaster here at Eleanor West's Home for Wayward Children. Can I help you?"

The naked girl swung around to face him, dropping her arms and beginning to gesticulate wildly. The fact that she was now talking to two boys, in addition to the two girls who had been there when she fell out of the sky, didn't appear to trouble her at all.

"I'm looking for my *mother,*" she said loudly. "She was here, and now she's not, and I have a problem, so find her and give her back *right now,* because I need her more than you do!"

"Slow down," said Kade, and because he made the request sound so reasonable, the stranger stopped shouting and simply looked at him, blinking wide and slightly bewildered eyes. "Let's start with something easy. What's your name?"

"Onishi Rini," said the stranger—said Rini. She really did look remarkably like Sumi, if Sumi had been allowed to live long enough to finish working her way through the kinks and dead-end alleys of puberty, growing tall and lithe and high-breasted. Only her eyes were different. They were a shocking shade of orange, for the most part, with a thin ring of white around the pupils and a thin ring of yellow around the outside of the irises.

She had candy corn eyes. Kade looked at them and knew, without question, without doubt, that she was Sumi's daughter, that in some future, some impossible, broken future, Sumi had been able to make it home to her candy corn farmer. That somewhere, somehow, Sumi had been happy, until somehow her past self had been murdered, and everything had come tumbling down.

Sometimes living on the outskirts of Nonsense simply wasn't fair.

"I'm Kade," he said. "These are my friends, Christopher, Cora, and Nadya."

"I'm not his friend," said Nadya. "I'm a Drowned Girl." She bared her teeth in mock-threat.

Kade ignored her. "It's nice to meet you, Rini. I just wish it were under slightly better circumstances. Will you come back to the house with me? I manage the school wardrobe. I can find you something to wear."

"Why?" asked Rini peevishly. "Are you insulted by my vagina too? Do people in this world not have them?"

"Many people do, and there's nothing wrong with them, and also that's your vulva, but it's considered a little rude to run around showing your genitals to people who haven't asked," said Kade. "Eleanor is in the house, and once you're dressed, we can sit down and talk."

"I don't have time to talk," said Rini. "I need my mother. Please, where is she?"

"Rini—"

"You don't *understand*!" Rini's voice was an anguished howl. She held out her left hand. "I don't have time!"

"Huh," said Nadya.

That was the only thing any of them said. The rest were busy looking at Rini's left hand, with its two missing fingers. They hadn't been cut off: there was no scar tissue. She hadn't been born that way: the place where her fingers should have been was too obviously empty, like a hole in the world. They were simply gone, fading from existence as her own future caught up to the idea that somehow, someway, her mother had never been able to conceive her, and so she had never been born.

Rini lowered her hand. "Please," she repeated.

"This changes things," said Kade. "Come on."

RINI WAS TALL and thin, but many of the students were tall and thin: too many, as far as Cora was concerned. She didn't like the idea that people who already had socially acceptable bodies would get the adventures, too. She knew it was a small and petty thought, one she shouldn't have had in the first place, much less indulged, but she couldn't stop herself from feeling how she felt. Rini had the fashion sense of a drunken mockingbird, attracted to the brightly colored and the shiny, and that, too, was not uncommon among the students, many of whom had traveled to worlds where the idea of subtlety was ignored in favor of the much more entertaining idea of hurting people's eyes.

In the end, Kade had coaxed her into a rainbow sundress, dyed so that the colors melded into each other like a scoop of sherbet in the sun. He had given her slippers for her feet, both in the same style and size, but dyed differently, so that one was poppy orange and the other turquoise blue. He had given her ribbons to tie in her hair, and now they were sitting, the five of them, in Eleanor's parlor.

Eleanor sat behind her desk, hands laced tight together, like a child about to undertake her evening prayers.

"—and that's why she can't be dead," concluded Rini. Her story had been long and rambling and at times nonsensical, full of political coups and popcorn-ball fights, which were like snowball fights, only stickier. She looked around at the rest of them, expression somewhere between triumphant and hopeful. She had made her case, laid it out in front of them one piece at a time, and she was ready for her reward. "So please, can we go and tell her to stop? I need to exist. It's important."

"I'm so sorry, dear, but death doesn't work that way in this world," said Eleanor. Each word seemed to pain her, driving her shoulders deeper and deeper into their slump. "This is a logical world. Actions have consequences here. Dead is dead, and buried is buried."

Rini frowned. "That's silly and it's stupid and *I'm* not from a logical world, and neither is my mother, so that shouldn't matter for us. I need her back. I need to be born. It's important. *I'm* important."

"Everyone is important," said Eleanor.

Rini looked around at the rest of them. "Please," she pleaded. "Please, make the silly old woman stop being awful, and give me back my mother."

"Don't call my aunt a silly old woman," said Kade.

"It's all right, dear," said Eleanor. "I *am* a silly old woman, and I've been called worse with less reason. I can't fix this. I wish I could."

Cora, who had been frowning more and more since Rini had finished her story, looked up, looked at Rini, and asked, "How did you get here?"

"I just told you," said Rini. "My mother and father had sex before bringing in the candy corn harvest, the year after she defeated the Queen of Cakes at the Raspberry Bridge. You do have sex here, don't you? Or do people in a logical world reproduce by budding? Is that why you were so upset by my vagina?"

Kade put his hand over his face.

"Um," said Cora, cheeks flaring red. "Yes, we, uh, we have sex, and can we please stop saying 'vagina' so much, but I meant how did you get *here*. How did you wind up in our turtle pond?"

"Oh!" Rini held up her right hand, the one that still had all its fingers and had yet to start fading from existence. There was a bracelet clasped around her wrist, the sort of thing a child might wear, beads on a piece of string tied tight to keep her from losing it. "The Fondant Wizard gave me a way for back-and-forth, so I could get here and find Mom and tell her to stop doing whatever she was doing that was making me never have been born. I'm supposed to be sneaking through the Treacle Bogs right now, you know, to look for threats along our western border. Important stuff. So if we could hurry up, that would be amazing."

Silence followed her words, silence like a bowstring, stretched tight and ready to snap. Slowly, Rini lowered her arm and looked around. Everyone was staring at her. Christopher was swallowing hard, the muscles in his throat jumping wildly. There were tears in Nadya's eyes.

"What?" she asked.

"Why did you leave her here?" Kade's voice was suddenly low and dangerous. He stood, stalking toward Rini. "When Sumi got to the school, she was a *mess*. I thought we were gonna lose her. I thought she was going to slice herself open to try to get the candy out of her veins, and now here you are, and you have something that means you can just . . . just come here and go back again, like it's nothing. Like the doors don't even matter. Why did you leave her here? Why didn't someone come and get her before it was too late?"

Rini shied back, away from him, glancing frantically to Christopher and Nadya for support. Nadya looked away. Christopher shook his head.

"I didn't know!" she cried. "Mom always said she'd loved it here at your school, that she made friends and learned stuff and got her head straight enough to know that she wanted it to be crooked! She never asked me to come get her sooner!"

"If she had, you might never have been born," said Eleanor. She cleared her throat before saying, a little more loudly, "Dearest, please don't torture our guest. Done is done and past is past, and while we're looking for a way to change that, I think we should focus on what can still be done, and what hasn't already been omitted."

"Can those beads take us anywhere?" asked Christopher. "Any world at all?"

"Sure," said Rini. "Anywhere there's sugar."

His fingers played across the surface of his bone flute, coaxing out the ghosts of notes. No one could hear them, but that didn't matter. He knew that they were there.

"I think I know a way to fix this," he said.

THE BASEMENT ROOM that had belonged to Jack and Jill, before they returned to the Moors, and to Nancy, before she returned to the Halls of the Dead, belonged to Christopher now. He viewed it with a certain superstitious hope, like the fact that its last three occupants had been able to find their doors meant that he would absolutely find his own. Magical thinking might seem like nonsense to some people, but he had danced with skeletons by the light of a marigold moon, he had kissed the glimmering skull of a girl with no lips and loved her as he had never loved anything or anyone in his life, and he thought he'd earned a certain amount of nonsense, as long as it helped him get by.

He led the others across the room to the velvet curtain that hung across a rack of metal shelves.

"Jack didn't take anything with her when she left," he said. "I mean, nothing except Jill. Her arms were sort of full." Jack had carried Jill over the threshold like a bride on her wedding night, walking back into the unending wasteland that was their shared perfection, and she hadn't looked back, not once. Sometimes Christopher still dreamt that he had followed her, running away to a world that would never have made him happy, but which might have made him slightly less miserable than this one.

"So?" asked Nadya. "Jack and Jill were creepy fish."

"So I have all her things, and all *Jill's* things, and Jill was building the perfect girl." He pulled the curtain aside, revealing a dozen jars filled with amber liquid and . . . other things. Parts of people that had no business being viewed in isolation.

Christopher leaned up onto his toes, taking a gallon jar down from one of the higher shelves. A pair of hands floated inside, preserved like pale starfish, fingers spread in eternal surprise.

Kade's voice was frosty. "We buried those," he said.

"I know," said Christopher. "But I started having bad dreams after Sumi's family took her away to bury her. Dreams about her skeleton being incomplete forever. So I . . . well, I got a shovel, and I got her hands. I dug up her hands. That way, if she ever came back, I could put her together again. She wouldn't have to be broken forever."

Kade stared at him. "Christopher, are you honestly telling me you've been sharing a bedroom with Sumi's *severed hands* this whole time? Because boy, that ain't normal." His Oklahoma accent, always stronger when he was upset, was thick as honey.

Rini, on the other hand, didn't appear disturbed in the slightest. She was looking at the jar with wide, interested eyes. "Those are my mother's hands?" she asked.

"Yes," said Christopher. He held the jar carefully as he turned to the others. "If we know where Sumi is buried, I can put her back together. I mean, I can pipe her out of the grave and give her back her hands."

"What?" asked Cora.

"Ew," said Nadya.

"Skeletons don't usually have children," said Kade. "What are you suggestin'?"

Christopher took a deep breath. "I'm suggesting we get Sumi out of the grave, and then we go and find Nancy. She's in the Halls of the Dead, right? She's got to know where the ghosts go. Maybe she can tell us where Sumi went, and we can . . . put her back together."

Silence fell again, speculative this time. Finally, Eleanor smiled.

"That makes no sense at all," she said. "That means it may well work. Go, my darlings, and bring your lost and shattered sister home."

PART II

INTO THE HALLS OF THE DEAD

4 WHAT WE BURY IS NOT LOST, ONLY SET ASIDE

OF THE FIVE of them who were going on this journey—Nadya and Cora, Rini, Christopher and Kade—only Kade knew how to drive, and so he was the one stuck behind the wheel of the school minivan, eyes on the road and prayers on his lips as he tried to focus on getting them where they were going in one piece.

Rini had never been in a car before, and kept unfastening her seatbelt because she didn't like the way it pinched. Nadya claimed she could only ride with all the windows down, while Cora didn't like being cold, and kept turning the heat up. Christopher, meanwhile, insisted on turning the volume on the radio up as far as it would go, which didn't make a damn bit of sense, since usually the songs he played were inaudible to anyone who wasn't dead.

It was going to be a miracle if they got where they were going without getting themselves killed. Kade supposed that joining Sumi in whatever afterlife she was in—presumably one that catered to teenagers who'd gone through impossible doors—would be a bad thing. All of them winding up dead would upset

Eleanor, as well as leaving the school without a van. Kade ground his teeth and focused on the road.

This would have been easier if they'd been driving during the day. Sumi's remaining family lived six hours from the school grounds, and her body was interred at a local cemetery. That was good. Grave robbing was still viewed as socially inappropriate, and doing it when the sun was up was generally viewed as unwise. Which meant it was after midnight and they were on the road, and everything about this little adventure was a terrible idea from start to finish.

Nadya leaned over the seat to ask, "Are we there yet?"

"Why are you even here?" Kade countered. "You can't pipe the dead out of the ground, you can't drive, and we'd be a lot more comfortable with only three people in the backseat."

"I got doused in turtle water," said Nadya. "That means I get to come."

Kade sighed. "I want to argue, but I'm too damn tired. Can you at least stay in your seat? We get pulled over, we're going to have one hell of a time explaining the severed hands, or why Christopher keeps a human ulna in his pocket."

"Just tell them we're on a quest," said Nadya.

"Mmm," said Kade noncommittally.

"So are we there yet?"

"Almost. We are almost there." The cemetery was another five miles down the road. He'd looked it up on Google Maps. There was a convenient copse of trees about a quarter of a mile away. They could stow the van there while they went about the business of desecrating Sumi's grave.

Kade wasn't religious—hadn't been since he'd come back from Prism, forced into a body that was too young and too small and too dressed in frilly, girlish clothes by parents who refused to understand that they had a son and not a daughter—but he'd been to church often enough when he was little to be faintly worried that they were all going to wind up getting smote for crimes against God.

"Not the way I wanted to die," he muttered, and pulled off the road, driving toward the trees.

"I want to die in a bed of marigolds, with butterflies hanging over me in a living canopy and the Skeleton Girl holding our marriage knife in her hand," said Christopher.

"What?" said Kade.

"Nothing," said Christopher.

Kade rolled slowly to a stop under a spreading oak, hopefully out of sight of the road, and parked. "All right, we're here. Everybody out."

He didn't have to tell Cora twice. She had the door open before he had finished speaking, practically tumbling out into the grass. Riding in backseats always made her feel huge and worthless, taking up more space than she had any right to. The only reason she'd been able to stand it was that Nadya had been crammed into the middle, leaving Rini, still a virtual stranger, on the other side of the car. If Cora had been told she'd have to spend the entire drive pressed against someone she didn't know, she would probably have skipped having an adventure in favor of hiding in her room.

The others got out more sedately, even Rini, who turned in a slow circle, eyes turned toward the sky and jaw gone slack.

"What are those?" she asked, jabbing a finger at the distant streak of the Milky Way.

"Stars, stupid," said Nadya.

“I’m not stupid, I just don’t know stuff,” said Rini. “How do they stay up?”

“They’re very far away,” said Kade. “Don’t you have stars in Confection?”

“No,” said Rini. “There’s a moon—it’s made of buttercream frosting, very sticky, not good for picnicking on—and there’s a sun, and a long time ago, the First Confectioner threw handfuls of candy into the sky, where it stuck really high, but it’s still candy. You can see the stripes on the humbugs and the sugar speckles on the gumdrops.”

“Huh,” said Kade. He looked to Christopher. “We need a shovel?”

“Not if she’s willing to dance.” Christopher’s fingers played over his bone flute, sketching anxious arpeggios, outlining the tune he would play for Sumi. “If she’s willing to dance, she’d move heaven and earth to come to me.”

“Then lead the way, piper.”

Christopher nodded and raised his flute to his mouth, taking a deep breath before he began to play. There was no sound. There was never any sound when Christopher played the flute, not as far as the living were concerned. There was only the idea of sound, the sketchy outline of the place where it should have been, sliced out of the air like a piece of chocolate pie.

No one knew how far he could be from the dead and still call them out of the grave, and they weren’t sure exactly where in the cemetery Sumi’s body was buried, and so he played as they walked toward the gates, putting everything he had into calling her and only her, Sumi, the wild girl who died too soon and too cruelly, rather than all the sleeping bones the graveyard had to offer. It had been too long since he’d been to a proper dance, one where the women wore garlands of flowers low on their hips and the men rattled their finger bones like castanets, where the dancers traded garments and genders and positions as easily as trading a blossom for a bolero. It was tempting, to call all the skeletons of this place to him, to lose himself in a revel while the moon was high.

But that wouldn't save Rini, and it wouldn't be what he had promised Miss Eleanor he'd do. So he played for an audience of one, and when he heard Cora gasp, he smiled around his flute and continued fingering the stops, calling Sumi from her slumber.

She came, a lithe, delicate skeleton wrapped in a pearlescent sheen, like opal, like sugar glass. The cemetery gates had been designed to keep the living out, not the dead in; she stepped sideways and slipped right through the bars, her fleshless body fitting perfectly in the gap. Christopher stopped walking but kept playing as Sumi, risen from the grave, walked across the field to meet them.

"Where's the *rest* of her?" demanded Nadya.

"He doesn't pipe flesh, only bone," said Kade. "He's called what will listen to him." The flesh, softened by time, if not yet rotted away, must have shrugged away like an old overcoat, leaving Sumi shining, wrapped in rainbows, to answer Christopher's call.

Rini raised her hands to cover her mouth. Another of her fingers was gone, replaced by that strange, eye-rejecting void. "Mom?" she whispered.

Sumi cocked her head to the side, more like a bird than a girl, and said nothing. Christopher hesitated before lowering his flute. When Sumi didn't collapse into a pile of bones, he let out a long sigh, shoulders slumping with relief.

"She can't talk," he said. "She doesn't have lungs, or a voice, or anything." At home in Mariposa, she would have been able to speak. The magic that powered that land was happy to give a voice to the dead.

But this was not his home. Here, skeletons were silent, and only the sliver of Mariposa that he carried always with him was even enough to call them from the grave.

"She's dead," said Rini, like she was realizing this for the first time. "How can she be dead?"

"Everyone is, eventually," said Christopher. "This next part is harder. Cora, can you open the jar with her hands, please?"

Cora grimaced as she knelt and wrested the lid off the jar, spilling sharp-smelling liquid onto the ground. She looked to Christopher. On his nod, she dumped the jar's contents out, jumping to her feet and stumbling back to avoid the splash.

Christopher raised his flute and began to play again.

"I'm going to barf," announced Nadya.

The flesh on Sumi's hands began peeling back like a flower in the process of opening, revealing clean white bone. As they all watched, the bone grew bright with rainbows, like the rest of Sumi's skeleton.

When the flesh had peeled away entirely, Christopher tucked his flute into his belt and bent to pick up the two skeletal hands. He offered them to Sumi. She leaned forward and touched the severed ends of her wrists to the base of the carpals. The rainbow glow intensified. She leaned back again, and she was whole, every bone in its place, every piece of her skeleton where it belonged.

"If we're trying to get to an Underworld, starting from a cemetery seems like the best way to do it," said Christopher.

He looked to Rini. "You can tell those beads where to take us, right?"

"I can tell them who I want, and they get me there," said Rini. "I couldn't find my mother, no matter how hard I looked, so I looked for Miss Ely. That was who Mom always said made the school go."

"Okay," said Christopher. "Tell the beads to take us to Nancy."

"I don't know Nancy," protested Rini.

"Nancy's smart," said Kade. "She's quiet, so sometimes people don't know she's smart, but the smart's always there."

"She can stand so still she looks like a statue," said Christopher.

"She has white hair with black streaks in it and she says it isn't dyed and her roots never grew out so she probably wasn't lying," said Nadya. The others looked at her, and she shrugged. "We weren't *friends*. I had one group therapy session with her, and stayed out of her way. Too dry for me. Dry as bones."

Cora, who had come to the school after Nancy was already gone, said nothing at all.

Rini frowned at each of them in turn. "What about the sugar?"

"Red," said Kade. "They mix it with pomegranate juice. It's bitter, but it still sweetens." His gaze remained steady, fixed on her. The fact that he had never seen the sugar in Nancy's world didn't matter. He knew what it *should* be, and that was as good as knowing what it *was*.

Rini nodded before lifting her wrist to her mouth and taking one of the beads on her bracelet between her teeth. She bit down hard, the bead shattering with a crunch, and swallowed.

"Wait," said Nadya. "*Those* are sugar, too?"

"Where I come from, everything is sugar," said Rini. She reached imperiously in front of herself, grasping an invisible doorknob. "Come on. They never stay open long, and sometimes they don't match up very well."

"Hence the falling out of the sky, one assumes," said Christopher.

Rini nodded, and opened the door that wasn't there.

The other side was a grove of trees with dark green leaves and gently twisted trunks. Their boughs were heavy with red fruit. Some of it had split open, showing the ruby seeds within. The grass around the trees looked soft as velvet, and the sky was no sky at all, but the high, vaulted ceiling of an impossible hall.

"The pomegranate grove," breathed Kade.

"It's the right place? Good," said Rini. "Come on." She stepped through the door, with the skeleton of her mother close on her heels. The others followed, and when it swung shut behind Cora, it wasn't there anymore, just like it had never been there in the first place.

5 PLACES OF THE LIVING, PLACES OF THE DEAD

THE SIX OF THEM—five living, one dead—walked through the velvety grass, making no attempt to disguise their gawking. Christopher kept his bone flute in his hand, fingers tracing silent arpeggios. Sumi stayed close to her daughter, bones clacking faintly, like the distant whisper of wind through the branches of a tree. Rini tried her best not to look back. Every time she caught a glimpse of Sumi she shuddered and bit her lip before looking away again.

Nadya reached up with her single hand and traced the outline of a pomegranate with her fingers, biting her lip and staring at the fruit like it was the most beautiful thing she had ever seen.

"Nancy said she spent most of her time as a statue in the Lady's hall," said Kade, pushing forward until he was in the lead. No one questioned him. It was good to have *someone* willing to be the leader. "I suppose that means she might be there now."

"Is the Lord of the Dead going to be happy to see us?" asked Nadya, finally taking her hand away from the pomegranate.

"Maybe," said Kade. "He's got doors. He's got to be used to people stumbling in without an invitation."

"But you only find doors you're suited to," said Cora. "We didn't *find* this one. We made it. Won't he be upset about that?"

"Only one way to find out," said Kade, and started walking.

"Why do people always *say* that?" muttered Cora, trailing along at the rear of the group. "There's always more than one way to find something out. People only say there's only one way when they want an excuse to do something incredibly stupid without getting called on it. There are *lots* of ways to find out, and some of them even involve not pissing off a man who goes by 'the *Lord* of the *Dead*.'"

"Yeah, but they wouldn't be as much fun, now would they?"

Cora glanced to the side. Christopher had dropped back to walk beside her. He was grinning, looking more at ease than she had ever seen him.

"Why are you so happy?" she asked. "Everything here is dead people."

"That's why I'm so happy," he said. "Everything here is dead people."

Somehow, when he said it, it wasn't a complaint, or even an observation: it was virtually a prayer, packed with hope and homecoming. This wasn't his world, wasn't Mariposa, and the only skeleton who danced here was poor Sumi. But it was closer than he had been in a long, long time, and she could see the joy coming back into his body with every step he took.

"Do you really want to be a skeleton?" she blurted.

Christopher shrugged. "Everybody's a skeleton someday. You die, and the soft parts drop away, and what's left behind is all beautiful bone. I just want to go back to a place where I don't have to die to be beautiful."

"But you're not fat!" Cora couldn't keep the horror from her voice. She didn't even try. Growing up fat had meant an endless succession of diets suggested by "helpful" relatives, and even more "helpful" suggestions from her classmates, ones that suggested starvation or learning to vomit on command. She'd managed to dodge an eating disorder through luck, and because the swim team had needed her to stay in good shape: if her school hadn't offered endurance swimming as well as speed, if she'd been expected to slim down to be allowed into the water, she would probably have joined the girls behind the gym, the ones who died slowly on a diet of ice chips, black coffee, and cigarettes.

"It's not about fat or thin," said Christopher. "It's not . . . oh, fuck. You probably think this is about dieting, don't you?" He didn't wait for her to reply before he continued: "It's not. It's really not. Mariposa is a land of skeletons. As long as I have skin, as long as I'm like this, they can make me leave. Once the Skeleton Girl and I marry, once she cuts my humanity away, I can stay forever. That's all I want."

"That's all any of us want," admitted Cora.

"You were a mermaid, weren't you? That's what Nadya said."

"I still am," said Cora. "I just have my scales under my skin for now."

Christopher smiled, a little lopsided. "Funny. That's where I keep my bones."

The pomegranate grove was coming to an end around them, the trees growing less frequent as they approached a high marble wall. There was a door there, tall and imposing, the sort of door that belonged on a cathedral or a palace; the sort of door that said "keep out" far more loudly than it would ever dream of saying "come in." But it was standing open, and when they drew nearer, no one appeared to warn them off. Kade glanced back at the others, shrugged, and kept walking, leaving them no choice but to follow.

And then, with so little warning that Cora thought the people who lived here—who existed here—would be fully within their rights to be angry, they were in the Halls of the Dead.

The architecture was exactly what a thousand movies had told her to expect: marble pillars holding up impossible ceilings, white stone walls softened with friezes and with watercolor paintings of flowering meadows. The colors were muted, whites and pastel greens and grayish pines. They somehow managed not to become twee, but to project an air of solemnity and silence instead. The only sounds were their feet tapping against the stone floor, and the clacking of Sumi's bones.

"You were not invited, and none of Our doors have opened, nor closed, in this last day," said a woman from behind them: she was between them and the doorway that might have led them back to the pomegranate grove. Her voice was low and husky, like blackberry brandy given a throat. "Who are you? How are you here?"

Cheeks burning, feeling like a child who'd been caught sneaking to the kitchen for a midnight snack, Cora turned, and beheld the Lady of the Dead.

She was short and curvy, with skin the color of polished cypress and hair that fell down her back in a cascade of inky curls, stopping just below her waist. Her eyes were like pomegranate seeds, deep red and as impossible as Rini's candy corn irises, yet just as undeniably real. Her gown was the same color, some loosely draped Grecian style that complimented every curve she had, and made Cora yearn for a fashion as forgiving.

"Well?" asked the Lady. "Have you all been struck silent by

My presence? Or are you thinking of excuses? I suggest you not lie to Me. My husband has little patience for those who offer trespass and insult both in the same hour."

"I'm sorry, ma'am," said Kade, pushing his way forward. The relief from the rest of the group was almost palpable. Let someone else take the blame, if there was blame to take. "I know we came uninvited, but we weren't sure how to ring the bell."

"You taste of Fairyland, little hero," said the Lady of the Dead, wrinkling her nose. "All of you taste of something that isn't meant for here, all but him." She pointed to Christopher. "Mirrors and Fairylands and Lakes. Even the skeleton tastes of Mirror. The taint lingers past death. You have no business ringing Our doorbell."

"We're here to beg a favor, ma'am," said Kade doggedly. "This is Rini."

Rini raised her hand in a small wave. She was down to a single finger and her thumb, and half of her palm had melted away, replaced by that same eye-burning nothingness.

"The skeleton is her mother, Sumi, who died before Rini could be born, and now Rini is, well, disappearing," continued Kade. "One of our old classmates lives here with you. We were hoping she might be able to help us find where Sumi's spirit went after she died, so that we can try to put her back together and keep Rini from disappearing altogether. Er. Ma'am."

The Lady of the Dead's eyes widened fractionally. "You're Nancy's friends," she said.

"Yes, ma'am."

"I'm not," said Nadya. "I'm a Drowned Girl."

"So you are," said the Lady of the Dead. She gave Nadya a thoughtful look. "You went to one of the Drowned Worlds, the underground lakes, the forgotten rivers. Many of them touch on Our borders. They aren't Underworlds, but they're under the rest of the world."

Nadya paled. "You know how to get to Belyyreka?" she asked, voice barely above a whisper.

"I didn't say that," said the Lady. "We have no power over the Drowned Worlds. I wouldn't—couldn't—open a door there if you asked Me. But I know the place. It's beautiful."

"It is," agreed Nadya, and started to cry.

The Lady of the Dead turned back to Kade. "You come uninvited, to trouble a handmaiden who still stings from her time in your company. Why should We grant you an audience with her? Why should We grant you anything at all?"

"Because Nancy told us you were kind," said Christopher. He was staring at her in quiet awe, like he hadn't seen anything so beautiful in years. "She said you never made her feel like she was broken just because she was different. You and your husband, you're the reason she wanted to come back here and stay forever. You made this place home. I can't imagine anyone who'd be that kind to Nancy could be cruel enough not to help us."

"Mariposa, wasn't it, for you?" asked the Lady, looking thoughtful. "So many different doors, and yet here you are, all of you together, trying to accomplish the impossible. I'll let you talk to Nancy."

"Thank you, ma'am," said Kade.

"Don't thank Me yet," said the Lady. "There are conditions. Eat nothing; drink nothing. Speak to no one save for Myself, My husband, and Nancy. The living who choose to spend their years in these halls do so because they're looking for quiet, for peace, for solitude. They don't need you reminding them that they were hot and fast once. Do you understand?"

"Yes, ma'am," said Kade. The others nodded, even Rini, who looked more confused than anything else. She was doing an excellent job of holding her tongue. For a Nonsense girl in a world full of rules, that was just this side of a miracle.

"Good," said the Lady. "This way."

She turned then, and walked back into the door to the grove, leaving the rest of them to follow.

THE TREES WERE GONE. In their place was a long hall, the sort that belonged in a palace or a museum, its walls lined with statues, all of them standing beautifully still in their frost-white draperies. No, not statues—*people*. People of all ages, from children barely old enough to have shed their infant proportions to men and women older than Eleanor, their faces seamed with wrinkles, their limbs thinned out by time and trials. There was a certain vitality around them that betrayed their natures, but apart from that, they might as well have been the carved stone they worked so hard to imitate.

Rini shuddered, stepping a little closer to Kade, like she thought he could protect her. "How can they hold so *still*?" she whispered, voice horrified and awed. "I'd twitch myself into pieces."

"That's why this was never your door," he said. "We don't go where we're not meant to be, even if we sometimes get born the wrong place."

"There was a boy," said Rini. "When I was small. His parents mined fudge from the northern ridge. He didn't like the smell

of chocolate, or the way it melted on his tongue. He wanted to be clean, and to follow rules, and to *understand*. He disappeared the year we all started school, and his parents were sad, but they said he'd found his door, and if he was lucky, he'd never come back, not ever, not once."

Kade nodded. "Exactly. Your mother and I were born in the same world, and it wasn't right for either of us, so we went somewhere else." He didn't ask what sort of lessons would be taught at school in a Nonsense world. His own world had been Logical, and what made perfect sense to Rini wouldn't make any sense at all to him.

The people on their pedestals and set back in niches in the walls said nothing, did nothing to show that they were even aware that anyone was nearby. The Lady kept walking, and the rest of them kept following, until she reached a pair of wide marble doors. Leaning forward, she tapped them ever so gently with the tip of her left forefinger, and stood back as they swung open to reveal a room that was half cathedral and half cavern.

The walls were naked gray stone, unshaped, unworked, sweeping upward to a crystal-studded bell of a natural vault. Lights hung from the ceiling, their bases set between great spikes of purple amethyst and silvery quartz, and the floor was polished marble, creating a strange melding of the natural and the manmade.

At the center of the room, well away from any of the walls, was a freestanding dais. Two thrones rested atop it, and short pedestals surrounded it, three to either side, each holding one of the living statues.

The statue closest to the door was Nancy.

Nancy at peace: Nancy in her element. She stood tall and calm and strong, one arm raised in a graceful arc, her chin canted slightly toward the ceiling, calling attention to the delicate line of her neck, the organic sculpture of her collarbone. She wore a long white gown, like so many of the other statues, but unlike them, there was a wine-red, pomegranate-red ribbon tied around her neck, casting the rest of her into monochrome relief. Someone had styled her white and black hair, arranging it so that the black streaks left by the Lord of the Dead's fingers were perfectly displayed, like the badge of honor that they were.

Christopher whistled low. "Damn, girl," he said.

Kade said nothing. He only stared.

Both thrones were currently empty. The Lady of the Dead led them toward the dais, stopping when they reached Nancy, who must have been aware of their presence, but who did nothing to betray that knowledge.

"Nancy," said the Lady softly. "Please move for Me. You have company."

Nancy moved like frost melting: slowly at first, almost imperceptibly, and then with more speed, until she finished lowering her arm and chin and turned with something approaching, yet far greater than, human grace. She allowed herself to look at the people clustered around the base of her pedestal, and her eyes widened, ever so slightly.

"Kade," she said. "Christopher . . . Nadya?" She looked at the others without recognition. "What are you all doing here? Is everything all right? Are you . . ." She stopped herself. "No, you're not dead. If you were dead, you wouldn't be here."

"We're not dead," said Kade, and smiled. "It's good to see you, Nancy."

"It's good to see you too." She glanced to the Lady of the Dead, seeking permission. The Lady nodded, and Nancy dropped to her knees, sliding into a graceful kneeling position atop her pedestal. It was a practiced, easy motion; she had done this before. "I'm sorry I didn't say goodbye."

"I don't think most of us would," said Kade. "You happy?"

Nancy's smile was brief but brilliant. Artists would have died for the chance to paint that moment of pure, unfettered bliss. "Always."

"Then all is forgiven." Kade gestured for Rini to step forward. "This is Rini. Sumi's daughter."

"What?" Nancy's expression faded into puzzlement at the mention of her former roommate. "Sumi didn't have children. She was too young. She would have told me."

"She was *supposed* to come back to Confection and save the world and get married and make a baby," said Rini. She held up her arm. Her hand was entirely gone now; her flesh ended at the wrist, and at the tear her disappearance was leaving in reality. "She needs to stop being *dead* and come home and have sex until I exist again!"

"Um," said Nancy, looking nonplussed.

"This is Sumi," said Christopher, gesturing to the shimmering skeleton beside him. "We were hoping you might know where the rest of her is."

"You mean her *ghost*?" asked Nancy.

"Yes," said Christopher.

Sumi said nothing, but she cocked her shining skull to the side in a gesture that was a pale shadow of her constant curious motion before she had died, her skin and flesh stripped away, leaving her in silence.

"Even if . . ." Nancy glanced to the Lady, who nodded permission. "Even if I could find Sumi's ghost for you, even if she was *here,* how would you put her back together? You'd still be missing all the . . . squishy bits."

"Let us worry about that," said Kade.

Nancy looked to the Lady again. Again, the Lady nodded her assent. Nancy looked back to the others.

"Not all ghosts come here," she said. "This isn't the only Underworld. She could be in a thousand places, or she could be nothing at all. Sometimes people don't want to linger, and so they just disappear."

"Can we try?" asked Kade. "It seems like dying when you still had a world to save might be cause enough to stick around for a little while. And you were roommates when she was alive. Sumi never did like to be alone."

"Even if you can find her ghost, that's just the part of her that's waiting to be reborn," said Nancy. "Who she *was* isn't going to be here."

"We have to try," said Rini. "There's nowhere else to go."

Nancy sighed, a deep, slow sound that started at her toes and traveled all the way up her body. She uncurled her legs and slid down from her pedestal, landing without a sound. As she fell, her skirt rode up just enough for Kade to see that her feet were bare, and that there was a ring on every one of her toes, shimmering and silver.

"Follow me," she said, and bowed to the Lady, and walked away. Every step she took chimed like a bell as the rings on her toes struck the ground.

Kade followed her, and the rest followed him, and they left the remaining statues and the Lady of the Dead behind.

KADE STOLE GLANCES at Nancy as they walked, trying to memorize the new shape of her face. She was thinner, but not alarmingly so; this was the thinness of a professional athlete at the top of their game, the thinness of someone who did something physical every hour of the day. Her hair was still white, her eyes were still dark, and she was still beautiful. God, but she was beautiful.

Nadya shoved her way between them, demanding, "So is that all you do all day? You *stand* there? You left a whole world full of shit to do and people to talk to so you could *stand* there?"

"It's more than just standing there," said Nancy. "Hello, Nadya. You're looking well."

"I'm drying out, and this world has no good rivers," said Nadya.

"We have a few." Nancy shook her head. "I don't 'just stand there.' It's like a dance, done entirely in stillness. I have to freeze so completely that my heart forgets to beat, my cells forget to age. Some of the statues have been here for centuries, slowing themselves to the point of near-immortality for the sake of gracing our Lord's halls. It's an honor and a calling, and I love it. I love it so much."

"It seems stupid."

"That's because you weren't called," said Nancy, and that was true, and simple, and complete: it needed neither ornamentation nor addition.

Nadya looked away.

Kade took a breath. "Things have been going well at the

school," he said. "Aunt Eleanor's feeling better. She hardly uses her cane these days. We have some new students."

"You brought one of them with you," said Nancy. She laughed a little. "Is it weird that I kind of feel like that's more disturbing than you bringing a skeleton?"

"Her name's Cora. She's nice. She was a mermaid."

"Then she still is," said Nancy. "There's always hope."

"Sumi used to say that hope was a four-letter word."

"She was right. That's why it never goes away." They had reached another closed door, this one a filigree of silver, containing an infinity of blackness. Nancy raised her hand. The door swung open and she continued through, into the dark—which was, once entered, not so total after all.

Gleaming silver sparks swirled through the air, darting and flitting around the room, as swift and restless as the rest of the Halls of the Dead were still. They would fly close to a nose or a cheek, only to jerk away at the last second, never quite touching living flesh.

Rini gasped. Everyone turned.

Sumi was covered in the dots of light. They clustered on her bones, hundreds of them, with more arriving every second. She was holding up her skeletal hands like she was admiring them, studying the shimmering specks of light that perched on her phalanges. Dots of light had even filled her eye sockets, replacing her empty gaze with something disturbingly vital.

"If she's here, she's one of these," said Nancy, spreading her arms to indicate the room. "The souls who come to rest here arrive in this room first. They dance their restlessness away before they incarnate again. Call her, and see if she comes."

"Christopher?" said Kade.

"I play for skeletons, not souls," protested Christopher, even as he raised his flute to his mouth and blew a silent, experimental note. The specks of light abandoned Sumi, rising into the air and swirling wildly around him. He continued to play, until, bit by bit, some of the light peeled away and returned to the air, while some of the light began to coalesce in front of Sumi's skeleton. Bit by bit, particle by particle, it came together, until the glowing, translucent ghost of a teenage girl was standing there.

She wore a sensible school uniform, white knee socks, plaid skirt, and buttoned blazer. Her hair was pulled into low braids, tamed, contained. It was Sumi, yes, but Sumi rendered motionless, Sumi stripped of laughter and nonsense. Rini gasped again, this time with pain, and raised her remaining hand and the stump of what had been its twin to cover her mouth.

The specter of Sumi looked at the skeleton. The skeleton looked at the specter.

"Why is she like that?" whispered Rini. "What did you do to my mother?"

"I told you, we have her ghost, but not her shadow—not her heart. Her heart was a wild thing, and this isn't where the wild things go," said Nancy. "If it were, I wouldn't be here. I was never a wild thing." She looked at the shade of Sumi with regret and, yes, love in her eyes. "We're all puzzle boxes, skeleton and skin, soul and shadow. You have two of the pieces now, if she'll go with you, but I don't think her shadow's here."

"Mama . . ." The word belonged to the lips of a much younger girl, meant for bedtimes and bad times, for skinned knees and stomach aches. Rini offered it to Sumi's shade like it was a promise and a prayer at the same time, like it was something precious, to be treasured. "I need you. Please. We need you. The Queen of Cakes will rise again if you don't come home."

The Queen of Cakes would never have been defeated: Sumi had died before she could return to Confection and overthrow the government. Rini wasn't just saving herself. She was saving a world, setting right what was on the verge of going wrong.

The carefully groomed shade of Sumi looked at her blankly, uncomprehending. Nancy, who understood the dead of this place in a way that none of the others did, cleared her throat.

"It will make a mess if you don't go with them," she said.

The shade turned to look at her before nodding and stepping forward, into the skeleton, wreathing the bones in phantom flesh. Rini started to reach for her with her sole remaining hand, and stopped as she saw that two more of her fingers were gone, fading into nothing at all.

"We have to hurry," she said.

"You have to pay," said a new voice.

All of them turned as one. Only Nancy smiled when she saw the man standing in the doorway. He was tall and thin, with skin the color of volcanic ash and hair the color of bone. Like his wife, he wore a flowing garment, almost Grecian in design, which drew the eye to the length of his limbs and the broadness of his shoulders.

"Nothing here is free," he said. "Eat nothing, drink nothing; visitors are told that upon arrival. What makes you think we would give our treasures away, if we will not share our water?" His voice was deep, low, and inevitable, like the death of stars.

"What do you need us to pay, sir?" asked Kade warily.

The Lord of the Dead looked at him with pale and merciless eyes. "One of you will have to stay behind."

6 WE PAY WHAT WE PAY; THE WORLD GOES ON

"NO," SAID KADE, without hesitation. "We're not for sale."

"This isn't a sale," said the Lord of the Dead. "This is an exchange. You want to take one of my residents on a fool's errand. You want to promise her that she can be alive again, when there's no possible way. I would forbid you entirely if I thought you would listen, but you're not the first among the living to seek to play Orpheus and lure what's mine away. Putting a price on the process is the only way to keep you people from robbing me blind."

"Sir," said Nancy, and curtseyed, deep and low. She froze when she was folded fully forward, becoming a statue again.

The Lord of the Dead smiled. He looked strangely human, when he smiled. "My Nancy," he said, and there was no doubting the fondness in his tone. "These are your friends?"

"From school," she said, rising. "This is Kade."

"Ah. The fabled boy." He turned to Kade. "Nancy speaks highly of you."

"Highly enough for you to give us a freebie?"

"Alas."

"Wait." Nadya took a step forward, nervous, glancing around at the others. Her hair, dry after so long away from either bathtub or turtle pond, was a fluffy brown cloud around her head. "Mr. Lord of the Dead, do you have turtles here? Not ghost turtles, I mean. Real turtles, the kind that swim in ponds and do turtle stuff."

"There are turtles in the River of Forgotten Souls," said the Lord of the Dead, looking faintly baffled.

"Okay," said Nadya. "Okay, okay. Because your, um, your wife, she said she knew Belyyreka. That's where my doorway led. To a Drowned World, where I was a Drowned Girl. I still am. It's too dry where I come from. The air doesn't forgive."

"I know the place," said the Lord of the Dead solemnly.

"Doors can open anywhere if the worlds are close enough together, can't they? Rini"—she gestured toward the sniffling girl with the candy corn eyes—"said a boy from the world she comes from found his door and went away, to someplace where he was better suited. If I stayed here, and Belyyreka wanted me back, could my door still find me?"

"Nadya, no," said Cora.

"Yes," said the Lord of the Dead. "And for that, for Belyyreka, I would let you go. For that, I would stand aside and release all claim to you."

Nadya looked around at the others. "I've been at the school for five years. I'll be seventeen in a month. A year after that and then I graduate, and my family starts expecting me to go somewhere, to make something of my life. I can't live on a countdown. I want to go *home,* and that means waiting until Belyyreka calls me back. I'm not a political exile like Sumi. I'm not a cultural exile like Kade, either. I just got caught in the wrong current. I want to go *home.* I can wait here just as well as I can wait on campus."

"Nadya, *no,*" said Cora, with more desperation. "You can't leave me. You're the only real friend I've got."

Nadya's smile was uneven and quick. "See, that's the best reason for me to stay here. You need to make more friends, Cora. I can't be the only estuary in your waterway."

"Aunt Eleanor's going to kill me," muttered Kade.

"Not when you tell her it was my choice, and that this place is closer to Belyyreka than the school ever was," said Nadya, dismissing his concerns with an airy wave of her hand. She turned to the Lord of the Dead. "If you'll let my friends go, and you'll let me take my door home when it appears, I'll stay with you. I'll haunt your rivers and terrorize your turtles and I'll never be still, but you don't want someone still, or you wouldn't have asked for any of us. You just want someone to stay so you feel like you're in charge of everything."

"Guilty as charged," said the Lord of the Dead, with a very faint smile. "You will stay?"

"I'll stay," said Nadya.

Kade closed his eyes, looking pained.

"The compact is sealed." The Lord of the Dead turned to the group. "Your payment is given; the shade may go with you. Nancy?"

"Yes, milord?"

"Show your friend to the river."

"Yes, milord," said Nancy, and turned to Nadya. "Follow me."

The others stood, silently watching, as the girl who had left them to grace her master's hall led Nadya the Drowned Girl away, toward the river, toward the future, whatever that future might entail. Neither of them looked back. Neither of them said goodbye. The shade-shrouded skeleton of Sumi was a patient reminder of why they had decided to meet this price, and of what it would have to redeem.

"Thank you, sir," said Kade finally. "We'll be going now."

"Wait," said Christopher.

The Lord of the Dead turned to him. "Yes, child of Mariposa?"

"I can pipe the bones of the dead out of the earth, and back in Mariposa, that's enough: nothing's missing. Something's missing with Sumi. The nonsense didn't come here, Nancy said. Where did it go?"

"The same place nonsense always goes," said the Lord of the Dead. "It went home. Even when a door never opens during the lifetime of a wanderer, they find their rest after death."

"Home . . ." said Kade slowly. He turned to Rini. "All right. Take us to Confection."

Rini's eyes lit up. She didn't hesitate, just raised her bracelet to her mouth and bit off another bead, crunching loudly as she swallowed.

The door opened directly under their feet, swinging wide, and then they were falling, four living teenagers and one glimmering skeleton. Rini laughed all the way down. The door slammed shut behind them.

The Lord of the Dead looked at the place where it had been and sighed before waving his hand, sending the specks of light dancing around the room. The living were always in such a hurry. They would learn soon enough.

RINI'S DOOR HAD opened above what Cora would have called an ocean, had it not been bright pink and gently bubbling. Christopher curled into a ball as he fell, using his entire body to protect his flute. Kade fell like an amateur, all flailing limbs and panic. Rini was laughing, spinning wildly in the air, like she didn't really believe that gravity would hurt her. Sumi's skeleton merely dropped. Dead people probably didn't worry too much about drowning.

Cora, once the surprise powerhouse of her school swim team, curved her body into a bow, arms stretched out in front of her, hands together, head tucked down to reduce the chances of her neck snapping on impact. That didn't happen often. She didn't often see divers leap from this height.

I'm flying, she thought giddily, and who cared if the sea below her was pink and the air around her smelled of sugar and strawberry syrup? Who *cared*? The school had a turtle pond and bathtubs big enough for her to sink down to her nose, only the small islands of her knees and the peak of her belly standing above the surface, but there was no pool, there was no ocean. She hadn't been swimming since she'd left the Trenches, and every molecule of her body yearned for the moment when she would be surrounded by the sea.

They hit the surface all at the same time, Kade and Christopher with enormous splashes, Rini and Sumi with smaller ones, and Cora slicing through the surface of the waves like a harpoon, cutting down, down, down into the pink, bubbling depths.

She was the first to burst back into the air, the force of her mermaid-trained kicks driving her several feet above the pinkish foam as she sputtered and exclaimed, "It's *soda*!"

Rini laughed as she came bobbing back up. "Strawberry rhubarb soda!" she cheered. One of her ears was gone, following her fingers into nothingness. She didn't appear to have noticed. "We're home, we're home, we're home in the foam!" She splashed Cora with her remaining hand, sending soda droplets in all directions.

Kade was sputtering when he surfaced. Sumi's bones simply floated to the top, buoyant beyond all human measure.

Cora frowned. "Where's Christopher?" she asked, looking at Kade.

"What do you mean?"

"I saw where everyone was when we were falling." She had been the only one composed enough to check. The others had been panicking, or plummeting, not trying to get their bearings. She couldn't blame them. Everyone's lives prepared them for something different. "He was right next to you."

Kade's eyes widened. "I don't know."

There wasn't time to keep talking: not if she wanted this to end well. Cora took a deep breath before she dove, wishing briefly that she had a hair tie, or better yet, that she had her gills.

The sea of strawberry rhubarb soda—and who *did* that? They were all going to get horrible urinary tract infections after this—was translucent, lighter than normal water. The bubbles stung her eyes, but she could deal with the pain. Chlorine was worse.

(It was hard not to think about the damage that sugar and

carbonation might do—but Rini wasn't worried, and this was Rini's ocean, in Rini's Nonsense world. Maybe things worked differently here. Things seemed to work differently everywhere she went. Anyway, things had to be at least *slightly* different, or they wouldn't have been able to stay afloat.)

A long eel swam by, seemingly made of living saltwater taffy. The strange shape of its body called to mind the concept of peppermint sharks and turtles with jawbreaker shells, of fish like gumdrops and jellybeans, a whole ecosystem made of living sugar, thriving in a place where the rules were different, where the rules had no concern for how things worked elsewhere. Elsewhere was a legend and a lie, until it came looking for you.

Down, down, down into the strawberry rhubarb sea Cora dove, until she saw something falling slowly through the sea. It looked too solid to be made of candy, and too dark to be prepared for a children's goodie bag. She swam harder, instinctively pressing her legs together and dolphin-kicking her way downward. Even in the absence of fin and scale, she had been the hero of the Trenches, the mermaid who swam as though the Devil himself were behind her. Quickly, she was at Christopher's side, gathering him out of the soda.

His eyes were closed. No bubbles trickled from his nose or mouth. But he was holding his bone flute tightly in one hand. Cora hoped that meant he was still alive. Wouldn't he have let go, if he were already gone?

He wasn't going to let go of the flute. Normally, she would have hooked her hands under his arms, using his armpits to drag him with her, but if that caused him to lose his grip, he was going to insist on going back down to try to find his last piece of home. She could understand that. So she held him to her chest in a parody of a bridal carry, or of the Creature from the Black Lagoon carrying his beautiful victim out of the water. Christopher didn't stir.

Cora kicked.

Sometimes she thought she had always been a mermaid: that her time among the two-legged people had been the fluke, and that her reality was her, well, flukes. She was meant to live a wet and watery existence, free from the tyranny of gravity—which had been trying to ruin her day even more than usual, starting with Rini's fall into the turtle pond. She kicked, and the sea responded, propelling her ever upward, turning effort into momentum.

This, right here, this was what life was supposed to be. Just her, and an environment where her size was an asset, not an impediment. Her lungs were large. Her legs were strong. She was flying, and even having Christopher clutched in her arms did nothing to slow her down.

They broke the surface of the sea in a spray of soda and bubbles. Rini and Kade were still bobbing there, waiting, as was Sumi's skeleton, which floated like a bath toy for the world's most morbid child.

Christopher's head lolled, his mouth hanging slackly open, a trickle of pink soda running from lips to chin. Cora cast wildly around until she spotted the distant streak of the shore. It wasn't so far: maybe fifty yards. She could do that.

"Come on!" she shouted, and swam, rapidly outpacing her companions. That didn't matter. *They* didn't matter. Christopher was the one who was drowning, who had already drowned. Christopher was the one she had to save.

In what felt like the blink of an eye, she was staggering back onto her unwanted legs, carrying Christopher out of the fizzing waves and onto the shore. It was made of brown sugar and cake crumbs, she realized, as she was in the act of throwing him down onto it. Still he didn't move. She rolled him onto his side, pounding on his back until a gush of pink liquid burst from his mouth, sinking rapidly into the sugary shore. Still he didn't move.

Cora grimaced, realizing what she had to do, and rolled him onto his back, beginning to go through the steps of CPR. She had taken all the lifeguard courses between ninth and tenth grade, intending to spend the summer sitting by the pool, keeping kids from drowning. Maybe even protecting the shyer, fatter ones from their peers, who would always find reason to make fun.

(She hadn't been counting on her own peers, who had been even more inclined to make fun than their younger brothers and sisters. She hadn't counted on the notes stuffed into her locker, crueler and colder than the ones she received at school, where at least the other students were used to her, had had the time to learn to think of her as something other than "the fat girl." She had never put on her red swimsuit or her whistle. She had done . . . something else, instead, and when she had woken up to find herself in the Trenches, she had thought the afterlife was surprisingly kind, not realizing that this was still the duringlife, and that life would always find a new way to be cruel.)

She breathed for him. She pushed against his chest until finally, it began moving on its own; until Christopher rolled onto his side again, this time under his own power, and vomited a second gush of fizzing pink liquid onto the sand. He began to cough, and she leaned forward, helping him into a sitting position, rubbing slow, soothing circles on his back.

"Breathe," she said. "You need to breathe."

There was a commotion behind her. She didn't turn. She knew what she would see: two people who didn't swim enough staggering out of the waves, with a skeleton following close behind. When that had become the new normal, she couldn't possibly have said.

Christopher coughed again before his head snapped up, eyes widening in alarm. Cora sighed.

"It's in your hand," she said. "You didn't drop it. I wouldn't let you."

He looked down, relaxing slightly when he saw the flute. He still didn't speak.

Cora sat back on her calves, knees folded beneath her, sticky pink liquid soaking every inch of her, and for the first time since leaving the Trenches, she felt almost content. She felt almost like she was home. Turning, she told Kade and Rini, "He's going to be all right."

"Thank God," said Kade. "Aunt Eleanor will forgive me for Nadya deciding to stay behind in an Underworld that might border on her own, but she wouldn't forgive me for a drowning."

"Why wouldn't he have been all right?" asked Rini. "It's just sugar."

"People who don't come from here can die if they breathe too much liquid," said Cora. "It's called 'drowning.'"

Rini looked alarmed. "What a dreadful world you have. I wouldn't want to live in a place where mothers die and people can't breathe the sea."

"Yeah, well, you work with what you have," muttered Cora, thinking about pills and pools and drownings. She turned back to Christopher. "Feel like you can get up?"

He nodded, still silently. Leaning forward, Cora hooked her hands under his arms and stood, pulling him along with her, providing the leverage he needed to get his feet back under himself. Christopher coughed one more time, pressing a hand to the base of his throat.

"Burns," he rasped.

"That's the carbonation," said Cora. "Don't breathe soda. Don't breathe water either, unless you're built for it. Chlorine fucks you up pretty bad too. It'll pass."

Christopher nodded, lowering his hand and letting it join its partner in gripping the bone flute, which was already dry and didn't appear to have been stained by its passage through an infinity of pink dye.

The same couldn't be said for the rest of them. Kade's formerly white shirt was now a pleasant shade of pink, and Rini's dress was less "melting sherbet" and more "strawberry smoothie." Cora had been wearing dark colors, but her white socks weren't anymore. Even Sumi glittered with tiny beads of pink liquid, like jewels in the sun.

"This just keeps getting weirder and I'm not sure I like it," muttered Cora.

Kade gave her a sympathetic look before running a hand back over his hair, releasing a sticky wave of soda. "Try not to think about it too hard. We don't know how much logic this place can handle, and if it starts trying to break us because we're applying too many rules, we're going to have a problem." He turned to Rini. "We're on your home turf now. Where do we go to find your mother's nonsense? We're going to need that if we want to put her back together."

Cora swallowed a cascade of giggles. They would have

sounded hysterical, she knew: they would have sounded like she could no longer cope. And that wouldn't have been entirely wrong. She was a solid, practical person, and while she had accepted the existence of magic—sort of hard not to, under the circumstances—there was a lot of ground between "magic is real, other worlds are real, mermaids can be real, in a world that wants them" and "everything is real, women fall out of the sky into turtle ponds, skeletons walk, and we left my best friend in the underworld."

When she got back to the school, she was going to draw herself a hot bath, curl up in the tub, and sleep for *days*.

"This is the Strawberry Sea," said Rini uncomfortably, looking around. "The Meringue Mountains are to the west, and the Big Rock Candy Mountain is to the east. If we chart a course between them, through the Fondant Forests, we should come to the farmlands. That's where my home is. There's where my mother's supposed to be. If her nonsense were going to go anywhere, it would probably go there."

"Just *how* Nonsense is this world, Rini?" asked Kade. "None of us went to nonsensical places, and Nonsense, it tends to reject what doesn't belong inside of it. We tend to haul logic in our wake, like dirt on our shoes."

"I don't understand," said Rini.

"If people don't normally drown when they breathe water here, and Christopher almost drowned, that's logic seeping in," said Kade. "We need to fix your mother and get out of here before the world decides to shove us out."

"Where would we go?" asked Cora.

"That's the sort of philosophical question that my aunt loves and I hate," said Kade. "Maybe we'd go back to the school, or back to the Halls of the Dead, and get stuck hanging out watching Nancy play garden gnome forever. Or maybe we'd get knocked back through our doors." His mouth was a thin, grim line. "Good for you. Not so good for me."

Cora didn't know all the circumstances of Kade's door, but she knew enough to know that he was one of the only students who had no desire to go back. While the rest of them searched, he sat back and watched, content to know that the school would be his home for the rest of his life. That was good. Someone needed to keep the lighthouse fires burning, because there would always be lost children looking for the light. It was also terrible. No one should find the place where they belonged and then reject it.

"Confection is Confection," said Rini, sounding confused. "Mom always said it was Nonsense, and then she'd laugh and kiss me and say, 'But things still do what they do, and babies still get born.' "

"So it's a Nonsense world with consistent internal rules," said Kade, sounding relieved. "You're probably near the border of Logic, or have a strong underpinning of Reason. Either way, we're not likely to get spit out unless we start trying to deny the reality around us. No one talk about nutrition."

"Wasn't planning on it," said Christopher.

Cora, who was slowly coming to realize that she was a fat girl in a world made entirely of cake—something the students at her old school would probably have called her deepest fantasy—said nothing as her cheeks flared red.

The five of them trudged along the crumble and sugar beach, moving toward the graham cracker and shortbread bedrock up ahead. Only Sumi seemed to have no trouble with the uneven ground: she was too light to sink into the sand, and walked blithely on the top of it, leaving bony footprints behind her. She was a strange double-exposure of an impossibility, rainbow skeleton and solemn black-and-white teen at the same time, and just looking at her was enough to make Cora shudder. Either of the images Sumi currently presented would have been bad. Both of them together was somehow offensive, too contradictory to be possible, too concrete to be denied.

"How far is the walk to your farm?" asked Kade.

Rini thought a moment before saying, "No more than a day. 'A good day's journey is like baking soda: use it well, and the cake will rise up to meet you.'"

Christopher blinked. "You mean the world rearranges itself so that everyplace you want to go is within a day's walk from where you are?"

"Well, sure," said Rini. "Isn't that how it works where you're from?"

"Sadly, no."

"Huh," said Rini. "And you call *my* world nonsensical."

Christopher didn't have an answer to that.

Cora's calves were aching by the time they reached the end of the beach, and it was sweet relief to step up onto the solid bedrock of baked goods, feeling them firm beneath her feet. The graham cracker and shortbread had more give to it than rock would have, like walking on the rubber-infused concrete at Disneyland. She still desperately wanted to sit down, but if all the roads here were like this one, she would be okay for a while.

They hadn't walked very far when the first of the vegetation began to appear—if you could call it that. The trees had gingerbread and fudge trunks, and spun-sugar leaves surrounding clusters of gummy fruit and jellybeans. The grass looked like it had been piped from a frosting bag. Rini paused to lean up onto her toes and grab a handful of cake pops off the lower branches of a tree, beginning to munch as she resumed walking.

"It's never a good idea to eat the ground," she said blithely, cake between her teeth and frosting on her lips. "People walk on it."

"But if the dirt here is edible, what does it matter if somebody's feet are dirty?" asked Christopher.

Rini swallowed before giving him a withering look and saying, "We still *pee*. People pee, and then other people step in it, and they walk on the ground. I don't want to eat something that has somebody's *pee* on it. That's gross. Do they eat pee where you come from?"

"It's not a given!" protested Christopher. "None of the skeletons in Mariposa do . . . that. They eat sometimes, and they still enjoy the taste of wine and ginger beer, but they don't have stomachs, so everything goes straight through them."

Cora blinked at him. "But *you*—"

"Don't ask." Christopher shook his head. "It was messy and unpleasant and we worked it out eventually, and I don't want to talk about it."

"Rini," said Kade, before she could ask Christopher to explain further, "how is it that everything here's made out of candy except for the people?"

"Oh, that's easy." Rini bit into another cake pop, swallowing before she said, "Confection is like a jawbreaker. Layers and layers and layers, all stacked on top of each other, going all the way down to the very middle, which is just this hard little ball of rock and sadness. Sort of like your world, only smaller."

"Thanks," said Kade flatly.

Rini didn't seem to notice. "It's a world, so even though nobody lived there, somebody eventually had a door that led there. She looked around, and she thought, 'Well, this is awful,' and then she thought, 'It would be better if I had some bread,' and then she found a stove and all the stuff she needed for bread, because Confection was already wanting to be born. So she baked and baked and baked. She baked all the bread she could eat, and then she baked herself a bed, and then she baked herself a house to put her bed in, and then she thought, 'Wouldn't it be nice if I had something softer to walk on,' and she baked enough bread to go all the way around the world twice, so that the stone was gone, and she had a whole kingdom out of bread. It was still pretty small, though, and eventually she got bored and baked herself a doorway home, and she never came back." She paused. "But her daughter did. And her daughter didn't much care for bread, on account of how she'd been a baker's daughter all her life, but wow, did she like cookies. . . ."

Rini's story went on and on, spinning out the creation of Confection in great, lazy loops as the bakers—what seemed like an endless succession of bakers, one after the other—came through the door the Breadmaker had baked. Each of them stayed long enough to add another layer to the world, becoming the next name in the long pantheon of Confection's culinary gods.

". . . and after the Brownie-maker put down *her* layer of the world, plants started growing. I guess that's just what happens when you have that much sugar in one place."

"No," said Cora. "No, it's usually really not." She wanted to say more, like how bread got stale and moldy, and ice cream wasn't usually stable enough to serve as the basis for a glacier, no matter *how* cold it got, but she bit her tongue. The rules were different here, as they had been different in the Trenches, and in the Halls of the Dead, and in all the worlds on the other side of a disappearing, impossible door.

Rini would probably be horrified to hear about bread mold and freezer burn and all the other things that could happen to the base materials of her world on the other side of the door. And maybe that explained the conception of Confection. Maybe the first baker, the girl who just wanted to make bread, had come from a place where there was never enough food, or where the bread went bad before she could eat it. So she'd baked and baked and baked, until her stomach wasn't empty anymore, until she wasn't afraid of starving, and then she'd gone home, having learned the only lesson that a small and empty world had to teach her.

According to Rini, Confection was like a jawbreaker. Cora thought it was more like a pearl, layers on layers on layers, all surrounding that first, all-encompassing *need*. Hunger was about as primal as needs got. What if all worlds were like that? What if they were all built up by the travelers who tripped over a doorway and found their way to someplace perfect, someplace hyperreal, someplace they could *need*? Someplace where that need could be *met*?

The beach was too far behind them now for the sound of the waves to reach, although the air still smelled faintly of strawberry. Cora supposed that could be a consequence of the soda soaked into their clothes, which was drying sweet and sticky on the skin. A fly buzzed over to investigate, its body made of a fat black jellybean, its legs strands of thinly twisted licorice. She swatted it away.

Rini, her cheeks still bulging with cake pop, stopped walking. "Uh-oh," she said, voice rendered thick and gooey by the contents of her mouth. She swallowed hard. "We have a problem."

"What is it?" asked Kade.

Rini pointed.

There, ahead, coming over a hill made of treacle tart and whipped meringue, rode what seemed like the beginnings of an army. It was impossible to tell at this distance whether their horses were real or some extremely clever bit of baking, but that didn't really matter, because a sword made of sugar can still be sharp enough to cleave all the way to the bone. The knights who rode those implacable steeds wore foiled armor that glittered in the sun, and there was no question of their intentions.

"Run, maybe?" said Rini, and turned, and fled, with the others close behind her.

OF COURSE THEY TRIED to run: to do anything else would have been foolish.

Of course they failed. Of the five of them, only Cora ran with any regularity, and while she could be remarkably fast when she wanted to, she was more interested in endurance than in sprinting. Sumi was skeletal, lacking the large muscles that would have made it possible for her to take advantage of her light frame. Rini ran like someone who had never considered exercise to be a required part of daily life: she was slim but out of shape, and was the first to fall behind.

Kade and Christopher did the best they could, but the one

was a tailor and the other had just come within a stone's throw of drowning; neither of them were very well equipped to run. In short order, they were all surrounded by armored knights on horses.

Seen up close, the horses were clearly flesh and blood, although their armor appeared to have been made from hard candy and peanut brittle, wrapped in foil to keep it from sticking to human skin or horse hair.

"Onishi Rini, you are under arrest for crimes against the Queen of Cakes," said the lead rider. Rini bared her teeth at him. He ignored her. "You will come with us."

"Well, shit," said Christopher, and that was exactly right, and there was nothing more to say.

PART III

BAKE ME A MOUNTAIN, FROST ME A SKY

7 PRISONERS OF SOMEONE ELSE'S WAR

THE KNIGHTS PRODUCED A surprising amount of spun-sugar rope and bound their captives, slinging them over the backs of their horses like so much dirty laundry. They seemed afraid to touch Sumi, in all her skeletal glory; in the end, they had to sling a loop of rope around her neck, like she was a dog. That seemed to be enough to make her docile: she trailed behind the slow-riding group without protest or attempt to break away.

They were all searched thoroughly before they were tied up, and anything that might be viewed as dangerous was quickly confiscated, including Rini's bracelet and Christopher's bone flute. Cora tried not to think too hard about what the loss of the bracelet could mean for the rest of them. Surely the wizard who had given it to Rini would be able to make another one, something that would let them all go back to Miss West's when this was over. Surely they weren't about to be trapped behind someone else's door, in a world that was even less right for them than the one where they'd been born. She still couldn't think of the school as "home" any more than she could consider going back to the house where her family waited for the day when she'd be cured of all the things that made her who she was, but . . .

But she couldn't stay here. This wasn't a fantasy adventure. This was a nightmare of a candy-coated wonderland, the place the kids she'd gone to school with would have expected her to dream of finding beyond an impossible door, and she wanted nothing to do with it. Nothing at all.

The riders rode, and the captives dangled, and everything began to blur together, like the landscape was accelerating around them. That was the logical nonsense of Confection coming into play, where everything was no more than a day's journey from everything else, no matter how fast you traveled or how big the world became.

(It felt a little bit like cheating—but then, to someone like Rini, airplanes and sports cars probably felt like cheating too, like a way to have all the distance in the world and not be forced to account for any of it. Cheating was always a matter of perspective, and of who was giving out the grades.)

Kade gasped. Cora twisted against her bonds as much as she could, craning her neck until she could see what he saw. Then she gasped as well, eyes going wide while she tried to take it all in.

In some ways, the castle that had appeared in front of them was nothing more nor less than a gingerbread house taken to a dramatic new extreme. It was the sort of thing children were coaxed to build at the holidays under the watchful eyes of their parents, getting flour and frosting absolutely everywhere. But true as that idea was, it didn't do justice to the towering edifice of cake and cereal brick and sugar. This was no kitchen-craft, meant to be devoured with sticky fingers after Christmas dinner. This was a monument, a landmark, an architectural marvel baked with the sole intent of standing for a thousand years.

The walls were gingerbread so dark with spice that it verged on black, hardened with molasses and strengthened with posts of twisted pretzel treats. The sugar crystals studding the walls were larger than Kade's fist, and sharpened to wicked points, until the entire structure became a weapon. The battlements looked like they had been carved from rock candy, and the towers were impossibly high, ignoring the laws of physics and common sense alike.

Rini moaned. "The castle of the Queen of Cakes," she said. "We're doomed."

"I thought your mother defeated her," hissed Cora.

"She did and she didn't," said Rini. "Once Mom died before coming back to Confection, everything started to come undone. The Queen of Cakes returned the same time the first of my fingers disappeared. *She* came back all at once, maybe because Mom killed her all at once, and she made me one ingredient at a time. I took nine months to bake. I might take nine months to disappear, one piece at a time, until all that's left is my heart, lying on the ground, beating without a body."

"Hearts don't work that way," said Christopher.

"Skeletons don't walk around," said Rini.

"All of you, silence," snapped one of the knights. "Show some respect. You're about to go before the rightful ruler of all Confection."

"There is no rightful ruler of all Confection," said Rini. "Cake and candy and fudge and gingerbread don't all follow the same rules, so how can anyone make rules that work for everyone at the same time? You follow a false queen. The First Baker would be ashamed of you. The First Oven would refuse to bake your heart. You—"

His fist caught her full in the face, snapping her head back, leaving her gasping for breath. He turned to glare at the rest of his captives, eyes resting on each of them in turn.

"Show respect, or pay the price: the choice is yours," he said, and the horses trotted on, carrying them ever closer to the castle, and to the impossible woman waiting there.

THE MAIN HALLWAY of the castle continued and fulfilled the promise of its exterior: everything was candy, or cake, or some other form of baked good, but elevated to a grace and glory that would have made the bakers back home weep at the futile nature of their own efforts. Chandeliers of sugar crystals hung from the vaulted, painted chocolate ceiling. Stained sugar glass windows filtered and shattered the light, turning everything into an explosion of rainbows.

Cora could close her eyes and imagine this whole place in plastic, mass-produced for the amusement of children. That made it a little better. If she just pretended none of this was happening, that she was safe back in her bed at the school—or better, that she was sleeping in her net of kelp in the Trenches, the currents rocking her gently through her slumber—then maybe she could survive it with her sanity intact.

The jagged sugar point of the spear at her back made it a little difficult to check out completely.

Rini was limping. From the way she wobbled, it looked like her toes were starting to follow her fingers into nothingness, leaving her off-balance and unstable. Kade and Christopher were walking normally, although Christopher looked pale and a little lost. His fingers kept flexing, trying to trace chords on a flute that wasn't there anymore.

Only Sumi seemed unbothered by the change in their situation. She plodded placidly onward, her skeletal feet clacking softly against the polished candy floor, the thin screen of her shade continuing to look around her with polite disinterest, like this was by no means a remarkable situation.

"What are they going to do to us, Rini?" asked Kade in a low voice.

"Mom said the first time she faced the Queen of Cakes, the Queen forced her to eat a *whole plate* of broccoli," said Rini.

Kade relaxed a little. "Oh, that's not so bad—"

"And then she tried to cut Mom open so she could read the future in her entrails. You can't read the future in candy entrails. They're too sticky." Rini said this in a matter-of-fact tone, like she was embarrassed to need to remind them of such a basic fact of life.

Kade paled. "See, that's bad. That's very bad."

"Silence," snapped one of the knights. They were approaching a pair of massive gingerbread doors, decorated with sheets of sugar glass in a dozen different colors. Cora frowned. They were colorful, yes, and they were beautiful, covered in tiny sugar crystals that glittered like stars in the light, but they didn't go together. None of this did. That was why she kept thinking of children playing in the kitchen: there seemed to be no sense of unity or theme in the castle. It was big. It was dramatic. It wasn't *coherent*.

This is a Nonsense world, she thought. Coherence probably wasn't a priority.

A small hatch popped open next to the door, and a pretty dancing doll sculpted from peppermint spires and taffy popped out, holding a scroll in its sticky hands.

"Her Majesty, the Unquestioned Ruler of Confection, Heir to the First Baker, the Queen of Cakes, will see you now!" proclaimed the doll. Its voice was high, shrill, and sweet, like honeyed syrup. "Be amazed at her munificence! Be delighted at her kindness! Be sure not to bite the hands that feed you!"

The doll was yanked suddenly backward, as if by a string around its waist. The hatch slammed shut, and the doors swung open, revealing the brightly colored wonderland of the throne room.

It was like Confection in miniature: a children's playroom version of the wild and potentially dangerous world outside. The walls were painted with green rolling hills topped by a pink and blue cotton candy sky. Lollipop trees and gumdrop bushes grew everywhere. The floor was polished green rock candy, like grass, like the rolling hills.

A step, and Cora saw that the walls weren't painted. They were piped frosting, puffed and placed to create the illusion of depth. Another step, and she saw that the bushes and trees were in jawbreaker pots, their roots trimmed to keep them from growing out of control.

On the third step, a veil of transplanted sugar vegetation was drawn back, and there was the Queen of Cakes, a thin, pinch-faced woman in a gown that was also a six-tiered wedding cake, its surface crafted from frosting and edible jewels. It didn't look like it could possibly be comfortable. Cora wasn't even sure the woman could move without cracking her couture and forcing it to be re-baked. She was holding a scepter in one hand, a long, elaborate stick of blown sugar and filigreed fondant, matching the crown upon her head.

The Queen looked at each of them in turn, eyes lingering for a moment on Sumi before finally settling on Rini. She smiled, slow and sweet.

"At last," she said. "Your mother did not invite me to your first birthday party, you know, and I the ruler of these lands. The first slice of cake should have been mine, to take as proper tribute."

"My mother offered the first slice of cake to the First Baker, as is right and proper, and she didn't invite *any* dead people to my party," said Rini smartly. "Not that we'd have invited you if you hadn't been dead. She always said you were the sort of person who never met a party she couldn't spoil."

The Queen of Cakes scowled for a moment—but only for a moment, her face smoothing back into pleasant placidity so fast that it felt like the scowl might well have been a lie. "Your mother was wrong about so many things. I can still remember her pouring hot grease on my hands. My beautiful hands." She held them up, showing that they were perfect and intact. "She thought to stop me, but look at me now. I'm here, healthy and hale and resuming my rule, and you, her precious little potential, you're fading away to nothing. How long do you think you have before the world realizes that you never existed and swallows you completely? I'll want to know when to plan my *own* party. The one to celebrate living forever."

"You were one of us," said Cora wonderingly.

The Queen of Cakes turned, eyes narrowed, to face her. "I don't recall inviting you to speak, *dear*," she said. "Now shut that fat mouth of yours, or I'll fill it for you."

"You were one of us," Cora repeated, not flinching from the venom in the word "fat." If anything, it was too familiar to really hurt. She'd heard that sort of hatred before, always from the women in her Weight Watchers groups, or at Overeaters Anonymous, the ones who had starved themselves into thinness and somehow failed to find the promised land of happy acceptance that they had always been told waited for them on the other side of the scale.

"One of who?" asked the Queen, venom in every word, a poisoned slice of fudge waiting to be shoved past Cora's lips.

"You found a door. You're not *from* here any more than Sumi was." Cora glanced to Kade, looking for confirmation, and felt hot validation fill her chest when he nodded, ever so slightly telling her that his suspicions were the same. She looked back to the Queen. "Were you a baker? Sumi wasn't a baker. She was . . ."

"A violinist," said Kade. "She didn't want to bake cakes. She just wanted to do something useful with her hands. She needed Nonsense, and I guess Nonsense needed her, with you trying to make it follow rules it never wanted."

The Queen of Cakes pursed her lips. "You must be from Sumi's world," she said primly. "You're just as obnoxious as she was. She's quiet now. How did you make her that way?"

"Well, she died, so that was a large part of it," said Kade.

"Dead people normally stay in their graves, out of the way of the rest of us. This, though . . ." The Queen smiled. "What a gift you've given me. No one will ever stand against me again when they see that my great enemy has been reduced to a shadow over a skeleton. How did you achieve it? I'll let you all go home, if you'll only tell me."

It would be a lie to say that the offer wasn't, in some ways, tempting. They had each been called upon to save a world and save themselves in the process, but not *this* world. Not even Rini had been called upon to save *this* world. She was trying to save her mother, which was something very different, even if it was still very admirable. They could go back to the school and wait for their doors to open, wait for the chance to go back to the worlds where things made sense, leaving this place and its nonsense behind. This wasn't their fight.

But Sumi was a silent skeleton, wreathed in shadows and rainbows, and Rini was disappearing an inch at a time, fading away according to the rules of her reality. If they left now, they couldn't save Rini. They could only leave her to be unmade, piece by piece, until there was nothing left but a memory.

(Would even that endure? If she had never been born, if she had never existed, would they remember her after she disappeared? Or would this whole madcap adventure be revised away, filed under things that never actually happened outside of a dream? What would they think had happened to Nadya, if Rini faded completely? Would they think she had found her door, gone home again, another success story for the other students to whisper about after curfew, hoping that their own doors would open now that someone else's had? Somehow, that seemed like the worst possibility of all. Nadya should be remembered for what she'd done to help them, not for what people invented to fill the space where she wasn't anymore.)

"No, thank you," said Cora primly, and she spoke for all three of them, for Kade, standing stalwart and steady, for Christopher, shaking and pale.

He didn't look well. Even Rini looked better, and she was being written out of existence.

"I didn't think you would, but I had to offer," said the Queen, leaning back in her throne. A chunk of her dress fell off and tumbled to the floor, where a butterscotch mouse with candy floss whiskers snatched it up and whisked it away. "I ask again: how is my old enemy here? What's dead is dead."

None of them said a word.

The Queen sighed. "Stubborn little children find that I can be a very cruel woman, when I want to. Did it have something to do with this?" She reached behind herself, pulling out Christopher's bone flute. "It's an odd little instrument. I blow and blow, but it doesn't make a sound."

The effect on Christopher was electric. He stood suddenly upright, vibrating, the color returning by drips to his cheeks, until they burned like he had a fever. "Give it to me," he said, and his voice was an aching whisper that somehow carried all the same.

"Oh, is this yours?" asked the Queen. "It's a funny color. What is it made of?"

"Bone." He took a jerky step forward, knees knocking. "My bone. It's *mine,* it's made of *me,* give it *back*."

"Bone?" The Queen looked at the flute again, this time with fascinated disgust. "Liar. There's no way you could lose a bone this big and still be whole."

"The Skeleton Girl gave me another bone to replace it and it's mine you have to give it back you have to *give it back*." Christopher's voice broke into a howl on his final words, and he took off running, the rope still dangling from his neck, launching himself at the Queen of Cakes.

His hands were only a few feet from her throat when one of the knights stomped on the end of the rope, jerking him backward. Christopher slammed into the floor, landing in a heap, and began to sob.

"Fascinating," breathed the Queen. "What terrible worlds you must all come from, to think this sort of thing is normal, or should be allowed to continue. Don't worry, children. You're in Confection now. You'll be safe and happy here, and as soon as that"—she indicated Rini—"finishes fading away, you'll be able to stay forever."

She snapped her fingers.

"Guards," she said, sweetly. "Find them someplace nice to be, where I won't have to hear them screaming. And leave the skeleton here. I want to play with it."

The Queen of Cakes leaned back in her throne and smiled as her latest enemies were dragged away. What a lovely day this was shaping up to be.

8 THE TALLEST TOWER

"SOMEPLACE NICE," IN THE castle of the Queen of Cakes, was a large, empty room with gingerbread walls and heaps of gummy fruit on the floor, presumably to serve as bedding for the prisoners. There had been no effort to chain the four of them up or keep them apart; the guards had simply dragged them up the stairs until they reached the top of what felt like the tallest tower in the world. The only window was almost too high for Cora to reach, and looking out of it revealed a rocky chocolate quarry, studded with the jagged edges of giant almonds. Oh, yes. They were stuck. Unless they could open the door, they weren't going *anywhere*.

Rini was slumped against the wall, eyes closed, the slope of one shoulder gone to whatever sucking nothingness was stealing her away one fragment at a time. Alarmingly, she wasn't the one in the worst condition. That dubious honor belonged to Christopher, who was curled into a ball next to the door, shaking uncontrollably.

"He needs his flute," said Kade, laying the back of one hand against Christopher's forehead and frowning. "He's freezing."

"Is it really made from one of his bones?" Cora dropped back to the flats of her feet and turned to face the pair.

Kade nodded grimly. "It was part of saving Mariposa, for him. He told me when I was updating the record of the world."

In addition to his duties as the school tailor, Kade was an amateur historian and mapmaker rolled into one, recording the stories of all the children who came through the school. He said it was because he was trying to accurately map the Compass that defined Nonsense and Logic, Virtue and Wickedness, all of the other cardinal directions of the worlds on the other side of their doors. Cora thought that was probably true, but she also thought he liked the excuse to talk to people about their shared differences, which became their shared similarities when held up to the right light. They had all survived something. The fact that they had survived different somethings didn't change the fact that they would always be, in certain ways, the same.

"Can it be put back?"

Christopher shook his head, and muttered weakly, "Wouldn't want it. There was something wrong inside. A dark thing. The doctors said it was a tumor. But the Skeleton Girl piped it away and freed me. Owe her . . . everything."

"But . . ."

"It's still *mine*." There was a flicker of fierceness in Christopher's voice, there and gone in an instant, like it had never existed in the first place.

Kade sighed, patting Christopher on the shoulder before he rose and walked over to stand next to Cora at the window. Dropping his voice to a low murmur, he said, "This doesn't happen as much as it used to—I guess the universe figured out it was an asshole move—but it's happened before. Kids who went through doors and came back with some magical item or other that still worked in our world, where there isn't supposed to be much magic at all."

"So?"

"So you want magic in *our* world, you pretty much have to be paying for it out of your own self, somehow. Most of the time, the magic item'd been tied to the person with blood or with tears or with something else that came out of their bodies. Or, in this case, a whole damn bone. The magic that powers the flute is Christopher. If he doesn't get it back . . ."

Cora turned to gape at him, horrified. "Are you saying he'll die?"

"Maybe not die. He's never been separated from it for more than a few minutes. Maybe he'll just get really sick. Or maybe the cancer will come back. I don't *know*." Kade looked frustrated. "I interview all the newbies, I write everything down, because there are so many doors, and so many little variations on the theme, and we don't *know*. He might die if we don't get it back. He wouldn't be the first."

Their stories were written down too, by Eleanor before his time, or by the other rare scholars of travel and consequence, of the space behind the doors. They wrote about girls who wasted to nothing when they were separated from their magic shoes or golden balls, about boys who burned alive in the night when their parents took away their cooling silver bells, about children who had been found at the bottom of the garden, magically cured of some unthinkable disease, only for the sickness to come rushing back ten years later when a sibling or one of their own children broke a little crystal statue that they had been instructed not to touch.

Travel *changed* people. Not all of the changes were visible, or even logical by the rules of a world where up was always up and down was always down and skeletons stayed in the ground instead of getting up and dancing around, but that didn't make the changes go away. They existed whether they were wanted or not.

Cora, whose hair grew in naturally blue and green, all over her body, looked uneasily over her shoulder at Christopher, who was huddled in a pile of gummi bears, shivering.

"We have to get his flute back," she said.

"How do you suggest we do that?" asked Rini. Her voice was flat, dull, devoid of sparkle or whimsy. She had given up. The resignation was visible in every remaining inch of her, slumped and shattered as she was. "The Queen of Cakes has an army. We have . . . nothing. We have nothing, and she has us, and she has my mother, and it's over. We've lost. I'm going to be unborn, and then I won't have to worry about this anymore. I hope you can get away. If you can, go to the candy corn fields. The farmers there will help you hide from the Queen. She hates them and they hate her, but candy corn isn't like most crops. It won't burn. So she leaves them alone as much as she can, and you'll be okay."

Rini paused for so long that Cora thought she was done talking. Then, in a hushed tone, she said, "I'm sorry. I shouldn't have brought you here. This is all my fault."

"This is the fault of the person who killed your mother, and of the *stupid* Queen of Cakes for being all 'rar look at me I can be a despot of a magical candy world aren't I great?' " Cora kicked the wall in her frustration. The gingerbread dented inward. Not enough to offer her a way to freedom—and even if it had, the way to freedom would have involved a long, long fall. "We agreed to come because we wanted to help. We're going to help."

"How?" asked Rini. "Christopher's too sick to stand, and he's the only one of you who's been useful."

Cora opened her mouth to object, paused, and shut it with a snap. She turned to Kade. "You," she said. "You're a tailor and you write stuff down, but what did you do when you went through your door? What was on the other side?"

Kade hesitated. Then he sighed and looked out the window, and said, "Every world has its own set of criteria. Some of them are . . . pickier . . . than others. Prism is considered a Fairyland. Technically it's a Goblin Market, which means they can control where the doors manifest. Every world chooses the children who get to visit, but Prism *curates* them. Prism watches them before they sweep them up, because Prism usually keeps them. Prism is one of the worlds we mostly knew about because of the hole it made in the compass, before I went there and got myself thrown out."

Cora said nothing. Speaking would have broken the spell, would have reminded Kade that he was talking to an audience. He might have stopped then. She didn't want that.

"In Prism, the Fairy Court has been fighting a war against the Goblin Empire for thousands of years. They could have won a hundred times. So could the goblins. They don't, because the war is all they know anymore. They have so many rituals and ceremonies and traditions wrapped up in fighting that if you took their war away, they'd be lost. I didn't know that, of course. I just knew that I was going to have an adventure. That I was going to be a hero, a savior, and do something that mattered for a change."

Kade's face darkened. "The Fairy Court always snatched little girls. The prettiest little girls they could find, the ones with ribbons in their hair and lace on their dresses. They liked the contrast we made against the goblin armies."

Cora jumped a little at the word "we." "What—"

"Oh, come on." Kade gave her a half-amused sidelong look. "You said Nadya was your best friend. There's no way she didn't tell you that."

"I . . . but, yes, but . . . I . . ." Cora stopped. "I don't have the vocabulary for this."

"Most people don't, until they need it, and then they need the whole thing at once," said Kade. "My parents thought I was a girl. The people in Prism responsible for choosing their next expendable savior thought I was a girl. Hell, *I* thought I was a girl, because I'd never had the time to stop and think about why I wasn't. It took me years of saving a world that stopped wanting me when I changed my pronouns to figure it out."

"But you saved the world," said Cora.

Kade nodded. "I did. The Goblin King made me his heir when I killed him. He called me the Goblin Prince in Waiting, and that was when I realized how long I'd been waiting for someone to *see* me, to really understand who I was, under the curls and the glitter and the things I didn't want but couldn't refuse."

"So you know how to use a sword," said Cora.

"Yes." Kade paused, looking at her warily. "Why?"

Cora smiled.

THE FIRST STEP was moving Christopher into the middle of the room, where he'd be easily visible from the door. Getting something heavy was the second. In the end, Cora had licked her fingers and driven them over and over again into the hard-packed frosting between the baked bricks of the wall, eroding it until she'd been able to punch one of the bricks clean out. After that, it had been easy to pry another one free, jagged edges and all.

Now, she rushed the door and beat her fists against it, shouting, "Hey! Hey! We need Christopher's flute! Hey! We need *help*!"

She kept hitting, kept yelling, until her hands hurt and her throat was sore. The door might be made of hardened shortbread, but the key word there was "hardened": it was still enough to hurt her. Still, she kept going. The plan only worked if she kept going.

Eventually, as she had hoped, footsteps echoed up the stairs outside, and a voice shouted, "You! Stop that! Be quiet!"

Cora was very good at ignoring people who told her to do foolish things. She kept hitting the door and yelling.

The door slammed open without warning, hitting her in the nose and knocking her back several feet into the tower room. That was fine. It hurt, but she had been anticipating a little pain, and she was an athlete. She was used to mashing her nose against the side of the pool, to skinning her knees and scraping her fingers. She staggered to her feet, trying to look cowed without looking overly terrified.

"We need Christopher's flute," she whined. "He's dying. Look." She pointed at Christopher, who was performing his part in their little play with distressing ease. All he had to do was lie there and look terrible. He was doing both, and they hadn't even needed to ask.

The guard at the door frowned dourly and took a step into

the room, past the threshold. Cora moved fast, slamming into his side and bearing him away from the doorway. Kade, who had been hidden by the angle of the door itself while it was open, stepped forward and slammed his chunk of edible masonry as hard as he could into the back of the guard's head. The man made a gagging noise and fell down.

Rini, who had been slumped against the wall, was suddenly there, back on her feet to deliver a solid kick to the fallen guard's throat. He made another gagging noise but didn't raise his hands to protect himself.

"You should go," she said, eyes on the man's still form. "I can watch him while you go."

"By 'watch him,' do you mean—"

Rini raised her head, candy corn irises seeming even brighter and more impossible than they had back at the school. "He doesn't want to be here," she said. "The world is reordering itself so the Queen of Cakes was always, and my family was never. But there isn't supposed to be a Queen of Cakes, which means he's supposed to be someplace other than here. I'm going to tie him up, and then I'm going to find out whether he knows where he's supposed to have been this whole time. But you should take his armor first."

Kade nodded uncertainly and began stripping the man's armor away. It was gilded foil over hard chocolate: it should have melted from the heat of the guard's skin, if nothing else, but it was still fresh and sound. Cora wrinkled her nose. Some things seemed like a misuse of magic, and this was one of them.

Christopher hadn't moved throughout the commotion. She turned and knelt next to him, checking his throat for a pulse. It was there. He wasn't gone yet. He might be going, but he wasn't gone.

"We're going to get your flute," she said softly. "It's going to be okay. You'll see. Just hang on. This would be a *stupid* way to die."

Christopher didn't say anything.

When she stood, Kade was dressed in the guard's gilded-foil armor, and was studying the guard's sword.

"It's weighted differently than I'm used to," he said. "I think it's toffee under the chocolate. But it's got an edge on it. I can make this work."

"Good," said Cora. "Let's go save the day."

9 DANCING WITH THE QUEEN OF CAKES

KADE MARCHED CORA into the throne room, one hand clenching her shoulder so hard that it verged on painful, the stolen sword sheathed at his hip. The Queen of Cakes, sitting on her throne with her chin propped on her hand, sat up a little straighter, seeming torn between irritation at the intrusion and relief that she had something to be annoyed about.

"What are *you* doing here?" she demanded. "I didn't call for any of the prisoners to attend on me."

Sumi was tethered to the base of the throne, a braided licorice rope around her skeletal throat, and the sight of her was enough to put steel in Cora's spine. They couldn't afford to get this wrong. If they did, then this would become the reality in Confection: a woman who thought that torturing the dead was appropriate and just.

"I asked to come," said Cora quickly, before Kade could have been expected to speak. "I wanted . . . I wanted to talk to you." She thought of Rini standing naked in the turtle pond, proudly telling Nadya that her vagina was a nice one, and felt the hot red flush rise in her cheeks. Being easily embarrassed could be a weapon, if she was willing to use it that way. "I thought maybe you could . . . I thought we might have something in common."

The Queen of Cakes raked her eyes up one side of Cora and down the other. Cora, who had endured many such inspections over the years, forced herself to stand perfectly still, not flinching away. She knew what the Queen was seeing. Double chin and bulging waistline and thighs that pressed against the fabric of her jeans, wearing them out a little more every day. She knew what the Queen *wasn't* seeing just as well. She wasn't seeing the athlete or the scholar or the friend or the hero of the Trenches. All she was seeing was fatty fatty fat fat, because that was all they ever saw when they looked at her that way. That was all that they were looking for.

The Queen of Cakes sighed, her face softening. "Oh, you poor child," she said. "How cruel this place must seem to you. The temptation of it all—unless that's what drew you to Confection? Are you looking to eat yourself to death on the hills and leave your body where no one will ever find it?"

"No," said Cora. "I wasn't drawn to Confection. I came to help Rini get her mother back. I didn't understand what Sumi had done to this place. We were wrong."

The Queen of Cakes narrowed her eyes. "Go on," she said.

"This wasn't Sumi's world, and that means it isn't really Rini's, either. They're too . . . I don't know. Too illogical to take care of a place like this. A place like this needs a firm hand. Someone who understands willpower and discipline." She needed to be careful not to lay things on too thickly. Overselling it would lead to suspicion, and suspicion would ruin everything.

The Queen of Cakes started to smile and nod. "Yes, exactly," she said. "This place was a mess when I found my own door."

"I can believe it," lied Cora, fighting the urge to remind the Queen that she had already tried to have this conversation. When people wanted to think that they knew more than she did, she found that it was generally best to let them. "You seem so perfect for what you are. This world must have needed you very badly."

"It did," said the Queen. She leaned back in her throne. A chunk fell off of her dress and tumbled to the floor. "It called me here to bake cookies—cookies! Who wants to put more cookies into the world? No one needs that sort of disgusting extravagance. It wanted to make me fat and lazy and awful, like all the people who came before me. Well, what *I* wanted was bigger, and better, and I won, didn't I? I won. What do *you* want, little renegade?"

"I want to learn to be . . ." Cora looked at the Queen's trim waist, wreathed as it was in cake, and swallowed bile at the hypocrisy of what she was about to say. *For Christopher,* she thought, before saying, "I want to be like you."

"Bring her closer," said the Queen. "I want to see her eyes."

Kade obediently marched Cora across the room. There were two guards, one to either side of the throne, neither close enough to intervene if things went south. That was good. Both guards had a spear, in addition to their swords. That was bad. Cora took a deep breath and kept her eyes on the Queen of Cakes, trying to focus on how necessary this all was.

When they were close enough, the Queen leaned forward, gripping Cora's chin in bony fingers and tilting her head first one way, then the other.

"You could be pretty, you know," she said. "If you learned to control your appetite, if you understood how important it was to take care of yourself, you could be pretty. I've never seen hair quite like yours. Yes, you could be a striking beauty. Staying here will help you. The best way to become strong is to surround yourself with the things you can never have. The daily denial reminds you what you're suffering for."

Cora said nothing. She was used to having people assume that her size was a function of her diet, when in fact it owed more to her metabolism and her genes, neither of which she could control.

The Queen smiled. "Yes," she said, letting go of Cora's chin and sitting back in her throne. "I think I'll keep you."

"Thank you," said Cora meekly, and took a step backward, putting herself behind Kade. "Truly, you're a monarch to be emulated—and overthrown. Now!"

Kade had been trained as a hero and a warrior, and had earned the title of Goblin Prince in Waiting with his good right arm. His sword was free of its sheath before Cora finished speaking, the tip coming to rest at the hollow of the Queen's throat, pressed down just hard enough to dimple the surface of her skin.

"Don't move, now," he drawled, behind the safe shield of his helmet. "You want to hand over that flute you took from our friend? He's sorely missing it. Cora?"

"Here." She stepped forward, holding out her hand. The Queen of Cakes scowled before sullenly reaching into her dress and slapping the flute, now smeared with frosting, into Cora's palm. Cora danced back before the Queen could do anything else.

"You'll pay for this," said the Queen, in an almost-conversational tone. "I'll have your bones for gingerbread, and your candied sweetmeats for my dinner table."

"Maybe," said Kade. "Maybe not. Neither of your guards seems to be coming to save you. That tells me a lot about the kind of place you've got here." Indeed, the guards were standing frozen at their posts, seemingly unable to decide what to do next.

Cora walked over to where Sumi was tethered, leaving Kade with the Queen. Sumi turned her head to look at Cora, spectral eyes over glistening bone, and Cora suppressed her shudder. This was not the sort of thing she was prepared for.

"Hang on just a second," she said to Sumi, and walked on, stopping when she reached the first guard. "Why aren't you trying to defend your boss?"

"I don't know," said the guard. "I don't . . . None of this feels right. None of this feels real. I don't think I'm supposed to be here."

Probably because he wasn't supposed to be. He was meant to be tending a candy corn farm of his own, or fishing for some impossible catch within the waves of the Strawberry Sea. The Queen of Cakes was a dead woman as much as Sumi was, but unlike Sumi, she was dressed in skin and speech, still talking, still moving through the world. That had to warp things. For her to have a castle, she would need courtiers, and guards, and people to do the mopping-up.

"There are too many dead people here," muttered Cora. Louder, she said, "Leave, then. If you're not willing to defend her, you don't have to be our enemy, and you can go. Get out and let us fix the world."

"But the Queen—"

"Really isn't going to be your main problem if you don't get the hell out." Cora bared her teeth in what might have been a smile and might have been a snarl. "Trust me. She's not going to be in a position to hand out punishments."

The guard looked at her uncertainly. Then he dropped his spear, turned, and ran for the door. He was almost there when the other guard followed suit, leaving the four of them—two truly among the living, two more than half among the dead—alone.

Cora turned and walked back to Sumi, who was still waiting with absolute patience. She dug her fingers into the braided licorice rope, feeling it squish and tear under her nails, until it gave way completely, ripping in two and setting Sumi free.

Sumi didn't seem to realize that she was free. She continued to stand where she was, shade over bone, staring straight ahead, like nothing that was happening around her genuinely mattered, or ever could. Cora wrinkled her nose before taking Sumi's hand, wrapping her fingers tight around the skeletal woman's bare bones, and leading her gently back to where Kade was holding the Queen.

"Those traitors will bake for what they've done to me," snarled the Queen of Cakes.

Kade cocked his head. "That's almost a riddle. Will you bake them, or are you going to sentence them to some suitable length of time in your cookie factory? Not that it actually matters either way, since you're not going to be giving any orders for a while." He leaned forward and grabbed her by the arm. "Come with me."

For the first time, the Queen looked afraid. "Where—where are you taking me?"

"Where you belong," said Kade. He pulled her across the throne room to the door, shedding chunks of her dress with every step, and Cora followed, Sumi walking silently beside her, bony feet tapping on the floor.

CHRISTOPHER WAS STILL breathing when they reached the tower room, and Rini had tied their captive guard up so tightly that he was more a cocoon than a captive, propped in the far corner and making muffled grunting noises against the severed gummi bear leg she had stuffed into his mouth. She raised her head when the door opened, eyes widening in relief. Well. Eye. Her left eye was gone, replaced by a patch of nothingness that somehow revealed neither the inside of her skull nor the wall behind her. It was simply gone, an absence masquerading as an abscess on the world.

"Did you . . ." She stopped herself as Sumi stepped into the room behind Cora. "Mom."

"She's still dead," spat the Queen of Cakes, struggling against the taffy rope Kade had wrapped around her wrists. "Nothing you do is going to change that."

"I don't know," said Kade. "Killing her early seems to have brought you back just fine. Seems like cause and effect aren't all that strict around here."

He shoved the Queen of Cakes forward, until she stumbled and fell into a frosted, crumb-covered heap.

"Tie her up," he said to Rini, holding his stolen sword in front of him to ward off any possible escape attempts.

Cora stepped around him, moving toward Christopher, who looked so small, and so frail. The blood seemed to have been leeched away from his face and hands, leaving his naturally brown skin surprisingly pale, like scraped parchment stretched over a bucket of whey. She knelt, careful not to jostle him, and lifted the dead starfish of his hand off the floor.

"I think this is yours," she said, and pressed the bone flute into his hand.

Christopher opened his eyes, inhaling sharply, like it was the first true breath he'd been able to take in hours. The color came back to his skin, not all at once, but flooding outward from his hand, racing up his arm until it vanished beneath his sleeve, only to reappear as it crept up his neck and suffused his face. He sat up.

"Fuck me," he said.

"What, here? Now? In front of Kade?" Cora put on her best pretense of a simpering expression. "I'm not that kind of girl."

Christopher looked startled for a moment. Then he laughed, and stood, offering her his left hand. It was probably the only hand he was going to have free for a while. The fingers on the right were clenched so tight around the bone flute that they had gone pale again, this time from the pressure.

"Thank you," he said, with all the sincerity he had. "I don't think I had much time left."

"All part of the job," said Cora.

"Chris? You all right?" called Kade. He pressed the tip of his sword down a little harder into the hollow of the Queen's throat, dimpling the skin. "You say the word and she's gone."

The Queen said nothing, frozen in her terror while Rini wrapped more and more pulled taffy and gummy candy around her. She looked like all of this had suddenly become genuinely, awfully real, like it had all been a game to her before.

And maybe it had been, once. Maybe she had stumbled through her door into a world full of people who grew candy corn from the chocolate and graham soil and thought that none of them were real people; like none of them truly mattered. Maybe she had played at becoming despot instead of baker because she hadn't believed that there would be consequences. Not until another traveler came along, a fighter rather than a crafter, because Confection hadn't needed another baker, not with their last one sitting on a throne and demanding tribute. Not until her death at Sumi's hands . . . but even that had been reversed, forgiven by the world when Sumi died before she could return and start a proper revolution.

Until this moment, even into death and out of it again, the Queen of Cakes hadn't truly believed that she could die.

"I'd say something about being the better man, but fuck, man, I don't know," said Christopher. He stretched before slumping forward and groaning. "I feel like I've been dragged behind a truck for the last hundred miles. This is the worst. Let's never come here again."

"Deal," said Cora.

Christopher looked at Kade and the Queen of Cakes, and the room went slowly still. He took a step forward.

"I never got offered a door to this place," he said. "I'm not a baker, and I wouldn't have liked it here. Too sweet for me. Too much light, not enough crypts. I like my sugar in skull form, and my illumination to come from lanterns hung in the branches of leafless trees. This place isn't mine. But the place I *did* go, the place that *is* mine, it sort of screwed with my ideas about life and death. It made me see that the lines aren't as clear as the living always make them out to be. The lines *blur*. And you, lady? I don't want you to be dead, because I never want to see you again."

He looked away from the shaking Queen of Cakes, focusing on Kade. “Let’s get the hell out of here,” he said, and turned and walked out of the room.

When the others followed, they left the Queen of Cakes and the one captive guard bound and gagged, to be found or forgotten according to the whims of fate. If the Queen had thought to order her prisoners fed, she might be rescued.

Or she might not. Whatever the outcome, it no longer mattered to the rest of them. They were moving on.

10 THE CANDY CORN FARM

"BEING DEAD FOR A while really messes with your staffing," said Cora, as they emerged from the castle's kitchen door and into the wide green frosting grass fields beyond. No farmers worked here, although there were a few puffy spun-sugar sheep nipping at the ground. "I figured we'd get caught at *least* twice."

"Once was enough for me," said Kade grimly. He had shed his stolen armor, but still carried his stolen sword. There was blood on the hard candy edge, commemorating that one brief encounter, that one hard slash.

Cora turned her face away. She had never seen someone die like that before. Drowning, sure. Drowning, she knew intimately. She had pulled a few sailors to their deaths with her own two hands, when there wasn't any other way to end a conflict, when the waves and the whispering foam were the only answer. She was *good* at drowning. But this . . .

This had been a stroke, and flesh opening like the skin of an orange, and blood gushing out, blood everywhere, hot and red and essentially animal in a way that seemed entirely at odds with the candy-colored wonderland around them. The people who lived here should have bled treacle or molasses or sugar syrup, not hot red animal wetness, so vital, so unthinkable, so, well, *sticky*. Cora had only brushed against one edge of one shelf stained with the stuff, and she still felt as if she would never be clean again.

"How far from here to your farm?" asked Christopher, looking to Rini. He was holding his flute in both hands now, tracing silent arpeggios along the length of it. Cora suspected that he was never going to let it go again.

"Not far," said Rini. "It usually takes most of a day to get to the castle ruins, so Mom can show me what they look like when the sunset hits them just so, and she can tell me ghost stories until the moon mantas come out and chase us away. But it never takes more than an hour or two to get back to the edge of the fields. There's not as much that's interesting about walking home, not unless robbers attack or something, and that almost never happens."

"Nonsense worlds are a little disturbing sometimes," said Christopher.

Rini beamed. "Why thank you."

Sumi's rainbow-dressed skeleton was still plodding faithfully along, neither speeding up nor slowing down, not even when she put her foot down in a hole or tripped over a protruding tree root. When that happened, she would stumble, never quite falling, recover her balance, and continue following the rest of them. It wasn't clear whether she understood where she was or what she was doing there. Even Christopher lacked the vocabulary that would allow him to ask.

"Do you know yet?" asked Cora, glancing uneasily at Rini.

"What you're going to do with her? You have to do *something* with her."

"I'm going to find a way to make her be alive again, so that I can be born and the Queen of Cakes can be overthrown and everything can be the way it's supposed to be." Rini's tone was firm. "I like existing. I'm not ready to unexist just because of stupid causality. I didn't invite stupid causality to my birthday party, it doesn't get to give me any presents."

"I'm not sure causality works that way, but sure," said Kade wearily. "Let's just get to where we're going, and we'll see."

Cora said nothing, but she supposed they would. It seemed inevitable, at this point. So she, and the others, walked on.

RINI WAS TRUE to her word. They had been walking no more than an hour when the land dipped, becoming a gentle slope that somehow aligned with the shape of the mountains and the curve of the land to turn a simple candy corn farm into a stunning vista.

The fields were a lush green paean to farming, towering stalks reaching for the sky, leaves rustling with such vegetative believability that it wasn't until Cora blinked that she realized the ears of corn topping each individual stalk were actually individual pieces of candy corn, each the length of her forearm. Their spun-sugar silk blew gently in the breeze. Everything smelled of honey and sugar, and somehow that smell was exactly appropriate, exactly right.

Beehives were set up around the edge of the field, and fat striped humbugs and butterscotch candies crawled on the outside, their forms suggesting their insect progenitors only vaguely, their wings thin sheets of toffee that turned the sunlight soft and golden.

Like the castle of the Queen of Cakes, the farmhouse and barn were both built of gingerbread, a holiday craft taken to its absolute extreme. Unlike the castle, they were perfectly symmetrical and well designed, built with an eye for function as well as form, not just to use as much edible glitter as was humanly possible. The farmhouse was low and long, stretching halfway along the edge of the far field, its windows made of the same toffee as the wings of the bees. Rini smiled when she saw it, relief suffusing her remaining features and making her look young and bright and peaceful.

"My father will know what to do," she said. "My father always knows what to do."

Kade and Cora exchanged a glance. Neither of them contradicted her. If she wanted to believe that her father was an all-knowing sage who would solve everything, who were they to argue? Besides, this wasn't their world. For all they knew, she was right.

"Come on, Mom!" said Rini, exhorting Sumi to follow her into the candy corn field. "Dad's waiting!" She plunged into the green. The skeleton followed more sedately after, with the three visitors from another world bringing up the rear.

"I always thought that if I found another door, to *anywhere,* I'd take it, because anywhere had to be better than the world where my parents were asking me awful questions all the time," said Christopher. "There was this telenovela about a bunch of sick kids in a hospital that my mother made me watch like, two whole seasons of after I got back, giving me these hopeful little looks after every episode, like I was finally going to confess that yes, the Skeleton Girl was another patient with an eating disorder, or a homeless girl, or something, and not, you know, a fucking *skeleton*."

"Let's be fair here," said Kade. "If my son came back from a journey to a magical land and told me straight up that he wanted to marry a woman who didn't have any internal organs, I'd probably spend some time trying to find a way to spin it so that he wasn't saying that."

"Oh, like you're attracted to girls because you think they have pretty kidneys," said Christopher.

Kade shrugged. "I like girls. Girls are beautiful. I like how they're soft and pretty and have skin and fatty deposits in all the places evolution has deemed appropriate. My favorite part, though, is how they have actual structural stability, on account of how they're not *skeletons*."

"Are all boys as weird as the two of you, or did I get really lucky?" asked Cora.

"We're teenagers in a magical land following a dead girl and a disappearing girl into a field of organic, pesticide-free candy corn," said Kade. "I think weird is a totally reasonable response to the situation. We're whistling through the graveyard to keep ourselves from totally losing our shit."

"Besides," said Christopher. "You don't choose your dates based on their internal organs, do you? Settle this."

"Sorry, but I have to side with Kade if you're dragging me into your little weirdness parade." Cora relaxed a little. This was starting to feel more like one of her walks around the school grounds with Nadya than a life-threatening quest. Maybe Rini was right, and her father would fix everything. Maybe they'd be able to go home s—

Cora stopped dead. "The bracelet."

"What?" Kade and Christopher stopped in turn, looking anxiously at her.

"We didn't get Rini's bracelet back from the Queen of Cakes," said Cora. She shook her head, wide-eyed, feeling her chest start to tighten. "We were so worried about getting Christopher's flute that we didn't look for the bracelet. How are we going to get back to the school?"

"We'll figure it out," said Kade. "If nothing else, the wizard she got the first set of beads from will be able to take care of us. Breathe. It's going to be okay."

Cora took a deep breath, eyeing him. "You really think so?"

"No," he said baldly. "It's never okay. But I told myself that every night when I was in Prism. I told myself that every morning when I woke up, still in Prism. And I got through. Sometimes that's all you can do. Just keep getting through until you don't have to do it anymore, however much time that takes, however difficult it is."

"That sounds . . ." Cora paused. "Actually, that sounds really nice. I'm not that good at lying to myself."

"Whereas I am a king of telling myself bullshit things I don't really believe but need to accept for the sake of everyone around me." Kade spread his arms, framing the moment. "I can make anything sound reasonable for five minutes."

"I can't," said Christopher. "I just refuse to die where the Skeleton Girl can't find me. I don't think this is the sort of world that connects to Mariposa. It's too far out of sync."

"What do you mean?" Cora started walking again, matching her step to theirs.

"You know Rini isn't the first person to come to our world—call it 'Earth,' since that's technically its name—from somewhere else, right?" Kade paused barely long enough for Cora to nod before he said, "Well, every time it's happened and we've known about it, someone's done their best to sit them down and ask a bunch of questions. Getting a baseline, getting more details for the Compass. Most of them, they have their own stories about doors. They knew someone who knew someone whose great-aunt disappeared for twenty years and came back the same age she'd been when she went away, full of stories that didn't make sense and with a king's ransom in diamonds in her pocket, or salt, or snakeskins. Currencies tend to differ a bit, world to world. And what we've found is that there are worlds *to* and worlds *from*."

"What do you mean?"

"Confection, it was made by the doors. Its rules were set by the bakers, and maybe those bakers came from Logical worlds, but what they wanted out of life was Nonsense, so they whipped themselves up a Nonsense world, one layer at a time. Half the nonsense probably comes from having so many cooks in the kitchen. Thirty people bake the same wedding cake, it doesn't matter if they're all masters of their craft, they're still going to come up with something that tastes a little funny."

Cora nodded slowly. "So this is a world *to*."

"Yes. Earth, now, we're a world *from*. When we get travelers, it's people like Rini, people who didn't have a choice, people who've been exiled, or who are looking for an old friend who came *to* a long time ago, and hasn't made it back yet, even though they said they were going to." Kade paused. "Earth isn't the only world *from*. We know of at least five, and that means there are probably more out there, too far away for us to have much crossover. Worlds *from* tend to be mixed up. A little Wicked, a little Virtuous. A little Logic, a little Nonsense. They may trend toward one or the other—I feel Earth's more Logical than Nonsensical, for example, although Aunt Eleanor doesn't always agree—but they exist to provide the doors with a place to anchor."

"All the worlds *to,* they connect to one or more of the worlds *from,*" said Christopher, picking up the thread. "So Mariposa and Prism both connect to Earth, and get travelers from there. And maybe they also connect to a few similar worlds, like how Nadya's world touches on Nancy's, and maybe they connect to another world *from,* so they can get the travelers they need without drawing too much attention. But when they connect to another world *to,* it's always one where the rules are almost the same."

"And the rules here aren't like the rules you had back in Mariposa," said Cora slowly.

Christopher nodded. "Exactly. Mariposa was Rhyme and Logic, and this place is Nonsense and Reason. I can't say whether it's Wicked or Virtuous, but that doesn't really matter for me, because Mariposa is Neutral, so it can sync to either. What it can't handle is Nonsense."

"My head hurts," said Cora.

"Welcome to the club," said Kade.

They had reached the end of the candy corn field. The trio stepped out of the green, onto the hard-packed crumble of the dirt in front of the farmhouse. It was impossible to tell what it was made of without tasting it, and Cora found that her curiosity didn't extend to licking the ground. That was good. It was useful to know that there were limits to how far she was willing to commit to this new reality. Or maybe she just didn't want to eat dirt.

There was Rini, in front of the farmhouse, with her arms around a man who was taller than she was by several inches. He must have towered over Sumi even when she was a fully grown adult woman, and not the teenage skeleton standing silently off to one side. His hair was yellow. Not blond: yellow, the color of ripe candy corn, the color of butterscotch.

"The people here are made of meat, right?" murmured Cora.

Kade glanced down at the patch of blood on his trousers and said, "Pretty damn sure."

"How do they not all die of malnutrition? How do they still have any *teeth*?"

"How did your skin not rot and fall off when you spent like, two years living in saltwater all the time?" Kade flashed her a quick, almost wry smile. "Every world gets to make its own rules. Sometimes those rules are going to be impossible. That doesn't make them any less enforceable."

Cora was silent for a moment. Finally, she said, "I want to go home."

"Don't we all?" asked Christopher mournfully, and that was that: there was nothing else to say. They walked toward Rini and her family, hoping for a miracle, hoping for a solution, while the fields of candy corn grew green all around them, reaching ever for the sun.

RINI WAITED UNTIL her friends—were they her friends now? Had they bonded sufficiently in adversity that they could use that label? She'd never really had friends before, she didn't know the rules—were almost upon her before letting go of her father and stepping back, letting him see them, letting *them* see *him*.

He was tall. They'd been able to see that from a distance, along with the unnatural yellow of his hair. What they hadn't been able to see was that his eyes were like Rini's, candy corn somehow transformed into an eye color, or that his hands were large and calloused from a lifetime spent working in the fields, or that his face had been tanned by the sun until he was almost as dark as his daughter, although his undertones were different, warm where hers were cool, ruddy red and peach, not amber and honey. They looked nothing alike. They looked absolutely alike.

Kade, who had known Sumi better than either of his companions, looked at Rini, and looked at her father, and saw Sumi in the differences between them, the places where she had been added to the recipe that, when properly baked, had resulted in her daughter.

"Sir," he said, with a very small bow. It seemed appropriate, somehow. "I'm Kade. It's a pleasure to meet you."

"Thank you for bringing my daughter home," said Rini's father. "She tells me you've had quite the adventure. The Queen of Cakes is back to her old tricks, is she? Well, I suppose that was the only thing that could happen in a world where my Sumi never made it back to me." He sounded less sad than simply resigned. This was the way he had always expected the world to go: snatching joy out of his hands for the sheer sake of doing it, and not because he, personally, had done anything to earn the loss. "My name is Ponder, and it's a pleasure to have you on my farm."

"This is no time for manners and moodiness, Daddy," said Rini, with a little of her old imperiousness. Being near her father seemed to be bolstering her spirits, enough to remind her that, fading or not, she was still here; there was still time for her to fix this. "I found Mom. I found her bones in a world that didn't know how to laugh, and I found her spirit in a world that didn't know how to run, and now I need you to tell me how to find her heart, so I can stick them all back together again."

Rini smiled at her father when she finished, guilelessly bright, like he was the answer to all her prayers: like he was going to make things right again.

Ponder sighed deeply before reaching over to touch her cheek—not the one with the emptiness where her eye had been, but the one that was still whole and sound, untouched by the nothingness that was eating her up from the inside.

"I don't know, baby," he said. "I told you when you went that I didn't know. I'm just a candy corn farmer. My only part in this play was loving your mother and raising you, and I did both of them as well as I could, but that didn't make me worldly, and it didn't make me wise. It made me a man with a hero for a wife and a daughter who was going to do something great someday, and that was *all I wanted to be.* I never saved the day. I never challenged the gods. I was the person you could come home to when the quest was over, and I'd greet you with a warm fudge pie and a how was your day, and I'd never feel like I was being left out just because I was forever left behind."

Rini made a small sound, somewhere between a gasp and a sob, and covered her face with what was left of her hands.

"The Lord of the Dead said that Sumi's nonsense came home," said Christopher abruptly. "Mr. Ponder, Rini told us about the Bakers. How they come and make Confection bigger and stranger in order to do what they need to do. Do you know where the oven is? Where they bake the world?"

"Of course," said Ponder. "It's a day's journey from here."

Christopher smiled wanly. "I guess it would have to be," he said. "Can you show us the way?"

PART IV

THIS IS WHERE WE CHANGE THE WORLD

11 SUGAR AND SPICE AND PAYING THE PRICE

PONDER HAD GIVEN THEM each a bag of provisions and an item he thought they might find useful: a small sickle for Cora, a jar of honey for Kade, something that was either a white rock or a very hard egg for Christopher. What he had given Rini was less clear, since she walked side by side with her mother's skeleton, hands empty, eyes fixed on the horizon.

Cora sidled over to her. "Are you all right?" she asked.

"My father gave us gifts because he had to, not because they're going to help us in the here and now," said Rini. "You can throw them away if you like."

"I don't know," said Cora, who had never owned a sickle before. She thought it was pretty. "Maybe it'll come in handy someday."

"Maybe," Rini agreed.

Cora frowned. "Okay, seriously. Are you all right?"

"Yes. No. I don't know. I've never been to see the Baker," said Rini. Her voice was low, even awed. "I always thought I'd do it someday, maybe, when I felt brave enough, but I haven't done it yet, and I'm a little scared. What if she doesn't like me? Or what if she likes me so much that she wants me to stay with her for always, to be her kitchen companion and kept thing? I would do it. For my mother, for my world, I would do it. But I'd die a little more inside every hour of every day, until I was just a candy shell filled with shadows."

"Wait." Cora glanced at Kade and Christopher, alarmed. The boys were talking quietly as they walked, Christopher's fingers still tracing silent songs along the length of his flute. She looked back to Rini. "We're not going to see the Baker. We're going to see the oven the Baker used when she made the world. Big difference."

"Not really," said Rini. "You can't go into someone's kitchen while they're using it and not expect to see them."

Cora stared at her. "I thought you said the Baker left a long time ago."

"I said *a* Baker left a long time ago. One of them did. Lots of them did. The current Baker, though, she's only been here since I was a little girl. She came through a door and started making things, and she's been making things ever since." Rini shook her head. "I guess she's probably still here, even though the Queen of Cakes is alive again, because the Queen was never a Baker, not really, but she was supposed to be, and the world needs to be kept up if we don't want it to fall down."

"Oh sweet Neptune I am getting such a headache," muttered Cora, massaging her temple with one hand. "All right. I . . . all right. We're going to see a god. We're going to see the god of this messed-up cafeteria of a reality, and then we're going to go the hell back to the school and stay there until our own doors open. Yes. That's what we're going to do. We're going to do that."

"Cora?" called Kade. "You all right?"

"I'm fine," said Cora. "Just, you know. Coming to terms with the idea that we're about to go hassle someone who is *functionally divine* in this reality. Because that's exactly how I was planning to spend my afternoon."

"Could be worse," said Kade. "Could be the first god you were meeting."

Cora frowned. "This *is* the first god I'm meeting."

"Really? Because I assumed you were using the word to mean 'absolute arbiter of the rules of the reality I'm standing in.' Were you?" Kade cocked his head. "If you were, you've already met at least one god, and possibly two. *Probably* two. The Lord and Lady of the Dead, back in Nancy's world, remember? They didn't get those titles in an open election."

Cora blanched. "Really?"

"If you ask me, they probably got the same deal the first Baker here did. Just a couple of confused kids who stumbled into a dead world and decided, for whatever reason, that they should stay." That, or the world refused to let them go. That could happen, too. Worlds could put down roots, winding them through the heart and drawing tighter with every breath, until "home" was an empty idea with nothing on the other side of it.

"Fuck." Cora shook her head, looking back to Rini, and to the silent, narrow shape of Sumi, wrapped in her own ghost. "I did *not* sign up for gods."

"None of us signed up for any of this," said Christopher. "I just wanted to live to see my sixteenth birthday."

"I just wanted to have an adventure," said Kade.

Sumi, voiceless, said nothing, and maybe that was for the best. She had been like Cora, a savior, a tool, someone who was called and offered a wonderful new existence in exchange for doing just one thing: saving the world. She'd done it, too, before she'd been killed too soon and had all her hard work revised away.

Nonsense was exhausting. Cora couldn't wait to get back to the school, where everything was dry and dreadful, but where things at least made sense from one moment into the next.

The road was made of sandy crushed graham crackers, and wound its way through a pastoral landscape that would have been impressive even if it hadn't been crafted entirely from living sugar. Kade paused to pick a handful of sugar buttons off a bush, and munched idly as he walked.

Cora frowned. "Rini," she said. "If the Bakers made the world and then went home, where did the people come from? Like your father? I mean, he's clearly enough like the people from my world for Sumi to marry him and have you, but that doesn't make *sense,* not really. Everything else is sugar."

"Oh, there were people who didn't want to be where they were, and the world was getting so big that the Baker was spending all her time—we had the First Confectioner then, and she was *very* busy doing sugar work—fixing things. So she opened all the doors she could, and told the people who were scared or hungry or lonely or bored that if they came through, they'd never be able to go back, because the doors wouldn't open for them, but that she could give them candy hearts to make them a part of this world, and then they could stay here and be happy and fix all the things she didn't want to fix, forever." Rini shrugged. "A lot of people came, I guess. She made them new hearts, and they found places to be, and they made homes and planted fields and built ships, and now there's me, and my father has a candy heart and my mother had a meat one, and they both loved me just as much as the moon loves the sky."

"The Pied Piper of Hamelin," said Christopher, almost wonderingly.

Cora, who had never considered that there might be less personal doors, doors that swallowed entire populations whole—with or without their consent—chewed anxiously on her lip, and kept walking. She was getting *tired* of walking. It had never been one of her top ten ways to exercise. It might not even be top twenty, although she wasn't sure there *were* twenty ways to exercise worth considering, unless she started counting every swim stroke and every dance style as a different category. Worse yet, this was *necessary* walking. She couldn't complain if she wanted to.

(And even though she wanted to, she never *wanted* to. If the fat person was the first one to say "hey, I'm tired" or "hey, I'm hungry" or "hey, can we sit down," it was always because they were fat, and not because they were a human being with a flesh body that sometimes had needs. Maybe Christopher had the right of it, going someplace where people had figured out how to do without the fleshy bits, where they would be judged on their own merits, not on the things people assumed about them.)

Christopher stopped, putting one hand up before bending forward and resting both hands on his knees, flute jutting out at a jaunty angle. "Just a second," he said. "Almost died a few hours ago. Need to catch my breath."

"It's okay," said Cora magnanimously. She kicked her left foot back and reached down to grab it, pulling it up into a stretch. The muscles in her thigh protested before they relaxed, letting her work out the incipient knots.

When she glanced up again, Kade was looking at her, impressed.

"You're more flexible than I am," he said.

"Swimmer," she said. "I have to be."

Kade nodded. "Makes sense."

Rini turned and glowered at the three of them. It was an odd expression, with her one remaining eye and her half-faded cheek muscles, but she managed it all the same. "We need to keep moving," she said. "I'm running out of time."

"Sorry," said Christopher. He straightened. "I'm okay."

"Good," snapped Rini. She started walking again, and the others hurried to keep up with her.

Kade moved to walk on her left side, sparing only a brief glance for Sumi, walking on her right. He focused on Rini's face, trying not to look away from what wasn't there anymore. She deserved more than that. She deserved at least the pretense of her dignity.

"I know you can't say for sure how much farther, but we'll be there soon," he said. "The Baker will help us, and then you can go home to your family, and things will be better. You'll see."

"Time kept happening here and it didn't happen for you. I'm later than you. My mother's younger than I am," said Rini bitterly. "If we fix her, does that fix *me*? Or do I keep fading, since now she's too young to be anything but a child bride for my father—and he'd never do that, he would never have *done* that, even before he had a daughter of his own. Even if we get her back and she's this much younger than me, do I still lose everything?"

"The prophecy—"

"Only said that she'd defeat the Queen of Cakes and usher

in an era of peace and peanut butter cookies. It didn't say *when* she would do it, or that she'd for sure get to marry her true love and have a ravishingly beautiful daughter named Rini who'd get to grow up and find a true love of her own." Rini's mouth twisted in a bitter line. "Nobody promised me a happy ending. They didn't even promise me a happy existence."

Kade looked at the road. "We'll fix this," he said again.

"We'll try," said Rini.

They kept walking. One moment, they were passing through the pastoral fields of green frosting and sugar flowers; the next, they were approaching the gates of what looked very much like a junkyard, if junkyards were made of the discarded remains of a thousand kitchen projects. Fallen soufflés, pieces of trimmed-off cake, and slabs of cracked fudge were everywhere, heaped into mountains of discarded treats behind a chain link fence of braided fruit vines. Kade blinked.

"This where we're going?" he asked.

Rini nodded, expression almost reverent. "The Baker is here," she breathed.

The five of them walked toward the gate. It swung open at their approach, and silently, they stepped inside.

THE JUNKYARD WAS impossibly large, stretching on toward forever, like it had its own laws about things like geometry and physics and the way the land should bend. The four travelers walked close together, their hands occasionally touching, like they were afraid that even a moment's separation might result in one or more of them disappearing into those towering piles of debris and never being seen again.

As they walked, the piles grew fresher. There was no mold—things didn't even seem to go truly stale—but there was a scent to fresh-baked goods that was missing from the heaps around the edge, a homey mixture of heat and sugar and comfort food that promised safety, security, and sweetness on the tongue.

They turned a corner, and there she was. The Baker.

She was short, and round, and had skin a few shades darker than Christopher's, and a pretty blue cloth wrapped around her head, concealing her hair. She looked no more than seventeen. Her skirt brushed the ground as she bent to remove a pie from the oven in front of her. Somehow, she had constructed a free-standing kitchen in the middle of a junkyard—or maybe she had created the junkyard around her free-standing kitchen, building it one broken cookie and discarded cupcake at a time.

Rini was staring at her, open-mouthed, a tear in her eye. Sumi actually took a step forward without being prompted, and a piece of biscotti cracked under her bony foot.

The Baker looked up from her oven and smiled. "There you are," she said, turning to put her pie down on the nearby counter. Had that counter been there a moment before? Cora wasn't sure. "I was hoping you'd make it."

Rini made a stifled gasping sound and turned her face away.

The Baker stepped out of her kitchen, walking across the broken-biscuit ground toward Rini, seemingly unaware of how the cracks smoothed out under her feet, how the cookie colors brightened, how the sugar shone. She was healing her world through her mere presence—but that presence was required. She could create. She could repair. She couldn't be everywhere at once.

"My poor sweet girl," said the Baker, and reached for what

remained of Rini's hands. "You found her. You found our Sumi, and you brought her home."

"Can you fix her?" Rini sniffled. Tears were leaking constantly from her eye, running unchecked down her cheek. "Please, can you fix her? The Lord of the Dead said her nonsense would be here. That's all we need to put her back together again. Can you?"

"Oh, my dear," said the Baker, and let go of Rini's hands. "Nonsense returns to where it's made, that's true, but it's like flour in the air: you can't just pull it back. You have to let it settle. It goes back into everything. It makes the world continue turning. If your mother's nonsense is here, I can't reclaim it."

"Well, can you make more?" asked Cora. "You're the Baker. You're the one who makes this world what it is. Can't you just . . . whip up a new batch of nonsense?"

"It's not like gingersnaps," said the Baker.

"So it *is* like flour and it's *not* like gingersnaps and you're still the person in charge of this whole world, so why can't you just decide that what you're baking now is a happy ending for everyone involved?" Cora folded her arms, resisting the urge to scowl. "I'm tired, I'm confused, and I'm not made for a Nonsense world, so I'd be really pleased if you'd just fix it."

"Sometimes you say 'nonsense' like it's an idea and sometimes you say it like it's a proper name," said the Baker. "Why is that?"

"You found a door," said Kade.

The Baker turned to him, blinking. He shrugged.

"Maybe it was in the back of the pantry, or maybe it was in your bedroom, or heck, maybe it was in the middle of the street, but you found a door, and when you went through it, everything was different. You had a kitchen, and all the supplies you could want, and a world that wanted you to bake it a future."

"I do that literally," murmured the Baker. "The prophecies that make the future run the way it should? I pipe them onto sugar cookies and toss them to the wind for distribution. It takes a lot of time. Frosting isn't a good medium for lengthy dissertations on fate."

"I guess it wouldn't be," said Kade. "But you found a door, and it brought you here, and you know you're not the first person to work in this kitchen, so I'm guessing you're afraid that the door will come back one day and send you back to wherever you came from."

"Brooklyn," said the Baker, and just like that, she wasn't a god, or a creator figure, or anything of the sort: she was a teenager in a hijab, with flour on her hands and a downcast expression on her face. "How did you know that? Are you here to take me back?"

"We'd never do that to anyone," said Cora. "Ever. But you asked why we talk the way we do."

"If your door ever reappears, if you ever find yourself back in a world that you don't want any part of, look up Eleanor West's Home for Wayward Children, and see if you can get your parents to send you there," said Christopher. "You'll be with people who understand."

The Baker frowned. "Right," she said finally. "But that's not going to happen, because I'm going to stay here forever."

Cora and Christopher, who both knew better, exchanged a look, and said nothing. There was nothing appropriate to say.

"That's lovely for you, miss, but we'd like to get back to school and back to the business of looking for our own doors," said

Kade politely. "Can't you whip up a new batch of nonsense for Sumi, so we can put her all the way back together?"

"I don't know *how,*" said the Baker, sounding frustrated. "Nonsense happens on its own. It's in the air, the water—the ground."

"Which is made of graham crackers," said Cora.

"Exactly! It makes no sense, so it makes more nonsense. I can't just whip up a batch of something that doesn't have a recipe."

"Can't you improvise?" Cora shook her head. "Please. We've come so far, and we've already paid for this. Sumi needs help. Sumi needs a miracle. Right now, you're the one who makes the miracles. So please."

The Baker looked to each of them in turn, finally stopping on Rini, who was still weeping, even as she seemed less and less tethered to the world.

"All right," she said. "I'll try."

WHEN THE BAKER had beckoned to Sumi, Sumi had gone willingly. How could she do anything else? This was the divinity of her chosen world calling her home, and even as a combination of skeleton and shade, she knew where she belonged.

Kade had helped the Baker lift Sumi up onto a long metal table that looked, if seen from the right angle, disturbingly like the autopsy table that used to occupy the basement, the one where a girl named Jack had slept and dreamed of a world defined by blood and thunder. Then he had stepped back, along with the others, and watched as she got to work.

The kitchen had no walls, and no pantry. When she needed

something, she would step outside its bounds and reach down into the junkyard surrounding, coming up over and over again with the right ingredients in her hands. Eggs, milk, flour, butter, vanilla beans and ginger roots, they were all there, waiting for her to scavenge them out of the dust. She didn't seem to understand that this was strange, that when the rest of them looked at the junkyard, they saw only failures, not the building blocks of new successes. This wasn't their place. There was no question that it was hers.

Bit by bit, she had built up Sumi's limbs with rice cereal mixed with melted marshmallow and honey, covering each layer with a thin sheet of modeling chocolate, until the combined confection began to look like human musculature. She was working on Sumi's shoulders when the timer dinged on one of her ovens. She crossed to it, opened it, and withdrew a sheet of sugar cookie organs, each dusted with a different color of sugar.

"It helps that bones don't melt," she said, using a spatula to slide the organs off the cookie sheet and onto a cooling rack. "I don't need to worry about putting something hot on top of them and losing the whole structure. That happens with the volcanos around here sometimes. It's really tedious."

"Um," said Christopher. "All of this is cool to watch, if a little nightmare fuel–esque, but people are usually made of meat, not Rice Krispy treats. We need a functional Sumi. You're making a cake that looks sort of like her."

"Baking something transforms it, and anyone who's ever eaten a piece of cake will tell you that sometimes we can take baked goods and turn them into a part of ourselves," said the Baker serenely. She was in her element: she knew exactly what she was doing, and was content to continue doing it until the job was done. "If this works, she'll be made of the same stuff as you and I."

Cora, who had heard plenty of jokes about cake and brownies going straight to her thighs, looked down at her short-clipped fingernails, picking at them to dislodge the last bits of sticky pinkness left over from the Strawberry Sea, and said nothing at all.

"Huh," said Christopher.

The Baker laughed. It was a bright, utterly joyful sound. "I love baking," she said. "It lets you make the world you want, and it makes everything delicious." She picked up a large pastry bag, beginning to pipe frosting intestines into the hollow of Sumi's gut.

Bit by bit, the glittering bone disappeared under layers of pastry. Bit by bit, the structure of the Baker's creation was built up to overlap the silent, almost disapproving shade, until the Baker was using modeling chocolate to sculpt the fine angles and planes of Sumi's face. Layers of yellow cake had been laid down for the fatty tissue, covered by a slightly thicker layer of gingerbread which was covered in turn by a fondant shell, dyed a few shades darker than Rini's skin.

"Hair, hair, hair," hummed the Baker, and leaned out of the kitchen, snatching a fistful of what looked like black candy floss out of the mess. She held it up and beamed. "You never know when you're going to need black cotton candy. Shouldn't eat the stuff, though. It'll dye your tongue black for a week." She stuck out her own tongue, which was currently a cheery shade of blue, before beginning to apply the filmy black material to the top of Sumi's head. When it was on, she picked up a roll of parchment

paper and draped it delicately over the body. "She's almost ready to go into the oven. Let's hope this works."

"What happens if it doesn't?" asked Rini.

The Baker sighed. "We try something else, I suppose."

"Her skeleton will be fine," said Christopher. "I don't know whether you can bake the ghost of somebody's boring side, but the skeleton won't care unless that oven is *way* too hot."

"I'm not into cremating my cookies," said the Baker.

"There you go," said Christopher. "No worries."

The Baker laughed. "All right, I like you people. Someone come and help me lift her into the oven."

The cake, cereal, and chocolate had added so much weight to the skeleton that it took Cora and Kade working in concert to help the Baker shift the baking sheet into the oven. The heat that flowed out when she opened the door was intense enough to make them shy back, the small hairs on their arms crisping as they drew closer.

"In she goes," said the Baker, and slid the tray—and Sumi—smoothly inside. The door swung closed behind her.

"Now what?" asked Cora.

"Now we wait," said the Baker. "We wait, and we hope."

12 THE BAKER'S STORY

THEY SAT ON A broken gingerbread wall, feet dangling, sipping glasses of cool, surprisingly unmodified milk. It was sweet in the way milk was always sweet, but it wasn't malted, or chocolatey, or anything else that would have made it fit better into the world. Cora gave the Baker a curious look.

"Where did you get the milk?" she asked.

"It grows on trees," said the Baker serenely.

Cora stared.

"No, really," said the Baker. "In these big white fruits that look sort of like eggs. One of the previous Bakers came up with *that*. I just enjoy it." She took another sip of her milk. "Ah. Refreshing *and* bizarre."

"Are you religious?" asked Christopher.

The Baker turned to blink at him. "Excuse me?"

"Your . . ." He waved a hand around his head. "I know that's a religious thing a lot of the time. Are you religious?"

"My family is," she said. "I think maybe I will be someday, but mostly I wear the hijab because I enjoy not having to worry about my hair getting in the cake batter."

"Functional *and* fashionable," said Christopher, his tone an intentional mirror to hers when she had been speaking of the milk fruit. "So is it weird for you? Being a god?"

The Baker hesitated before putting her milk down. "Let's clear this up," she said. "I am *not* a god. I'm a baker. I bake things. Any magic in my food comes from the world, not from me, and I can't help it if here, my brownies are always perfect and mysteriously double as roofing materials."

"Sorry," said Christopher. "I just thought—"

"I'm not here to convert people, or to preach, or to do anything but make a lot of cookies. A continent of cookies. When I'm done, if the door opens and sends me home, I suppose I'll make cookies there."

"Do you have a name?" asked Kade.

"Layla," she said.

"Nice to meet you," he replied. "I'm Kade. These are my friends, Cora and Christopher. Rini, you already know."

Layla nodded to each of them in turn. "Nice to meet you. You all had doors of your own?"

"Goblin Prince," said Kade.

"Mermaid," said Cora.

"Beloved of the Princess of Skeletons," said Christopher.

Layla blinked. "I was with you right up until that last one."

Christopher shrugged easily. "I get that response pretty often."

Rini didn't say anything. She was miserably flicking chocolate chips from the wall, sending them clattering down into the junkyard below them. Layla sighed and leaned over to put her hand on Rini's shoulder.

"Breathe," she said.

"I think one of my lungs has stopped existing," said Rini.

"So breathe a little more shallowly," said Layla. "Just keep breathing. The baking will be done soon, and then we'll see what we'll see."

"Rini was worried," blurted Cora. Rini and Layla both turned to look at her. "About the timing. Um. If Sumi died before she was born, and we bring Sumi back to life *now* . . ."

"Oh, that's simple," said Layla. "You bring Sumi back to life now, and she returns to school with the rest of you. For us, Sumi is a grown woman, not a teenage skeleton. She'll have a few years with you before her door opens again."

"Are you the one who opens it?" asked Kade.

"No," said Layla. "I get here a year after Sumi does."

There was a momentary silence before Christopher asked, "If we're in the future—our future—right now, does that mean that if I looked you up on Facebook once I have Wi-Fi again, I'd find you, like, twelve years old and living in Brooklyn?"

"I didn't have a Facebook when I was twelve, but it doesn't matter," said Layla. "Please don't look me up. Please don't try to find me. I don't remember that happening, which means it didn't happen for me. If you change my past, my door might never open, and I might not get to bake all these cookies. I'd been waiting my whole life to bake all these cookies."

Everyone who wound up at Eleanor West's School—everyone who found a door—understood what it was to spend a lifetime waiting for something that other people wouldn't necessarily understand. Not because they were better than other people and not because they were worse, but because they had a need trapped somewhere in their bones, gnawing constantly, trying to get out.

"We won't," promised Kade.

Layla relaxed.

In the kitchen, a timer dinged. Layla stood, brushing cocoa powder off her knees and bottom, before saying, "Let's see what we've got," and starting back. The others followed, Rini walking slower and slower until she was pacing slightly behind Cora.

Cora turned to look at her quizzically. "Don't you want to see your mom?" she asked.

"She won't be, not yet," said Rini. "If this worked, she's not my mother today, and if it didn't, she won't be my mother tomorrow. Is it better, in Logic? Where time does the same thing every day, and runs in just one line, and your mother is always your mother, and can always wipe your tears and tell you that there, there, it's going to be all right, you are my peppermint star and my sugar syrup sea, and I'll never leave you, and I certainly won't get killed before you can even be born?"

Cora hesitated.

"Not always," she said finally, and looked away.

Rini looked relieved. "Good. I don't know if I could live with the idea that everyone else had it better and we had it worse, just because we didn't want to always do things in the same order every day."

Kade paused at the edge of the kitchen, turning and looking back over his shoulder. "Well, come on," he called, beckoning. "We need to get Sumi out of the oven before she gets burnt."

"We're coming," said Cora, and hurried, Rini beside her, up the hill.

A RUSH OF AIR flowed out of the oven when Layla pulled it open, hot and sweet and smelling of brown sugar, cinnamon, and ginger. She took a step back, laughing in evident relief.

"Oh, that's a *good* smell," she said. "That's a right-and-ready smell. No charcoal or char."

"How can we help?" asked Kade.

"Grab a pair of oven mitts and lift," said Layla.

She didn't put on oven mitts before reaching into the oven: she simply grasped the metal end of the tray in her bare hands and pulled. There was no smell of burning, and she didn't make any sounds that would indicate that she was in pain. She might not do magic, but this world *was* magic, and it said that the Baker was important: the Baker would be protected.

Kade had never been very fond of cooking. Too much work for something that was too transitory. He much preferred tailoring, taking one thing and turning it into something else, something that would *last*. His parents had taken his interest in sewing after he got home from Prism as a sign that he was a little girl after all, until he'd started modifying his dresses, turning them into vests and shirts and other things that made him feel more comfortable.

He'd stuck his fingers with pins and cut himself with scissors more times than he could count. If someone had offered him a place where he could just sit and sew for a while, with all the fabric and findings he could ever want, with tools that wouldn't do him harm, no matter how careless he got, well. The temptation would be more than he could handle.

Rini hung back, unable to trust her grip with so much of her hands missing, but the others lifted as Layla ordered them, two to a side, like pallbearers preparing Sumi for her final rest. They set the tray on the baker's block at the middle of the kitchen, and Layla motioned them to step away before she reached for the sheet of parchment paper covering Sumi's face.

Cora realized she was holding her breath.

The parchment paper came away. Sumi had been gone before Cora came to the school: there was nothing there for Cora to recognize, just a beautiful, silent, teenage girl with smooth brown skin and long black hair. Her eyes were closed, lashes resting gently on her cheeks, and her mouth was a downturned bow, mercurial even when motionless.

Rini gasped before starting to cry. "Wake her up," she begged. "Please, please, wake her up."

"She needs to cool," said Layla. "If we woke her now, she'd have a fever bad enough to cook her brains and kill her all over again."

"She looks . . ." Kade reached out with one shaking hand, pulling back before he could actually brush against her skin. "She looks perfect. She looks *real*."

"Because she is real," said Layla. "The hair proves it."

"How's that?"

"If the oven hadn't wanted to put her back together, she wouldn't have hair now." Layla beamed. "She'd have a sticky black mess attached to a bunch of melted fondant—you're not supposed to bake fondant, by the way, or frosting, or most of the other things I put onto her skeleton. Confection wanted her back, so Confection gave her back. I'm just the Baker. I put things in the oven, and the world does as it will."

It seemed like a very precise way of avoiding accusations of magic. Kade didn't say anything. Getting into an argument with someone who was helping was never a good idea, and in this case, making Layla doubt her place in Confection could result in a door and an expulsion, and then all of this would have been for nothing.

Sumi looked so real.

"Was making a new body out of candy and cake and everything enough?" asked Cora. "Will that give her back her nonsense?" Or would Sumi's quiet, solemn ghost open her new eyes and ask to be taken home—not to the school, but to the parents who believed that she was dead, the ones who'd been willing to send their daughter away when she turned out to be someone other than the good girl they had raised her to be.

"I don't know," said Layla. "I've never done this before. I don't know if anyone has."

That was a lie, but it was a necessary one. Of course someone here had done this before. This was Confection, land of the culinary art become miracle: land of lonely children whose hands itched for pie tins or rolling pins, for the comfortable predictability of timers and sugar scoops and heaping cups of flour. This was a land where perfectly measured ingredients created nonsensical towers of whimsy and wonder—and maybe that was why they could be here, logical creatures that they were, without feeling assaulted by the world around them. Kade remembered his aunt's tales of her own Nonsense realm all too well, including the way it had turned against her once she was old enough to think as an adult did, rigidly and methodically. She would always be Nonsense-touched, but somewhere along the way, time had caught up with her enough to turn her mind against the realm that was her natural home.

Confection wasn't like that. Confection was Nonsense with rules, where baking soda would always leaven your cake and yeast would always rise. Confection could be Nonsensical *because* it had rules, and so Logical people could survive there, could even thrive there, once they had accepted that things weren't quite the same as they were in other worlds.

Layla reached over and carefully touched the first two fingers of her right hand to the curve of Sumi's remade wrist. She smiled.

"She's cool enough," she said. "We can wake her up now."

"How?" asked Christopher.

"Oh." Layla looked at him, eyes wide and surprised. "I thought you knew."

"I do," said Rini. She walked toward the table, and the others stood aside, letting her pass, until she was standing in front of Sumi, looking down at her with her sole remaining eye. She rested the back of her hand against her mother's cheek. Sumi didn't move.

"I finally had an adventure, Mama, like you're always saying I should," said Rini softly. "I went to see the Wizard of Fondant. I had to trade him two seasons of my share of the harvest, but he gave me traveling beads so I could go and bring you back. I went to the world where you were born. I breathed the air. . . ."

On and on she went, describing everything that had happened since she'd fallen out of the sky as if it were the greatest adventure the universe had ever known. How she had argued with the Queen of Turtles and bantered with the Lord of the Dead, how she had been there for the cleverest defeat of the Queen of Cakes, when a Mermaid and a Goblin Prince had conquered her at last. It was all lords and ladies and grand, noble quests, and it was magical.

Quests were a lot like dogs, Cora thought. They were much more attractive when seen from a distance, and not barking in the middle of the night or pooping all over the house. She had been there for every terrible, wearying, bone-breaking moment of this quest, and it held no magic for her. She knew it too well.

But Rini described it for Sumi like it was a storybook, like it was something to whisper in a child's ear as they were drifting off to sleep, and it was beautiful. It was truly beautiful.

". . . so I need you to wake up now, Mama, and go with your friends, so you can come back here, so you can marry Papa, so I can be born." Rini leaned forward until her head was resting on Sumi's chest, closing her eye. "I want you to meet me. You always said I was the best thing you'd ever done, and I want you to meet me so you can know it's true. So wake up now, okay? Wake up, and leave, so you can come home."

"Look," whispered Kade.

Sumi's hands, which had never once in her life been still, were twitching. As the others watched, she raised them off the table and began stroking Rini's hair, her eyes still closed, her face still peaceful.

Rini sobbed and lifted her head, staring at her mother, both eyes wide and bright and filled with all the colors of a candy corn field in full harvest. Cora put her hands over her mouth to hide her gasp. Christopher grinned, and said nothing.

"Mama?" asked Rini.

Sumi opened her eyes and sat up, sending Rini stumbling back, away from the table. Sumi blinked at her. Then Sumi blinked down at her own naked, re-formed body.

"I was dead a second ago, and now I'm naked," she announced. "Do I need to be concerned?"

Kade whooped, and Christopher laughed, and Rini sobbed, and everything was different, and everything was finally the same.

PART V

WHAT CAME AFTER

13 TIME TO GO

RINI HELD FAST TO her mother's hands, squeezing until Sumi pulled away, taking a step backward.

"No and no and no again, girl who says she's a daughter of mine, in the some bright day when I get to come home, instead of coming wherever and whenever this is: don't damage the merchandise." Sumi shook her hands like she was trying to shake Rini's touch away before tucking them behind her back and shifting her sharp-eyed gaze to Layla. "The door you've baked, you're sure of where it goes?"

"I told the oven what I wanted," said Layla.

The door was gingerbread and hard candy, piped with frosting details that looked like golden filigree and dusted with a thin veneer of edible glitter. It looked like something that would open on another world. Nothing else entirely made sense.

"You're the Baker." Sumi shook her head. "Always thought you were a myth."

"When you're saving our world, I am. I come after you," said Layla, and smiled, a little shyly. She turned to look at Kade. "Remember what I said. Don't look for me. I need to find my door, and that means I need everything to go just the way I remember it going. Leave me alone."

"I promise," said Kade.

"If you ever find yourself back in Brooklyn, give us a call," said Christopher. "We take students throughout the year, and it'd be nice to know that you were going to where there were familiar faces."

"I'll keep you in mind," said Layla, and flicked her hand toward the door, which swung lazily open, revealing nothing but a filmy pinkness beyond. "Now get out of here, so the timeline can stop getting tied into knots."

"Wait!" said Rini. She darted forward, pulling Sumi into a rough hug. "I love you, Mama," she whispered, before letting the younger woman go and turning away, wiping her eyes with her fully restored hand.

Sumi looked bemused. "I don't love you," she said. Rini stiffened. Sumi continued: "But I think I'm going to. See you in a few years, gumdrop."

Turning, she started for the door, with her classmates tagging after her.

The last thing Layla and Rini heard before the door swung shut behind them was Sumi asking, "So why didn't Nancy come?"

Then the door was closed, and the strangers were gone. Bit by bit, the door crumbled away, joining the debris that covered the ground. Layla looked at Rini and smiled.

"Well?" she asked. "What are you waiting for? You have about a day's walk between here and home, and I bet your parents want to see you."

The sound Rini made was half laugh, half sob, and then she

was off and running, leaving the junkyard and the girl who only wanted to make cookies behind, racing into the bright Confection hills.

FOUR STUDENTS HAD LEFT and four students returned, even if they weren't the same ones, stepping out of a door-shaped hole in the air and onto the dry brown grass of the front lawn. Eleanor was standing on the front porch, smiling wistfully—an expression that transformed into a gasp of open-mouthed delight when she saw Sumi.

"Sumi!" she cried, and started down the stairs, moving faster than such a frail-looking woman should have been able. "My darling girl, you're home!"

"Eleanor-Ely!" cried Sumi, and threw herself into Eleanor's arms, and held her tight.

Kade and Cora exchanged a glance. There would be time, soon enough, to tell Eleanor about everything that had happened: about leaving Nadya behind, about Layla, who might someday join them at the school, about the ways that Nonsense could be underpinned with Logic, and how this changed the Compass. There would be time for Kade to find Layla's family, to seize the chance to watch someone—from a distance, never interfering—who was about to be chosen by a door. There would be time for so many, many things. But for right now . . .

For right now, the only thing that mattered was an old woman and a young girl, embracing in the grass, under a bright and cloudless autumn sky.

Everything else could wait.

14 THE DROWNED GIRL

WELL. PERHAPS NOT *EVERYTHING*.

Nadya sat on the bank of the River of Forgotten Souls, one leg drawn up against her chest so she could rest her chin atop her knee. Turtles basked on the bank around her, their hard-shelled bodies pressing against her hip and ankle. They followed her everywhere she went, a terrapin train of devoted acolytes keeping her company in this most uncompanionable of places.

It was nice, being in the company of turtles again. The turtles back in the pond at school (which seemed more like a dream with every endless, languid day that passed here, time defined by the lapping of the water against the riverbanks, by the occasional sound of music drifting from the Hall) had never wanted to spend time with her. There wasn't enough magic in the world of her birth. Some magic worked there—Christopher's flute, or Nancy's stillness, back when she'd been a student, although Nadya had to admit that it was nothing compared to what Nancy could do here, in her natural habitat—but most magic was just too much for the local laws of nature to bear.

These turtles, though . . . these were proper, magical turtles.

They didn't talk to her, not like the turtles back in Belyyreka, and the largest of them was only the size of a dinner plate, instead of being wide enough to ride upon, like her beloved Burian, who had been her steed and dearest companion in the Drowned World, but they were still willing to let her tickle their shells and stroke their long, finely pebbled necks. They let her exist among them, ever-damp and ever-weeping, and she loved them all, and she hated them all, because they were a constant reminder that what she had here was not enough. This, none of this, was enough.

"I hate everything," she said, and grabbed a stone off the bank and skipped it hard across the water, watching it hit the surface three, four, five times before it plopped and sank, joining the others she had already thrown to the bottom. Then she froze.

She had grabbed the stone with her right hand.

Nadya had been born without anything below the elbow on her right arm, a teratogenic trick of something her birthmother had been exposed to back in Mother Russia. Three mothers for Nadya: the one who bore her, the country that poisoned her, and the one who adopted her, American tourist on a misery tour of the rest of the world, well-meaning and well-intentioned and willing to take on a "special needs" child who liked nothing more than to flood the orphanage bathroom playing with the taps.

Her third mother had been the first to fit her with a prosthetic hand, which had pinched and dug into her skin and done nothing to improve her quality of life. The only things she hadn't been perfectly capable of doing with one hand were things the prosthetic didn't help her do *anyway,* lacking the fine motor control necessary to apply nail polish or thread a needle. If she'd been younger, maybe, or if she'd wanted it more, but the way it had been presented, like it was a great gift she wasn't allowed to refuse, had only served to remind her that in the eyes of her adoptive family, she would always be the poor, pitiful orphan girl with a missing hand, the one they needed to *help*.

She had never wanted that kind of help. She had only wanted to be loved. So when the waterweeds by the turtle pond had looked like a door, so open and inviting, she hadn't watched her footing on the muddy bank. She'd gotten too close. She'd tumbled in, and found herself somewhere else, somewhere that didn't want to help her. Somewhere that wanted *her* to do the helping, and promised to love her if she only would.

She had spent a lifetime in Belyyreka, and they had always called her a Drowned Girl, even when she was away from the water, and she had never considered how literal that might be, not until she had fallen into a river and felt hands yanking her by the shoulders, away from the surface, away from the real world, back into the false one, where mothers left her, one after the other, where nothing ever stayed.

In Belyyreka, she had chosen her own prosthetic, a hand made of river water, which she could decorate as she liked, with weeds and small fish and once, with a tadpole that had grown to froghood in the sheltering embrace of her palm, looking at her with a child's love before hopping away to find freedom. In Belyyreka, no one had called her broken for lacking a flesh and bone hand: they had seen it as an opportunity for her to craft a tool, a weapon, an extension of her own.

It had dissolved when that helpful neighbor had seen her floating face-down in the pond and pulled her to supposed "safety." She had thought it lost forever.

Slowly, Nadya raised her right hand to her face and stared at it, its translucent flesh, its rippling skin. There was nothing inside it. She reached down with her left hand, laying it against the surface of the water. A turtle the size of a quarter crawled into her palm. She lifted it to her water hand, sliding it through the surface. It swam a content circle before poking its head up to breathe, nostrils breaking the "skin" between the left and right knuckles.

Nadya stood. The light reflecting on the water had formed the shape of a doorway, or a grave. It was eight feet long by three feet wide, and she knew that if she dove in here, no one would come to save her. Had she really been drowning the whole time she was in Belyyreka? Had it all been a lie?

But the school was real. The school was real, and Christopher could raise the dead, and Cora's hair was like a coral reef, bright and impossible, and if magic was real, if her water hand was real, then she had only started to drown in truth when someone sought to pull her back. All she had to do was believe. All she had to do was be sure.

"We're going on a journey, little friend," she told the turtle in her palm. "Oh, I can't wait for you to meet Burian."

Nadya backed up, giving herself room for a running start before she leapt into the air, feet pointed downward like knives, set to slice through the surface of the water. She landed squarely in the middle of the dream of a door, eyes closed, hands lifted above her head, and she slid into the river without splash or ripple, and she was gone, leaving nothing but the turtles who loved her behind.

There is kindness in the world, if we know how to look for it. If we never start denying it the door.

ABOUT THE AUTHOR

Beckett Gladney

SEANAN MCGUIRE is the author of the Hugo, Nebula, Alex and Locus Award–winning Wayward Children series; the October Daye series; the InCryptid series; and other works. She also writes darker fiction as Mira Grant. Seanan lives in Seattle with her cats, a vast collection of creepy dolls, horror movies, and sufficient books to qualify her as a fire hazard. She won the 2010 John W. Campbell Award for Best New Writer, and in 2013 became the first person to appear five times on the same Hugo ballot. In 2022 she managed the same feat again!